PASSPORT
TO MURDER

OTHER BOUCHERCON ANTHOLOGY TITLES

Blood on the Bayou (2016)
Murder Under the Oaks (2015)
Murder at the Beach (2014)

PASSPORT TO MURDER

Bouchercon Anthology 2017

EDITED BY
JOHN MCFETRIDGE

Down & Out Books
3959 Van Dyke Rd, Ste. 265
Lutz, FL 33558
www.DownAndOutBooks.com

The characters and events in this book are fictitious. Any similarity to real persons, living or dead, is coincidental and not intended by the author.

Cover design by JT Lindroos

ISBN: 1-946502-05-7
ISBN-13: 978-1-946502-05-6

To Librarians,
who feed both the mind and the soul

CONTENTS

Introduction
John McFetridge

Anything to declare?

Welcome to Toronto. Welcome to the Bouchercon 2017 anthology, *Passport to Murder*.

Our call for submissions asked that stories have "actual travel or the desire to travel with or without passports," and "a strong suggestion of murder or a plan to commit murder," and the writers delivered.

The guidelines also said, "All crime sub-genres welcome," and that could also be a theme for the convention.

My first Bouchercon was in Madison, Wisconsin, 2006. I was very nervous about attending, mostly because I didn't know anyone else who would be there, but also because of something that happened just a few weeks before the convention.

My first novel had just been published and I was at my first industry event. It was exciting but also intimidating. I got to chatting with another writer who asked me what genre I wrote in and I didn't really know. So he said to me, "Who's your guy?" I didn't understand the question so he said, "The detective, the PI, the main character, who is he?" I said there wasn't really a main character, it was more of an ensemble. "Okay," the guy said, "who solves the murder?" I had to think about it for a minute and then I said, "Well, a few people get killed." Now he was starting to get annoyed and he said, "But the main murder, the one that gets solved, who solves it?" Again I had to think about it and said, "No one. It doesn't get solved."

Now the guy was staring at me like I was crazy and I was starting to think maybe I was. I said, "There are a lot of cops and a lot of bad guys but it's really a novel about opportunity and how some people see it everywhere and some people never recognize it and..." I realized he'd stopped listening and I couldn't really blame him.

So, with that book and a lot of trepidation under my arm I showed up in Madison expecting to get the same reaction from everyone. I had been told before by agents and publishers (over twenty years of rejections, actually) that my books fell between the cracks; not literary enough to be literature, not gritty enough to be hardboiled, so that's what I expected to hear at Bouchercon.

That's not what I heard at all.

What I discovered within five minutes at my first Bouchercon was that it's a place where people come together with a shared love of books—all books. I made friends at my first Bouchercon that I'm still friends with today and that's happened at every Bouchercon since.

And I've discovered books I likely would never have found any other way. Some of my now favorite books. Many of them fall between the cracks and can't be defined by genre.

Of course, if you want to it's still possible to get into a heated discussion about genre and sub-genres at Bouchercon. In that case, this anthology will be able to help you in two ways; one, there are excellent examples of many genres, from cozy to noir, and, two, many stories cross genre and show why no labels really work.

A few years ago I took part in a Flash Fiction Challenge organized by Patricia Abbott, Gerald So and Aldo Calcagno (the Mystery Dawg), all people I met at Bouchercon. Patti described the challenge as:

*Write the first paragraph of a story, send it to me by
January 20th. I will stir the pot and send it back out to another
writer. Write a 750 (or so) word story using it.*

The paragraph I received mentioned a writer and that immediately made me think of Bouchercon. So, to begin this anthology that includes so many genres, here is that flash fiction.

Cozy/Noir
John McFetridge and Sandra Scoppettone

The first time George Heartwell e-mailed the writer, Margaret Roberts, on June 22nd, he suffered all morning. He re-read the letter over and over and wished to hell he hadn't ever done such a stupid thing. Christ, what was she going to think?

Well, she was going to think she was being blackmailed, sure, but what would she think of the *writing*?

"There are cameras everywhere, Margaret, in phones, in pens, in computers—some even look like cameras. There was one on the eleventh floor of the Lord Baltimore Radisson at Bouchercon."

He wanted it to be the fewest words possible, noir style, none of that purple prose like her cozies. Her bestselling-around-the-world cozies.

Now here it was almost winter and George was driving Highway 21, looking for the entrance to a closed provincial park for his meeting with Margaret. They'd gone back and forth for months, she'd answered his email with a simple, "What do you want?"

That surprised him, he'd expected a denial or some excuses, some convoluted story about it being a misunderstanding, how there was nothing going on really, but she got right to the point. Not very cozie-like at all.

She must've read his hardboiled flash fiction online.

Back then George'd wanted to get her help with agents and

publishers but she pointed out their writing didn't really have anything in common, people would suspect something was going on between them if she started showing his work around—her husband would find that suspicious for sure.

So he settled for money and Margaret asked him to meet her at the Ipperwash Provincial Park on Lake Huron. It had been closed since a group of Native protestors took it over, claiming it was on Native land—it probably was for all George knew—and Margaret and her husband lived in an old farmhouse somewhere nearby.

He'd expected more trouble getting into the park but he just drove in like Margaret told him in her email. Typical Canada, there was a sign that said, "Closed," but no locked gate or anything. He drove a few miles through the woods until he came to the Park Store, the building boarded up and falling apart. The parking lot was surrounded by trees, the perfect location for a drop. Well, not perfect like it would have been in one of George's books, some back alley all gritty and dark, or a massage parlor.

George parked and waited. He had a copy of Margaret's latest book with him and he thumbed through it. The author photo was pretty good, she looked great for a woman a little over fifty and he liked the first page; a woman walking her dogs comes across a guy who committed suicide in his car, attached a vacuum hose to the exhaust pipe with tape and ran it through the trunk.

Everyone bought the suicide except the woman walking her dogs. George couldn't believe these cozies, amateur sleuths, the woman was a professional dog walker and now she's investigating a homicide. Who buys this crap?

He was well into the book when a dog barked and he almost had a heart attack.

There was Margaret Roberts, walking out of the woods behind two dogs, a German Shepherd and some small fluffy thing. Maybe that photo wasn't retouched, she looked good.

George got out of his car and said, hey. Margaret nodded at him, said, hello, as she was opening the black bag she had over her shoulder. It was the bag from Bouchercon, the Charmed to Death logo in white, the bracelet with the little charms, the skull, and the gun and the switchblade.

She took out a thermos and asked George if he'd like some tea. He said no and Margaret said, "How about a little Bushmills then?"

"Sure, why not."

Margaret poured a little into the thermos lid and handed it to George. He drank and coughed a little and said, "Very good." Then he said, "Do you have my money?"

"Get right to the point why don't you?"

George drank the rest of the Bushmills and Margaret poured him some more, saying, "Don't you think it's beautiful out here?

George said, "I guess," and Margaret said, "Not like one of your hardboiled stories, of course, but like a cozie."

"Yeah."

"I suppose people get blackmailed in hardboiled stories all the time?"

George said, yeah they do. He couldn't believe this chick, hadn't she ever read Hammet? Or even Robert B. Parker?

"People sometimes get blackmailed in cozies," Margaret said. "But do you know what happens more often?" She was looking right at him now but going out of focus, saying, that's right, "They get poisoned."

George's knees started to give way and he was falling over, his face hitting the gravel hard, but he was already numb.

He could see Margaret getting something out of the black Charmed to Death bag, a vacuum cleaner hose and a roll of tape.

She said, "Not everyone gets published, George, it's no reason to kill yourself."

The Divide
Janet Hutchings

Her first sight of the girl was in the student union, where she was tacking a notice to the ride-share board.

Gabriella touched her shoulder.

"Where you go?" she said.

A little roll of baby fat formed between the girl's jeans and top as she brought her arm down. "Vegas," she said, surveying Gabriella doubtfully. "But...*we're students*. Probably not what you're looking for."

When Gabriella said she'd be willing to take a donkey as long as it was headed west, she got an eye-roll instead of a laugh, but the girl tore a tab off her posting and scrawled an address where they'd meet Wednesday, nine sharp.

They were merging onto the interstate before Gabriella stopped looking back at the giant red-brown slabs of the Flatirons, jutting behind town like a theatrical backdrop. The sudden acceleration pressed her stomach into the back of her seat, shifting her attention to the van. The driver had black curly hair and a jagged, lightning-bolt earring. Beside him, the pixie-haired blonde reached into his shirt pocket.

Gabriella might have been a passenger on public transit for all the attention they paid her. She'd been assigned the middle seat, next to a cooler and a brown grocery bag. At first, she thought she was being cold-shouldered because of her age, but behind her, in the van's last row of seats, a boy was sprawled, bobbing his head to the rhythmic *tish* that escaped his ear buds, and he, too, had received little more than a nod from the pair.

Snatches of conversation drifted in and out of the weave of her thoughts: a concert the driver, whose name was Darren, didn't want to miss; hints that the girl, June, was counting on winning at the casinos.

Then the highway narrowed and Gabriella saw a sign cautioning a downhill grade. Again, she was pressed back as the driver took the opportunity to dodge ahead of slowing traffic.

Before she could stop herself she let out a small shriek.

"Ohmygod! We didn't mean to *scare* you...! Watch it, Darren!" the girl said, turning around.

Gabriella felt the van slow and with it the pounding of her heart. "I no used to these mountain," she said.

"So where you from?"

Gabriella had seen in the looks the couple exchanged earlier that the girl was more intrigued than worried by her. The girl had even tossed some extra camping equipment into the van on seeing Gabriella didn't have any. But Darren found her unsettling.

"*Italia*...Long-a time before you two are born. After thirty year in this country I decide I gonna make it to the other coast!"

The girl laughed. "Well, you don't want to miss everything in between, do you?

"Hey, Darren," she said, thumb going to her phone. "If we go along here a little farther we get to an exit for Independence Pass, and...cool...It's only another hour from there to Aspen...We could stop—"

"No, no," Gabriella said, catching a glimpse of Darren's face.

"Quit worrying about your stupid concert, Dar," the girl insisted. "We've got two days to get there...You never think of anyone else—"

"What I'm thinking is that those two signed up to get where we said we're going!"

"Let's ask them, then! Jason!" she shouted to the back of the van.

As the boy pulled the earbuds down around his neck and sat up, pushing wispy long hair back behind his ears, Gabriella thought it was like seeing a giant come to life in a fairy tale.

"Hey, Jason, we're thinking about stopping in Aspen... where I'm going to buy dinner for *everyone*, case money's an issue. That okay?"

When the big boy shrugged assent, the matter was settled. They climbed for more than an hour, past timberline, until the earth began to look like the top of a balding man's head—little strands of low grassy shrubbery holding on here and there but mostly bare.

The switchback eventually opened to a place where there seemed to be no life at all except for patches of brownish green that hugged the earth as thin and tight as skin. Here the girl said, "I think we must be coming to the Continental Divide, Dar...Case you didn't know, that's the line where on one side all the water flows to the Pacific and on the other it all goes toward the Atlantic." When he didn't answer, she yanked gently at the back of his hair and pointed to a parking area ahead. "Let's stop. It's cool...Think about it. A raindrop that just *happens* to fall to the east of this point's going to flow east—*forever*. Just a fraction of an inch the other direction, it can only go west..."

This time she got a mocking "*Whoo-ooh*," followed by, "You want to try selling that to Hallmark, maybe you should also work in that once they evaporate they get a chance at a whole new life."

"Yeah? Well, that's what I wish *I* had right now, Darren. *A whole new life!*"

They pulled into the lot and tumbled out of the van,

9

quibbling as they drifted off on their own, leaving Gabriella to admire the panorama of snow-capped mountains and Jason to light up what Gabriella recognized, after two weeks in Colorado, as a joint.

She spotted a restroom and quickly headed for it, afraid they might leave without her.

The break didn't help.

"Hey, you don't like it," Darren said, when they were back on the road, "you're free to go." He flicked the door locks up and slowed down.

Gabreilla's heart quickened. If her husband had ever invited *her* to leave so coolly, it might not have taken her three decades to do it. But this hard little bud of a woman seemed to have no illusions at all. Her reaction was to calmly reach out and give his earring a vicious ping, making the metal dance.

It must have stung, Gabriella thought, and she held her breath. The canyons were so deep here, she felt that even her weight leaning one way or the other could tip them over.

Darren swatted the girl's hand away and the van lurched dangerously close to the edge.

Gabriella's stomach filled with butterflies. She was the cause of this! Once they were parked, and there was no further danger of a dispute erupting on these perilous roads, she would get the girl aside. Tell her she really did want to stick to their plan.

They didn't stop till they reached Aspen, however, and by then, Gabriella was glad June had insisted on the detour. Her joints screamed, and when she got out of the car and looked around, something about the town tugged at her memories— the hanging baskets of flowers, the ring of mountains...a little like the village where her *nonna* had lived. A soda fizz of happiness bubbled up in her.

Her sense of foreignness had increased with every mile she'd traveled west, as questions about where she came from, never uttered at all in New York, became almost universal. But in this town the sounds of French and Italian seemed to waft from every passing group of tourists. How pleasant it would be to walk a little.

June caught her eye and saw she'd been right. She pointed down the street to some shops. But her partner intervened.

He had dark glasses on now, which Gabriella thought strange, since he'd never once worn them during the sunny drive through the mountains. And there was something else about his looks she didn't like: an incongruous freckle-faced, gap-toothed boyishness.

None of them, not even the big boy from the back of the van, contradicted Darren when he said it was time to eat or questioned his choice of a sidewalk cafe with a neon sombrero, where molded plastic armchairs surrounded glass tables.

As they sat, June picked the cocktail menu from its stand. "Ooooh!...Guys?" she said, showing the card around.

When they'd all had a few sips of salt-rimmed margaritas, Gabriella noticed that the girl's eyes had begun to wander to the other diners. Like a beautiful lizard, June licked seductively at the edge of her glass, then caught the eye of an older man at a table nearby and shrugged an apology for her goofiness. It was enough to bring him over, glass in hand, an offered "Good, aren't they?" while his other hand went out in introduction: "I'm Max. May I?"

June nodded, and Max reeled over a chair, placing it next to Gabriella's.

He was a rich man—Gabriella could see that from the quality of his clothes and rings—and he had the air of a regular at the café.

The blind eyes of Darren's sunglasses pinned June to the back of her chair, which she'd slid down in to rest her neck, but she ignored Darren and elaborated on the places she'd heard of in nearby Utah and Arizona. Max took the bait and told them about red rocks and purple canyons somewhere to the south.

The waiter came, and Max ordered another round of drinks.

Little darts of anger passed silently between June and her partner. Max noticed: It showed in the way he tried to draw Darren out.

Of Gabriella Max asked many questions, too. All of them about Italy. None about what she sensed he most wanted to know: what she was doing traveling with this threesome less than half her age.

She was already regretting it. If she'd taken a bus, she'd be in California tomorrow. It had been foolish to try to save a few dollars this way. She'd only stumbled on the notice-board by accident, while ambling around the picture-postcard campus.

When the check finally arrived, Max scooped it up and pulled his fat wallet out before June—with the reptilian slowness she'd acquired as the meal wore on—could claim it.

Darren put a toothpick in his mouth and sat coldly waiting to see what June would do when the folder came back with Max's change. Gabriella thought Max must have found his pose threatening because he didn't invite them back to his house, as she'd been certain he'd intended to. Instead he accepted their thanks, wished them good luck, and headed slowly off down the street.

"Congratulations, June," Darren said, "you got him to pay without even having to fuck him—"

"Just shove it, will you!"

"Let's go," he said, kicking one of the chairs out of his way.

"We have to know *where* we're going first!"

"You said there was a campsite near here."

"Yeah, but GPS might not work once we're out of town."

He chewed the toothpick menacingly as she ran off, saying, "I'll ask Max."

From where they were, they could see her stop the older man and gesture. Gabriella was certain she saw Max give June something that she shoved into her jeans pocket, but when June returned, she didn't say a word, just cocked her head at the van.

At the campsite, Darren and June pulled out a pup tent that Gabriella could hardly believe would sleep two and handed her one like it.

It was spring, mild during the day, but the temperature had dropped dramatically now. Gabriella struggled to set up the tent. Finally she got it, rolled out the flimsy sleeping bag assigned her, and crawled in. The little bit of privacy was a relief, but soon she began to quiet enough to hear the others. There was low talk from one side; from the other, tinny music. As she shifted to find a comfortable bit of ground, a hump of earth pressed so that she became aware of her bladder. She thought of holding it, but knew she'd be afraid to get up after everyone was asleep.

When she slithered out of her tent, and moonlight peeked from behind a cloud, she saw them—like bulgy braided snakes trying to shed a single skin...

She woke to a shivering cold dawn, her nose and forehead, and the tips of her ears where they stuck out of the sleeping bag, numb. They would head for Las Vegas this morning, she thought. The couple would be back in harmony after all that mambo-ing.

But when she arrived at the building where a little line was forming for the sinks, June waved her over to where she'd piled her toiletries and stood splashing cold water over her face.

There was a smug look about her.

"So, Gab," she said. "Where'd you like to go today? That cool place Max was telling us about isn't too far off our route. You ever been to a national park?"

Gabriella shook her head. "But, the boys—"

"Don't worry about them." She rubbed her face energetically. "Dar's gonna do what I tell him. And that other guy— Earbud-man—if he doesn't want to go, we can drop him in town."

Gabriella shook her head. "Please..."

"What've you got waiting for you, Gab? It took a lot of work to change Darren's mind, believe me. And I did it for you. We'll call it Gabriella's Day, okay?"

"No..." Gabriella said. "Is no for me!"

"Okay, how about this, then. You relax for one day, just roll with it, and I swear we'll get there tomorrow. We have to be there tomorrow night anyway, 'cause Darren's got tickets to some stupid concert he's freaking out about. I want to see some of these places, too. We can call it 'June's Day' if that's what you want."

Voracious from the night in the open air, they stopped first for a farmer's breakfast. The smell of the coffee nearly made Gabriella swoon, and she couldn't help smiling as she sucked down hot biscuits, and butter ran from the corners of her mouth. By the time big platters of eggs clattered down onto the table, even poker-faced Darren was becoming boisterous. Gabriella's anger at June's tactics all but disappeared and a satisfying tingle began to creep through her. She hadn't sought this day, but she'd given in to it, and suddenly she yearned for it to be one of happiness: an adventure—in a life with too few moments of spontaneous fun.

June hadn't yet told them exactly where they were going, and her elusiveness lent a whiff of enchantment to the meal.

The sun shone brightly over the mountains when they

stepped outside, Darren again putting the question of where they were headed, June only looking at her phone and winking.

As he drove, they played games like *I spy with my little eye*—sardonically, and then in earnest.

Until what June spied was a sign for Grand Junction, where she insisted Darren turn off. And here, when they'd rolled into town, she would not be denied the shopping she'd missed the day before, roaming from shop to shop until even Gabriella was weary.

The boys lounged in the sun. Darren, whose eyes were covered by the sunglasses again, betraying his irritation by the twitch of his lips.

"What kind of crap you pick up now?" he said when June finally plopped down next to him with her bags.

She feigned a scowl, pushing him away when he attempted to look in one of them, and pulled from it a box in which a silver necklace inlaid with turquoise gleamed.

"You put any more a' that shit on, you're gonna look like a Christmas tree."

Gabriella laughed. June *did* have ornaments everywhere: several rings per ear, and one in the side of her nose. Three bracelets on one arm, two on the other. Her latest purchase, however, was of an altogether better quality. Gabriella wondered where the money for it had come from.

Her own treasure was pinned inside her clothes, disguised by a bulky shirt.

As if she could read Gabriella's mind, June pulled a receipt from her pocket, displaying it with pride. When she'd done the clasp on the necklace and let it fall against her clavicle, she pulled out her phone and took a selfie.

"We done?" Darren asked.

"Not hardly." She shot Gabriella a don't-dare-object look and said, "Back to 70, driver."

They drove for more than an hour, crossing into Utah,

then turning onto a smaller highway. The ground all around had been transitioning to fiery clay as they went, the rocks rising at the edge of the horizon becoming luminous.

When finally they pulled up inside the park, Gabriella couldn't believe her eyes: arch after arch glowing salmony red, most large enough to march armies under. Everywhere another triumphal structure, a gallery of them, covering a space as vast and otherwise barren as the surface of an alien planet.

As they climbed down from the van even June and Darren were stunned to a respectful hush.

Gabriella wandered away by herself. An undertow of worry that her past would catch up to her, ensnaring her in public shame, had threatened to pull her under for nearly two thousand miles. Here, in the shadows of the giant rocks, it finally let her go.

She was agile for her age and scrambled up the bases of the more horizontal arches, reassured by the flank of the sun-warmed stone. As the minutes stretched she felt she might simply dissolve into the earth, the air, and the lowering sun, without a single regret.

The sun was casting long shadows among the arches before June came to find her.

"Park's closing in a few minutes, Gab," she said gently.

"Yeah...Okay." Gabriella slid off the side of the rock, waited for her wobbly legs to steady, and, feeling as light as the desert air, put an arm around the girl's shoulder.

They set their tents in a wide arc around a campfire that night, unpacking hot dogs and s'mores. When Darren couldn't find his Gerber knife to cut cooking twigs, Gabriella pulled a girly pink army knife from her pack and offered it.

Laughing, Darren took it, his distrust of her forgotten...for a moment.

The spell cast by the massive arches lasted through dinner. Or maybe it was the hypnotic dance of the campfire flames. Whatever it was, confidences were shared that in daylight would pass only between intimate friends.

Gabriella talked about her husband—how they'd hardly known each other when she came with him to America. How her life had been bounded, suffocatingly, by his domineering family and her job as maid to a wealthy old woman. How, finally, she had walked out the door without even letting him know where she was going.

How Darren and June and Jason had their whole lives before them and shouldn't waste it being afraid to try new paths.

It was an opening for Jason to say, "Right, well here's something *you* should try," as he passed her a joint. "Say hello to mary jane."

Gabriella waved it away at first, then, to prove her point, took it and tried to inhale, coughing until she got the hang of it. Later, she couldn't recall much of their talk in detail; every momentary thing—the snap of the fire, the howl of some creature out in the canyons behind them—seemed to suck all of her attention into itself. She would vaguely remember bits of June's story—her hardscrabble childhood with a single mother, how Darren's family had cut him off from a sizable allowance, believing June was after his money—but the drug proved a garbler of certainty.

Who knew how long they sat like that, smoking and talking and watching the fire. Eventually Gabriella was aware that Darren had folded his jacket and laid his head down. June's arms crept around Jason's neck and soon the two of them drifted quietly away from a snoring Darren. At that moment, this new pairing seemed natural to Gabriella: the conclusion to a day of peace and love.

When, much later, she made it to her tent, she left the flap open and stared into the vast sky. It had been a good day,

June's day. Or maybe it had been Gabriella's day after all—one of the best of her life.

It was sometime in the middle of the night that things started to go wrong. By first light what had wakened Gabriella as a snarling murmur had risen to shouts. As she tested her stiff joints, she heard the girl scream, "It's not as if *you* never shagged anyone else, Dar!"

Gabriella found her toothbrush and headed for the sinks. She took as long as she could, hoping to reclaim the serenity of the previous evening, but June caught up to her.

"You got it right, Gab," she said. "*Just walk out the back, Jack...*"

Gabriella blushed, recalling some of what she'd told them about Mario. Hoping she hadn't mentioned how she'd finally been overcome by such rage—from the years of dismissals, prohibitions, and neglect—that it changed her till she could hardly recognize her own face.

"You no gonna leave him now!" she said. "What we gonna do out here, middle'a nowhere?"

June, now finished washing, ignored her and turned away.

When Gabriella got back to the tents, Jason was moving about, warily avoiding Darren. Soon June and Darren, between violent outbursts, were throwing things into the van, and Gabriella scrambled to keep up. Jason, with the same speed, furled his tent and slipped quietly into the backseat.

They traveled for several hours in hostile silence, punctuated by stops for gas, before the landscape changed again, this time to cracked brown flats of earth—like a never-ending pan of brownies, Gabriella thought. And finally June spoke.

"We'll be there in about an hour, guys."

The remark was addressed to Gabriella and Jason, whom

she'd turned to as if Darren didn't exist. But Darren said: "Before we get there, *June*, it's your turn to fill up the tank."

"Can't. I'm out of money. Spent it all in Grand Junction."

"Cut the crap," he said, pulling off a few minutes later at a service area.

The girl gave him a filthy look, but went inside to pay.

They were back on the road and the buildings of a city had appeared on the horizon when Darren pulled his wallet from his pocket, awkwardly searching through it with one hand.

"Weird...I'm sure I put the Drake tickets in here."

June shrugged, but a tic beneath her eye betrayed her.

"You got them?" he said.

Another shrug.

"The fuck are you playing at, June?"

"I told you I didn't have any money...Soooo, I made a deal with the clerk back there. It's a sold-out concert, Dar. He couldn't believe his luck."

As he smacked her hard below the eye, the van swerved out of its lane and horns blared.

Dead silence followed, and then, without so much as touching her injured cheek, June said: "You need to take Gab to the bus station, Darren, and drop Jason wherever he wants. And then...*you and I are going to talk.*"

It was late afternoon, dark closing in. Gabriella hoped there'd be a bus headed for California.

At the station, Darren got out, threw the sliding door open, and ordered them out. He tossed their bags after them, then flung the front door open and yanked June out by the arm.

"What?! You can't do this, Dar! I'm broke! What'm I gonna do?"

But he was away before they knew it, in a screech of tires.

They all stood looking at one another for a moment, and then Jason, silently saluting goodbye, made for the cabs in front of the station.

Gabriella started to say something—a thank you for the magic of Gabriella's Day—but the girl was sorting frantically through her purse, throwing things onto the pavement. And so, glad to escape her turbulent orbit, Gabriella went on into the station.

In the middle of the night, as her bus wooshed its way west to L.A., then north to San Francisco, Gabriella began to notice rain trickling down the window—one of many manifestations of June. A girl who'd said she wished she could be transformed like a simple drop of rain.

But that could never be.

When her bus pulled in to San Francisco around nine, they were waiting for her—two uniformed cops requesting her attendance at the police station.

So, she thought, June had talked. She could hardly believe that in the hours since she'd left Vegas, past midnight, they'd tracked her down, but she went with them without protest.

Outside, gulls swooped in the flat grey sky. She felt the detective benignly watching as her eyes ran over the room, finding steel—table, chairs, window frames, doors.

She wasn't a suspect, he said; this was a routine interview in cooperation with the Las Vegas Metropolitan Police. There'd been a homicide, and she was thought to be one of the last people to see the victim.

The shock left Gabriella breathless.

June Matine's body had been found in an empty field behind the bus station, he said. She'd been stabbed—and then a coyote had gotten to her during the night.

Photographs were laid on the table.

The coyote had made a meal of the girl's middle, and for a moment Gabriella thought she was going to be sick.

"Darren Spiegel, your driver, says they had a fight," the detective said. "Says he dropped June off, with you and Jason

Marks, at the bus station. Tell me about it. When did you last see her?"

"When he leave us there," Gabriella said. "By the curb."

The questions that followed focused on Darren's violence toward the girl, Gabriella insisting he was unlikely to have come back and killed her.

"Ah, but he *did* come back," the detective said. "When he was unloading at his hotel he noticed her phone on the passenger seat. Up till then, he figured she'd just call some guy she had on a string and get a ride back to Boulder. Like the man who paid for your dinner in Aspen, Max Olstead. A real operator, by all accounts. Speigel says he found his card in June's clothes, and there were texts on June's phone, inviting him to join her in Vegas.

"Anyway, without a phone *or* money, Speigel thought June might be in danger. So he went back to find her. And she was gone. That's his story, and if there weren't a better suspect, either he or Max Olstead might be in custody..."

Gabriella flinched, and with a mild smile the cop said, "No, not you, Mrs. Bellini.

"Witnesses put June in a bar less than a half-hour after Speigel dropped you off. It's not the kind of place you'd expect to find a college student. She left with an older guy who's got a conviction for assault. Maybe he expected her to put out and she started to scream..." He shrugged. "Guy like that'd be inside again in a minute if a student cried rape. He's a lot more interesting for this than Speigel or Olstead, since it would've been hard for June to hook up with either of them without her phone."

Gabriella let out a sigh. She'd had plenty of time to think about June's string of Darrens and Jasons and Maxes—and now there was this new one.

It was on the tip of her tongue to say that the detective was probably right about the motive—somebody'd had too much to lose—and to add that June had been too young to know how much more dangerous the desperation of middle-age is than the ruthlessness and recklessness of youth.

Gabriella hadn't known that herself until last night.

But she pressed her lips together and shook her head. She hated having to lie. The cop deserved the truth. But she couldn't summon the courage to tell it.

"Well, that should be all, Mrs. Bellini," he said. "We're just dotting some i's for the LVMPD."

When Gabriella emerged onto the street, the sky was clearing and the sun was sending down warming rays. She shook with relief.

When her hands were steady enough, she slung her pack over her shoulder and clutched it tightly, remembering June's words as she'd sidled up to Gabriella in the empty station restroom, near midnight last night: "Oughta be more careful with those jewels, Gab."

Gabriella hadn't realized until that moment that her treasure was no longer pinned inside her clothes, and when she recovered from the shock of seeing June there, she grabbed her pack, wondering if she'd been in such a stupor from Jason's mary jane that she'd thrown the jewels in there when she'd undressed at the park—and June had rifled through it as she slept.

"So, Gab," June continued, "where ya headed? If you haven't got enough cash to buy me a ticket, too, I noticed a pawnshop near the bar I was just in.

"Looks like the kind of place you wouldn't be questioned about where you got those diamonds. It wasn't from your husband, was it? More likely from that old lady you told us about..."

Sweat had broken out all over Gabriella's body. Her hand groped in her pack, but it was her army knife her fingers closed on. When her fist emerged white-knuckled around it,

June's eyes went wide—not with fear, but with Gabriella's betrayal.

Now, as the remaining clouds floated tranquilly apart over the bay, Gabriella felt the whole thing could almost have been a dream, in which she'd only imagined she might have *used* that blade.

But then the beast of her despair rose again inside her, savage to protect her little bit of freedom, and she knew it didn't matter. She'd as good as killed June anyway.

Because the last time she'd seen the girl, from the window of the station waiting room, she'd been running from the shelter she'd hoped to find back into the devouring night.

Montezuma's Revenge
Michael Bracken

Back then it was easier to cross the border with a corpse in the trunk than it was to cross with a lid of grass in the glove compartment. Cadaver dogs didn't work the checkpoints, Customs officers were more interested in hassling hippies than bothering businessmen, and white Anglo-Saxons entering the U.S. from Mexico did not trigger racial profiling. My partner would have appreciated the ease with which we crossed the border on our way home if he hadn't been the corpse.

Arnie and I had entered Mexico from Texas several days earlier, hired to find one of Willard "Jumbo" Johnson's former employees, a bookkeeper who had disappeared with a quarter-million-dollars taken from Jumbo's safe. We planned to recover the cash, eliminate the bookkeeper, and return home without ever contracting Montezuma's revenge.

Almost three decades earlier, Arnie and I had met as front-line grunts slogging through Europe while driving Heinies back to the Fatherland, and we'd worked together ever since. Though we had no marketable job skills when we returned home from Europe, we landed jobs as bouncers at the Blue Note, one of Jumbo's Houston jazz clubs, and began doing collections work on the side. Before long we gave up bouncing and concentrated on collections, hiring out to low-level bookies and loan sharks around the city, and we were surprised when Jumbo retained us twenty-five years after we'd left his employ. Rumor was the police department provided his muscle, so we didn't understand why Jumbo needed us until we learned we'd be traveling south of the border.

After finishing one last collection for Manny Goldstein, we left Houston in my black Cadillac Sedan de Ville, and soon after crossing the border realized what a poor choice it was for traveling unpaved Mexican back roads. Jumbo's former bookkeeper was last seen at a wide spot in the road on the Gulf coast of Mexico, a village the color of dirt just large enough for a cantina, a church, a bodega, a service station, and a six-room posada, and we drove straight through. Upon arrival the following evening, we rented one of the rooms at the posada, cleaned up, and then found Frankie Sherman downing tequila shots in the nearby cantina.

She was last-call beautiful—the kind of woman you'd take home after a night of drinking but wouldn't want to awaken next to the following morning—and it was obvious she had once been a looker. Though still blonde and blue-eyed, age and alcohol had worn at her, and she'd gone native, wearing a loose-fitting, multi-colored cotton peasant dress and huarache sandals. Her hair hung limply to her shoulders, held away from her face by a pair of silver combs, and she wore no makeup.

Arnie was no beauty either. His nose had been broken twice and never properly reset, and his face had grown doughy with age, even as his hairline retreated and his weight settled around his waist. Like me, he wore a lightweight blue suit over a white button-front dress shirt and a skinny black clip-on tie. Our flattops had been touched up just before leaving Houston, but they drooped in the sweltering heat, and our black wingtips were coated in dust—the same dust that covered my Cadillac—after our short walk from the posada.

We settled onto wooden stools on either side of Jumbo's former bookkeeper. My knuckles were still bruised from giving the what-for to a late-paying greengrocer with a rock-solid jaw, and Frankie eyed them as we introduced ourselves.

"You look thirsty," Frankie said. She attracted the attention of a man the color and texture of worn leather, ordered a trio of tequila shots, and pushed one to each of us.

"I wondered when you'd find me."

She lifted her glass in silent toast.

After we all downed our drinks, I asked, "Where's Jumbo's money?"

"You just drank it."

"How's that?"

"I spent most of it on new I.D. that didn't fool anyone or you wouldn't be here."

"Jumbo says you took him for a quarter mill."

"He lied," she said. "Nineteen thousand and change."

"He inflated his loss?"

"And likely kept the difference."

"Fertitta won't like hearing that."

"Not my problem."

Arnie was a little slow to follow the conversation, and he said, "So there's no money to recover."

Frankie turned to Arnie and put one hand on his knee. "Not from me."

To the back of her head, I said, "We'll have to confirm that ourselves."

Frankie motioned to the bartender, bought a bottle of tequila she paid for with pesos, and led us to the two-room adobe casa where she'd been living since her arrival. A threadbare couch and a chair separated by an end table occupied one half of the front room. A kitchenette with a wooden table and four unmatched wooden chairs occupied the other. The back room contained a bed, a wardrobe, and a six-drawer dresser. A rust-red Volkswagen Beetle with Texas license plates and two flat tires was parked next to the wooden privy a dozen steps from the back door.

We slung our jackets over a kitchen chair and turned our attention to the interior, where an oscillating fan moved tepid air around the front room, neither cooling us nor interfering with the fly buzzing around as we tore the place apart looking for any sign of the stolen money. While we worked, Frankie settled at the kitchen table, opened the tequila bottle, poured two fingers into each of three water glasses, and waited.

We dumped everything on the bed. Shoes, skirts, blouses, dresses, and women's underthings joined a variety of cheap and inexpensive jewelry, several blank ledger books, and a variety of pens. Three empty purses and a wallet containing identification under two different names joined the pile, as did the contents of a make-up bag and some rather flimsy nightwear.

During our search, Arnie found a dozen hundred-dollar bills and I found several dozen pesos. When we finished taking Frankie's place apart and found nothing more, we joined her at the kitchen table and threw the cash in front of her.

While Arnie smelled his fingers and made a face, I said, "You told us it was gone."

"As good as," Frankie said as she nodded toward the cash. "How long do you think that pittance will last, even down here?"

She pushed the glasses toward us, so we sat.

I'd warned Arnie not to drink the water, so he quenched his thirst with tequila, matching Frankie shot-for-shot. I didn't.

After we'd emptied most of the bottle, Frankie told us more. "I kept the books for all of Jumbo's clubs. He was laundering money for the Fertitta family, and he kept a stash of cash in his office safe. I learned the combination by accident."

"So you knew it wasn't Jumbo's money?"

"I knew," she said, "and I didn't care."

"Fertitta is holding him accountable for the loss."

"Serves him right."

"Not just the loss, but Fertitta's charging Jumbo a substantial vig."

"Still not my problem."

"What do you think Jumbo wants from you?"

"I sold my soul when I went to work for that man," Frankie said, "so I'm guessing you're here to collect it."

By then, I'd had enough to drink and I was tired from having done most of the driving. I left Arnie alone with Frankie and returned to the posada, where I killed one of two cockroaches startled by the light before I put myself to bed.

The next morning, I woke to find Arnie passed out on the other bed.

I shook him awake and asked, "You learn anything after I left?"

"That woman can out-drink a fleet of sailors," he said as he sat up, "and she insists she doesn't have Jumbo's money."

"I don't believe her."

Arnie stared at me. "You see how Frankie's living? You think she'd live like that if she had the money?"

"I would," I said. "I wouldn't want to draw attention to myself."

Arnie repeated himself. "She swears she hasn't got it."

"What's going to happen if we go back without Jumbo's money?" I asked. "One of them is lying, and it doesn't much matter which one. If she has the money and we take it back, we're golden. If we go back empty-handed, Jumbo will tell Fertitta we failed. Either way, Fertitta wants his money from Jumbo, and Jumbo's going to take it out on us."

Arnie shook his head. "What's Jumbo ever done for us?"

"He gave us our first jobs."

"Making ugly faces at mugs and throwing drunks to the curb."

"We didn't have anything better," I said.

29

"He didn't like it much when we went freelance, told us we'd never work for him again."

"And yet here we are," I said. "Sometimes he needs guys like us who can get their hands dirty."

"But a woman?" Arnie asked. "We've never hurt a woman."

"We were hired for a job," I said. "We need to finish it."

The posada had indoor plumbing, and we took advantage of it before we tore apart Frankie's Volkswagen, finding nothing more than pocket change and breath mints.

Then Arnie spent the rest of the day drinking with Frankie in the cantina. I spent my time visiting with the locals. Between my broken Spanish and their broken English, I learned that Frankie—Señora Smith to them—had arrived several weeks earlier, had paid six months in advance for the casa, and had spent the time since her arrival sitting in the cantina drinking tequila and awaiting the inevitable.

"Jumbo was using her," Arnie told me when we met for dinner at the cantina that night. "She had to get away. When she saw the chance, she took it."

"Using her for what? We've heard all kinds of sob stories," I reminded Arnie. "What makes her story more believable than all the others?"

"Frankie hasn't asked us for anything and she admits she took Jumbo's money."

"Not all of it."

"She was keeping two sets of books. She said Jumbo was planning to double-cross Fertitta and pin it on her. When she saw a chance to get away, she took it."

"And all she took was nineteen and change?"

"That's all there was in Jumbo's safe the night she hightailed it out of town," Arnie said. "She says she can prove it. She has life insurance."

I stared into Arnie's eyes for a moment and then said, "You're sweet on her, aren't you?"

He looked away without answering. I'd seen that evasive non-answer before, and each time Arnie had fallen for a woman she'd broken his heart.

"Don't get involved," I said. "Not this time. Not with her."

My admonition came too late. When Frankie arrived a few minutes later, Arnie finished his rice and beans and left our table to sit with her at the bar. She'd done something with her hair, applied a little make-up, and accented her drab apparel with a silver and turquoise necklace.

"Dos tequila," she told the bartender, pointedly ignoring my presence.

Using a corn tortilla, I mopped up the last of my dinner, tossed some money on the table, and headed outside. Arnie must have said something funny because Frankie's laughter followed me into the night.

Our usual approach was simple. When sent to collect past-due funds, Arnie and I braced the welcher, gave him the opportunity to make good on his debt, and listened politely to excuses and promises before providing a physical reminder of why falling behind was a bad idea.

The greengrocer who had been our last assignment before leaving Houston had been so desperate that he offered us a night with his wife. That so enraged Arnie we gave the man a beating far worse than we otherwise might have before we emptied his store's cash register and suggested to his wife that she double his life insurance before our next visit.

Arnie was right. Frankie had offered us nothing, and we didn't have the heart to smack her around. Neither of us had ever hit a woman, and we weren't keen on starting with Frankie. Instead, Arnie was playing a different game, and I wasn't certain which part of his body was doing the thinking.

* * *

Arnie did not return to the posada that night, and I waited until after breakfast of huevos rancheros, corn tortillas, and bitter coffee before I went looking for my partner. I found him in Frankie's front room, naked and pressing a bloody towel against his abdomen with one hand, a bottle of tequila in the other. He said, "I'm getting too old for this."

"What happened?"

"You warned me not to drink the water," Arnie explained. "I didn't listen. Gave me horrible stomach cramps and I felt almost as bad as I do now."

He coughed, spit up blood, and then rinsed his mouth with a swing of tequila.

"You were right," Arnie said. "She's had Jumbo's money all along."

"Where'd you find it?"

"In the privy out back," he said. He had been stuck there earlier that morning. While bracing himself for a second wave of abdominal cramps, he cut his palm on the tip of a screw coming up through the thick wooden seat shelf from below. When he finished, Arnie reached through the opening he had just vacated and found a hook screwed into the underside of the shelf. From it hung a large macramé handbag. When he brought the handbag inside and dumped the contents on the bed, Frankie shot him with a derringer we had overlooked in our zealous search for Jumbo's money.

"Where's Frankie now?"

"On the bed."

I checked and found Frankie just as naked as Arnie, but dead. Arnie had broken her neck. I also found a single-shot derringer, a yellow macramé handbag, a ledger book filled with numbers written in a feminine script, and twenty-three straps of one-hundred-dollar bills, all of it smelling of Montezuma's revenge.

I returned to the front room. "I can't take you to a hospital," I said. "There isn't one."

We passed the tequila bottle back and forth until Arnie could no longer lift it to his lips, and a few minutes later he exhaled his last breath.

Frankie, the derringer, and the handbag went into the privy. Then I wrapped Arnie in a blanket and put him, the ledger, and the money in the trunk of my Cadillac.

My partner was ripe by the time I arrived in Houston the next day, but I convinced a quack with a gambling habit to sign a death certificate citing natural causes. A mortician struggling to pay the vig on a business loan was happy to accept double his usual rate for a same-day cremation, and a guy who had served with us in Europe detailed my car without question.

After a shower and a change of clothes, I made an appointment to meet with Jumbo.

Jumbo was sitting behind his desk and Fertitta was sitting on the black leather couch when I arrived. Jumbo didn't bother introducing us. He said, "You got my money?"

I tossed a dozen privy-scented hundreds on his desk.

"That's it?"

"That's all Frankie had left," I told him. "She said she only took nineteen thou and change."

Jumbo's face turned red as he slapped the desktop and rose from his seat. "The lying bitch!"

Fertitta finally spoke. Turning to me, he asked, "You believe her?"

"Doesn't matter if I do or I don't," I said as I motioned toward the money, "but that's all Frankie had when we found her."

"And where is she now?"

I told them what had happened to Arnie without mentioning what he had found, and I told them where I'd left Frankie.

"She also had this," I said as I handed Fertitta the ledger Frankie had cooked after her arrival in Mexico, the life insurance she never had the chance to cash in.

I don't know what happened to Jumbo—that was above my pay grade—but a few weeks later someone else was fronting the Blue Note.

I spent the next few years hiring out to the same low-level bookies and loan sharks as before, but work wasn't the same without Arnie at my side. So, I took his ashes and quietly retired to Puerto Vallarta.

It's amazing how long two hundred and thirty grand will last in Mexico if you don't do anything to draw attention to yourself.

Jerusalem Syndrome
Hilary Davidson

Suzanne Horne fell in love with Tel Aviv at first sight. She'd dreamed of visiting Israel for years, long before she and her husband joined Pastor Ted's church. The long series of flights—from Houston to Chicago to New York to Tel Aviv—hadn't sapped her energy, or her enthusiasm. From the air, the city glittered like a jewel at the edge of the Mediterranean. Up close, on the bus drive in from the airport, she was just as impressed. Every way she looked, there were palm trees and names that resonated with Biblical weight, along with modern skyscrapers and a palpable sense of energy.

"Look to your left," Pastor Ted said as they were getting off the bus beside the hotel. "That's the ancient port city of Jaffa. Four thousand and five hundred years old and still going strong."

"Jaffa! Where Jonah was swallowed by the whale!" called out Minday Serle. She poked her teenage daughter, Mercy, in the shoulder. "Remember that?"

Of course you remember that, Suzanne thought. You've gone on Pastor Ted's Tour of the Holy Land every year! Then she caught Mercy's eye and felt guilty. The girl gave an uncertain nod and her eyes slid to the ground. Minday might be a piece of work, but her daughter was never anything but gentle and shy.

"Exactly, Minday. All right, everyone. Tonight we have dinner and prayer circle," Pastor Ted said.

"Do we have time to take a short walk on the beach?" Suzanne asked. She could already imagine soft sand under her feet while the Mediterranean lapped at her toes.

Pastor Ted's smile remained plastered on his face, but his eyes narrowed. "No, you don't. You just have time to take your luggage up to your room now."

Suzanne wasn't ready to give in. After four years of waiting for a spot to open up on Pastor Ted's annual Tour of the Holy Land, she and her husband Bobby had snagged spaces, thanks to their work on—and donations to—the presidential campaign. It wasn't that Pastor Ted was a big fan of the candidate—behind the scenes, he referred to the man as a *Mormon moron*—but certain services were expected if you wanted to rise in that circle. While Bobby thrived in that environment, Suzanne struggled to fit in.

"What time, exactly, is Prayer Circle?" Suzanne asked.

Pastor Ted shot her a look that telegraphed what a patently foolish woman she was. "If you wanted to walk on the beach, Suzanne, you should have gone to California for Christmas." The tone of his voice was soft but there was steel under it.

"With all the sinners bound for hell," Minday added.

"It looks so beautiful..." Suzanne mumbled.

"Of course it's beautiful," Pastor Ted said. "God created it as the Holy Land. It is a blessed patch of earth."

"Why did you have to ask that?" Bobby was beside Suzanne, head down, pulling their wheeled suitcase behind him. "You know how he is. You won't get to set foot in the sand. Maybe none of us will."

"Sorry," Suzanne murmured. "I was just so excited."

"Just don't open your mouth, okay? Because whenever you do, you put your foot in it."

Suzanne's shoulders slumped. She was always putting her foot wrong around the church crowd, especially Pastor Ted.

She managed to keep her mouth closed for the rest of the

evening, except to eat the modest meal provided by the hotel: couscous and vegetables with a few beans mixed in, plus a few strips of flatbread with hummus.

"How much did we pay for this trip?" Bobby whispered to her. "They're sure not spending it on the food."

Suzanne shook her head.

"Do they serve wine with dinner here?" Bobby asked the man on the other side of him.

"No, you have to pay for the wine yourself if you want that," announced Minday Serle. She was well up the inverted U-shaped table, sitting as close as she could get to Pastor Ted's right hand, her owlish husband nodding frequently but not saying a word. Minday had ears like a fox.

"Does someone want to order wine?" Pastor Ted said. "I thought we were all full of the Holy Spirit tonight."

"Just curious," Bobby muttered.

"Not that there's a crime in a glass of wine," Pastor Ted went on. "But, as our Lord teaches us, *Wherefore be ye not unwise, but understanding what the will of the Lord is. And be not drunk with wine, wherein is excess; but be filled with the Spirit.*"

"Ephesians!" Minday called out loudly. She nudged Mercy, who was seated on her left, the only thing between herself and the pastor. "Remember that?"

"Yes, Mom," Mercy mumbled. Suzanne saw the girl as a fig leaf—a way for Pastor Ted and Minday to deflect attention from their too-close relationship. It was impossible to miss the fact that Pastor Ted's wife *wasn't* on this trip.

Bobby's jaw tightened, but he didn't say anything. He shot Suzanne a dark look that spoke volumes to her. *Don't say a word.*

"While we're on the subject of Ephesians," Pastor Ted added, "Let us contemplate the Scripture. Giving thanks always for all things unto God the Father in the name of our Lord Jesus Christ. Submitting yourselves one to another in the fear of God. And wives, submit yourselves unto your own husbands, as unto the Lord. For the husband is the head of the wife, even as Christ is the head of the church, and he is the savior of the body." Pastor Ted smiled around the room. "Let us all meditate on that. Shall we pray?"

It was dark outside before the twenty-five parishioners were able to escape back to their rooms. Suzanne and Bobby's was a tiny little cell, but it had a balcony and a spectacular view of the Mediterranean. "Do you think it's too late to walk down to the beach?" Suzanne asked. "It's so close. We could…"

"Shut up," Bobby said. "You're the one who put him into a bad mood. Now Ted's taking it out on me."

"All I did was mention the beach."

"I don't want to hear your carping."

Suzanne bit her tongue and counted to ten, just like the counselor at the church had told her to. They'd had to take counseling sessions when they'd joined the church, and Suzanne had never managed to graduate from them. The cost of the ongoing counseling was another source of friction between them. Pastor Ted insisted on it, saying that the modern world messed with women, making them believe foolishness instead of seeing the world as it was meant to be.

"I'm sorry," she said finally.

"Don't be sorry," Bobby said. "Just stop ruining this for me. You know how important this is."

They'd joined Pastor Ted's church five years earlier, within months of their move to Montgomery County for Bobby's job. At first, they'd joined a Methodist church, but then some of Bobby's colleagues made it clear that executives on the inside track were all members of Pastor Ted's congregation. Their CEO was a longtime member of that church.

"I know. But Pastor Ted doesn't always act in a godly way."

They'd had plenty of arguments about Pastor Ted. After

they joined his church, Bobby banned Suzanne's brother from visiting them. *We don't need any of his twisted San Francisco lifestyle around our kids,* Bobby had insisted. *We don't even have kids yet,* Suzanne had argued back. *We will one day. And this is how it's going to be.*

Suzanne had grown up with the idea of Jesus as a loving figure, the perfect embodiment of kindness and understanding. At Pastor Ted's church, members sometimes circulated messages with Jesus in jungle camouflage, holding an Uzi.

"Look, Suzanne," Bobby said. "You know I'm up for a promotion. If things don't go well on this trip..."

"It's ridiculous that Pastor Ted has any influence over that."

"No one cares what you think." Bobby loomed over her, grabbing her shoulders and squeezing hard. "Stop making problems for me. If you don't shut up, I'll make you shut up."

He gave her a hard shake, shoving her back so that she collided with the small writing desk next to the balcony. He stormed out of the room without looking back.

Suzanne swallowed hard and stepped out onto the balcony. There was a hard knot in the center of her chest, squeezing her heart tight. Bobby hadn't always been that way. Five years under Pastor Ted's guidance had warped something inside him.

Lord, please show me the way, she prayed. Help me to do what's right. Make me Your instrument. Help me to be strong enough to deal with whatever comes my way. That was one of her little rebellions since she'd joined Pastor Ted's church. There were prayers that she was supposed to recite, renouncing the sinful modern world and promising to live as a proper woman should. Instead, Suzanne prayed as she always had.

When Bobby returned, he'd settled down a bit—a few drinks could have that effect on him—and when he pulled her onto the bed and she showed no resistance, that seemed to mollify him. He was peaceable enough the next day, when the bus took them to the Sea of Galilee. It was at the edge of a hillside city called Tiberias, and there was a boardwalk by the water. It was beautiful, there was no doubt of that, but what stunned Suzanne was its size.

"It's so tiny," she said, staring at it. "It's not a sea. It's maybe a lake. You could *swim* to the other side."

"Is that what impresses you, Suzanne?" Pastor Ted asked. "Swimming in Galilee, the very place where Jesus walked on water?"

"No, I just meant..."

"I guess you're thinking about the beach again, while the rest of us are thinking of Christ's ministry." Pastor Ted held up one arm. "Behold, the very spot where our Lord and Savior delivered the Sermon on the Mount."

Suzanne stared up the hillside. Somehow, she'd always imagined that *the Mount* meant there was a mountain. Instead, there was just the hillside. She bit her tongue.

"Do you have to say every stupid thought that comes into your head?" Bobby whispered to her on the bus, when they were bound for Nazareth.

"It just came out. I mean, weren't you surprised about how small it is?"

"That's not the point. Shut up."

Suzanne kept that in mind while they were in Nazareth. She was shocked by it, too, but in a different way. It was a living, breathing city, filled with people, but one of the first things she noticed was a large poster with three boys, each dropping a weapon—a gun, a knife, a chain—into a bin. It was an anti-gang ad she wouldn't have been surprised to see in Houston, but it jarred her in the Holy Land. The beautiful shrines were more in line with what she was expecting to see. They were crowded, and she couldn't help but overhear tour guides with other English-speaking groups.

"Can any good thing come out of Nazareth?" asked a gap-toothed man with a smile.

A group of older ladies with him laughed. "What a terrible thing to say!" said one, mock-tsking.

"That's what Nathanael asks in John 1:46," the guide said. "And people still ask today."

"It's amazing, coming here," another woman said. "You get such a different understanding of the Bible."

Suzanne wished that were true for her. She followed the group, taking in the magnificent sights, but it didn't touch her soul, not in the way she'd expected. The next day, they went to Bethlehem, which was in Palestinian East Jerusalem. She had looked forward to seeing Jesus's birthplace as long as she could remember, but the day was marked mostly by waiting in one security line to get into Palestinian territory, and then by an infinitely longer one to return to Israeli territory.

It wasn't until the third day of touring that her heart started to lift. That was the day they were to see Jerusalem itself, the glittering jewel they'd all waited for. Their first stop was Gethsemane on the Mount of Olives, where a majestic church marked the site where Jesus had surrendered himself to the Roman authorities. It was a beautiful structure, with Corinthian columns and stone statues and a spectacular gold-infused mosaic above its entrance. But what captured Suzanne's heart was the olive grove outside, with its ancient trees with massive, gnarled trunks.

"Some of these trees have stood here for more than a thousand years," she overheard a guide say to another group. Was that true? Somehow, it made her heart beat faster. It wasn't that long, in Biblical terms, but it made her feel as if she were getting closer to what she was searching for. She couldn't picture Jesus, exactly, but in her heart she felt an echo of his sacrifice: he'd stood in the Garden of Gethsemane and decided not to run but to embrace God's plan. There was nothing greater that Suzanne could imagine.

But that feeling was impossible to sustain on the bus after Pastor Ted got up to speak. "Our next stop is the Wailing

Wall," he announced. "The Jews like to call it the Western
Wall, so you'll see that on signs. There's a separate entrance
for ladies and gentlemen, and you can expect to be searched,
okay? It's not unusual for ladies to get full-body searches
here. And ladies, there are some special rules you need to
follow at the Wall. The first one is, you're not allowed to
pray."

"What?" Suzanne gasped.

"You can say whatever you want in your head," Pastor
Ted clarified. "But you're not allowed to pray aloud. Or to
talk. Or to sing. If that happens, men have been known to
throw chairs into the ladies' section."

"Throw...chairs?" Suzanne repeated.

"Also, you can't go near the main section of the Wall.
There's a special section for ladies."

"What special section?"

"You'll see," Pastor Ted answered. "It's separate, but
equal in importance."

When Suzanne did finally see the women's section, it broke
her heart. The Western Wall was behind a wire fence, where
male guards monitored tight entryways. The section of the
Wall for men was massive, so much so that there was space
for every man who wanted to touch the Wall to walk right up
to it and pray aloud if the Spirit moved him. The women's
section was miniscule—a fifth of the size of the men's—and
packed to the gills with silent women waiting their turn to get
close to the Wall.

Suzanne's first instinct was to make a break for the men's
side of the Wall. But the guards shouted at any woman who
went near that entryway, so she followed a group led by
Minday Serle into the women's side. They stood waiting for
the women ahead of them to have their turn and get out.

"Do women's prayers matter less than men's?" Suzanne
muttered.

"Shh!" Minday hissed. "Don't talk!"

Mercy leaned closed to Suzanne. "When I was little, my dad was able to take me into the men's side." She gazed at it wistfully through the fence.

There were a few women who'd parked themselves in chairs in front of the Wall. They weren't budging, but most of the women standing behind them seemed to be waiting just to have a few seconds to make contact with the Wall.

It wasn't right, Suzanne thought. None of this was right. As she got closer, she could see tiny bits of paper, thousands of them, tucked into the crevices of the Wall. Was *that* how women were supposed to pray? Write to God, as if God were a distant pen pal? She looked to her left, through the section of fence dividing the men's and women's portions. Bobby and Pastor Ted and the other men in their group were walking up to the Wall and praying aloud.

More women entered their tiny pen, pressing her from behind. That made Suzanne push forward, desperate for a moment with the wall. As she got closer to it, she stretched out one hand, even though it was well beyond her reach.

Then three women who were ahead of her each unfurled a fabric scroll. Suzanne couldn't read what was on them, only that the letters were Hebrew. The women began to pray aloud.

The reaction was swift. Shouts rang out from the men's side of the Wall. Behind Suzanne, guards shoved their way in, pushing women to the side, and grabbed the praying women, forcibly dragging them out. A man ran up to one and kicked her in the side. The guards didn't give him a glance, but they were rough with the women who'd been trying to pray.

More guards poured in. They positioned themselves in front of the Wall, shoving the women back. They shouted in a few different languages, but the only word Suzanne understood was "Closed!"

"No!" Suzanne cried. She was taller and more muscular than most of the women, but the crowd carried her back with it. Her chance to touch the divine was being swept away, and there was nothing she could do about it. "There is neither Jew nor Greek," she called out. "There is neither bond nor free, there is neither male nor female, for you are all one in Jesus Christ."

Minday slapped her across the face. "Are you trying to start a riot?" she demanded. She grabbed Suzanne by the arm as if she were a child, as she stormed over to where the men of their group were waiting for them.

"You'll never guess who started quoting Scripture at the wall," Minday said.

"This is insane," Suzanne said. "Does anyone here really think this is what God wants? Women cast off into a chicken coop, then beaten if they pray out loud?"

"Look everyone," Pastor Ted said. "We have our first case of Jerusalem Syndrome."

Minday cackled beside him. "Suzanne thinks God is talking to her!"

"I didn't say that!"

There were murmurs and chuckles from the group.

"This city can do that to people," Pastor Ted said. "The weight of history is heavy. It causes weak-minded people to have delusions. Sometimes they think they suddenly know what God wants."

"What makes you think *you* know what God wants?" Suzanne demanded. Her words shocked the church group into silence.

"Enough!" Pastor Ted shouted. "You're going back to the hotel now, Suzanne. Obviously, this is all too much for you."

Suzanne looked at Bobby, but he wouldn't meet her eyes. He stayed silent.

"The rest of you are seeing what I'm seeing, aren't you?" Suzanne asked. "You think this is okay?"

"That's your delusion talking, I'm afraid." Pastor Ted

pointed at the exit. "You can get a taxi. We'll discuss this at Prayer Circle tonight."

Suzanne felt like a sleepwalker as she headed for the exit. Was what she had said so terrible? It was always like this with Pastor Ted and his cabal: they picked on anyone who wasn't like them. She was the scapegoat for the group.

When she got outside the gate, she headed for a taxi, but then stopped in her tracks. Why would she go back to the hotel because Pastor Ted told her to? She was in the holiest city in the holiest of lands. Why not explore it herself? She walked around the ancient walls of Old Jerusalem until she came to the Jaffa Gate.

When she thought of it later, that was the moment her trip to Israel truly began. Without a map, she found the Church of the Holy Sepulcher, which marked the place where Jesus was crucified and buried. She meandered through the narrow streets, up and down short staircases and through bazaars selling scarves and jewelry and religious paraphernalia of all types. The city was divided into quarters—Jewish, Christian, Muslim, and Armenian—and she followed her feet through each one. She found the Via Dolorosa and marked the stations of the cross, then stumbled into a restaurant in the Muslim Quarter that served the best meal she'd eaten on the trip. Old Jerusalem was tiny and close, with archways that frequently blocked out the sunlight, but it made her imagination soar.

She bought a small wooden cross for her brother, because she wished, more than anything, that he were there to see this. At the same time, she felt ashamed, because she had let Pastor Ted and his twisted interpretation of scripture squeeze the joy out of her life. No more, she thought.

When she finally got into a taxi, it was late. The driver was an elderly Jewish man, and they chatted all the way back to Tel Aviv. He seemed to get a kick out of playing tour guide, and told her about the sights she absolutely had to see. "By now, you've probably noticed, in Israel, every lake is a sea, every hill is a mountain, and every town is a city," he told her. She laughed for the first time in what felt like forever. Her perspective wasn't the problem. It really was Pastor Ted.

When she got to the hotel, she headed up to Pastor Ted's room, which was on a higher floor than the parishioners. She rang the bell, but he didn't answer. It was after midnight, so Prayer Circle was long over. He had to be in there, and come hell or high water, he was going to hear what she had to say. So she rang and rang and rang the bell, and finally she heard footsteps. "What the hell do you want?" he called.

She didn't answer, except to ring the bell again.

Pastor Ted opened the door a crack. He frowned when he saw who it was. "I have nothing to say to you."

"Well, I have a lot to say to you," Suzanne said, surprising him as she pushed past him and into the room. Then she stopped in her tracks, realizing this room wasn't like the others: it was a suite, with a living room and a dining room. There had been a feast there, given the dishes on the dining table, but it looked like it was for three, complete with steak and champagne. "You've been living quite the life here, haven't you?" Suzanne said, moving closer to the table. There was lipstick on two of the glasses, the same pinkish-red shade.

"That's none of your business. Get out."

There was a low moan behind a closed door. Suzanne moved toward it but Pastor Ted jumped in front of her, blocking it.

"Who's in there?" Suzanne asked. "Because I know it's not your wife."

"No one."

"Let me guess," Suzanne said. "I bet it's Minday. Shall we check?"

He shoved her back. "Get out."

"You're rotten to the core," Suzanne said. "You use God

to further your own ends. You're the worst kind of hyp-
ocrite."

"And you're going to rot in hell for all eternity."

"Nothing you can say will scare me," Suzanne said.
"There's one thing I realized today. No one has a monopoly
on God." She raised her voice. "Hey, Minday, why don't you
come out?"

To her surprise, the bedroom door opened. Only it wasn't
Minday who was standing there, but her teenage daughter.

"Mercy?" Suzanne could barely catch her breath. The girl
was naked. Her eyes were downcast, and her expression
broke Suzanne's heart. "What are you..." Her voice trailed
off. *What are you doing here,* she was going to ask, but there
was no question in Suzanne's mind what the answer was. Her
head swiveled around. *Three* glasses on the table. Pastor Ted
grabbed her, knocking her off balance and through the doorway.

"No one is going to miss you," Pastor Ted said. "Your
husband will have no trouble finding a much more suitable
wife. An obedient wife."

The balcony door was open and he dragged her through it.
They were about the same height, but he was heavier. He
shoved her against the wrought-iron railing. "Everyone saw
you having your psychotic break today," he hissed. "No one
will be surprised that you jumped off the balcony. You'll be a
sad cautionary tale."

Suzanne fought back, but he was stronger. Inch by inch,
her torso edged over the balcony. She grabbed his body, determined to take him down with her. Then Pastor Ted cried out
and let go. Suzanne saw Mercy standing in the doorway,
holding a steak knife.

"You cut me?" Pastor Ted shifted his shoulder forward
and stared at it. The wound wasn't large, but it was bleeding.

"You're a monster," Mercy whispered.

Pastor Ted grabbed for the knife. Suzanne took a step back

and shoved him with all her might. He toppled over the balcony and flew down eighteen stories.

Instead of panic, Suzanne was filled with a sudden sense of calm. She knew exactly what to do. "Let's get you into a bathrobe, okay, honey?"

Mercy nodded mutely. Suzanne gently pried the knife out of her hand and helped her into a terrycloth robe. "What happened to you is a crime."

There were tears on Mercy's cheeks. "Mama said I had no choice."

Suzanne hugged her. "We're going downstairs to the front desk. We're going to tell them that Pastor Ted assaulted you and I got you out of his room. But we're not going to tell them..."

"That he accidentally fell off his balcony?" Mercy interrupted. "No, we won't."

Suzanne knew she should feel terrible about what happened, but she didn't. The only thing she felt bad about was that Mercy didn't want to get her mother in trouble. When the police came, she couldn't tell them that horrible woman had been pimping out her fourteen-year-old daughter. Instead, she had to watch her pretend to weep, knowing full well that what Minday Serle was grieving was her special seat atop Pastor Ted's corrupt pyramid.

Just wait until we get home, Suzanne thought. Because your reckoning isn't over yet, Minday.

She kept that part to herself. She knew she had to be grateful that the Tel Aviv police seemed to appreciate the surface story—fundamentalist clergyman caught raping a child and then decides to kill himself—without searching for undercurrents beneath it.

"I can't believe Pastor Ted raped that poor girl," Bobby muttered.

"Yes, you can," Suzanne said. "We all can. We knew there was something wrong with him, but we never tried to stop him." She headed for the front door of the hotel.

"Where are you going?" he called.

"It's time I went for that walk on the beach."

She crossed the road in front of the hotel and slipped off her sneakers when she got to the sand. She walked to the water and let the waves lap at her feet. She looked at her watch. It was almost eight in the morning. She counted back in her head. That meant it was midnight in Houston, and ten o'clock in San Francisco. She pulled out her phone and called her brother.

"Suzanne?" he sounded surprised to hear her voice. "Is everything okay?"

"It is. I just wanted to tell you I love you. And I'm sorry for...for a lot of things. I've missed seeing you. There are so many things I've wanted to tell you."

He was quiet for a moment. "I've missed you, too. Tell me what's going on. I thought Mom said you were going to Israel for Christmas?"

"That's where I am now. It's been a life-changing experience. But I'll have to wait till I see you to tell you how."

"They say travel's supposed to expand your mind."

Suzanne thought of Pastor Ted hurtling down eighteen stories. "It's been liberating," she said.

Clean Getaway
LD Masterson

"Nine-one-one. What is your emergency?"

The sound of the dispatcher's voice brings everything into focus, which both calms and terrifies me. "Please. I need help. My brother...he's hurt bad. Someone...He's not breathing. I'm going to start CPR."

I hit the speaker button, lay the receiver on Evan's desk, and turn back to the still form on the plush carpet behind me. The puddle of blood under his head turns the dark hunter green to black.

"Sir? Sir? Please stay on the line."

The woman on the phone is yelling questions but I ignore them except to confirm the address. She'll send the police as well as the rescue squad. I roll Evan onto his back, trying not to look at his crushed skull, and begin chest compressions. But they won't do any good, he's dead already.

I know. I killed him.

I didn't want to. I mean, I've never liked him but he is... was my brother. And my business partner. Which is why I had to kill him. I don't know how he got ahold of that ledger, all my little under-the-table dealings, but I knew he wouldn't let it go. He was always such a damn Boy Scout.

"One, two, three, four, five..." I'm counting off just loud enough for the nine-one-one operator, still on the line, to hear me. And waiting for the sound of sirens. I look around my brother's office, mostly in shadow outside the harsh light of the desk lamp. Did I think of everything? Wiped my prints off that ugly stone sculpture—heavy enough to do the job without much effort on my part—but left the blood and bits of... oh Christ, what a mess.

"One, two, three, four, five..." I had to call it in. Couldn't pretend I hadn't been here. Too many people in the building when I arrived. Hell, I talked with a couple in the elevator. I just hope no one saw him. I have to sell the cops on the idea he was attacked before I got here and I tried to save him.

"One, two, three, four, five..." And the ledger. It has to go with me. Can't let the cops find that. That's my insurance policy. That and all the money I've squirreled away in off-shore accounts. It was a sweet setup but it's all over now.

I was a little frantic trying to figure how to get it out of here until I saw Baxter's crate. Baxter was in the office when I arrived, right by Evan's side like always. In fact, I'd walked over to pet him when I saw what Evan was reading. But when things got heated, the dog got agitated and Evan put him in the conference room. I can hear him there now, that soft whimper. Does he know? Does he understand what's happening in here?

"One, two, three, four, five..." I hear them now, coming down the hall. The muffled sounds of stomping feet and voices I can't quite make out. The door's unlocked and they push their way in. A couple EMTs drop down on either side of Evan, the one next to me putting his hand on my arm.

"Sir. It's okay, sir. We've got him. We'll take it from here."

I let them push me away and rock back on my heels. I don't have to fake being exhausted. Faking CPR was hard enough.

A cop helps me to my feet and leads me around Evan's desk to the big leather chairs in front. He eases me onto one and sits on the edge of the other.

"Sir, I'm Officer Greene. I have to ask you a few questions."

Yeah, he looked pretty green. That should help. "Yeah, okay."

"You called nine-one-one, correct."

I nodded.

"This is your brother?" He glanced at the desk and Evan behind it. The EMTs were still back there but they weren't doing CPR.

"Yeah. Evan. Evan Sullivan. I'm Ian Sullivan."

"Can you tell me what happened here?"

Okay. Here we go. "I don't know. I had meetings all day, off site. I got back about seven. Sara, our receptionist, was already gone but the outer door was still unlocked. I went into my office to check my messages and...you know, end of day stuff. Then I came over to talk to Evan and...he was there. And all that blood. I tried to...he wasn't breathing. So I called nine-one-one and I started CPR."

"You both work here?"

"Yeah. We're partners. Sullivan Imports."

The EMTs are packing up, closing their heavy cases. They aren't taking Evan. One of them shakes his head at Officer Greene. The other gives me a pitying look. I lower my face into my hands. It feels like an appropriate gesture and gives me some protection in case my expression gives me away. Damn it, Evan. Why couldn't you just let it go?

Officer Greene gets up without speaking and walks away. I hear the EMTs leaving but others are arriving. Coroner's office, I guess. Someone drops heavily into the other chair. It's not Officer Greene. I wait for him to speak but the silence drags on and I have to lift my head to see him.

The new guy is in plain clothes, older, with a world-weary look about him. I've got to be careful with this one.

"Mr. Sullivan, I'm Detective Borough. I'm sorry for your loss."

His voice is flat, the words without meaning. I just nod.

"I need you to take me through everything that happened tonight."

"But I already told that officer. Greene."

"Yes, I know. Now I need you to tell me."

I go through it again, being careful to mix up the wording so it doesn't sound rehearsed.

He's making notes in a little flip pad. "And you didn't see your brother, didn't hear anything when you got back?"

"No. Nothing. I knew he was still here because the outer door was unlocked. But his office door was closed and I didn't go in. Like I said, I wanted to check my messages and stuff first."

"And how long did that take? Checking your messages and *stuff?*"

Crap. I told Greene I was in my office fifteen to twenty minutes. That would jive pretty well with when I called nine-one-one if anyone saw me come in. But what if this guy decides to check my phone or my e-mail? He'll know I didn't open either one. Well, I can't change my story now. "I'm not sure. About fifteen to twenty minutes, I think. I didn't look at the clock."

"Mr. Sullivan, do you know anyone who would want to kill your brother? Did he have any enemies?"

Ironic. This is the one question I can answer honestly. "No. No one. Evan was an honest, likable, really decent guy. I can't think of anyone who would want to hurt him."

"Was he married?"

"Divorced. But it was...amicable. You know, as much as divorce ever is. She had an affair, wanted out so she could marry the other guy. Evan didn't fight it. He even let her take the kids to live on the coast, although he has joint custody. Like I said, a decent guy." A thought strikes me. "Um, should I call...?"

"No, we'll take care of that."

I'm glad. I never had much use for his ex, but it isn't a call

54

I want to make. Borough scribbles in his little pad while I wait.

"Sullivan Imports. What is it you import?"

"Rugs. Tapestries. Art objects. We work with a lot of high-end decorators."

"How's business? Any problems with customers, suppliers, that sort of thing?"

"Nothing major. Usual little stuff. Business is good." Yeah, it was good. Plenty of Evan's legitimate imports that I could use to disguise my not-so-legitimate ones.

"You're partners. Just the two of you?"

I nod. I know where this one is going.

"Who gets his half of the business?"

"Well, I take over operations, but his kids, my nephews, own his half in trust until they're twenty-one, then they can come in as active partners or I buy them out—their choice."

Hah. No motive there.

"Do you keep much cash on hand or valuable merchandise?"

"No. Sara has a petty cash box but..." Here's my opening. I let my eyes wander around Evan's office like I'm looking for something he could have been killed over, then I jump to my feet. "Baxter!"

Boroughs gets up with me. "What?"

"Baxter. Evan's dog. That's his travel crate. He must be here." I do a quick turn around the office, heading for the conference room door. "Baxter. Where are you boy?"

I find Baxter cowering under the big table, a mass of shaggy white fur. He wasn't a brave dog at the best of times, and I guess getting locked away from Evan and all the commotion and maybe the smell of blood had been too much for him. I drop to my knees, shoving a chair out of the way so I can reach him.

"It's okay, boy. It's okay." I manage to coax him out and he half climbs into my lap. Whatever he understands about what just happened, it doesn't look like he's blaming me. I'm glad. I like Baxter. And he's my ticket out of this mess.

Borough is standing over me. "This is your brother's dog?"

"Yeah."

"Is it usual for him to be here?"

I crane my neck to look up at him. "It's not unusual... depends on Evan's schedule. But if he was going to be in the office all day, he'd usually bring Baxter. And I'll tell you something else, Evan wasn't surprised by whoever killed him. Baxter always slept next to Evan's desk. Evan only put him in here if he had a meeting or a visitor or someone came in who didn't want Baxter around."

"Wouldn't he have been barking?"

I turn my attention to the dog trying to hide his face against my chest. "No. Baxter doesn't bark. He's a rescue and Evan always figured he'd been abused in some way. I've never heard him make a sound above a whimper."

It works. I see it in Borough's eyes. I've planted the idea of someone else. I'm being helpful. I'm sitting on the floor with my brother's dog in my lap. I may not be off the suspect list completely but I've got some wiggle room. A little window. That's all I need.

"Detective, can I go? I'd like to take Baxter home with me. And I need to..." I gesture at my clothes, which I managed to smear with Evan's blood.

I try not to hold my breath until he answers.

"Yeah. You can go. And take the dog. But don't go far. I'll have some more questions for you tomorrow."

I get up and scoop Baxter into my arms. He's a little heavy, thirty—forty pounds, but I don't want him trying to find Evan or sniffing at the drying stain by the desk. Like I said, I like Baxter. And he loved Evan. More than I did, I guess.

I carry him to the crate and drop to my knees, setting Baxter on the carpet. I unlatch the door and lay my hand over the front of the pad inside, holding it down over the ledger I had hidden underneath. "Come on, boy. Inside." He enters without hesitation, turns around, and settles onto the cloth covered bed. I can barely feel the outline of the book through the thick pad. He doesn't seem to notice it at all. I secure the door, stand, and pick up the crate. Borough is talking to one of the crime scene guys in white coveralls. Officer Greene asks if I need any help. I tell him no, thanks. I leave my briefcase on my desk. A sure sign I'll be back tomorrow.

Moments later I'm sliding Baxter and the ledger into the back of my SUV. The sky is clear and loaded with stars. A warm breeze stirs the air and sets Baxter's nose twitching. I get in and lower the tailgate window for him. Then we head out. But I'm not heading home.

At the first intersection I stop and pull the battery out of my cell phone. I know cops can track some phones even if they're turned off. The guy I'm going to see wouldn't appreciate my leading any cops to his door. It takes about thirty minutes to get there. It used to be a nice neighborhood, small neat homes on tiny well-kept lots. Now the houses are falling apart and the lots are strewn with junk. I leave the back window open a crack for air, lock the car and walk around back.

He isn't happy to see me.

"Sorry, Stu, but it's a bit of an emergency."

"You running?"

"Yeah. The game's up. I gotta blow."

He looks suspiciously toward the window. "You better have not brought any cops down on me."

"No. Don't worry. I was careful. I wasn't followed. I need the papers and my bag."

Stu is the best around when it comes to forged IDs and passports. I had him make mine up about six months ago and just hold them for me; the papers and a carry-on bag already packed with a change of clothes and the usual necessities. I figure everything else I can buy new.

The papers look good. I put the passport in my bag, the

driver's license in my wallet and dump everything with my real name in the trash.

"You still owe me," Stu says. "Final payment."

He brings up a money transfer app on his phone already set to his off-shore account and hands it to me to enter my codes. For a second I think about using the Sullivan Imports account, let Evan pay this one last bill for me...but this is no time to be fooling around. I've got to walk away clean.

Hmm. Clean. I glance out the window. An older-model dark sedan sits in the drive. "I need a clean car, Stu. Just in case they come after me before I can get clear."

He follows my gaze. "Yeah, she's clean. Runs good, too."

We negotiate a price. "Just give me a couple days before you report it stolen," I ask.

"Nah. When you get where you're going, send word where you left it and I'll have one of my boys pick it up."

"And you'll take care of mine?"

"It'll be disposed of. No problem."

I transfer Baxter in his crate to the back seat of the sedan. I trust Stu but I'm not going to pull that ledger out in front of him. Better to leave it tucked away for now.

Heading for Chicago. Should take about six hours. I can get a direct flight from there to my nice, new, non-extradition home, and even if Borough is watching for me, he's not likely to be covering O'Hare. Traffic is light this time of night and I'm making good time. I'm almost sorry when I get to the rest stop.

"Okay, boy, end of the line for you."

There are a few semis in the truck lane, drivers catching some sleep. I'm the only car. I park as far into the shadows as I can get and open the back door. Baxter's waiting patiently, tail thumping as I open the crate. I slide my hand under his bed to retrieve the ledger and stuff it into my carry-on. Then I leave the bag, close the crate and lift it out of the car. Damn. I really don't want to do this. I thought of just dumping him somewhere. He's a cute dog, someone would take him in. But that's just it. He's too cute. If someone picked him up too soon…I'm sure Evan had him micro-chipped. It would be like calling the cops and telling them I'm flying out of O'Hare. *Hey, guys, catch me if you can.*

I walk out to where there are a few picnic tables scattered around and set him down on one. The big dumpster alongside the building will get the crate. I pull Baxter onto the table and run my fingers into the long fur around his neck. "Come, buddy. Let's get your collar off." Don't need any good Samaritan trying to call Evan to tell him they found his dog's body.

The collar is bulky and has a funny clasp. Takes me a couple tries to get it loose. I pull it out from under his fur and see the light. A small green flashing light on a box in the thickest part of the collar. I turn it toward the parking lot lights and read the label: PET FINDER GPS.

The memory hits me, clear and sharp. Evan's voice, all excited, telling me about his new toy, "It's a satellite tracking system and it'll send alerts to my phone if he wanders off so he can't get lost."

A pair of State Police cars swing into the lot and pin me with their headlights. I sit quietly, scratching Baxter behind the ear. Maybe they're not here for me. Maybe Borough isn't monitoring Evan's phone and these guys are just taking a break.

Two cops jump out, guns drawn. "Ian Sullivan, stay where you are. Put your hands on your head."

I set Baxter on the picnic table. He climbs into his crate as I raise my hands.

Commute
Michael Dymmoch

I'm not sure why the three-pound crowbar was in the car. I can't even remember when I'd put it there. Under the back seat. Out of sight. Out of mind. But when I cleaned the car out before leaving it with the dealer, I dropped the crowbar in the bottom of the large Crate and Barrel bag I use to transport light bulky things. The bag is clear polyethylene, so I wrapped the crowbar in a jacket. No sense alarming paranoid members of the public or wasting police time explaining what used to be an ordinary tool.

The car dealership was a short walk from a train station. A pleasant walk. Not too sunny. Not too hot. Daisies and white clovers grew beside the path. Birds serenaded.

Other passengers arrived. A retired man—by his graying hair and casual clothes; a millennial worshiping his pocket-god; a young Ms. Executive in a smart pants suit and spiky heels. When the train pulled up, Mr. Retiree stood back and let the rest of us precede him.

The car was crowded—no empty seats. Few with only a single passenger. We four newcomers ended up sitting near one another in aisle seats. I put my train pass in the holder. As the conductor strolled the aisle, punching tickets, I studied the other riders. Most seemed to be business people, starting their day on-line or continuing where they'd left off—earlier—at home. One or two of the young women could have been students, high school upper class or college. A grandmotherly older lady was quietly reading to a three- or four-year-old—a Dr. Seuss book. Two middle-aged women chatted amiably. A suit-type took out his iPhone, looked around, then headed for the door. I watched him through the window as he stood in the vestibule gesticulating and getting redder in the face. Finally, there was a praying man sitting alone in the seat across the aisle from me, right behind Ms. Executive. He was white, middle-aged, casually dressed and unremarkable except that his lips were moving, and from time to time he sighed and closed his eyes. Ms. Executive looked at her seatmate and rolled her eyes, then leaned closer to the guy as if to put more distance between herself and Praying Man.

Having inventoried my fellow passengers, I settled back to enjoy what I could see of the passing scenery. The gentle rocking of the train and the low murmur of conversations were soporific, and my eyes closed.

"*No, by God!*" shook me awake. It was loud enough to raise Lazarus.

Praying Man was standing, a shoebox swathed in duct tape gripped like a football beneath his left arm, a box cutter in his right hand. During my brief nap, he'd metamorphosed into a terrorist.

He dropped the shoebox on his seat and stepped into the aisle with a second scream that was unintelligible. Ms. Executive gasped and crowded against her seatmate. Which must have caught Praying Man's attention because he focused it on her. She paled.

He grabbed her hair and dragged her into the aisle, rolling his eyes, screaming, "Get Back!" He held the point of his box-cutter to her throat and glanced from side to side. "Stay back or I'll cut her." He waved the cutter back and forth, amplifying his claim.

Grandmother put herself between Praying Man and her grandchild. Millennial stared gape-mouthed as if taking in an action movie. Mr. Retiree faced Praying Man, wide-eyed, with his hands up and fingers spread. "No one's gonna move."

Praying Man responded with, "I'm the new unabomber!" He jerked Ms. Executive's hair and screamed, "I'm the *real* unabomber! Don't think I won't cut her and blow this train to Hell!"

His gaze darted maniacally from passenger to passenger, halting briefly on the men and younger women, skipping past the old folks. So I'm sure he scarcely noticed me. His mistake.

I knew he had a tragic story. They all do. No one's born a psycho. Most outgrow infancy's narcissistic rages before they're old enough to do much harm. This man was beyond that corrigible stage, almost certainly permanently damaged.

I found my own rage building. Rage at all the media attention the violent or rude or angry craved and fed on. Rage that the hourly news was always bad, all the time. Rage that Ms. Executive's life was being devastated by a sicko she'd likely never met before. *My* rage was suddenly as out of bounds as his, fueled by unprovoked attacks on people minding their own business.

I reacted like a triggered IED, unaware that I was grasping the crowbar, dropping the camouflaging jacket.

And having dismissed me as a non-threat, he didn't notice when I raised my weapon in a deadly arc above my head.

The downward trajectory didn't slow or miss. The bar smashed through his wrist with a sickening crack, leaving his hand swinging like a pendulum, his weapon clattering to the floor.

Ms. Executive screamed and fell away, saved from a horrific fall by the shell-shocked man who'd sat beside her.

The lunatic stared white-eyed at his mangled wrist, then turned to scream and lunge at me.

But I stopped his screams with the straight end of my crowbar, shoving it in the channel between his windpipe and his sternomastoid muscle. I jumped backward as the severed carotid artery sprayed his life out.

He was dead before anyone could punch in nine-one-one.

His "bomb" turned out to be full of crumpled incoherent drafts—the bomber's manifesto.

The Penitent
Victoria Weisfeld

The ancient bus wheezed into Rome's Tiburtina station, late again that Thursday. As it skirted the huge Cimitero del Verano and approached the last turn, a cloud of diesel exhaust ballooned forth, and new motes of grit wafted toward the unblinking eyes of the cemetery's stone angels.

The dozen or so passengers, stiff and bleary-eyed from dozing in the unairconditioned coach, staggered down the steps, wrinkled shopping bags and duffels clutched tight. Last off the bus bounced portly Father Nunzio Maratea, come to take up a post in the great papal basilica of Santa Maria Maggiore.

He descended awkwardly, thrown off balance by his heavy leather suitcase, a gift from his parents when he left home for the seminary some thirty years before. The color of a roasted hazelnut, the bag outweighed its sparse contents. His other hand clutched a prayer book, the well-thumbed pages of his favorite passages—those describing the annunciation and Jesus's birth—loosened from the binding and sticking out untidily.

As a priest in a rural village, Father Maratea hadn't dared dream he would one day serve in Rome, and the enigmatic workings of the Church would never reveal that confusion in a lower-level Vatican office had produced the invitation to him, Nunzio Maratea, instead of to Nicodemo Maratea of Livorno, a young priest rising bright as the sun through increasingly sensitive diocesan assignments.

A posted map suggested the walk to the Basilica's rectory would take less than an hour, and he set out, plodding past the cemetery and through the university. For comfort, he wore a loose black cassock, rarely seen nowadays, and the broad-brimmed, aptly-named *cappello saturno*. The long cassock hid his feet and, due to his stately gait, he appeared to grind along on slowly turning wheels, an obstacle in the rushing streams of students. Everything he passed demanded his attention. He reveled in the excitement—the prestige—of the summons to the Holy City. When he rounded a corner and first saw Santa Maria Maggiore enthroned on her hill, he thought his heart might burst.

He reached the rectory, overheated and perspiring. A grim-faced porter took his bag and grunted ahead of him up four flights to a disused garret room furnished with a large wooden crucifix, a bed hardly wider than the priest himself, a dresser with temperamental drawers, a slab of wood for desk and bookshelf, and three hooks on the back of the door. A lone window admitted copious afternoon sun, and the room felt hot enough to bake bread.

"This is temporary, Father. Soon you will be given more suitable quarters. Dinner is in the refectory in a half-hour." The porter clomped away.

Father Maratea struggled the dusty window open. Desiccated flies showered his feet. The plaza below bustled, and the curving stone walls of the basilica's apse seemed close enough to touch. Everywhere the stonework was interrupted by windows, balustrades, arches, pillars, and statues of martyred saints. His new home.

He turned away from the October sunlight and rested the back of his head against the sash. Bright light sometimes triggered one of the headaches he'd suffered since childhood. They started behind his right temple, preceded by fireworks in front of his eyes and numbness in his left arm and torso, the prickling heaviness of a limb gone to sleep. Occasionally, they produced frightening visions—vivid monsters, walls changing shape, the world closing in on him. Then agonizing pain, dizziness, and waves of nausea.

He'd grown up in a home where every life event, good or bad, was "God's Will," or, in rare cases when that was insufficient, "God's Mystery." His young boy's logic naturally concluded God sent him the headaches for a reason, for some sin he could not name, a crime of which he knew not.

Nunzio never dared reveal the extent of his affliction. People knew he had headaches, but people do have headaches from time to time, so his mother or the school director would give him an aspirin, or two or three, and let him lie down. He would sleep and be hard to wake. "His brain needs to rest," his mother would say, and everyone understood that as both diagnosis and treatment.

The call to Rome finally proved God had a plan for him, especially the assignment to Santa Maria Maggiore—the most spiritually rigorous of the city's four great basilicas and the one with the greatest emphasis on penance. Of all the aspects of faith working in him daily, being penitent remained chief among them. With this posting, he could save himself at last.

The next morning, a Friday, Father Maratea had an appointment to receive his assignment. Over breakfast, he worked out several modest scripts that would present his capabilities and his ideas for the basilica in the proper light.

Promptly at eight, he entered the basilica director's outer office and was shepherded through a heavy inner door carved with garlands of fruits and leaves. Father Maratea stepped into a spacious, high-ceilinged office paneled in dark wood. The man he'd come to see sat across the room, erect behind a mahogany desk, scrutinizing documents by the stingy light of a green-shaded lamp. He absently motioned his visitor into a chair.

Father Maratea waited, hands folded on his ample belly,

and studied the tapestry depicting the Annunciation that filled the office's back wall. The weavers had given Archangel Gabriel a benevolent expression, and Father Maratea imagined the graceful hand upraised in blessing was meant as much for him as for the kneeling Mary. A shuffling noise behind and to his left prompted him to turn. Two sleek young priests occupied large wingchairs pulled close to the wall. Father Maratea nodded, and they acknowledged him. The director looked up.

Father Maratea immediately spoke. "Good morning, Reverend Father. I am Father Nunzio Maratea, from Potenza, called to Rome by the Grace of God to participate in the great works of Santa Maria Maggiore." He struggled to keep his voice from quavering. A muffled sound that became a cough came from the chairs along the wall.

The head priest looked surprised. "Nunzio? Nunzio Maratea?" he asked. Father Maratea smiled brightly. The man riffled the papers, saying, "Welcome, Father, welcome. And, how were your travels?" He seemed still distracted by the sheets in front of him.

Father Maratea provided a lengthy recitation of his tedious journey. The director stared, pinned to his chair like a museum beetle. Taking my measure, Father Maratea thought. One of the young priests stifled a yawn.

"Well!" said the official, at the end of the journey. "Your duties here."

Father Maratea began one of his prepared speeches, but the other man quickly intervened. "We have the very thing for you." He set aside the folder in front of him and opened the desk's bottom drawer. He pulled out a single sheet and placed it in the circle of light. "Do you speak any other languages?"

"Only our mother tongue, in both her ancient and contemporary versions," the priest said, pleased with his elegant expression. Again that choking sound from the young priests. Father Maratea sensed the imminent opportunity to explain his plans. Yes, a bouquet of languages might afford a slight advantage, but surely most necessary would be the most beautiful rose of languages, his own Italian.

"We have decided—" and the way the head priest emphasized "we," it included him, all the basilica's priests, the archpriests, the cardinals, the Pope himself, and the two callow young priests there in the room, "—you should assist Monsignor Goodnard in attendance on our many visitors."

"Exactly my idea!" Father Maratea clapped his hands. "To persuade visitors to make our basilica their religious home, as a sign of their love for the Virgin. I have prepared several short speeches, Reverend Father, which I can—"

The head priest thrust out his chin and broke in gently. "Tourists, Father, I'm speaking of tourists. Not, alas, potential congregants." Making an approximate sign of the cross, he dismissed him. "Father Russo will take you to meet Monsignor Goodnard. Good luck. God bless you and your service."

One of the two young priests steered him toward the door. Father Maratea twisted his head to look over his shoulder and tried to think of a tactful objection to an assignment offering such limited scope. More quickly than he thought possible, Father Russo led him through a side door of the basilica, through a doorway at the rear of the gift shop, and into the office of Monsignor Goodnard, the man who ruled Santa Maria Maggiore's daily affairs.

Goodnard gave him a detailed map of the basilica, a booklet about its history, art, and religious significance, and, as he escorted Father Maratea to the sanctuary, told him to take the docent's tour that would begin shortly. Afterward, he should make himself visible and available to tourists with questions and direct them to the restrooms, the various chapels, the gift shop (especially)—he waved a hand in the general direction of these locations—and so on. Then he left.

Father Maratea stood in the basilica's soaring nave for the

first time, paralyzed with dismay. He clenched the map in his hand, wrinkling it. He'd dropped the booklet. *Tourists! Look approachable! Holy Mother of God.*

He asked a docent to direct him to the Pauline Chapel, and in front of the ancient icon of the Virgin Mary, added his woeful prayer to the millions addressed to her mercy.

At six-thirty Sunday morning, Father Maratea stood at his garret window contemplating the spotlit basilica. Because Santa Maria Maggiore stands on the summit of the Esquiline hill, its tower is the highest in Rome. The light of the rising sun first strikes the bell tower, then gradually descends, warming the basilica's buff-colored stones, while the rest of the street remains cloaked in early morning shadow. To Father Maratea, it was a thrilling daily acknowledgment of the basilica's magnificence by the cosmos itself.

Yet, he walked across the piazza dreading the day's work. *The questions people ask!* Hardly any visitors spoke Italian and compensated for their ignorance by shouting at him. He'd learned the basics of the basilica's interior and could wave in the general direction of what he guessed people were seeking. Mosaics. The Sforza Chapel. The Sistine Chapel—no, not the Michelangelo one, *en il Vaticano.* Papal tombs.

He never suggested they visit the place he held most sacred—the crypt tucked under the high altar that housed relics of the Holy Manger, which he persisted in regarding as his private place. Two curving stairways led down to the crypt, and each time he reached the bottom, he nodded to the kneeling statue of Pope Pius IX, marble fingertips touching in eternal prayer. Compared to the nave full of noisy activity, the crypt felt intimate, peaceful. Its dark walls, lined with rich sienna-colored marble, reflected and multiplied the flames from ranks of candles. Their waxy smoke filled the air.

Set into the wall at the rear of the crypt, behind a small

altar, was a glass-fronted niche lined with carmine silk that held a resplendent silver and gilt reliquary, the size of a small cradle. Through its crystal windows, Father Maratea thought he could make out its contents, the real joy of the crypt for him—five precious sycamore fragments from Jesus's crib.

As the centerpiece of his penance, Father Maratea had spent Saturday evening memorizing the special prayer for the Holy Crib. Each time he recited it, he would earn two hundred days of indulgence. With the hour for the basilica's public opening approaching, he sank to his knees in front of the rope separating visitors from the crypt's altar and began: "*I adore Thee, O Word Incarnate, true Son of God from all eternity, and true Son of Mary ever Virgin in the fullness of time. Whilst then I adore Thy Divine Person and the Humanity which is thereunto united, I cannot but venerate...*"

At that moment, several juvenile representatives of that humanity clattered down the steps. He persevered: "*...the poor manger which welcomed Thee...*"

"Where's Baby Jesus's manger?" a little girl asked in—he guessed—English, piercing his concentration.

Out of the corner of his eye, the priest saw a seven-year-old pointing at the brightly lit reliquary and shouting something. He squeezed his eyes shut.

"Let's go!"

The father said something mollifying and flipped the pages of a guidebook.

"*...when an Infant, and which was truly the throne of Thy love.*"

A small hand pulled on the priest's sleeve.

"Caroline, stop!"

Father Maratea sighed and abandoned his prayer. The child thrust her face within inches of his; her warm milky breath brushed his cheek. In a stage whisper she asked, "Where's Baby Jesus's manger?"

Father Maratea pointed to the reliquary.

The father found the place in his travel guide. "Yes, that's it."

"That's *it?*" Two high-pitched voices in unison. The boy sounded unconvinced. He bounced away, saying something about dead Popes.

The children clattered up the steps chanting, "Popes! Popes! Popes! Popes!" and pressed past the docent accompanying visitors to one of the world's most sacred relics.

Father Maratea attempted to pick up his prayer again. *Let me prostrate myself before it, with the simplicity of the shepherds, with the faith of Joseph, with the love of Mary!* but the jostling of the new group was too much. He'd have to finish the prayer later. His headache briefly reached out then retracted a claw, a reminder it still occupied its space over his right temple. To him it was a heavy, live thing, resting, waiting.

By late afternoon, he'd been asked about toilets in at least twenty languages and reminded himself to smile scores of times, with dubious success. The basilica was emptying, and he visited the crypt again. While shutting out visitors' intrusions was becoming easier, the onset of one of his headaches was hard to ignore. As he knelt in prayer, stars exploded behind his closed eyelids. A guide marched her charges back up the stairs, and the noise around him subsided.

*Let me incline myself in lowly veneration of this precious memorial of our salvation with the same spirit of mortification, poverty, and humility with which Thou, though the Lord of heaven and of earth, didst choose for Thyself...*A man standing alongside him brushed his sleeve...*a manger as a receptacle of Thy poor infant limbs.* In another minute, Father Maratea finished the petition and lifted his head. The swarthy young man wore a thin pony tail and the leather outfit of a motorcyclist.

Father Maratea shuddered involuntarily as the room spun a little. Expanding spirals of light changed everything directly in front of him into pulsating smears of color. The visitor eyed him intently. They were alone.

"So this is where a poor man will find our Lord's crib," the man said quietly, speaking Italian, "Thanks be to God."

"*Sì, sì.*" Father Maratea touched the visitor's arm, in part to steady himself, and swept his other hand toward the brightly lit reliquary. The motion created a wave of dizziness. "Come with me." He clutched the young man's arm and, stepping awkwardly over the rope, led him closer. "The unique glory of our basilica—the beginning. Christ's birth." A note of pride infused his strained voice. The veins in the brown-red marble wove like sea grass. He planted his feet and steadied himself against the altar.

The visitor knelt next to him and crossed himself, revealing an elaborate snake's head tattoo on the back of his hand, its body spiraling up his forearm. Softly, he said, "Amen." He slipped behind the altar. He spread his hands to the cinnabar pillars that framed the niche and bowed his head. He ran his hands up and down the sides of the niche. It looked as if the inky snake were writhing along the pillars. Uneasy, Father Maratea pulled his mind into focus and tried to form the words of an objection.

"It is a wonderful thing—" the young man glanced over his shoulder, "—that after two thousand years, these holy relics exist here, in our city."

"A miracle." *How can I make him leave?*

The man was using a large, odd-looking camera, and Father Maratea bitterly regretted taking him behind the rope. Yet he didn't have the strength—or at that moment, the composure—to stop him. The swirling patterns in the marble walls closed in. He backed away from the altar in shuffling steps, arms held out for balance. With difficulty, he stepped over the rope and continued to retreat.

Once out of the cave-like crypt, his claustrophobia decreased, just as the visual distortions began to recede.

"Beautiful. So beautiful," the young man said, still on the wrong side of the rope. Father Maratea steadied himself against the stairway balusters and directed an anguished glance at the statue of the kneeling Pope Pius. Another group of tourists gathered at the top of the steps, eager to see one of the most valuable relics in all Christendom.

The young man was suddenly beside him. "Bless you for letting me see it with you."

The priest breathed a sigh of relief. *No one had witnessed his indiscretion.* They climbed the stairs, the priest gripping the railing, the man holding his elbow. They paused a moment at the top for the priest to catch his breath. "Your camera...I've not seen one like it."

The young man clasped the camera to his chest, where it nestled, protected by the snake's head. "I'd imagine not. It belongs to my...*padrino*. Another relic, but not a holy one."

"Your godfather. How nice. God go with you."

"And with you, Father."

The priest watched the young man walk away. His visions had faded, but the familiar numbness crept down his left side, and he needed to cling to the curved balustrade a while longer. Giving the interested young man a close view of the crypt surely was not so terrible, even if it was absolutely forbidden. But words from the Book of James flowed into his heart: "For one who knows the right thing to do and does not do it, it is a sin." And he trembled.

Early Thursday morning, Father Maratea was settled at the refectory table, one week into his assignment. The high arched window framed a patch of royal blue sky, rapidly lightening— another clear and sunny day to come. He hurried through breakfast, eager to be in the basilica. Monsignor Goodnard had allowed one of the maintenance staff to show him which electrical switches served the crypt. If he arrived early enough, he could spend private time there.

And Thou, O Lord, Who in Thine Infancy didst deign to lay Thyself in this manger, vouchsafe at the same time to pour into my heart one drop of that joy which both... Passing the docent's station and crossing the nave to the crypt stairways, Father Maratea rehearsed the special prayer.

When noon arrived, the tourists departed the basilica in response to some undetectable signal, like a school of fish flashing a changed direction. Monsignor Goodnard and the rest of the basilica's hierarchy also left and wouldn't drift back until nearly two, whereas he, the bottom rung of that hierarchy, had to stay. At the table in the staff room he ate the lunch the refectory cook had packed for him. When he emerged, everything was peaceful. An ideal time to slip down to the crypt.

...the sight of Thy lovely Infancy, and the miracles which accompanied Thy Birth, must have caused. In virtue of that holy Birth, I now implore Thee—a noise above distracted him, but he persisted—*to grant to all the world peace and goodwill; and I desire, in the name of the whole human race, to render*—Only a single line of the prayer remained, but he could no longer ignore the commotion upstairs. He might be the lowest rung of the basilican ladder, but he was nevertheless a rung, and his mote of authority might be needed.

Two men in Vatican maintenance uniforms and hardhats had set up safety barriers marked "Do Not Cross" atop both sets of crypt stairs.

"What—?" Father Maratea looked up at them from the bottom of the steps.

"Good afternoon, Father." The shorter of the two, a remarkably pale man, smiled broadly. "We're here to repair the wiring under the crypt floor."

Father Maratea climbed the steps toward them. "The—?"

"The wiring under the floor."

He reached the top, carefully stepped around the barrier,

and gestured to the crypt below. "It works perfectly."

"Hard to tell, Father. The chief inspector stopped by last week with his voltage tachometer and detected uneven current. It's only a matter of time until we have a fire or—"

"His what?"

"Voltage tachometer, Father." The pale man spoke quickly, and his voice turned serious. "Only a matter of time until—"

Though Father Maratea didn't understand any of this, he'd caught the one unexpected word. "Fire? This building is stone. Stone doesn't burn."

"Sure, the parts we see are stone, but underneath there's subflooring and sub-subflooring. Who knows what flammable materials they used hundreds of years ago and in all the renovations since? And there's the wires themselves. Fire can race down those wires until it finds something that *will* burn."

"But you can't do this *today*. It's the twenty-fifth, the monthly anniversary of Jesus's birth. People come specifically to see the crib. From all over the world."

"We have to do it today." The man pulled out a letter and held it up for the priest to read, not letting go. "Emergency work. Thursday is a light visitor day."

"Thursday may *usually* be a light day," Father Maratea began doubtfully. This was his first Thursday, and he didn't know whether it should be light or not. "But *this* Thursday is the twenty-fifth. Not light at all."

"We have to do it today. We can't expose hundreds of weekend tourists to the risk of a major combustion event, toxic fumes."

The tall man nodded. They were young, sure of themselves. Father Maratea shifted from one foot to the other.

They let him think for about a half-minute before the pale one glanced around and sniffed the air, as if a malodorous smoke might even then be curling up the crypt stairs. "The quicker we get started, the sooner we're done."

"Oh, all right," the priest said, perplexed.

"Thank you, Father." They each picked up a canvas bag.

"How long will this take?" Father Maratea's tone was peevish. Something about the pale man's hands nagged at him, but the thought wouldn't take shape.

The man glanced at his watch. "It's twelve-twenty now. I'd say, thirteen hundred or so."

Not too bad. They'll be done before Monsignor Goodnard returns. "Just be quick about it."

"We will. Would you make sure no one comes down here? Interruptions slow us down." The man touched his hard hat in a respectful gesture, and the two descended the steps, securing the barrier behind them. The tall one said loudly, "Okay, first we put up the dust shield."

When Father Maratea returned a few minutes later, top to bottom across the crypt opening was stretched what looked like bedsheets sewn together. Pope Pius, marble hands folded in entreaty, stared at the blank screen dragging the floor.

A sharp tap on his shoulder. "What's going on?" Monsignor Goodnard, back early.

"Oh." Father Maratea caught his breath. "The Vatican sent a couple of men to repair the wiring under the crypt floor."

"What wiring?"

"The old wiring isn't working right. They're afraid it might cause a fire."

"What's that?" Goodnard pointed.

"The dust shield." Father Maratea was pleased he remembered the technical term.

"Who authorized this, today of all days?"

Father Maratea suddenly understood his mote of authority might be even smaller than he'd supposed. He steadied himself with a hand on the balustrade. "They have a letter from the Vatican maintenance department. They have to fix it today so they—we—don't expose weekend visitors to a, a...

major combustion and toxic fumes event."

Goodnard stared at him. "Call them up here."

Father Maratea looked doubtfully at the barrier blocking the steps. True, the men's work was authorized by the Vatican, but their masters were across town, while Goodnard stood stiffly beside him. He moved one end of the barrier, edged through the opening, descended the steps, and stopped outside the dust shield.

He cleared his throat. "Excuse me?" A tool thumped the floor.

"Yeah?"

"Excuse me, *signore*, but Monsignor Goodnard wants to see you."

"Who?" Thick work gloves moved the curtain slightly aside. The bulky safety glasses did not hide the pale man's angry flush.

"Monsignor Goodnard." Father Maratea lifted his chin toward the top of the stairs. "He's in charge. Of the building."

The workman stomped up the stairs, and Father Maratea followed. But when he approached the monsignor, his manner was ingratiating. "I'm awfully sorry we have to disrupt you." He handed Goodnard the letter. "Our inspector stopped by here last week. It's a shaky situation down there. There's old wires and potential combustibles under the floor—"

Goodnard interrupted. "I'm going to call this—" he studied the letter's signature, "—'Aurelio Conti' and make sure this work is really necessary. Today."

"He may be back in the office before too long. When we left the shop around lunchtime, he was on his way out to a church in the suburbs. Water leak," the man confided. "Tough. Hard to trace." He proceeded cheerfully, "We'll just stay set up here until you have a chance to talk to him."

Goodnard studied him, then handed back the letter. "Get it over with."

"I know you're extra-busy today, so we'll do our best not to set off any alarms." The workman scanned the crowd slowly returning to the basilica. "Wouldn't want to cause a stampede. But there's all kinds of scrambled wires down there."

"I'll shut the alarm off. But finish as quickly as you can. This is a terrible inconvenience."

"We will, monsignor. With your help."

Goodnard swept away toward his office. The priest shrugged an apology for his rude superior.

"Bureaucrats," the pale man hissed, "the same everywhere."

Father Maratea couldn't entirely suppress a complicit smile and watched the workman hurry down the stairs. Something about those gloves and the scaly pattern on the man's arm still puzzled him, but the thought wouldn't come.

Over the next half-hour, he heard enough noises from the crypt to know the men were hard at work, but apparently they weren't finishing fast enough for Monsignor Goodnard. He returned, and ordered Father Maratea to check on progress.

"How long do we have to put up with this?" He glared at the dust shield and, muttering, strode away toward his office.

Father Maratea made his way down the crypt stairs, coughed politely, gripped the edge of the sheet with a pudgy hand, and stepped behind it.

"You should be nearly—" His glance automatically went to the niche, but the precious reliquary wasn't there. "Oh." He gasped, as he struggled to make sense of what he saw. "Where—? What—?"

Eyes wide with surprise, he looked to the men for answers. The pale man moved quickly to stand alongside his partner. Their goggles and heavy gloves littered the floor, but behind them he glimpsed the large canvas bag gaping open. From inside came a glint of silver that pierced him like an arrow.

"Oh!" Overcome by a wave of weakness, he wavered where he stood. "Oh, no!"

He took a step backward. The tall man was instantly there—to steady him, he thought. He started to thank him, but the man gripped his neck in the vise of one elbow and closed his mouth so tightly his teeth cut the inside of his lip. Blood filled his mouth and dribbled down his chin. Smooth as a boxer, the man wheeled him toward his partner.

The pale man's arm thrust toward him. The snake tattoo that covered the back of his hand was visible through a thin rubber glove, its sinuous body wound up his arm, and a knife blade flicked out of its mouth, a deadly steel tongue.

Just like the man with the camera. The man he'd let see the crib...when he'd broken the rules.

The pale man plunged the knife into the priest's belly—punching hard, going deep—and jerked the knife sideways, severing the abdominal aorta. He jumped aside, escaping the startling arc of bright blood.

Father Maratea crumpled to the floor, his broken heart more painful than any wound the man could inflict. He lay motionless, his gaze fixed on the canvas bag as if still able to see the beloved reliquary inside. His lips soundlessly moved, *...all thanks and all honor to the Father, and to the Holy Spirit, who with Thee liveth and reigneth one God world without end.* As his eyelids drifted closed, Nuzio Maratea finally understood the true and deep meaning of repentance. With his life's last breath, he sighed "*Amen.*"

Pick-Up and Delivery
Eric Beckstrom

Tommy the Curb is the kind of guy who's always telling you he knows where your mother or your sister lives. That's how he keeps you in line. I don't blame him for it. In fact, really it's kind of nice of him to give a guy fair warning. He's really just stating a fact, after all—"I know where your mother lives"—and just supplying you with useful information when he tells you things like that.

Because, sure as death and Mondays, the Curb is the kind of guy who would go find your ma or your sister or your girlfriend if you fell out of line. I've seen him do it. Or at least seen the results. So it's actually pretty thoughtful of him to let you know ahead of time. I know you probably won't understand this, and maybe you'll think it's crazy thinking it's so kindhearted of him to drop awful hints like that. But take it from me, I know guys who on purpose don't give you fair warning. Instead they just go out and do something to somebody a guy cares about, and do it slowly, without giving a guy the option of preventing it. I mean, it's effective, it gets the job done, it gets you in line. But the Curb's way is more humanitarian, if you know what I mean. In that kind of life, killing you quickly was the last nice thing somebody might ever do for you.

I should tell you why they call him the Curb. It's because of the time he made a whole bunch of bad guys go away, just him by himself. I mean, they're all bad guys—heck, I guess

I'm a bad guy, too—but the definition of "bad guy" my employers used was somebody from a rival gang or family. Somebody who was "impeding commerce," the Curb would say.

That always used to crack me up: "impeding commerce." And it always cracked the Curb up that it cracked me up. The Curb was mean, but he was nice, if you know what I mean.

So anyway, one time the Curb—only back then they still called him by just his first name, Tommy—so Tommy is standing on the side of the street in front of the head honcho's club—standing on *the curb*, get it?—and this whole carload of bad guys drives up thinking to make some trouble. Maybe mess up some of our guys, or act edgy so as to scare off customers, and generally impede commerce. And so Tommy, he squares his shoulders, steps up to the very edge of the curb, right up to their car, and folds his arms all confident-like.

And then he says, or so the story goes, "Despite appearances, that ain't a public street your wheels are holdin' down, this ain't a public sidewalk, and you ain't welcome here. You're also parked in front of a hydrant, and you ain't put no money in the meter. Plus, I know where all your mothers and sisters live. Now beat it."

And they did. Their grins fell, and they beat it.

That's not me saying "ain't," by the way, that's the Curb—Tommy, at the time. I'm just quoting. I never say it. I made it through eighth grade and I know it ain't a word, ha ha.

Anyway, let me just say, I heard all this secondhand because it happened years before I ever showed up on the scene. But I know it's true. Tommy probably *did* know where all their moms and sisters lived—he was big on research that way, still is, far as I know. The other reason I know it's true is because I saw him do the same thing to some cops once.

They had rolled up, two whole carloads of cops, meaning to "have lunch" in the club. In other words, meaning to nose around, harass, and, what else, you got it, you're catching on: impede commerce. Only, when they pulled up in front of the club (in front of the hydrant, no less), the Curb—because by then that's what everybody called him—steps up to the curb, squares his shoulders, and crosses his arms, just like that other time. And do you know what? Those cops never even got outta their cars. They just sort of smirked and laughed, trying to make it look like it was their own idea to leave, as though the cholesterol options at McDonald's suddenly looked healthier.

But I knew the truth. There's just something about the way Curby squares himself up that makes a guy (or even a bunch of guys with cuffs, guns, and night sticks) want to just go about some other business, maybe rearrange their To Do list and put "Messing with the Curb's boss" on the very bottom.

So after that first time, when Tommy made a bunch of bad guys go on their way just by standing there on the curb, some of the boys at the club started thinking up names for him. Charlie Choppers told me how it went.

They call him Choppers because he lost all his teeth in a fight when he was twelve, and was the only sixth-grader with dentures. In the twenty years since then, he had learned to rattle them around in a way where the rattling makes a song. The William Tell Overture is his specialty. He's never had a girlfriend as far as I know—you can guess why—but the girls still love it when he plays music on his fake teeth.

Anyway, Choppers said all the guys were lounging in the back of the club. The back is the darkest part, and the part where everybody always knows what everybody else is doing and thinking, because the only safe secrets are the ones the boss keeps, and he doesn't want any other kind. He'll send the Curb after you if he thinks you have one.

So Choppers tells me the guys were sitting in the back of the club retelling for the hundredth time in two days how Tommy scared away a whole carload of bad guys.

Somebody said, "How about we call him Tommy the Terrible?"

"That's stupid," somebody else said.

"Tommy the Door Man."

"Better. Not good, but better."

"Tommy the Sentinel."

"What the hell's a sentinel?"

"Tommy Stands with Arms Folded."

"He's not a friggin' Native American, moron."

"Bull! Tommy, ain't you one-sixteenth or something?"

"What's with that whole fire hydrant bit, how about Tommy the Meter Maid?"

Tommy, who had been silent up until then, jumped up and almost tore that last guy's jaw out of his head.

After things calmed down, and ice packs had been applied to just about everything above the guy's ankles—not Tommy, but the other guy, naturally—somebody said, "Tommy the Curb."

And that was that. It stuck.

Tommy the Curb was annoyed with his new name—being named after a strip of concrete that people stand on and spit on and piss on and who knows what else on, bugged him I guess—but he took to heart what the boss told him later.

"Being named is an honor," the boss told him. "It means people respect you, and they know something important about you; something worth knowing. In your case, your name has nothing to do with that damn curb. Now people know that you don't bluff, and they know that you are without fear. That kind of reputation is priceless. Dangerous—probably get you killed eventually—but priceless."

I don't know if that's really a word-for-word quote, but it's pretty close to what Choppers told me the boss said, and Chops has a pretty good memory for a guy who got all his teeth beat out of his head when he was twelve. Good old Choppers. He took a beating that would have killed most people, but he lived. I guess the boss would have said that was something worth knowing about the guy.

I wish I could have met the boss, but I never made it through the ranks. He seemed like a guy who knew things worth knowing.

So anyway, I did a lot of traveling for Tommy the Curb, running packages. Which is to say I ran packages for the boss, only like I said, I never met the boss, so it was sort of once removed, if you know what I mean. It was mostly just around the boroughs, and sometimes Jersey. One winter, twice in one week, I flew to Omaha, Nebraska, and that was about as exotic as it got. That's a whole nother story. Maybe I'll tell you someday, but it was Nebraska, for Jeez sake, so how exciting could it be?

I always wanted to travel someplace exotic, but I was a pretty safe player—a homebody—which is one reason they trusted me. I knew my place, and my place was one hunk of the coast, except for the two trips to Corn Land. Knowing your place is important in that business. The threat of death, in case you forgot your place, was always hanging over your head, but most guys got used to it so they didn't much notice it after a while.

I knew a guy who rented the basement of an old house, and it wasn't a place meant to be lived in. The ceiling beams were less than six feet off the floor, so this guy, who was kind of tall, always had to walk around stooping. He had a scar on his forehead from when he forgot once, but after that he got used to it. When you'd visit him you could tell he didn't even know he was stooping anymore. In fact, out on the streets he was always walking around kind of bent over, which is why they call him Scotty Hang Head.

It was kind of like that running packages for the Curb, only I never quite got used to stooping. I did it, but I was always kind of scared, deep inside where ulcers live. Curby liked me, but he knew where *my* sister lived, too, and he knew where I lived, and he knew I knew he knew, if you know what I mean.

Anyway, it was always the Curb who gave me the package and the drop point. He never told me what was in the package, and why should he? It wasn't my business. But I knew—only a brainless idiot wouldn't have known—that it was either money, or contraband, or copies of photos or records somebody wouldn't want going public, or to the cops.

Sometimes it was something worse. Something that would put a real scare into somebody.

One time, they didn't seal up the package so good, and halfway to Queens a little blood leaked out from between where the tape held the brown wrapping paper together. I did the best I could with that one. I stopped at a grocery store, bought some gallon food bags, and dropped the whole package into one of them. Then I rewrapped it all in a bigger box, an empty one from a candy display at the same store.

I think I knew generally what was in the package. Maybe something off a mom or a sister or somebody. But it was none of my business. I felt bad for whoever got hurt; but *I* didn't do the hurting, so I tried not to feel too bad. I mean, I felt bad, but not too bad, I guess.

Only sometimes I wished I could stoop for other people, too.

I used to pick up and deliver packages at all kinds of places. Since I'm only five feet three "standing on a box of matches," is what Curby used to say, and look younger than I am, I could actually pass for a delivery kid. Also, I kept my razor really sharp, so that after I shaved I looked like I'd never had a whisker on me since birth.

"You're cute. You look sweet and innocent," the Curb would say. I didn't like that so much, but it was the Curb, so what was I gonna do?

And actually, you know, the Curb wasn't famous for his sense of humor. I mean, he understood a joke if you told him one—he'd "get it"—but he just didn't think there was anything funny about the pope, a rabbi, and an atheist walking into a bar.

"Not with me standing on the curb, they ain't getting in," he'd say.

So the fact that he would tease me a little now and then, and the fact that he got a kick out of me getting a kick out of him saying "impeding commerce," well, I took it as a compliment.

So anyway, I used to run packages all over the place, traveling from one end of town to the other, and on account of me being short and young-looking and passing for a kid, plus the official-looking delivery uniform I'd sometimes wear, I could get into almost anywhere. And because of that, everybody and his cousin knew me. I sort of blended in with the background, the way bricks disappear into a wall, if you know what I mean. They're right there in front of you, but nobody pays any attention to them. They only see the wall.

And sometimes I'd get some pretty good-sized tips. The Curb was nice about that. He let me keep every penny of them. It always killed me when I'd be delivering a package to some poor schmoe—a box that I could tell contained something not so nice—and before he knew any better, the schmoe would give me a good tip. I always laughed over that with the Curb.

But afterwards, when I'd be thinking things over, I always felt kind of bad, like maybe I should give the schmoe his tip back. One time, and I guess it was that first time a package leaked for me, I felt so bad that I actually dropped the tip—an especially big one, which I guess is why I felt especially bad—into the cup of some blind guy begging on the sidewalk. I found out later he wasn't really blind, he was just a scammer. But I didn't mind. It was the thought that counted.

Another time, not too long ago, I was delivering something during a posh convention at some hotel. On the way out, I spied a fifty-dollar bill just sitting there on the floor right in the middle of the lobby, like a bonus tip. Beneath it was the most expensive carpet I had ever walked on, and hanging over it was the biggest chandelier I'd ever seen. I mean, this thing must have been fifteen feet from tip to top. And right between the carpet and the chandelier sits this fifty.

All kinds of richies are coming and going, only no one makes a move for it. At first I thought maybe everybody just had the wrong angle on it and didn't see it. Maybe it was sort of camouflaged by the carpet pattern. But then I noticed how the eyes of almost everybody who walked toward it flicked down to that bill. Sometimes somebody would even slow down just a bit to think about it. You could hardly tell they'd slowed down, but they had. Everybody there was rich, or on their way to being rich, but they all still wanted that fifty bucks.

Everybody sees it, everybody wants it, nobody picks it up.

At first I thought they were all nuts. But then I finally figured out that they just didn't want to lower themselves to pick up money off the street, so to speak. They were worried about what their fellow richies might think.

You might think I laughed at them for acting this way, and sort of looked down on them, but I didn't. In fact, I admired them for it. It must have been hard for all those rich people to pass up free money, even if it was just fifty dollars. I mean, to them it was nothing, right? Something to light a cigar with or snort something with. But you just know it was hard for them anyway, and that they suffered over it. After all, they didn't get rich by passing up opportunities.

But, like the Curb told me, "Reputation is everything. Why do you think no one messes with me? Why do you think no one messes with *you*, my pick-up and delivery guy? It's because of that day on the curb. And behind *us* stands the boss's rep."

So what did I do? Well, I tell you one thing, I didn't leave that fifty—what you might call my biggest tip of the day—sitting there getting scuffed under the soles of thousand-dollar shoes. But I also remembered what the Curb had said, and I let it sink in that every one of those richies was thinking the same way the Curb did, that reputation is everything.

I went up to the desk and asked if they had a piece of tape I could use to fix a delivery receipt that had torn. I was wearing my uniform that day. They were happy to oblige. A big hotel like that can afford lots of tape.

Then I hurried off to the side, out of the stream of traffic, hoping one of the hoity-toities wouldn't decide he didn't care a rat's patooey about reputation, and increase his personal fortune while I messed around by the ficus trees, making the tape into a loop and sticking it to the bottom of my shoe.

I paced myself just right so I wouldn't have to break stride. I walked right over that fifty and planted my right foot on it. I didn't check to see if it had worked. I just kept right on walking, smooth and casual.

Outside and down the block, I figured I had a loose shoelace. I bent down to tighten it, and there it was, stuck to the bottom of my humble shoe. I took off the tape and stuck it to the edge of a garbage can that sat there on the corner—I hate it when people litter—and put the fifty in my wallet.

I usually told the Curb when unusual stuff happened to me. We'd have a laugh over it, or he'd say things like "reputation is everything" and "impeding business." Sometimes I could tell he admired something I'd done, or the way I'd handled some situation.

But I didn't tell him about the fifty. Not because he'd want his share—I already told you he didn't operate that way. I think I didn't tell him because I knew he'd admire me for how I didn't make it look like I was desperate for fifty dollars, and because I also wasn't so dumb as to pass up free money either. I didn't tell him because for maybe the first time I decided I needed to admire myself for something without somebody else knowing about it. I don't know if that makes any sense to you, but it's how I felt. Looking back, I kind of wish I had told him—it's kind of a great story—but I'm still glad I didn't. I never told anyone about it, not until now, anyway.

That night, while I was thinking things over like I always do before I fall asleep, I thought about how some rich guy probably saw that fifty spot disappear under my foot, and how he must have thought, "That lucky jerk." And it made me curious to think that some rich, successful guy might think that I'm the lucky one.

That was the night before I delivered my last package. Only no one knew it was going to be my last one, not even me.

Same as usual, I stopped by the club in the morning to pick up the first one of the day. I always delivered them only one at a time. That way, in case I ever got caught, I wouldn't be busted with more than I had to be, and the law could only come down on me just so hard. Well, really, it was because that way the boss wouldn't lose anything more than he had to, but I like to think part of it was for my sake.

So Curby hands me this package, and I could tell it was something bad for whoever was getting it. The little brown box was too small to hold money, or the kind of contraband I knew they sometimes had in them. This package contained a message of some kind, and since it wasn't Valentine's Day I knew it wasn't chocolates.

It was for a guy I usually picked up from. I had never delivered anything to him before that day. He never tipped, but he wasn't a bad guy. On the elevator ride up to his corner office on the top floor, I remembered he hadn't had anything for me the last couple of times I'd stopped by for a pick-up. Tommy the Curb had not been happy.

So this guy had missed a couple of payments, and I was dunning him. I wasn't worried for me—no one ever messed with the Curb's pick-up and delivery guy—and I wasn't even worried for the guy. I was worried for his mom or his sister or his wife. You see, the Curb's different from some guys you've heard of. He didn't go in for breaking the knee caps and knuckles of people who didn't pay. All that did was impede commerce. Guys who owe you just have a harder time paying if they can't hustle or work.

I was halfway down the wide hallway, passing a bunch of glassed office doors, and had almost gotten to the client's— that's what the Curb called them, "clients"—when I noticed red syrup dripping onto the white and blue floor tiles. The box was leaking from one corner. Only I knew from the last time I had a leaky package that it wasn't syrup, any more than the red, white, and blue on the floor meant it was Independence Day.

I can think pretty quick in situations, so I whipped a hanky from my pocket and held it to my nose as if it were bleeding. I also leveled the box off so it wouldn't drip so much. It was a good thing too, because a woman called out from behind me just then.

"Hey, you're dripping. Oh, it's you, hello."

And then, thinking it was me who was bleeding, she asked, "Oh my, are you okay?"

"I'm okay, just the dry weather making my nose bleed. I'll wipe it up."

"There's a restroom down the hall on your right. Do you need anything?"

"I'm fine, but thanks. Sorry for the mess."

But after "I'm fine" she disappeared back into an office reception area. I think she was in a hurry to get away from me because she knew who had sent me, and maybe even why. It kind of made me sad because it's in my nature to want to be friends with everybody, and to chat. But that's not in the job description, and you can maybe guess who told me that.

Anyway, I locked the restroom door and held the box over the sink. Even though it was only leaking from one corner, the cardboard on the bottom was getting soggy. I don't usually get too upset, but I mean whoever boxed this up should have known better. The Curb would have said it was a "quality control issue."

But I'd learned my lesson the last time. Ever since that first leaky package, I had always kept a gallon-sized plastic bag in my pocket on work days. I never had a chance at Boy Scouts, but I live by their motto.

Except this time I stopped for a second, instead of just dealing with the problem and completing the delivery. Why I did the next thing—something I had never done before—I still don't know. I mean, if you get nosey, if you don't stoop, then *you* become the problem that's put in a box.

I looked anyway. The box was maybe the size of two decks of cards, so I figured whatever was inside couldn't be all that bad. I ran my pocketknife between the flaps of the package and slit the tape.

The finger wasn't a surprise. I mean, it's gruesome, but it's pretty standard fair. And it was just a warning. They had even left the custom-made, antique diamond wedding ring on it as a sign of good faith. She—the owner of the finger—I could tell it was a woman's finger, and not just a dainty man's finger, because of the kind of ring it was, and because of the red nail polish—was still alive, and she would stay that way as long as the client started having packages for me to pick up again, simple as that.

It was the ear lobes that really bothered me. So tiny and soft, but impaled with earrings by their owner, then cut off by a stranger, and finally made to travel across town with another stranger.

In each lobe was an earring with a perfect diamond, I'd say three carats each. The boss could have taken the jewelry and cashed it in for a small fortune. Instead, he'd told Curby and the packaging guys to leave it, and so had given the guy in the top floor corner office one last chance to pay what he owed in his own way. It was more generous than others would have been. Also, being flexible was just good business.

Both the finger and the ear lobes were very pale, and the cotton batting underneath them was gummy with blood. I guess whoever boxed them up just didn't think that three little bits could bleed that much. Then I lifted the batting and saw another set, for Jeez sake. This one looked older and more wrinkled than the set on top. On each of these three pieces were more high-end jewels. So this was a mother-daughter combo, probably. My knees got a little wobbly, but I think that was because I hadn't eaten breakfast that day. I hadn't ever felt that way before. I usually eat breakfast.

In that single tick of a clock, I saw two options, and I had to choose between them.

I could put everything back together, drop it into a nice leak-proof bag, and deliver it. The Curb would be impressed, and that would be nothing but good for me.

Or I could...

I slid the rings off their fingers. At first, neither would come off either the tip or stump end, but I used some hand soap and they loosened. One left a ring-shaped mark where it had been. It made me kind of sad to see that, I'm not sure why. I guess because it was a deep mark, which meant the ring had been there a while. It kind of symbolized her life. I don't know.

Then I took off the four earrings, which was easy. Well, not easy to do, but easily done, if you know what I mean.

I put everything except the jewelry back where it had been. The red polish on the one nail almost made me turn away. The little earing dimples on each of the four lobes, too. I closed up the box, and dropped it into the plastic bag.

Then I used more soap to clean the jewelry, and dropped the six pieces into my pocket. I washed my hands and left the restroom. Halfway down the hall I turned around, went back to the restroom, and washed my hands three more times.

I delivered the package.

Then I sold the jewelry to a guy I know, and left that city forever, using the jewelry proceeds as disappearing money.

See? I told you I think quick in situations.

I can tell you two things about where I traveled to, and where I am: One, it's exotic. And two, it ain't Nebraska.

And I can tell you two things about my new life: sometimes I have bad dreams; but I don't have to stoop anymore.

I forgot to tell you my name. It doesn't really matter, which is why I forgot. I'm just not that important. My name is Jerry, only Tommy the Curb used to call me "Little Jerry," because, like I told you, I'm only five feet three inches tall standing on a box of matches. Little Jerry's not really a name, though. It's just sort of a fact. Curby likes his facts.

But now I hear they call me Jerry the Jeweler, even though I'm gone. I guess I got kind of famous after I left, and sometimes the story about how the Curb got his name and the story about how I got my name are told together because everybody knows I was his main pick-up and delivery guy. The best he ever had, or so they say.

I kind of miss the Curb.

Jerry the Jeweler. I'm kind of proud of that, because like the boss said, it's an honor to be named. It says something about a guy.

This Ain't No Time For A Vacation
Gary Phillips

"Who the hell?" the skinny older man said. A towel around his waist, his personal-trainer-taut skin was damp from his shower. Automatically his eyes shifted to the bed, but his boy toy had been rendered unconscious and hogtied. His eyes returned to the stranger, but craftiness, rather than surprise, lurked behind them now. A lion in the boardroom he'd been dubbed by the business community.

"If it's money you want, I can help you out. And if you're a jilted lover, I can assure you the thing between me and Davey is purely professional." Davey was the man on the bed, various sex toys and a cat o' nine tails lay about.

"Sorry," Comstock said, "but those negotiations already happened without your participation." He then shot the man once through the eye with his semi-auto equipped with a suppressor. The body crumpled to the floor as if it were made of broken balsa wood.

Comstock had an edge. It wasn't picking locks or master of disguise, though he could be present yet unseen. His was a unique ability, and in his line of work, eliminating human beings from this troubled world, such was not insignificant. Unlike the other skills he'd honed over the years, this ability of his had been acquired quite by accident. It was while on his third tour of duty in Afghanistan as part of the Army's 17th

Convoy Sustainment Support Battalion that the incident happened that would, as the cliché goes, "change his life forever."

Not three klicks out of Forward Operating Base Rushmore, having made a successful delivery of material including petroleum, food stuffs and pallets of ammunition, the attack happened. The road was supposed to have been swept and cleared by the Afghan National Army, and confirmed by the U.S. brass less than a day before, but of course as was usual in the service, the information was not exactly accurate. Far from it.

Later they would calculate the IED that went off was at least two hundred pounds of "going boom," as the soldier slang went. Their RG-31 armored vehicle was equipped with a roller extended in front of it, an attachment of metal and rubber wheels that looked like something workers would use smoothing out a slurry of asphalt on a highway. But this was designed to explode the device before the vehicle was harmed. The roller did its job but the power of the blast tore through the cab, the air going black from dirt and soot, and a sharp chemical smell searing Comstock's and the others' noses.

"We're hit, we're hit," yelled the corporal into the mic screwed into his helmet.

"The front wheels are jammed up," yelled the PFC driving the vehicle. "We need to get the hell out."

While spilling out of the halted vehicle to dash to one of the others in the convoy, Comstock, a one-time solar panel installer in Phoenix, was tagged by a bullet that ricocheted off the side of the RG-31. Comstock went down and would vaguely recall his buddies carrying him low, his feet dragging across the ground to the relative safety of a companion armored vehicle. He was hauled in and dumped on his back in the thing. There was a jumble of voices above him, gunfire and his vision blurry due to the blood seeping from his head wound, bathing his face in a red sheen. Then he passed out.

Due to battlefield medical advances, and the docs discovered the round had creased his skull and brain but passed on without fragmenting, Comstock rated positive on all the tests they gave him when he was in recovery at Walter Reed. He didn't evidence brain damage and he was looking forward to being rotated out.

"You're one lucky man, soldier," winked his fortysomething nurse with the crooked nose.

"Yes, ma'am," he agreed.

Comstock figured he'd try and get a job driving a truck for the civilian side of the military contractor who supplied some of the vehicles for the CSSB. He'd made friends with one of the company's managers and the outfit had been nice enough to send him a basket of fruit to the hospital. Then one evening, after his physical therapy session, he was sitting in a chair in his hospital room. It was getting on late afternoon and the day had been overcast. Sitting there listening to a sports radio program, Comstock began to doze. Soon he was having a dream where he was floating along the hallway like a specter, unseen by anyone. But he could see and hear everyone.

He wafted through walls as if they were movie special-effects greenscreen projections. Comstock found himself in a darkened room full of medical supplies. His friendly nurse was there with a younger man, an orderly whose name tag read "Velasquez." It was obvious from the way they were buttoning up, they'd just finished making love. The orderly fired up a joint and shared a toke with her. Then after another pull, extinguished the weed and put it back in his pocket.

"See you on Friday, Alice," Velasquez told her.

"Yes you will," she replied huskily, letting her hand travel south of his belt buckle, giving him a lustful squeeze while she tongued him.

Comstock grinned crookedly and his eyes came open in his room. When the nurse made her rounds later, he mentioned off-handedly, "How you doing, Alice?" Figuring it was a private joke and he'd tell her she was in his dream, but he'd keep it chaste.

"How'd you know my first name?" Only her last name was stamped on the rectangular tag pinned to her uniform.

"I, uh, guess I must have overheard it."

She smiled sweetly and finished up.

The next time his astral form left his body, he knew it wasn't a dream. For that time he followed one of his doctors home to a split-level ranch house and noted the address. When he was released two weeks later, he had the cab driver take him there. The house matched what he'd seen as a wraith, his ghostly form not nude, but dressed as he had been in actuality. He decided then that driving a truck or going back to installing solar panels was not in the cards.

Now, several years on, Comstock was one of the highest-paid pro button men. Whatever that enemy bullet had done to his brain, and in his astral form he couldn't carry physical objects or touch things, his ability gave him one hell of a way to reconnoiter. Over time he'd learned the limits of his power. He had to be in physical proximity to his target to be able to focus on the person later. Generally, too, he found he could only project some fifty miles away. If he happened to see something shocking while tracking his prey, and this had occurred more than once, given what people do behind closed doors, he would instantly snap back into his body. The same would happen if he suddenly lost focus.

The commercial jet touched down in Dallas and Comstock got off the plane in the heat and humidity with the rest of the passengers. He rented a car using a driver's license issued to one of the various false identities he'd cultivated over the years and drove to his hotel. Along the way he activated his GPS jammer to block the signal the rental was sending. Not that he'd purposely leave any evidence linking "Walter

Monroe" to the killing that was going to go down soon, but he tried to be meticulous in erasing as much of his digital footprint as he could. That's why he'd memorize routes and byways in a city he was journeying to as opposed to using any of those apps that told you in a nice lady's voice where to drive, even though he always used burners or encrypted phones.

His target was the CEO of some sort of oil and gas concern. Because he commanded a high-end fee, his targets were one percenters who invariably found themselves in the crosshairs of their fellow swells. All said and done about loosening regulations that strangled business or renegotiating foreign trade deals, when it came down to it, how business really got done proved crime in the suites was more brutal than crime in the streets.

"Here you go, Mr. Monroe," the pert desk clerk said as she slid his card key across the marble countertop. Her nails matched her emerald eyes.

"Thank you," he said. She smiled her practiced response back at him. Comstock reminded himself not to be a spectral creep and follow the pretty woman home later to get a thrill as she undressed.

In his suite Comstock opened the shades to let the afternoon light in and checked his watch, adjusted to the correct local time. Pouring himself a glass of cranberry juice liberated from the mini-bar, he once again reviewed the information on fifty-four-year-old Geoff Ralston, head of Sunridge Petroleum, headquartered here in Dallas, not too far from this hotel. Back at the window he could see Sunridge's gaudy orange and yellow logo on the side of its highrise. He threw the security lock on his hotel door and sat in a comfortable chair. His being able to astral project didn't require him to sleep so much as to go inward, to envision the neural connectors in his brain, and as he did this, as his heart rate decreased and his breathing got shallow, he could send himself out. At

Hialeah horse race track in Miami a week ago, he'd positioned himself to briefly pass by the energy head.

Comstock sent his essence soaring, flying above the skyline, a sensation he never tired of experiencing. He entered one of the upper floors of the Sunridge building, watching the crisp men and women in their crisp suits go about their workday. He knew where the CEO's office was, as he'd been supplied the floorplans. There he found Ralston in his corner office with the magnificent view, joking on the phone with someone about a recent golf game. And so it went. Comstock sat cross-legged, floating in the room, watching. He knew from the past, the richer the man or woman, the more pressure they were under, the more they got their indulgences on. Married, divorced, whatever, none of them were celibate, they all had to get their release some kind of way. It didn't have to be sex, but damned if the percentages didn't usually say it was.

Sure enough, by the second day the way in which he'd eliminate his target became clear to Comstock. No surprise but Ralston had a squeeze on the side, Debi Namaras, a blonde who couldn't be more than twenty-five, he estimated. Ralston paid for her apartment on a street of leafy elms that ended at a cul-de-sac. From their conversations he understood she was a part-time bartender at a sports bar in the Bishop Arts District but wanted more of her life. Of course he'd promised her the moon, particularly when she was giving him enthusiastic head. He'd already bought her a used Camry, which Comstock located in her numbered parking stall. At one point, while the two cavorted, the non-corporeal Comstock studied the lock on her apartment door and the one at the entrance security gate downstairs. No lock expert, more than once he'd lingered at an apartment entrance, walking back and forth, gabbing on a cell phone, and when someone went in, followed or disabled the lock with super glue.

Over the years, Comstock had observed that various guys

and gals of the upper crust who got some on the side had their drivers take them to their assignations. Ralston was old school and drove his black BMW 6 Series to her place. Okay, Comstock concluded after noting the man's pattern with the young lady over several days, the hit would have to go down in daylight with possible witnesses. But not on the girlfriend's street he concluded. He withdrew his ghostly head from the engine compartment of the car, having scrutinized its electronic components. Comstock returned to his body and went down to the pool to have a swim and solidify his plan. Later he drove across town to a public library and reviewed the specs on Ralston's BMW, utilizing a site for hardcore aficionados.

Ralston whistled a tune when he left the blonde's apartment two days later. He beeped the alarm off, which also unlocked the car door of his Beemer. He got behind the wheel of the sleek machine, a satisfied grin on his face. The engine caught instantly and he drove away, diffused rays of the sun filtering tendrils of light through the leafy trees. Comstock trailed him in his rental, but not too close. He was pretty certain from his past observations of the route Ralston would take to get to the I-30 freeway and back into downtown and his office.

Just as the purring BMW cornered the commercial street that led to the on-ramp, the car suddenly stopped functioning, the engine shutting off with the rapidity of snapping your fingers. It was times like these that Comstock reflected on the types of devices to be obtained via the so-called dark web. Gadgets like the one he'd just used to disable Ralston's car. New vehicles were built with a kind of black box that recorded accident data. His gizmo, which looked like a two-way radio, activated in close enough range, sent a false message to the black box that it was being tampered with—a code telling it that thieves had stolen the car. This, in turn, meant the onboard computer would receive a signal from the black box and shut down the car's operating system.

Comstock wryly noted it was a good thing Ralston didn't favor rebuilt 1960s' muscle cars whose electrical components were by comparison uncomplicated and immune to hacking. He stepped closer to the stalled out BMW, wearing his worn mechanic's clothes. He'd timed it so that Ralston would have just enough inertia to steer toward a curb, which he had. The steering wheel locked once the front wheels stopped moving. Comstock's heart rate quickened, hammering in his ears. The old excitement still stirred him but he'd long ago learned to channel the jangles through and out his body like sending forth his astral form. Hand cool around the weapon in his pocket, eyes scanning his terrain, he lessened the gap to the car.

For surely a busy man like Ralston, women to juggle and kickbacks to oversee, would be happy to ask this grease monkey to take a look under the hood. And given nothing worked on the car, Ralston might be standing outside, the interior stuffy, as the power windows were up and there was no air conditioner. Or maybe Ralston was getting Triple A on the phone. But Ralston was unmoving behind the wheel, Comstock saw. Comstock had both hands in his pockets, his baseball-style cap pulled low on his forehead. He paused momentarily. Ralston's BMW was partially stopped in the driveway of an industrial store. Two men in clothes not dissimilar to Comstock's came out of the side of the store, guiding a large commercial refrigerator on a dolly toward a flatbed truck.

"Hey, mister," Comstock said just loud enough, knuckle sounding on the driver's side window of the BMW, "need a hand?"

Ralston lay back against the supple leather of the roadster's seat. His eyes were open, his mouth slightly agape. Frowning, Comstock unlatched the door and swung it open some, stepping around it in the same motion so as to strike instantly and be gone. Pressing two of his fingers to the big vein in Ralston's neck, he detected no pulse. He bent closer, detecting the smell of wine inside the recently deceased man's open mouth.

"Hey, we got a delivery to make," called out one of the workmen at the flatbed.

"I think this guy's had a heart attack," Comstock said. "Can you call nine-one-one, my phone is dead."

"Okay, hold on," the other one replied.

Comstock walked away briskly, not worried that he was leaving tell-tale fingerprints behind. Coated onto his hands was a clear plasticine-like material. He got back in his rental, parked down the street, and making a U-Turn, headed back toward the girlfriend's apartment. There was no such thing as a coincidence in his line of work. Ralston just up and croaked conveniently like that? Hell no, Comstock determined

Namaras' Camry was still in its space when Comstock walked around to the rear of her complex. He went to a side gate off the pool, having heard voices and splashing coming from there. He carried a tool box. Two women of a certain age were enjoying the water.

"Excuse me, would you mind letting me back in? I'm working on one of the forced air units."

"No problem," one of them said, a dark-haired forty plus in big shades and an endearing muffin top. She made a thing of sashaying over in her too-small bikini.

"Thanks a lot."

"My pleasure," she flirted.

He touched the brim of his cap like a cowboy might. He heard the two chuckling and whispering at his back at his went on. Namaras' apartment was in the second floor and out of the line of sight of the pool. He knocked lightly on the door, unrushed, conveying nothing too much out of the ordinary.

"Yes?" came her voice.

"It's about the flooding, ma'am."

"What?"

"Apartment 29, pipe burst." That was the unit to the right of hers. The layout of the place had her kitchen mirrored against 29's. If she'd lived here any amount of time, she'd know that. There was a pause and was that murmuring Comstock detected? Was she on the phone?

Namaras cracked the door and examined him through the sliver. "Is this going to back up into my place?'

"I want to make sure it doesn't."

"Okay, fine." She opened the door more and he stepped in.

"You did a hell of a job on Ralston," he said, aware of the exposed doorway behind him.

Her alert face clouded momentarily then cleared. "I guess you're not the plumber."

"And I guess you're not just a part-time bartender."

"Let's talk." She backed up some, her feet in sandals, wearing hip hugger jeans and a crop top. What was seen of her exposed belly was toned muscle.

Facing her, he reached behind and pushed the door closed. It didn't click in the frame.

"I'm guessing you're working for the wife," Comstock said. He held the tool box before him, hand clasped on the other wrist.

"Who are you working for?"

There was a shuffling, shoe leather making a soft scuff over the apartment's carpeting, and Comstock looked from Namaras to another woman who appeared from around the corner leading to the kitchenette. She must have been like a statue there, Comstock dimly recorded as the gun came up in her hand and she triggered off rounds at him.

He reeled sideways and went flat next to the small coffee table with a vase of flowers on it that exploded from a bullet.

Another bullet grazed his shoulder blade and yet another clipped him in the back, in the posterior deltoid, as he went prone. The lid of the tool box was rigged so that it flipped open on a spring release. The inner lid held another of Comstock's guns in a simple Velcro harness and the semi-auto was now in his hand. He shot the woman from where he was down on the floor. His first bullet slammed into her chest, staggering her backward, crimson spraying across the beige carpet like an abstractionist throwing paint on a canvass. His second entered her forehead off-center and she dropped to the floor heavily.

Fighting disorienting pain, he was up and flicking the muzzle of his gun about. He waved Namaras off from going for the Beretta that belonged to the dead woman. The piece lay near her open curled hand.

Comstock judged the woman he'd just killed was forty or so, in heels and a designer dress ensemble. Her mussed hair was coiffed and the jade bead necklace she'd worn had broken when she fell, the balls laying everywhere like an errant set of Tiffany marbles. She looked like a realtor who'd gone berserk. Or the late Ralston's once-trophy wife.

Comstock shook his head at Namaras. "Fuckin' amateurs," he grumbled. Excited voices drifted up to him from outside. His blood, his DNA was splattered over this crime scene and soon the police would arrive.

"Listen, I'll split the money with you," she began but didn't finish as Comstock shot her, too, once through the heart.

He started for the door but had to brace against the wall, a weakness like he'd felt when the bomb went off that time in Afghanistan, wobbling his legs. He sucked air in deep, and out the door and down the steps he went.

"Hey, man, you can't leave," a would-be Good Samaritan said to him, grabbing at his arm when he got downstairs. The man wore a tank top emblazoned with "Wall of California," and he reeked of skunky weed.

"Fuck off."

Comstock clubbed him viciously in the head and was past him as the man groaned, wilting to the ground. This being Texas, a state big on guns and self-defense, Comstock assumed the wife, partnered with Namaras, would have tearfully explained that this crazy man had broken in on them and what choice did they have but to shoot him? They'd have witnesses attesting that he pretended to be some sort of repairman.

For the first time in his professional career, Comstock was in a slow panic as he drove away. That second bullet that struck him was lodged in his upper back. While he could concentrate and avoid an accident, he couldn't leave it there to fester and infect him, fever him up and maybe kill him off with who-knew-what internal toxins. The slug had to come out. But the underground docs he knew, a few who'd lost their licenses due to drug habits or other such vices, none of them were in Dallas. The closest was in Fort Collins in Colorado.

He could make it, less than a thousand miles, that was like what, twelve, thirteen hours on the road? Less when he could gun it along sections of the highway. Like strolling to the corner grocery for a loaf of bread. Comstock psyched himself, steeling his mindset. Sweat salting his lips, he accelerated and tried for a few seconds to pretend the blinking lights in his rearview were just a hallucination. That chump he whacked must have seen him drive off. Now there were at least three cop cars behind him.

Shit.

Comstock wasn't going to be yet another moronic subject of breaking news, a hapless suspect no better than a liquor store stickup man, chased all over various freeways by vehicles and news copters for the enthrallment of reality show addicts munching on hot Cheetos. The object of conversation for maybe a half-hour to be replaced by the next titillation, be it the latest jaw-dropping tweet from the Oval Office or Bigfoot being spotted in the Walmart parking lot.

He pulled over and let the law swarm his car. Sidearms and shotguns pointing at him from every angle, he obeyed commands to "Show your hands...hands out the window now," and so on. He was roughly removed from his rental and thrown to the asphalt. A foot pressed on his back wound made him grimace and grit his teeth.

"Who the hell are you? You a Muslim, boy?"

"Why'd you kill those two women? Did you rape 'em?"

"You the boyfriend, asshole? Huh?"

On it went, Comstock remaining mum.

His fake ID was taken, and strapped and handcuffed to a gurney, he was finally hauled away. The beefy cop who rode with him in the back of the ambulance stared at him balefully.

"Just give me an excuse, son," he drawled.

At one point as they went along the vehicle humped over a substantial pothole. The ambulance lurched and the portable defibrillator crashed onto Comstock's head from its overhead rack. He wasn't sure, but he had an inkling the cop might have helped it slide off.

"Oops," the officer said, "you got a boo-boo."

"Your mama's got a boo-boo," a woozy Comstock croaked. Blood seeped into his eye from the fresh wound.

The EMT surprised a grin while the cop smoldered.

This being Texas, they love them some executions, Comstock understood, so he was given tip-top treatment at Parkland Hospital and sent to the jail ward for recovery. In that way he'd be in good shape when they gave him the hot shot.

"You dropped off the radar after the Army, Comstock," the detective with the trim waistline and deep-set eyes said to him as he lay shackled after his operation. "Given the woman who shot you was the wife of Geoff Ralston, who just happened to have what looks so far like a heart attack less than an hour before, and the other woman had been seen in his company, why don't you set me straight on what went down, pardner?"

"Can't help you, slick." The dryness of his voice surprised him.

The detective studied him with a practiced detached interest. "Uh-huh."

He left, both knowing he'd be back once he'd gotten the toxicology results from Ralston's autopsy and looked further into Namaras' life. Comstock damn sure didn't plan to be around for that return visit. On the second day toward late afternoon, he felt strong enough and left his body. It took more effort than in the past but he chalked that up to his current condition. Spooking away, he looked back at his body and the stitched-up wound on the side of his forehead.

Skulking about, he noted the cop assigned to guard his door was sweet on a curvy nurse. He would ease down the hall to chat with her at the nurse's station. Good to know, Comstock catalogued, pleased. There up toward the ceiling, he lolled, happy to feel whole, free, even if it was in his unsolid form. Hands behind his head, he did the backstroke, careening across ghostly waves. Then, as he came out of a loop, he saw an orderly at the door to his room. The cop, back at his post, and the orderly exchanged a nod and the orderly went inside. Comstock was about to drift further along but ice was settling in his belly. He double-backed to his room.

The orderly's name tag read "Velasquez" but this wasn't the man he'd seen with Alice. This one now stood quietly inside the room, gazing at Comstock's inert form, the only noise the steady hum of the monitor. Comstock figured he must have been sent by his employers to tie up loose ends. Comstock made to re-enter his body and yell his head off.

Only he couldn't seem to get back in. Like blowing your nose or scratching an itch, that's how easy it should have been. But his recent head wound, what had it done to him?

"Okay, be calm, you can do this," he said in his ethereal echo. The orderly stepped closer, a hypodermic in one hand while he extracted a fluid from a slim vial in his other.

"Shit," Comstock blared in his silent tone. "Shit, come on, this ain't no time for a vacation. Come on, get back in, get in," he yelled at himself.

The orderly raised the needle to inject its contents into the tube line from the saline solution into his arm.

"Now," Comstock screamed as he made a last dive toward his body, screaming all the way.

Zona Romantica
Susan Calder

Ashley puts her Mexican Tourist Card and passport into the condominium's safe. She won't need them for a month, unless Nicole sends an all-clear. On the dresser, Ashley counts out pesos for groceries and a taxi from Mega, the closest Canadian-style supermarket. She stashes the remaining bills in the safe and locks it with a combination number she'll never forget—Luke's birth date and month.

She changes from her travel clothes into a T-shirt and shorts. Nicole says even in November the nights are warm in Puerto Vallarta. Ashley secures the pesos in her zippered pocket. On her way from the bedroom, she dips in to the great room and revels in the two leather sofas, bookcase with travel literature on this coastal region, wall mounted TV, glass table and chairs, all for herself. Thirty-two years old and living alone for the first time, with more space than she needs. She pirouettes to the sliding doors.

On the balcony, she admires the views of the bay and hills rising from the Zona Romantica, this neighborhood of Mexican-style buildings and new development. An hour from now, in Calgary, Luke will get home from work and read her note. She doubts he'll report her missing, but neither he nor the police would think to search for her in Mexico. Her one fear is Nicole's husband showing up.

"He'll kill me if I try to leave him," Nicole said.

Chills rise up Ashley's arms. She returns to the great room, closes the door behind her and double-checks the lock. If Robert, the husband, does appear, Ashley has her story prepared.

Ashley became aware of Nicole in the changing rooms at Sears, when both emerged with their arms draped in clothes. Ashley hung her pile up on the discard rack; Nicole took hers to the cashier. Two days later, Ashley saw the same woman in Sporting Life, trying on jackets. The next week, Nicole was a few people behind her in line at Salad Express. Ashley collected her tray and claimed a table.

As she stirred milk into her coffee, a voice said, "Mind if I sit here? All the tables are taken."

Ashley looked up at the woman from Sporting Life and Sears.

"Go ahead," she told her.

The woman placed her shopping bags by the vacant chair and went to get her order. Sitting down, Nicole introduced herself. "Usually it's not this busy," she added.

"Friday afternoon," Ashley said. "More people in the mall."

"You come here often?"

"I work at Shoppers Drugs." Ashley nodded at the store across from Salad Express.

Nicole's face brightened. "That's why you look familiar."

Ashley couldn't recall seeing this woman with frizzy blonde hair at the prescription counter. Nor did her high-pitched voice strike a chord. Nicole's black and white scarf, tied in a bow, looked like one Ashley had fondled yesterday in The Bay Accessories.

She glanced at Nicole's shopping bags. Eddy Bauer. The Bay. Victoria's Secret. "Looks like a productive day."

Nicole shot the bags a glance. "I'll return most of it later."

She laughed. "Actually, all of it. My husband has a fit if I bring stuff home."

"He makes you return them?"

"I hide it before returning."

Ashley stared at Nicole, whose center hair part highlighted her heart-shaped face. She looked to be around Ashley's age. "Owning the things for a short while gives me a lift." Nicole laughed. "You think I'm crazy."

"No, I don't."

"Anyone would, including my therapist. Understanding the problem doesn't solve it."

Ashley owned the items for an even shorter time in the changing rooms, and shorter still when she picked objects up from store shelves. When she'd confided her urges to Luke, he suggested therapy.

"Have you called someone yet?" he kept asking.

"That nutty behavior was a phase," she finally said. "It's stopped."

Nicole finished her salad. She rubbed a napkin over her lips. "This has been fun."

Oddly, it was, Ashley realized.

"We should do it again," Nicole said. "What days do you work next week?"

They agreed on Tuesday, which led to Friday lunch, and Tuesday again. Ashley learned that Nicole was thirty-nine, older than her sweet face and voice suggested. She had dropped out of the university to marry Robert, a football-playing business major with a can-do approach to everything. He'd made it big with his firm, which produced some kind of pipeline part.

Each time, Nicole showed up in a different outfit and expensive-looking accessories—a scarf, purse or necklace she had managed to squirrel away from Robert.

"Our son's a chip off his father," Nicole said. "He started college this fall. Do you have kids?"

Ashley shook her head, her mouth full of grated carrot. "I've never been that interested and Luke doesn't want them. He says I'm enough."

"Robert treats me like a child, too."

"Luke's joking when says that." Or was he? "He has this idea I'll crumble without him, but I've wondered if that's him projecting."

"What do you mean?" Nicole's eyes narrowed.

Ashely chewed some lettuce slowly to avoid talking about the nights Luke had held her and said he'd die without her. Over a few beers, she'd made the mistake of confiding this to her mother shortly after she'd met Luke. Her mother's face had grown as fierce as Nicole's was now.

"I don't trust that man," her mother had said. "He's too handsome."

"What does that have to do with anything, Mom?"

"He's used to the world pandering to his every wish." Her mother clunked her bottle to the table. "You don't want to cross him."

Since then, Ashley had sometimes wondered, if she ever left Luke, would he be the type to stab her with a fishing knife, then turn the blade on himself?

Nicole speared a tomato. "Robert's the other side of the Luke coin," she said. "He'll kill me if I try to leave him."

Ashley shivered. "How do you know?"

"All I can do is escape now and then on my own to our place in Mexico. Robert hates Mexicans and the heat." Nicole pushed away the salad she'd barely touched. "We bought the condo as an investment and rent it out most of the year."

Ashley ran her tongue over her teeth to rid them of any spinach remains. "My only getaway is Luke's weekends at our cottage in Montana. I hate fishing and skiing, my excuse to stay home." It struck her the excuse part was true. She used to enjoy both activities; they'd met on a ski hill.

At their next lunch, Nicole mentioned her love of old

Hollywood movies. "Robert finds them weak on plot. How can he say that about *Roman Holiday, Casablanca...*?"

Ashley knew it was unprofessional, but she had looked up Nicole's prescription history at work. Nothing on record, but Shoppers sold more than drugs. Nicole might easily have seen Ashley there while buying something else. The important thing was that Ashley had stopped prowling other mall stores since acquiring a friend.

"Have you seen the film *Strangers on a Train?*" Nicole said. "Two strangers meet on a train, discover they both want to kill someone and agree to kill the other's target. Neither one has a motive, so isn't a suspect."

"Do they get away with it?"

"I don't remember. It gets complicated." Nicole toyed with her polka-dot scarf. "It made me think of you and me."

"I don't want to kill anyone." Ashley tittered. From nerves?

"Me neither," Nicole said. "But if we wanted to escape, there's your cottage in Montana and my condo in Puerto Vallarta. Luke wouldn't dream of looking for you there."

"I've never been farther than the USA."

"Montana's about the last place I'd visit."

Ashley moistened her dry throat with coffee. "What about the police, if Luke reported it? Can they check people who've crossed borders and flight records?"

"Probably." Nicole's fingers dropped from her scarf. "We could trade passports. If you frizz your hair and dye it blonde, you'd pass for me in a passport picture."

"That's illegal."

"If you're caught." Nicole laughed. She swirled lettuce around her plate. "Robert might search for me in Mexico, much as he hates it. He wouldn't find me at the condo."

"He'd find me."

"You'd be our renter from Airbnb. You only know me by e-mail."

"This is nuts."

"Isn't it?" Nicole giggled.

"You'd hate our cottage," Ashley said. "It's more of a shack. No Wi-Fi, TV or phone. Or stores for miles."

"That might cure me." Nicole touched her shopping bag from Sport Chek.

"Luke would think of checking the cottage," Ashley said. "How would you explain yourself? We don't rent on Airbnb."

"A detail to iron out."

"He'd know you have some connection to me and badger you until you give him my location."

"Lots of details before we make this work," Nicole said. "If we want to."

After a week in Puerto Vallarta, Ashley has her routine in place. Morning walks through the Zona Romantica and beyond; afternoons at the beach or pool; evening strolls on the Malecon boardwalk, where she feels safe after dark. Since day three, when she spotted a computer café, she's longed to go in and check her messages on a terminal that can't be traced to her. On day seven she decides she's held off long enough.

In the café, she clicks open the Hotmail account she set up. A blank inbox pops up. No message from Nicole saying she convinced Luke she was Ashley's colleague, using the cottage off-season for a writing retreat.

Ashley expects her heart to sink in disappointment. Instead, it flutters on her walk up Basilio Badillo Street, lined with restaurants she'd love to try if she were sure her pesos would stretch the month. In this hot, sunny land, Luke doesn't seem terrible, and not dangerous at all. It's been years since the day her mother implied he might go postal. When was the last time Luke told her he'd die if she left? And maybe that was simply his insecurity in their early years, an older man who'd stolen her from her boyfriend. Now they were settled into security. Complacency? For all she knew, the point of this trip might be revival, not the end of Luke and her.

She arrives at the Mexican neighborhood that feels miles from the touristy Zona Romantica. Everything in these shops is cheaper than the goods at Mega. Bananas cost less than five cents each and taste sweeter than the ones at home. She buys a bunch, along with vegetables for stir fry and fillets of fish. For variety, she returns along a street she missed before and stops outside a pet shop, the first one she's seen in Puerto Vallarta. Chickens, rabbits, budgies, mice packed in cages. She jumps backward, totters on the curb. Are these pets? Or food, and the mice food for other creatures?

Ashley hurries away, hoping the budgies aren't for eating and glad she chose fish over chicken for tonight. Onion aromas waft from a street food cart. For lunch, she buys two tacos—vegetarian.

In the condo's rooftop pool, Ashley floats, dipping the back of her head into the water. Refreshing. She bangs into a person and swivels around.

"Sorry," she says.

It's the woman in the Blue Jays visor, who's been here every time Ashley's come up. Like always, the woman is wearing a blue swimsuit and clunky blue earrings, although she and her husband are usually in lounge chairs, reading. From overheard conversations, Ashley gathers they're retired, like many others in the building. More than half of the residents seem to be Canadians.

"Isn't it beautiful today?" Blue Jay says.

They scan the horizon, where the ocean shines turquoise under pure blue sky.

"My husband's crazy to give this up for an adventure tour," Blue Jay says. "He's off on an ATV ride and zipline in the jungle."

Is she hinting to learn why Ashley is always at the pool alone? Ashley decides to test the story she brainstormed with Nicole, who stole the basics from a friend.

"My husband's back in Calgary at work." Ashley raises her feet from the pool bottom and treads water. "For my birthday, he gave me this month away to research and work on my novel."

Blue Jay's eyes light up. "You're writing a book?"

"About a woman who leaves a broken romance and escapes to Puerto Vallarta."

"Sounds like something I'd read," Blue Jay says. "Before you go, give me your name so I can buy it."

"Sure thing." Ashley paddles away. That was easy. She wants to e-mail Nicole and say the story works.

A man joins Blue Jay in the pool, an American, Ashley guesses as she breast-strokes past. They're discussing the café at the hotel next door.

"The food's amazing," the man says.

Blue Jay agrees. "Surprisingly good value."

Between swimming and reading the mystery novel she picked up from the condo book exchange shelf, Ashley's afternoon passes quickly. With reluctance, she leaves the lounge chair, puts on the cover-up she bought from a beach vendor and pads downstairs. She enters her unit to a blast of cold. She could swear she turned off the air conditioner when she went out. Under the arch to the dining area, a man appears.

Ashley retreats. "Who are you?"

The man edges closer.

She fumbles behind for the door handle. "Why are you here?"

The man halts. "You aren't Nicole."

"Are you in the wrong unit? How did you get in?"

Ashley's legs buckle. She leans into the door for support. A suitcase and laptop bag stand by the entrance. The man is tall, broad, fair-skinned. He wears a mauve business shirt and beige pants. Robert, Nicole's husband, and Ashley is acting bewildered and frightened, which is normal in this situation.

Her brain starts to focus. "Nicole is the person I dealt with to rent this place."

"My wife." He rubs his jaw. "I assumed... My apologies." He moves toward her.

Ashley grasps the door handle. He leans forward to pick up his cases.

"I have a printout of our e-mail agreement," Ashley says. "I can show you."

"My mistake." He smiles, like a grimace. "You're in the right. I apologize for the intrusion."

Baggage in hand, he's out the door. Ashley secures the lock behind him. In the great room, she sinks to a dining chair. Her heartbeat returns to normal. Robert showing up was inevitable, almost. Now he's gone; it's over. Nothing more to dread.

Still, she skips her evening Malecon walk. Robert has a key to this place. She'd spend the whole outing worried about coming back and encountering him again.

For the first time since arriving, Ashley has a bad night's sleep. Her mind won't stop reeling. Should she e-mail Nicole? No, nothing's happened that's unexpected. Ashley keeps waking from dreams of chickens, rabbits and mice chasing each other, biting heads and legs, while budgies swirl above them. A lump rumbles in her stomach. The fish? Was it rotten? Is this Montezuma's revenge?

In the morning, she's too tired to explore Puerto Vallarta beyond the rooftop pool. No diarrhea, thank the Aztec gods, but she should buy some medicine at a *farmacia* just in case. There's one on every block, selling drugs that would be more expensive or restricted in Canada.

After lunch, her stomach feels settled enough for an afternoon at the beach. Outside the condo building, her gaze strays to the café next door. Should she splurge tomorrow on its amazing cheap food? A man seated at a table looks up from his laptop screen.

Robert. She freezes. He waves, a salute.

She forces her legs toward him. "Still here?"

"Too late yesterday to catch a plane home," he says. "I figured, I might as well stay a few nights."

A huge margarita stands beside his open laptop. He wears a floral shirt that, somehow, looks cool on him. Black hair, even features, muscled arms, he's remarkably good looking.

"Have you eaten?" he asks. "I'm about ready to order."

She holds up her swimming bag. "I'm on my way to the beach."

"Have fun." He smiles. "*Buenos tardes.*"

Three hours later, she returns from the beach and glances at the café. There he is, at the same table, laptop open.

"You haven't moved?" she says.

"I've gone to my room a few times." He motions toward the hotel courtyard that's bursting with tropical foliage. "I made this unexpected trip and left work behind to deal with. This is my office for the day. I'm done now." He closes the laptop lid.

A waiter comes over. "*Senorita,* you join us for happy hour? Two for one margaritas."

"Thanks, but..."

Robert talks to the waiter in Spanish, his hands moving in large gestures.

"*Si, Roberto,*" the waiter says.

"*Gracias,* Javier."

The waiter leaves.

"You speak Spanish?" Ashley says.

"*Un poco.*" Robert makes the gesture for "small" with his thumb and index finger. "I ordered an appetizer platter. It only comes in one size—huge. You'll have to help me eat it."

Javier returns with a bucket of Coronas in ice. He pops a cap and holds the bottle out to Ashley. She's parched and hot from the beach and walk back.

"I owe you," Robert says. "After barging into your space." What would be the harm of sitting with him on this street patio? She sets her bag by the rattan chair, which molds to her back. The beer is cold and delightful. Facing her is a wall decorated with beaded masks. A leopard face looking over Robert's shoulder echoes his high cheekbones and narrow-set eyes.

"Nice hat," Robert says.

Ashley touches the floppy brim. "A beach vendor bargained me down to seventy-five pesos. It's a god-send in this sun."

"You look a little like Nicole, my wife," he says. "If I sounded strange when you came into the condo, that's why."

"You don't need to explain."

He strokes his beer bottle. "She left me for another man."

"She did?" Ashley sips beer to hide her surprise.

"It didn't occur to me, at first, they'd come to Mexico. Nicole doesn't like it."

She doesn't? Ashley guzzles the beer. "Why did you buy in Puerto Vallarta, then?"

"Honestly?" He glares. "I suspect she hoped I'd leave her alone for a few weeks a year. Who knows how long this affair has been going on?"

Ashley drains her bottle's last drops. Nicole's plan, like hers, was to leave a note with no specifics, saying she was gone. Has Robert assumed his wife's only possible reason for leaving him was someone else?

"Here is your salsa." Javier brings them bowls of guacamole, pico de gallo and other sauces. He shuffles the bowls and beer bucket to the side to make room for an enormous platter.

"I really should go," Ashley says, despite the savory aromas.

"What for?"

Her mouth waters. Does he know she's alone in Puerto Vallarta?

"It was her shopping that clued me in," Robert says. "This summer, she starts bringing home clothes, shoes, jewelry. Change of behavior."

Ashley realizes she's picked up a taco, which tastes even better than the one from the food cart.

"Now I know," Robert says. "She was buying her trousseau."

Ashley recalls her meetings with Nicole, those shopping bags of stuff to return. Evidently, Nicole didn't hide the stuff from Robert as well as she thought. One shopping bag was from Victoria's Secret. You can't return lacey undergarments.

"I'm not stupid," Robert says. "I did my research. When it finally hit me to check the condo reservation log, I see your name and figure'd she wrote it in to deter me."

Ashley spoons brown sauce onto a quesadilla. She's glad Nicole suggested registering Ashley under her real name, rather than exchange passports. Too criminal and risky, they concluded.

"You mean," Ashley says. "You flew here expecting to find your wife in the condo with—"

"Her lover." Robert's jaw clenches.

Ashley forks up a piece of quesadilla. Fire rips through her mouth. She grabs a Corona from the bucket.

Robert's jaw twitches. "Spicy tamarind takes some getting used to."

Ashley drinks; the heat in her mouth fades, slowly. She decides to shift the conversation from Nicole and her alleged lover to Robert, who seems more comfortable in Mexico than Nicole implied.

"Do you come to Puerto Vallarta a lot?" she asks.

"Three or four times a year," he says. "I'd get down more often if it weren't for work." He looks at his laptop case. "And if Nicole wanted."

Did Nicole get Robert wrong or was she lying? Why would Nicole confide "He'll kill me" to Ashley, a stranger, and withhold the relatively mundane detail about her affair? Or was Robert's research skewed by his assumption of another man?

Ashley tries changing the subject again. "That's interesting art behind you."

Robert cranes his head around. He explains that the beaded animal masks are handmade by Mexican peasants. They glue on the beads individually to create intricate patterns, like the lightening slash across the leopard's fore-head. While Ashley munches tapas, Robert segues into descriptions of his day trips from Puerto Vallarta. Rather than tours, he prefers to hire boats to take him to beaches and villages inaccessible by roads.

"It's unusual for a woman to travel alone to Mexico," he says.

Ashley starts at the non-sequitur. A chicken bit lodges in her throat. She washes it down with beer, and finishes her second bottle. She shouldn't go for a third, but her mouth is dry.

She clears her throat. "For a present, my husband gave me this month to work on a novel I'm writing, and research the place. The story's set here."

"At this hotel?"

Ashley glances at the courtyard. Why not right here? "This might suit my character. The hotel looks quaint." Stupid word. "I mean, boutique, Mexican-style."

Robert dips a piece of quesadilla into the tamarind sauce. "Inexpensive, too, with more atmosphere than your sterile place. I'll show you around the hotel, if you want to take notes."

"That's okay." Except that after two beers and an hour since the beach, her bladder's so full she's not sure she can make it to her condo next door. "I could use the washroom."

"It's off the atrium."

"You mean, the courtyard?"

She leaves for the open-air space. When she emerges from the washroom, Robert is standing by the atrium's central staircase. He points out the tree that twists four floors up, its leaves searching for sunlight. The trunk and branches press into the staircase railings, breaking them in spots. Rather than cut the tree down, the owners work around the problem. Robert adds that the strings of lights around the trunk illuminate the courtyard at night. When the café closes after happy hour, he says, they should move the tables and chairs to the atrium. The rooms are small, so guests spend the evening in the atrium, playing cards or trading travel experiences.

"You sound happy with the hotel," Ashley says.

"So, don't feel guilty for kicking me out of my condo."

She jerks back.

"Joking." He grins.

Stuffed from the food, Ashley doesn't need dinner. She sets out early for her Malecon walk, half expecting to see Robert in his usual chair. Instead, Javier is lifting Robert's table to move it inside.

"*Hola senorita,*" he says.

"*Hola.*" She really should learn more Spanish words.

On the pier, Ashley watches the orange, pink and red sunset hues build through layers of cloud. She walks the Malecon to its north end, in increasing darkness. Mexicans in town for the weekend party on the boardwalk and beach. They and other tourists snap photos of themselves climbing on sculptures and pose with the busker painted as an angel statue. Ashley hums along with a folklore group, a string quartet, two boys playing a melodica and electric piano. She tips them all a few pesos and buys a souvenir—a knit doll from an old woman peddler—to decorate her sterile great room. Odd that Robert put down his condo, when he could have chosen to buy a place with character. Unless Nicole didn't want that. How many of Nicole's confidences were untrue? Some of them? All?

Ashley leaves the boardwalk action for her quiet, dark street. She stops at the *farmacia* for a package of diarrhea medicine in case the tapas disagrees with her overnight.

From behind the hotel reception desk, Javier sees her and brightens. "*Senorita*," he says. "Roberto ask to meet you in the atrium. He has a surprise."

"What?"

Javier shrugs.

Ashley could snub the request, but she won't sleep for worry it's something about Nicole. She'll be safe with Javier here and all the guests sitting out on this clear night.

Robert sits alone at an atrium table, staring at his laptop screen. The strings of tree lights illuminate the space, but where are the other hotel guests?

He looks up, scrapes back his chair and stands. "It's about Nicole."

Ashley's legs waver. "What?"

"Look at this." Robert grabs her arm.

Ashley pulls away. "It's not my business—"

He shoves her down to the chair. She grips the armrests to hoist herself up, but his hand weighs on her shoulder. She opens her mouth. His other hand blocks her scream, feeds her bitter liquid. The atrium goes black.

Ashley wakes to dim light, Robert sitting on a bed beside her. She tries to move her arms and legs; can't. They're tied to a chair, not the rattan one in the atrium. This chair is hard with a straight back.

"Where am I?"

She knows. This is his room in the hotel. Single bed, dresser, café table, squeezed into the small space. She opens her lips, but no scream comes out. Too groggy.

"What did you give me?"

"You can buy anything in a *farmacia,*" he says. "Don't bother yelling. No one can hear back here."

Ashley doubts these old walls are soundproof, but she needs to gather energy for thinking.

Robert sits straighter on the bed. "Where is she?"

"Who?"

"Nicole's with him. You know where."

She coughs. Play along to escape. "I'm only the renter."

"The wife. How did she rope you in?" He gets up and switches on a ceiling light that blinds her. "My guess is he wouldn't leave you, so she stalked you, learned your habits, insinuated herself into your life."

"What are you talking about?"

He leans over her, narrow eyes staring. She turns toward the far wall that displays a beadwork mask. Not a leopard.

"You really don't get it," he says.

A monkey?

"Your husband's her lover."

But its ears are long.

"Luke, isn't it?"

Memories flood Ashley's brain. Nicole appearing in all those stores and at Salad Express. It seemed a coincidence, and then plausible and likely, due to their shared shopping habit.

"Where are they hiding out?"

Ashley smells his beer breath. "How would I know?"

"Why cover for that bitch? She betrayed you."

Nicole was her friend. No, she wasn't.

"Your husband, too."

I'll die if you leave me, Luke said, but that was years ago. Not lately. He was cheating. Nicole planned this, used her. They both did.

"Tell me their address."

Ashley eyes the door, her only exit. Robert raises his hand, palm to her face.

She cringes into the chair. *He'll kill me if I try to leave him.* Was this the one thing Nicole said that was true?

"You're a fool to protect them."

"Let her go," Ashley says. "She doesn't want you."

Robert slaps her face. Pain radiates to her forehead and neck. He presses his hand over her mouth, muffles her shriek. She squirms his hand off her.

His breathing is heavy, deep, labored. The beaded mask taunts from across the room. Long ears; it's the face of a rabbit, who will not be meat.

"Okay." She forces her voice steady. "Untie me first."

Robert touches her neck. "Run and you're a dead woman."

Ashley hurries through the atrium that's still empty. She reaches the hotel reception desk.

"*Buenos noches.*" Javier smiles.

If she reports Robert, he'll deny everything. Who would Javier believe? *Roberto,* for sure.

She makes it to her condo unit, hurls herself in, bolts the door and paces the great room. It will take Robert a full day to get to the cottage by plane and car. Could she phone the Montana police and say he's on his way there to kill his wife and her lover? Ashley has no proof. They'll think she's nuts. Despite the abduction and her slapped cheek, she's not sure herself. She's mainly going on the word of Nicole, a liar.

Ashley rifles through the folder of condo information. She

finds the page with instructions for connecting to the Internet and logs onto her Hotmail account. She types a message, keeping the details sparse, and ends with: *Get away. Take Luke with you, if you care about him.*

Nicole might go to town today and read the warning. If she doesn't, it's not Ashley's fault.

Ashley sleeps remarkably well that night and wakes up late. No response from Nicole, but she wouldn't expect it this soon. Over lunch on her balcony, Ashley basks in the view of the Zona Romantica stretching to ocean, hills and sky. She studies her Mexican Spanish phrase book and debates her afternoon activity: beach or pool?

"*Hola Senorita.*"

Ashley stops in front of Javier. She sets her beach bag by Robert's table, now unoccupied. The bag is heavier than usual with the books on the Puerto Vallarta region she borrowed from the condo shelf.

"Did Roberto check out?" she asks.

"This morning."

"*Bueno.*" Time to mangle a little Spanish. "After the beach—*la playa*—*vengo* for tapas and happy hour."

Javier grins. "Two for one margaritas."

"*Si.*" Ashley picks up her beach bag, which feels lighter.

Life is Good
John Floyd

Tony's so sweet to me, Judy thought.

He played with the kids, did his share of cooking and laundry, encouraged her career, brought her flowers.

He had also stopped his evil ways, just for her. They'd never talked much about his past—the years before they met—but Judy knew it had been situated firmly on the other side of the law. He'd even served some time, upstate.

But all that was behind them now. Tony seemed content with their marriage, their modest means, their simple lifestyle. Probably because of the chaos of his early years.

Bottom line was, he loved her and he showed it, every single day.

So she had decided to do something for him, in return.

Tony's mother, Mary Calucci, lived in San Francisco, almost three thousand miles away. Tony rarely saw her. A phone call now and then was their only contact, and Judy knew he missed his mother and worried about her. Especially now, with that new virus going around on the West Coast. Spread by rodents, apparently. Coughing, fever, then death.

And there she was, Tony's mother, sixty-three and alone in the most high-risk area of the country.

All of which led Judy to her decision: she would have Tony ask Mrs. Calucci to come east and live with them.

It would be a hardship in some ways, sure—that kind of arrangement always was. Financially, and otherwise. But it would have its benefits. His mother could be a help around the house, and with the children. She and Judy had always gotten along well. And it would certainly make Tony happy. He and his mother could even have the place to themselves for a while, since Judy and the kids were scheduled soon to visit her parents in Ohio for a week. It would give Mrs. Calucci time to get settled in.

The problem was, even if she were invited, she might not come. The virus scare wouldn't be a big issue, to her; Tony's mother lived and worked in a neat, middle-class suburb that had probably never seen a rat or mouse, and even if it had, nothing ever seemed to scare her. Besides, she'd been employed at the same accounting firm for fifteen years, and was fiercely loyal to the business and its owner. Judy doubted she'd ever quit.

Still, it was worth a try. His mother was in good health but she sure wasn't getting any younger, and yesterday's letter mentioned that a close friend of hers, someone named Winston, had recently passed away. There might never be a better time to leave those memories behind.

If Tony agreed, he and his brother could fly out and persuade her. If it didn't work, so be it—but Judy thought it would. He and David could talk their mom into anything.

Judy felt satisfied with her decision. She'd be doing something positive for her husband, her kids, her mother-in-law, maybe even herself. All in one swoop.

Life is good, Judy decided.

Now if she could just get Tony to pick up his socks...

Judy's so sweet to me, Tony thought.

The suggestion to go invite his mother to live with them was the nicest thing anyone had ever done for him. He'd been concerned about his mother anyway, for some time now—not only because of the Bay Area crime rate but because of this plague they kept hearing about.

But now that his mom had agreed to his invitation and he'd brought her back here, everything seemed to be working out. They had arrived last night and—in the rest of his family's temporary absence—had spent almost every moment together since.

He'd had to do a little work beforehand, of course. On the other end. Contacting his old friends in San Francisco, gathering information about the place where his mother worked, persuading his brother David to participate, acquiring the necessary equipment, and—finally—executing the plan. But when all that was done, the actual task of talking his mother into the move had been easy.

After all, she had nothing to stay there for, anymore. Most of her friends had been colleagues at her workplace. Another friend, some guy named Winton or Winslow or something, had apparently died the other day on his treadmill. Now she was here with her son, where she should be, safe and sound. And in a few days Judy and the kids would be home too, from their trip to her parents'.

He switched on the TV, leaned over to his mother's chair, and gave her a kiss on the cheek.

Life is good, Tony decided.

Now if he could just get better reception on ESPN...

Tony's so sweet to me, his mother thought.

It was a fine thing he'd done for her, he and David. Going all the way out there to ask her to come live here with Tony and Judy and the children. My, how she loved those children. It would be so good seeing them again. And until they got home from their trip, she and Tony had this roomy house of his all to themselves.

She wouldn't have come, though, except for what had happened at her job. The timing had been uncanny.

Two days ago, less than twelve hours before Tony and David had appeared on her apartment doorstep, the offices where she worked had burned to the ground in the middle of the night. And there was no question of rebuilding—a small fortune had been stolen from the fireproof safe, every penny old Mr. Burgin owned, after she had cautioned him a hundred times not to keep it there. Well, the money was gone now, for good, and so was Burgin, who had been working that night and perished in the fire. The police and the SFPD were saying it was arson, robbery, and murder; the intruders must've stolen the cash just before torching the place. All that, of course, was hard to believe. Everyone had liked Mr. Burgin and loved his store.

At any rate, Mary Calucci was suddenly free to leave, freed by a sad and tragic twist of Fate to come here with her darling sons and live with Tony and his darling family. And now, on the morning after their arrival at her new home, she'd received yet another surprise. Tony had bought her a car of her own—a new car and a new sewing machine and a new set of furniture for the spare bedroom (hers, now). He'd told her he was even building a swimming pool in the back yard, just so she'd be able to exercise. She'd had no idea he was so well off, financially.

She did miss Winston, of course. Her newly-purchased little hamster had dropped dead in his cage while running on that silly wheel of his. But staying in California wouldn't have brought him back. She was better off here.

She sighed and leaned back in her new recliner and thanked her lucky stars for such a fine son.

Life is good, Mrs. Calucci decided.

Now if she could just shake this cough...

The Queen-Size Bed
Rosemary McCracken

A torrent of Spanish from the hotel roof jolted Janet out of her poolside siesta. Her command of the language was limited to what she needed to navigate a food and beverage menu, but it wasn't difficult to figure out what was going on. A large bed frame was slowly being lowered from the roof on ropes. Workers guided it onto a third-floor balcony and—with some pushing and pulling—into the room.

They repeated the maneuver for a large mattress.

The crowd around the pool broke into applause when the sliding glass doors closed behind the mattress. "Olé!" cheered the Spanish-speaking guests.

"Bravo!" cried the francophones.

"Well done!" shouted the British contingent.

A smiling woman sauntered over to the man on the recliner next to Janet's. "The bed must for Len and Ruth," she said in a cut-glass English accent. "He's been complaining about their single beds."

The man groaned. "Len wants the entire world to know he's sleeping with Ruth. No fool like an old fool."

All the rooms at the Cuban hotel had twin beds. No doubles or queen-size. The resort was a three-star all-inclusive: cheap, clean and cheerful, exactly what the Babes on Bikes, Janet's daughter's bike club, wanted.

Janet opened her novel, dismissing Len and Ruth as an older guy and his trophy blonde.

* * *

She was sipping a mojito in the lounge a few hours later, thinking about Phil Redding, the man she'd been seeing back in Ottawa, and trying to tune out the hotel band playing "Yellow Bird," the only song it seemed to know. A few days before Janet had left Ottawa, Phil had brought up the M word. She'd told him they had a good thing going, why spoil it by getting married? Besides, Phil lived and ran his company across the country in Vancouver. Janet's family, her friends and her law practice were in Ottawa. "Give it some thought while you're on holiday," he'd told her.

She waved to her daughter Maddy when she came into the lounge with a group of tanned women. The Babes had left the resort at the crack of dawn to cycle the thirty-nine-kilometer loop from Cienfuegos to Pasacaballo, a route that had some challenging hills. Janet had pulled her pillow over her head when Maddy asked if she'd like to join them.

Maddy breezed over to Janet's table and kissed her cheek. "Come out with us tomorrow, Mom. An easy ride around the bay. We'll have a swim on our lunch break."

"I'm happy right here," Janet told her. "I have the pool, the beach, a good book. And the bar."

Maddy left the lounge shaking her head.

"You're Canadians!" a woman at the next table cried, clearly recognizing the accents.

Janet looked over at an elderly man and woman. They had snow-white hair and smiling, wrinkled faces like dried apples. The picture of kindly grandparents.

"From Ottawa," she said. "I'm Janet Quinlan."

"May we join you?" the woman asked. "There aren't many Canadians here this week. Mostly Europeans, some Brits."

"And some French Canadians," the man said.

"Who don't speak English," she countered.

Janet gave them a smile. "Please join me."

"I'm Len Brewster," the man said, pulling out a chair for his companion. "And this is Ruth Wyman."

Len and Ruth. Not what Janet had expected.

"We're from Carleton Place," Ruth said, naming a town not far from Ottawa.

They smiled and bobbed their heads. Ruth was the first to speak again. "Were you by the pool this afternoon?"

"Watching a bed go into a room?" Janet chuckled. "It certainly was dramatic."

Ruth lowered her eyes. "Lenny wants us to be comfortable, but I had no idea that moving a queen-size bed into our room would create such a spectacle." She raised her blue eyes to look into Janet's. "Everyone's talking about it. I'm embarrassed."

"Why be embarrassed, cookie?" Len put an arm around her. "Everyone shacks up before tying the knot these days. And many never get around to tying it."

Ruth smiled at him. "We're getting married in mid-January," she said to Janet. "We'll stay here over Christmas, and return to Canada just before the wedding."

Janet assumed this would be a second marriage for one or both of them, and she asked about their families back home. She learned that Len was a widower and Ruth was divorced. They each had two children, and several grandchildren between them.

Janet had worked with blended families in her law practice, and she knew that adult children can complicate second or third marriages. So she decided to focus on the grandkids. "Your grandchildren must be excited about your wedding."

Ruth opened her mouth to speak, then looked at Len and closed it. He took her hand.

Maddy appeared at the table, freshly showered and dressed for dinner. "Ready, Mom?"

Janet made the introductions, and Ruth asked the Quinlans to join them in the dining room.

Over dinner, Ruth peppered Maddy with questions about where she'd cycled on the island and what she'd seen. "What fun you girls are having," she said. "And Babes on Bikes is such a cute name for your group."

She placed a hand on Maddy's arm. "How old are you, dear?"

"Twenty-six." Maddy smiled back at the elderly woman.

"Have your adventures while you're young. You may not feel up to them when you're older."

"I intend to do just that," Maddy said and winked at her mother.

"Stay with your friends when you're on the road," Len told Maddy. "Most Cubans are friendly and helpful to tourists. But there are a few bad apples in every group."

Ruth's eyes filled with alarm. "Be careful, dear."

After dinner, Maddy announced that she was whacked, and took the staircase up to the Quinlans' room. The hotel's two elevators hadn't worked since they'd arrived.

Janet joined Len and Ruth in the lobby. "There's the hotel manager," Ruth said to Len, pointing at a man in a grey suit. "Ask him when the elevators will be running."

Len went over to him, and Janet heard them speaking in Spanish.

"What did he say?" Ruth asked when he returned.

"Mañana. Tomorrow."

She rolled her eyes. "That's what they tell us every day. Climbing the stairs to the third floor is a big hike for old folks like us."

Len took her arm. "Join us for a stroll along the beach, Janet? We're getting in shape for the stairs."

Janet followed them out the door.

"It's heaven down here," Ruth said, seating herself on a bench that faced the ocean. "We don't have to worry about slipping on ice or whether the roads are plowed after a snow-storm."

"Have you considered spending winters here?" Janet asked, sitting down beside her. Len took his place on her other side.

"We're giving it some thought," Len said. "We'll be back right after the wedding."

"Until things cool off," Ruth added.

Cool off? Janet wondered what she meant, but Ruth was turned toward Len and she couldn't see her face.

"We'll stay here till the beginning of April," Len said. "Then we'll go to my cabin in Quebec."

"Cabin, Lenny? You make it sound like a shack in the woods." Ruth smiled at Janet. "Len has a beautiful home on Lac Desmarais. Sauna, Jacuzzi, four bathrooms and three boats."

Len's vacation shack was on a prime lake in Laurentian cottage country. Janet wondered why they were staying at a three-star hotel in Cuba.

Len glanced at the Rolex on his wrist. "Time for a night-cap in the lounge."

Len and Ruth's room was down the hall from the Quinlans', and Janet found herself teaming up with the elderly couple every day. Their leisurely pace matched hers to a T. One morning they stopped at her table as she was finishing break-fast.

"Maddy's already on the road?" Ruth asked.

"She was gone by seven," Janet said.

"We're taking a taxi into town," Len said. "Why don't you come along?"

Janet ran up to the room and slipped into her walking shoes. Len and Ruth were waiting in an old-model cab outside the front entrance.

In town, they toured the cigar factory and walked through the old cathedral before settling into an outdoor café for lunch. Len suggested they try fritas, which turned out to be Cuban hamburgers that were much better than they sounded.

"I wanted to get away from the resort for a while," Ruth said when the food arrived. "I had a bad night. Woke up a little past one when I heard clicking noises at the door. Like someone trying to fit a key into the lock."

"Your imagination was running wild, cookie." Len reached over and touched her hand. "You got too much sun yesterday. Nobody came into our room, did they?"

She still looked worried.

They were getting up to leave when Ruth pointed to a woman across the street. "Isn't that Christine?"

The tanned brunette in a turquoise sundress and matching ball cap was hurrying down the sidewalk. Oversized sunglasses hid most of her face.

Len shook his head. "What would bring Christine to Cuba? It's not Bermuda or Aruba."

"Who is Christine?" Janet asked.

"Lenny's daughter-in-law."

They decided that a short walk would be good for them, and got out of the taxi down the road from the resort. Ruth walked ahead, while Len told Janet about the luncheon they planned to hold after their wedding ceremony. As they approached the hotel, Ruth ambled across the road toward the entrance. A souped-up vintage Chevy came roaring out of nowhere, headed straight for her.

"Ruthie!" Len yelled.

Two waiters were smoking outside the front door of the hotel. One of them sprinted over to Ruth and pulled her off the road.

The car roared by without stopping.

Len rushed over to Ruth and took her in his arms. Janet was right behind him. "Are you okay, cookie?" he asked. "You need to watch where you're going down here. They're maniacs on these roads."

She rested her head on his chest, breathing heavily.

"Did you see the driver?" Janet asked the waiter.

He shook his head. "Too quick. I want to get señora safe."

Len handed him several American bills and thanked him profusely. Then he turned back to Ruth. "You need to lie down, Ruthie. Let's go up to the room."

"No," she said. "Let me sit for a few minutes."

With the waiter hovering behind them, Len and Janet guided her to an armchair in the lobby. She sank into it and closed her eyes.

Janet took Len aside. "That car tried to run Ruth down."

He shook his head, looking puzzled. "Who would want to hurt Ruthie?"

Who would want to hurt Ruthie? The words played over in Janet's head as she waited by the pool for Maddy to return.

After dinner, she joined the Babes for a slide show of their adventures. There were dozens of shots of beaches, waterfalls and palm trees, with grinning women leaning against their bikes in the foreground. After the show, they all adjourned to the lounge where the band was playing—what else?—"Yellow Bird."

It was after eleven when Janet and Maddy left the table where several Babes were debating the merits of various bicycles. Janet walked Maddy to the staircase in the lobby.

"How would you feel if I married Phil?" she asked her daughter at the foot of the stairs.

Maddy's brown eyes widened. "Mom!" She paused for a few seconds. "Is that what you want? Would you move to Vancouver?"

"I wouldn't leave Ottawa."

"Could Phil move to you?"

"Probably not."

"Well...They say bi-city marriages are pretty sexy."

Janet gave her a friendly swat. "Get some sleep, Mads. We'll talk more tomorrow."

Maddy took the stairs two at a time. Janet headed down to the beach where she strolled along the water's edge as far as the large five-star hotel. She wondered if its rooms had double or queen-size beds, or even king-size. As she got closer, she heard a band playing "Yellow Bird."

As she turned back, she saw a woman hurrying along the lighted paved path above the beach that linked all the hotels on the strip. She had shoulder-length dark hair and was wearing a turquoise sundress. She was headed in the direction of Janet's hotel.

The woman in turquoise was nowhere in sight when Janet returned. The band had packed it in—perhaps it had moved to the five-star—and the lounge was nearly empty. Janet sat on a recliner beside the pool and looked up at Len and Ruth's darkened room.

Who would want to hurt Ruthie? Janet remembered the clicking sounds Ruth had heard the night before. The couple had a problem back in Canada. They were returning to Cuba right after their wedding. Until things cool off, Ruth had said.

Janet had a good idea what their problem was. Their kids didn't want them to get married. Late-life marriages present major complications for would-be heirs. Like what will happen to the couple's money after one spouse dies. Janet saw it frequently in her law practice.

And it was another problem she'd face if she married Phil.

Janet couldn't sleep. Her mind kept jumping from the pros and cons of marrying Phil, to Len and Ruth, who were marrying against their families' wishes.

She'd been tossing and turning for more than an hour when she heard footsteps on the tiled hall floor. She got out of bed, opened the door as quietly as she could, and looked down the hall.

A man dressed in white was bent over in front of a door down the hall. The door to Len and Ruth's room.

What the hell was going on?

Janet closed the door and went over to Maddy. "Wake up. Someone's trying to get into Len and Ruth's room."

Maddy groaned. "What?"

"Len and Ruth." Janet shrugged on her beach robe. "We've got to help them."

Maddy flung off the bedcovers. Janet handed her a pair of jeans, then grabbed the bicycle pump on the dresser.

The hall was empty, but light was coming from Len and Ruth's room. The door was ajar and Janet pushed it open. The man in white was standing over Len and Ruth, who were cowering on the bed. The blade of the knife he held flashed in the lamp light. Ruth gave a small yelp when she saw Janet and Maddy.

Before he could turn around, Janet jammed an end of the bike pump into the intruder's back. "I have a gun," she said.

He shrieked, and his knife clattered to the floor. Maddy picked it up.

"Down on your knees," Janet barked. "Kneel!"

As he knelt, she got a good look at his face. He was one of the waiters who'd been smoking outside the hotel that afternoon. Not the waiter who'd helped Ruth, the other one.

"Call the front desk, Len," she said. "Tell them you caught an armed intruder."

"No!" The intruder burst into tears. "No telephone. Señora, she pay me to come here. I need money. I have many children."

Len yanked the sash from a bathrobe on the back of a

chair. "Hold out your hands," he ordered.

The man groaned as Janet shoved the bike pump harder into his back. Len bound his hands tightly at the wrists. "Been doing this on my boats for years," he said with a grin.

Then he turned his attention back to the intruder. "Who was this woman who paid you to come here?"

"Señora from Canada."

"Christine," Ruth said. "It was her we saw in town today."

"Si," the man said. "Señora Christine."

Len looked at the knife in Maddy's hand. "She was paying you to kill us."

The man ducked his head. "She give me cell phone. Tell me call her when I finish."

"Where's the phone?" Janet asked.

"Pocket."

She took the cell out of his shirt pocket. "Tell the señora you've finished, and you need her to come here."

"Here?" he asked.

"Here. This room," she said. "Right now."

He gave Janet a telephone number. She placed the call and held the phone for him. From his end of the conversation, she gathered that Señora Christine didn't want to come to the room. But he insisted that she come. Right now.

Janet made sure the door was unlocked, and positioned herself in the bathroom beside it.

A few minutes later, a rap sounded on the door. "Benito?" a woman said.

"Come in, Señora," he called out.

The door opened, and the brunette in the turquoise dress walked into the room. Janet slipped out of the bathroom and locked the door.

"Hello, Christine," Len said.

"You!" She scanned the room. "Benito..." When she saw that his hands were tied, she made a run for the door.

Maddy came up behind her, and wrestled her to the floor. Janet stood over her with the knife.

Len made his call from the phone on the desk.

"Lenny's kids don't want us to get married," Ruth said.

"They think your marriage will wipe out their inheritances," Janet replied.

Ruth nodded, and Christine groaned.

"You might've got away with it, Christine," Len said when he hung up the phone. "Two more tourists murdered in the Caribbean. What wouldn't the locals do to get their hands on some cash and jewelry?"

"We didn't tell anyone we were going to Cuba," Ruth said. "Len found us this three-star so we wouldn't meet any friends of his family."

Len went over to Christine and looked down at her. "You got into our condo and found our travel itinerary. You knew we were in Cuba, but we'd changed hotels."

She grimaced and turned her head away.

"You're not staying here, are you?" he said. "This hotel's not swanky enough."

"Damn right, I'm not staying here." Christine glared at him. "The five-star down the road is bad enough. The elevator doesn't work and I'm on the eighth floor."

She fixed furious eyes on him. "The bed gave you away. I was sitting by the pool, the day it went into this room. I was checking all the hotels on the strip, and I knew that old farts like you wouldn't be out in the afternoon sun. Someone said the big bed was for Len and Ruth. The old love birds."

There was a knock on the door. The hotel manager and three uniformed police officers entered the room. Len spoke to them in Spanish.

The officers hauled Christine and Benito to their feet, and frog-marched them out of the room.

Len sat on the bed beside Ruth. "I never should have given my business to my sons. They thought it could run itself, and it wasn't long till it began to flounder. When I refused to sink more money into it, it went belly-up. Told the boys they'd get nothing more from me in my lifetime."

He shook his head sadly. His troubled face revealed what he wasn't saying. That his sons and their wives had plotted to kill him and the woman he loved.

"Maybe if I had money of my own..." Ruth said.

He put an arm around her. "Wouldn't have mattered, cookie. My kids are greedy. They want my money now."

He took her hands in his. "This settles it. We're getting married right here. Today, tomorrow, as soon as we can get a license and someone to officiate."

Ruth looked at Janet and Maddy. "Care to be bridesmaids, ladies?"

The Oldest Old Country
John Stickney

So, Michael, you're working in Henry's Crew. He treating you right?

Yes, Mr. Pascoe, Henry is a good man to work for.

Hear that, Lou, someone both polite and smart enough to lie.

Lou grunts.

I'm glad you like Henry, hell, we all like Henry, right, Lou?

Lou grunts.

Henry tells me you can shoot, he's used you as a shooter, right?

I can shoot.

Good, where'd you learn?

Some while growing up hunting, did a short stint around the first Gulf war and tried to keep at it.

Hunting?

Deer, rabbit, some varmints around the farm.

Varmints, huh, you catch that, Lou, varmints. We got enough of those around here.

Varmints, Lou says.

Henry said you do distance. We got plenty of guys can do the close in. Distance not so many. So, how far?

How far depends.

Depends on?

145

Weather, type of gun, type of charge, time of day, wind. Factors.

Factors, huh? Here's the question can you adjust, you're dropped down someplace, got no control of the factors, can you adjust, make the shot?

I can adjust, I can make the shot.

Damn, that's what I wanted to hear. So, here's the offer, ten upfront, fifteen on the backside after the job is done. If it goes well, maybe a bump up the ladder for you. This works out, the docks will need another crew, maybe here in Cleveland, maybe Lorain. It would be yours. You interested?

Yes, sir.

Get that, Lou, polite. Lou will lay it out. Nice talking to you, Michael, I'll see you soon.

Lou walks to the door, opens it, leads Michael "Mutt" Mutti down to a different, much smaller office, points to a chair, turns on the radio. It's some tenor enticing some soprano to do something.

You like music? Lou asks.

Sure.

Good, some friends of ours from back home asked a favor. We do this favor and we get some additional shipping and subsequent distribution coming our way. You pull this off, kid, you and the rest of us will be sitting pretty. But you have to be smart and careful. You got to make sure it is not traced back to us.

Who's the guy.

Right to it, huh. You know the name Vito Scopelliti?

No.

Wouldn't think you would, you're not from Canada.

Outside of Ashtabula, Ohio.

Right, not Canada. He is a boss from Toronto, a boss of bosses. He did a stint in the U.S. for a drug distribution conspiracy, like five. Got out, four months ago. Went back to Toronto and decided to reassert himself. While he was away, things kinda changed. New alliances with the old country, new product, new ways. Don't get me wrong, Vito was welcomed with open arms and a full account but for some guys there's nothing like being in charge. So, Vito is like one of those varmints on the farm, making his way into that silo, eating not only his but someone else's share of the corn cob.

Mutt and Lou laugh.

Two days later, Mutt finds himself sitting in a casino, feigning interest. The Akwesasne Mohawk Casino in Hogansville, New York, was the pick-up and drop off place. To get into Canada these days you needed a passport, you went through screenings, you left a trail. The way in and the out was, in the words of Lou, Injun country. Mutt was waiting for a guy named John Redfeather, which sounded like Lou was putting him on. Honest Injun, said Lou, Jim Fricking Redfeather. That guy's gonna take you through to where you gotta go. Leave your electronics behind, no cell phones, no computers, nothing they can locate later. No record, no trace.

Mutt checked in the hotel under a prearranged name, Sean Spicer. The room was comped, there was a thousand dollars in casino credit and a meal voucher.

Mutt was trying to get things straight in his mind. He had studied some of the pictures of Vito, carried the most recent one in his pocket, imagined the picture newly captioned, Vito in Happier Times. In celebration of his release and an upcoming birthday, the guys were taking Vito hunting. Lou said the guys Vito's with want him gone as much as everyone else, they won't even react. Take the shot, from as much distance as possible, doesn't even have to be a Moe Green.

Moe Green, said Mutt.

You don't know what a Moe Green is? Through the eye? The Godfather?

Oh, yeah, that Moe Green, Mutt said, like there was some

other Moe Green out there causing confusion.

So, journey out there across the border and into the middle of the woods guided by some unknown trailblazer, set up, shoot, and have said trailblazer take you back across the border where the balance of your payment will be waiting at the casino window. Cash out and viola, come back. Oh, by the way, no witnesses. Tonto, said Lou, has got to go to the feathered heaven of his forefathers.

Mutt was reaching for his virgin tonic water when a man said, Scott, Scott Spencer?

Spicer, said Mutt.

Right, right, my mistake, the man said, Spicer. Redfeather, Jim Redfeather. Grab your gear and let's go hunting.

Mutt went up to his room, changed into insulated jeans and a plain grey sweat shirt, camo jacket, hunting socks and boots, repositioned his ankle holster a little lower, grabbed his duffle and met the man who was standing outside, smoking a cigarette and speaking softly to a car attendant. Ah, he said, dropping the cigarette in a large outside ashtray, here's my hunter now. The attendant moved away without even looking.

In the truck, a beat up once red Ford, Mutt said, What's all this hunter stuff.

Glad you asked, Redfeather said, reaching across to the glove compartment, handing Mutt a lanyard with a crumpled paper in yellowed plastic attached, throw this around your neck. You are now officially authorized to hunt bear on Mohawk land. Anyone stops you, asks what you're doing, that's what you're doing. And me, Jim Redfeather, I am your guide.

They drove across tribal land while the sky and landscape grew dark. At one point Redfeather said, Hold your breath, rolled down a window and said, Okay, now breathe in the fresh Canadian air. At another point, Redfeather said, We'll overnight here, go out and do your business if you need. They slept upright in the car. At least once, maybe twice, Mutt caught Redfeather walking outside, smoking.

Time to get up, said Redfeather. They drank coffee from a thermos, ate some off-brand energy bars for breakfast.

Mutt said, Where's the rifle?

Redfeather produced a McMillian Tac 338, complete. You can add legs later, he said.

Someplace safe I can sight this in, Mutt said.

No problem.

They drove a bit farther, pulled off into a brush-filled dirt road and stopped in a clearing a half mile up, parking the truck. On foot from here, said Redfeather. Just so you know, this is bear country.

They walked about an hour and found another clearing. Redfeather walked out, made a big circle and came back. All clear, he said.

Mutt took the rifle out of its soft case and began the process of sighting it in. Redfeather stood and watched, smoking, then went out and set up some cans and empty water bottles at a variety of distances. Mutt sighted in, taking off his gloves to use a small screwdriver to adjust and attach the legs, all before loading. The trigger was surprisingly light. He hit everything no matter the distance. From behind him Redfeather said, Nice shooting, Tex.

They repacked the rifle, started walking, drinking bottled water and eating more of the energy bars. In the walk, Mutt learned Redfeather had grown up on Mohawk land, bouncing between the two countries depending on what family member would claim him. Redfeather learned Mutt's mother was Irish but from Erie, Pennsylvania, and his father from the old country. Redfeather said his family was from the oldest country.

Italy, Mutt said, I'm was from Italy.

Ah, Redfeather said, that explains why you look like you are someplace else.

After about an hour Redfeather said, Not far now. Within

a half hour they could see the cabin. Mutt took up a position where he could sight in on the front door. They waited and waited and the light started going. When the door finally opened, two guys came out, stumbling toward the outhouse. Neither one was the right one. Twenty minutes later, he showed in the doorway, surrounded by light. Mutt took the shot through the left eye and started gathering stuff up. Come on, come on, said Redfeather. People were starting to pour out of the house with flashlights and guns. Shots were being fired in their general direction.

What the hell? Mutt said.

You just shot their friend, what did you think they were going to do?

They started running, back into the woods, toward the truck. It was dark, and they stumbled and fell, and got up and ran some more. At one point Mutt dropped the rifle. The rifle, Mutt said, turning back.

We got to go, Redfeather said.

Along the way, they got separated, then joined up again. By dawn, they were at the truck. Redfeather started driving. Mutt planned to cap Redfeather when they crossed into U.S. territory. He didn't think he could drive the roads needed to get there. Redfeather said, Catch some shut eye, and Mutt did just that.

Wake up, Redfeather said.

Mutt opened his eyes, they were in the middle of nowhere.

So, Redfeather said, I know they want you to kill me, I saw the gun on your ankle at the casino. You might notice it is not there anymore. Mutt's leg felt lighter. I don't want to visit the great longhouse in the sky yet so we have to make a deal. You can say that you killed me, left me out in the woods with that rifle you dropped. Which rifle I picked up and can easily retrieve.

Mutt thought on it.

By the way, Redfeather said, they also wanted me to kill you, so...

Scott Spicer went to the casino, cashed out his chips, gave half to his gambling buddy Jim Redfeather and made his way home to Cleveland, Ohio, a wiser, wealthier man.

Making Tracks
KM Rockwood

Monroe never made it back from town Saturday night.

We didn't realize that until late Sunday morning.

The sun was up well before I crawled out of the small stone house where eight of us white guys slept. It was a company house, built for the family of an iron furnace worker, but who could afford a wife and children on what we made? So it had been turned into a bunkhouse.

Right now, it was filled with drunken snores. And the smell of vomit. Somebody hadn't handled their liquor well. More likely a few somebodies.

I stepped carefully as I made my way to the cookhouse.

Miss Lilly, our colored cook, shook her head when she saw me. She handed me a cup of her boiled coffee.

I'd prefer tea, but coffee was what she offered.

I ran my fingers through my mess of curly hair and sniffed the coffee. Black and tarry. But hot. I took a sip. Too hot. And bitter.

A frying pan sat on the stove. I peered into it. "Did I miss breakfast?"

She raised her eyebrows. "Heavens, Neil, are you sure you want breakfast?"

"Yeah. What have you got?"

"You Irish." She took a chunk of stale bread and dumped it into the hot bacon grease to fry. "Always ready to fight or eat."

I joined Sean at the rough table. He was picking at his chunk of bread and blowing on his coffee.

Sean grinned at me. "Good time last night, huh?"

I started to nod my head and thought better of it. I didn't get bad hangovers, not the way some people did, but I'd had a lot to drink and my head felt funny. No sense pushing my luck.

Gradually everybody crept out of their bunks. Most wanted coffee, but the smell of the fried bread gave some the heaves.

It was a Sunday, but church wasn't on our agenda. Everybody knew working at the iron furnace was an ungodly occupation, and usually we worked right through the Lord's Day. Right now, though, the entire operation was shut down for repairs.

Some people said the furnace itself ran on hellfire, and considered it the devil's work. None of the local churches wanted to see any of us darken their doorway. Even at our best, we looked and smelled like something just delivered from the brimstone abyss.

We sat around the tables, bleary-eyed. Someone asked, "Where's Monroe?"

He wasn't there. Old Zachariah, who hadn't gone into town with us, clambered to his feet and went back to the colored bunkhouse. He came out, his face a worried scowl. "He ain't there."

Tucked away in the foothills of Maryland, the furnace had run non-stop through Mr. Lincoln's war, producing cannon balls and pig iron. Now, a dozen years later, it still produced the pig iron, but time and overuse had caught up with it.

For us, the shutdown was a rare break from our twelve-hour shifts, six days a week. We wouldn't be paid again until the furnace was back in blast, which would be a problem, but we were making the most of our time off.

Given the demands of the operation, usually only three or

four of us were off work at a time. Now, though, the whole bunch was idle.

Yesterday some of us had trekked the four miles into Mechanicstown. We watched the Fourth of July parade, then drifted to the train depot to see an excursion train from Pen Mar, filled with folks in fancy clothes, roll through. We stayed in town until well after dark, when we ran out of money.

Maybe we were a tad rowdy. I know we were ragged and dirty—when you only have one set of clothes, and you work at an iron furnace, getting spiffed up to go into town isn't going to happen. We washed up in the creek before we left, but I don't think anybody seeing us would have realized we'd made the effort.

For sure, the townspeople didn't welcome us. When we tried to go to the bar at the Grand Hotel, they wouldn't let us in. So we went around the rear, off the alley.

There, the barback was sympathetic, but he knew they'd never let us in.

"Go around downtown. There's a big gray barn in the alley on the north end, where the railroad tracks head out," he told us. "Fellow who lives there keeps a still somewhere in the hills. He's got a supply in the barn, and he'll prob'ly sell you some. A lot cheaper than in the hotel bar, and, truth be told, it's a lot stronger, too."

We thanked him, and Monroe, who had more money than most of us, tipped him a nickel for the information. So I know Monroe was definitely with us at that point.

The barback looked at him kind of funny. I don't think he'd ever been tipped by a colored man before. But a nickel's a nickel, so he nodded and put it in his pocket.

We went through the alleys to the edge of town and found the property with the gray barn. A big dog barked ferociously at us, so we hung back.

As we waited for the owner, we watched a pretty colored

girl who was working in the garden, bending over to weed or pick vegetables.

Monroe couldn't take his eyes off her. He was too shy to say anything to her, and we all teased him unmercifully.

So he was with us then.

The man eventually came out and tied up the dog. He sold us some filled Mason jars from his stock. We took them and drank the contents along the railroad tracks, then headed back into town.

We got a little loud. A few of the guys whistled at some of the women outside the hotel, which got an immediate bad reaction.

A big group of men from the town gathered to "escort" us out of town.

By now it was full dark. We drifted along in front of the townspeople, permitting ourselves to be herded toward the road to the furnace.

They dropped off when we were a half mile along the road. A few of the guys decided they'd had enough and continued to the furnace. The rest of us circled back around town to the gray barn, where we bought a few more Mason jars.

By then, I'd run out of money. Monroe hadn't, though, so he bought a jar to share. He was pretty unsteady on his feet, and after a few sips, he gave the whole thing to me.

That was the last time I remembered seeing him.

I shifted uncomfortably on the hard bench. Even though Monroe was colored and I was Irish, he was the closest thing I'd ever had to a friend.

Monroe had lived at the iron furnace his whole life. His mother, a slave, was rented out by her master to work as a cook. When the slaves in Maryland were freed in 1864, she stayed on, collecting her pay herself, until her death.

Even though Monroe was about the same age as me— nobody knew his age for sure—he was a skilled gutterman and made better money than most of us. I hired on as a teamster, but soon I was reassigned to the casting house and became a gutterman's helper. Monroe showed me how to form the molds in sand to set the liquid iron into pig iron. We made a good team. Monroe, short and wiry, could handle the heat a lot better than I could. I was broad and well-muscled, and could heft and carry the pig iron with the best of them.

I looked around at the other men and stood up. "We need to look for Monroe." Those of us who could walk without falling over searched the area around the furnace.

No Monroe.

"Prob'ly passed out next to the road somewhere on the way back," Sean said. "He'll show up sooner or later."

I wished I could believe that. But no one could remember seeing him with us when we left town.

"I'm gonna walk back down the road. Maybe I'll see him." I looked around the group. "Who's coming with me?"

Everybody stared down at the table. Most of the men, including pretty much all the colored guys, were too hung over to be of much use. The Irish and the Germans, who maybe could have handled it, just shrugged and turned away.

I set off on my own.

The four-mile walk took a while, especially since I stopped to check in ditches and behind bushes close to the road. No Monroe.

When I got near town, I stuck to the alleyways. The town folk were in the streets, all dressed up in their Sunday-go-to-meeting best.

I crept up to the barn where the supply of moonshine was kept. The big dog was lying in the doorway to the barn, and he set up barking and growling as I approached.

The man who'd sold us came hurrying out of the house. The dog quieted down.

He looked me up and down. "No sales on Sunday."

I didn't have any money left anyhow, but that kept me from having to explain.

"Especially," he said, "after what happened last night."

"What happened last night?" I couldn't think of anything out of the ordinary beyond us being rowdy, but then my memory was pretty vague.

He drew himself up straight and cleared his throat. "That colored boy…"

Was it Monroe he was talking about? "What about the colored boy?"

"He attacked Mrs. Bishop. Tried to have his way with her. And set her on fire."

That didn't sound like Monroe, but with all the alcohol, who knows what could happen? I thought about him staring at the colored girl earlier.

I scratched my head. "Where was this?"

"Down by the covered bridge. She heard about you furnace workers raising Cain in town, and she set off to straighten everybody out."

"Why would she do that?"

"She's a teetotaler. And a suffragette. And a busybody. She's sure she's right, and everybody ought to agree with her."

"Is she gonna be all right?" I asked.

"Not hardly. She hasn't woke up. The doctor says it's just as well. Burns hurt something awful."

That's true. You don't work at an iron furnace without getting a few burns. They hurt like hell. "How'd they know who did it?"

"They found this colored boy lying in a ditch by the road. He smelled of smoke, and there were burn holes in his clothes.

Of course. We all smelled like smoke. And had burns in our clothes. "What did they do with the colored guy?"

"Put him in jail. Too bad the sheriff's away."

"Where's the sheriff?"

"Gone to Frederick on Friday for court. Case carried over

till Monday. His daughter lives down there, and he's staying with her."

"So they're gonna wait to do anything till the sheriff gets back?"

The man snorted. "I doubt that boy's gonna make it till then. A lot of people are up in arms over the whole thing. Talking about a lynching if Mrs. Bishop dies. Or maybe even if she doesn't die. Kid who's minding the jail won't be able to stop them."

I asked where the lady lived, and where the jail was.

He told me. Then he said, "Say, I'd appreciate it if you didn't say anything about where you got the booze yesterday. I could do without everybody blaming me."

I nodded, then set off across town, sticking to the alleys.

A vegetable garden separated the jail from the alley. No one was in sight. Picking my way carefully among the pole beans and cabbages, I snuck up under the barred window and crouched.

"Monroe!" I kept my voice low. "Monroe! Are you in there?"

Through the unglazed window, I heard someone scrabbling around. "Who's there?"

"It's me. Neil. You okay, Monroe?"

"Here I am, locked up in a white man's jail, and you want to know if I'm okay? No, I'm not okay."

"Well, how are you feeling?"

"Not so good."

"But aside from being hung over. You hurt?"

"Not yet."

"What'd ya mean, 'not yet?'"

"This guy in the office, he says come nightfall, a crowd of white men are gonna come and teach me a lesson."

"Isn't he gonna try to stop them?"

"Nah. He says he's not going to get hurt trying to save some ape that they're just gonna kill anyhow."

"What did you do to that white woman?"

"Me? Nothing. She got attacked about sundown. I was with you-all then. Things get a little hazy later. I guess I passed out. If I'd made it back to the furnace, nobody'd be saying I done nothing."

"Where'd they find you?"

"Next to the road. I started feeling mighty poorly, and thought I'd just lay down for a quick nap. You all went on ahead."

We'd done that. And no one noticed that Monroe wasn't with us.

"Next thing I knew," he said, "these white men were dragging me over here, saying I done something to this white lady. I didn't see no white lady. And I sure as hell didn't do nothing to one."

A voice called from the front room, beyond the cell. "Who you talking to?"

"Nobody, sir," Monroe called back. "I been praying. Out loud."

A harsh laugh reached us.

"Good idea. Chances are you're gonna meet your maker tonight."

"Be back later," I whispered, and slipped away through the garden.

The Bishops' big stone house was just off Main Street. I approached it from the alley, staying in the shadow of the neat barn at the end of the property.

A young colored woman stood at the edge of the garden, hanging laundry on the line.

Seemed like an odd thing for her to be doing on a Sunday, but what did I know about how rich people lived?

I crept closer. She worked for the family. She'd probably be loyal to them and not tell me much. Still, she'd know how Mrs. Bishop was doing and maybe tell me that.

"Excuse me, miss," I said, stopping a few feet away from her.

She looked up at me in alarm. Tears were streaming down her cheeks. Was she mourning her mistress?

"What do you want?" She backed up a few steps.

"I heard about last night. I wondered how the missus was doing."

The girl lifted her apron to her face and wiped her cheeks. "Not so well. She got burned bad. The doctor says it'll take a miracle to save her."

That didn't sound good. "Gotta be tough."

She nodded. "And they got me washing all these bandages." She swept her hand toward the clothesline. "On a Sunday. I just came to work here last week, and I never thought I'd be doing laundry on a Sunday. It's a sin."

"A sin?"

"Uh huh. My mama took me to church every Sunday of my life. 'Remember thou keep holy the Lord's Day.' God's gonna punish me for working on His day." More tears streamed down her cheeks.

"Well, if you're doing something that needs to be done, I don't think God would punish you."

"No?"

"No. After all, people got to cook on Sundays. And take care of their kids. And milk the cows. All sorts of work gotta be done on Sundays."

"But not laundry. That's heavy work. It could be put off till Monday. The Good Lord's gonna be mad at me."

"Not at you." I tried to think fast. "If He's mad at anybody, it'll be whoever made you do the laundry on Sunday. Not you."

"Really?"

"Yep. I'm almost sure of it."

"That would be Mr. Bishop. He told me to wash all these

bandages. And his shirt and coat." She held up a wet dark cloth.

"Why his shirt and coat?"

She shrugged. "They're all muddy and smoky-smelling. And I see they got some tears and burn holes in them. I'm gonna have to mend them. But not on Sunday."

How did Mr. Bishop's clothes get smoky and torn? I didn't think I'd better ask that. "How's the family taking it?"

She shook her head. "I don't know. Mr. Bishop is stomping around—I daren't say anything to him. The children are being very quiet. And Miss Ginny is taking over."

"Who's Miss Ginny?"

"She's Mrs. Bishop's niece. Came here when her mother died. They said to help with the children. But Mr. Bishop, he's taken a shine to her. If'n I was Mrs. Bishop, I'd have sent her away."

"He's showing too much interest in her?"

"Yeah. And she's showing it right back."

"Must cause problems."

"Sure does. What with Mrs. Bishop going to all those meetings, getting all worked up about men drinking and women voting, Mr. Bishop stays away from her as much as he can."

"I hear Mrs. Bishop set off last night to confront some rowdies in town about their drinking." I wasn't about to tell her I was one of the rowdies.

She raised her eyebrows. "Oh, I don't think she cared about the rowdies in town. She'd worked up a full head of steam over Mr. Bishop not coming home after the parade for supper, and staying out until near dark, so she set out to find him. Said he was probably at the hotel bar. But from what I hear, she never made it there."

"'Cause she was attacked?"

"I guess. Folks are saying it was a colored boy who works at the iron furnace, but I bet it was Mr. Bishop. If she dies, he can marry Miss Ginny. She don't care about drinking and voting at all."

"Are you gonna talk to the sheriff about that when he gets back?"

She gave a sad laugh. "It might cost me my job, but I done said something to that man who's keeping the jail when he came by. He said it don't matter what I say. Nobody'll listen to me. And even if some people did, the courts don't let a colored testify against a white man anyhow."

I left her hanging up Mr. Bishop's shirt and went to the yard behind the Grand Hotel. Because it was Sunday, the bar wasn't open, but the barback was sitting on an upturned half barrel, smoking a pipe.

He looked at me as I approached and took the pipe out of his mouth. "You furnace folks best stay away from town for a while," he said. "There's an ugly rumor that, come sundown, there's gonna be a lynch mob. Anybody who gets in the way'll be hanged along with that colored boy."

My fellow workers would be mad when they heard of Monroe's death, but I knew they wouldn't be willing to do much to defend him.

I stayed a distance from the barback. "Suppose he didn't do it?"

He shook his head. "Don't see that it matters much. Crowd's gonna decide he done it, and they're gonna hang him. They won't listen to nothing else."

"Was Mr. Bishop here last evening?" I asked.

"Yeah. Until somebody came to fetch him home 'cause his wife was hurt."

"What time was that?"

"Pretty late. I hear she lay under that bridge for a good bit. If'n she'd been found earlier, she might have a better chance of making it."

"And Mr. Bishop, he was here the whole time?"

The barback frowned. "Now that you mention it, I'm not sure."

"What'd you mean?"

"Mrs. Bishop, when she got upset with him, she'd come to the hotel and send somebody into the bar to fetch him out. Most of the men thought that was pretty funny. And he'd get embarrassed. So he usually left about dusk to go home, before she could show up."

"But not last night?"

"Well, I saw him leave the bar, and I thought he was going home. But then I saw him later on. Maybe he just slipped out to take a leak or something."

I went back to the jail and threaded my way through the garden. I crouched underneath the window, behind the pole bean teepees.

"Monroe! It's me again."

I heard him move in the cell. He must have climbed on top of the bunk, because I could see his dark face in the light of the late afternoon sun.

"Neil! Can you get me out of here?" His voice quavered. "They're gonna come get me after it gets dark."

"I'm sure gonna try. Where's the jailer?"

Monroe took a shuddering breath. "He's gone home to supper. Said there was no point feeding me. Said he'd be back around midnight."

"He just left you?"

"Uh huh."

"For the lynch mob?"

"Yep."

"He's really not gonna talk some reason into them?"

"No. He says he can't stop them. No sense even trying. Even if they prob'ly got the wrong man."

"He actually *said* that?"

"Yeah. Said the Good Lord'll take care of anything needs taking care of."

"Look, I'm gonna go figure out how to get in the office there and see if I can find the key."

"Shouldn't be hard. He left the front door unlocked, and the key on its hook. No point making anybody damage the sheriff's office trying to get in or opening the cell."

"Okay. I'm gonna sneak around front and wait till there's nobody passing by. Then get in the office. You take your blanket and anything else you can get your hands on. Try to make a dummy so they'll think you're still in there."

"In the bunk?"

"Under it, if you can. They'll think you're trying to hide. That you're scared."

"They'd be right. I'm damn scared."

I eased around the side of the building. The cell portion was stone, but the office was dingy white clapboard.

Raucous noises from a crowd reached me. They were coming from the square. I slipped through the door, closing it behind me.

The large iron key hung on a hook over the desk.

I reached up and took it, then went through the opening in the wall that separated the office from the cell area.

There were two cells. Monroe stood in one, his breath coming fast and the whites of his eyes showing, like a panicky horse.

I inserted the key in the lock. It didn't want to turn. I tried jiggling it. It still wouldn't turn.

Monroe's dark hands clutched the bars on the cell door. "I watched the man when he locked the door. He pushed the key in all the way, then pulled it almost out before he turned it."

Straightening the key in the lock, I shoved it all the way in, pulled it back toward me, and tried to turn it. It caught for a few seconds, then turned.

With a quick shove, Monroe opened the door and leapt out. "Let's get out of here."

"Wait a minute," I closed the door and twisted the key.

"We want them to waste some time trying to get in here." I managed to lock the door again and glanced at the cell. Monroe had tucked the slops bucket under the bunk, and draped the blanket over it so it did look like someone might be trying to hide there. Not much, maybe, but it might slow the mob down. A little.

I pocketed the key on its ring and peered out the front window. No one was in sight. We slipped out the door and back alongside the building. The dusk was deeper.

We could hear shouts from the square. Wavering light pierced the growing darkness. The crowd was lighting more torches.

When we'd stumbled through the garden and into the alley, Monroe wanted to turn back toward the furnace road.

"Are you crazy?" I grabbed his arm and pulled in the opposite direction. "That's the first place they're gonna be looking for you. We got to get out of here."

His arm was slick with sweat where I'd grabbed it. His voice trembled. "Where are we gonna go?"

I shoved him along in front of me. "The excursion train. We got to get to where it slows down just before town."

"And what?"

"And jump it."

"Jump a moving train?"

"Yeah. It's not that hard. You just can't pause. Just do it."

Monroe shook his head. "I can't do that. Never been away from the furnace. Except to Mechanicstown."

"And if that crowd catches up to you, Mechanicstown is where you're gonna die, too."

He didn't have an answer for that, but turned and trotted beside me along the alley toward the railroad tracks.

A half-block over, we could hear the mob beginning to move through the street, an excited roar of mingled voices.

When we reached the tracks where the train would slow down at a curve as it approached town, we hunkered down.

I pulled a piece of long grass and chewed on it. "Now, Monroe, listen. The train will slow down for the curve. It won't pick up speed until it's on the other side of town. The last car'll have this platform with railings for people to stand on. But this time of night nobody'll be on it. You got to run alongside it and grab the railing. Then swing your feet up and get some footing. If we're lucky, there'll be a ladder. We got to haul ourselves up to the roof."

He shivered. "Don't the train stop in town?"

"Only if somebody signals. Mechanicstown is a whistle stop. And just for a minute. But even if it does, there will be a lot of people around. Somebody'd be sure to see us."

"After we get on the train—*if* we get on the train—then what?

"Then we ride possum belly."

"What's that?"

"That's when you ride face down, lying flat on the roof. It's windy up there—you don't want to be blown off. And you don't want anybody to see you if you can help it."

"Won't they see us when we climb up the side? And hear us?"

"Train's too loud for them to hear much. Somebody might see us, but mostly they'll be looking toward the town. That's where the lights are. You can't worry about that."

"You gonna get up there with me?"

"Yeah. I'll go first and get out of your way as fast as I can."

"What then?"

"We ride the train to Baltimore. Then we try to catch a freight going north. We want to get out of state as fast as we can."

"I don't know nothing but furnace work. How're we gonna live?"

"Pennsylvania's got a lot of furnaces. Nice big one in

Cornwell. They always need skilled guttermen. You'll have no trouble getting hired."

Long and low, the train whistle sounded back in the hills. It was coming toward us.

I got into a crouch, waiting for it to pass.

When the last car was even with us, I sprinted alongside of it, grabbing the railing and bringing my feet up. Aware of Monroe right behind me, I reached hand over hand, moving toward the far side of the car.

The train was still slowing.

Monroe's dark hands grabbed the railing, but instead of his feet coming up onto the floor beneath the railing, they slid out from under him.

Looking into his terrified eyes, I reached over, grabbed the waistband of his pants, and heaved upward.

I heard a ripping sound, but managed to pull his butt up.

He scrambled for a solid footing, his boots finally landing on the railing.

We were in luck. This car had a ladder welded onto the side of the observation platform.

Without waiting to see if Monroe was following me, I scrambled up it and launched myself, belly down, on the roof of the car.

I lay there for what seemed like a long time, but Monroe didn't climb up with me. There wasn't much I could do about it if he'd fallen off, but I inched myself around until I was facing the back of the train, scooched over to the end and peered down.

Monroe hung onto the ladder, unable to make his way past the roof's overhang.

I reached a hand down to him. "You can't stay there." I'm not sure if he heard me above the sound of the train and the wind, but he grabbed my hand and hauled himself up, kneeling next to me.

"Get down!" I shouted, inching backward and pressing myself against the roof.

With a glance at the empty track behind us, Monroe lay down, his head just beyond mine.

We approached the station, dimly lit by a few lanterns. Although we couldn't see directly below us, the sound of people bustling around and shouting rose above the noise of the train. On one side, toward the jail, we could see the wavering light from torches.

With a shrill blast of its whistle, the train lurched forward. Away from Mechanicstown.

The Dead
Scott Loring Sanders

Me and my buddy Mush were tripping on blotter, trapped inside an amusement park while the Grateful Dead jammed "Fire on the Mountain" in the background, an appropriate song choice considering the sky had turned multiple shades of pinkish-reddish-purple, the clouds swirling in twisted patterns like Italian ice cream. And I don't mean the tune was pumping through the park's speakers, I mean the *actual* band stood on the amphitheater stage, well into their second set. Bug-eyed hippies danced and twirled around the grounds, or rode rollercoasters and log fumes next to Izod-wearing, penny loafer-clad dads and moms who'd brought their innocent children to ride bumper cars and swings and Tilt-O-Whirls, not expecting to encounter tie-dyed, long-haired freaks puffing joints and tripping their faces off.

By the way, we were in a different country. Also, there was a good possibility that a girl we'd only met hours before had overdosed in the back of my van, shooting venom into her veins that produced the nods, and worse, maybe stopped her heart, while me and Mush, with pupils the size of quarters, somehow decided—through the haze of LSD—that leaving her there and heading inside the venue was the best course of action, figuring the girl, named Melanie or Melody or something with an M, would snap out of it.

So there I was, in Canada's Wonderland, thirty miles (kilometers?) outside of Toronto, sitting atop a hundred-foot (meters?)-tall Ferris wheel, the Dead rocking as a killer sunset detonated the western sky. The woods, fields, and towns far beyond the park rippled and wavered like heat mirages. And I thought how amazing it was that the band had chosen that particular song at that particular moment, like how everything was interconnected, and how Melanie or Melody, earlier in the parking lot, had paid me a sincere compliment about my van, which meant a lot because I'd been self-conscious before then. It wasn't one of those cool VW microbuses all the Dead Heads had, but instead a decade-old '77 Econoline, a vehicle generally preferred by serial killers or kiddie diddlers. But she'd called it "wicked" in the most complimentary sense, which boosted my confidence, and I realized, in that instant, high above the grounds, how every person and every moment and every everything is related to the complex inner-workings of the entire world. It all made sense. It was all so beautiful.

Okay, so I'd probably eaten too much acid. But I was eighteen, aimless, and usually just followed along with whatever Mush—who was two years older—proposed. Like him suggesting we should travel with the Grateful Dead once school let out. "I already applied for my passport, Juan. For the Canada show. You should too. You gotta take some chances in life. Live a little."

I already had a passport from when my mother and I visited her native El Salvador a few years back. Which is why Mush called me Juan instead of John, my real name given to me by my estranged (and very white) father. Thanks to my parents, my skin was tinted a light walnut, easily my best feature on an otherwise skinny, featureless body. Mush, on the other hand, resembled yellow ·pine, complete with a thicket of blond hair curled into ringlets. We'd left our blue collar, furniture factory Jersey town a week before, spending several days in Alpine Valley, Wisconsin, where the Dead started their tour. So, yeah, I was more of a follower than a leader—following Mush, following the Dead, following the next party or high or dream. It's why I agreed to leave Melody (I'm just gonna go with that) in the van. If it had been my call, I would've made sure she was okay first, but Mush said, "That's just what the shit does. She'll be fine. Plus, this acid," he said, slowly waving his hand across his face, "is kicking in. I'm catching trails."

Hours before, Melody had appeared like a magic trick while me and Mush sat on the tailgate, cassette player cranking. Parking lot vendors hawked tie-dyes and tapestries and hologram spinning discs. Smoke from grilled meat and veggies wafted by, mixing with the aroma of kind-bud.

"What's going on?" she said, as if she'd known us forever. "Were y'all at Alpine?"

I was too nervous to respond, not used to talking to girls. Especially not a pretty older one with long strawberry hair and a freckled nose, wearing a thin, paisley dress and drinking a Molson.

But Mush perked right up. "Hell, yeah. We're doing the whole tour."

"Right on. Sweet locks," said Melody, squeezing one of Mush's curls as if carefully testing a fruit's ripeness. It never failed. That mop was his golden ticket. "And y'alls van is wicked."

Mush, never one to miss an opportunity, offered up a camping chair. Over the next few hours, we hung out, Dead tunes playing while high-pitched screams erupted from the distant rollercoaster. Melody explained she was from Virginia, had been married but, "Split from my old man when he busted my jaw. He come home early, saw a guy leaving the house. I told him the dude was selling magazines, but my old man was having none of it, beat me good, cracked three teeth." She paused right then, let her tongue probe the back of her mouth as if testing for lingering pain. "I reckon he's got a whole stack of *Sports Illustrateds* by now, a monthly reminder of how he fucked that one up."

She didn't offer her age, but I guessed twenty-five. "I ran off, stuck out my thumb, and last fall, stumbled onto Dead tour. Hey, Goldilocks," she said, "mind if I use your van to party?"

"No, it's cool," said Mush. "We're all about partying."

Let me just say, I resented how that always happened. How I always seemed to disappear. It was *my* van. It would've been nice if *I'd* been asked. Regardless, inside, she unzipped a small Guatemalan pouch, removed a needle and something resembling a deflated balloon. She went about her business, talking to us all the while as if casually mixing a drink. She spied my rolled sleeping bag and commandeered the strap without permission, as if it were her van, her property, and we her guests. But I'll admit, I was fascinated. Like how you sort of hope you'll see body parts when passing a car accident.

When Melody had the works prepared, she pushed the plunger. Then, just that fast, her head lolled. Her eyes stayed open but mostly went white. Me and Mush had no knowledge of heroin, of what was normal or not. Plus, within the first ten minutes of meeting Melody, she'd sold us a half sheet of acid. Mush had torn off four perforated hits, which we'd promptly split. So when he said, "Let's go into the concert" it seemed pretty logical, even if spittle had started trickling unnaturally from Melody's lips. We locked the van but cracked the windows. Figured she'd let herself out once she straightened up.

By the time we exited the venue, I'd pretty much come down. Sparkly flashes clouded my periphery as if camera blind, but I felt more-or-less normal. Normal enough to drive, anyway.

The van was locked, the windows still cracked, causing a short spurt of panic. But once I opened the door, my worst fears dissipated; Melody wasn't there. Yet, a part of me was disappointed. Back atop the Ferris wheel, I'd fantasized that maybe she'd be waiting for us. That maybe she would travel with us from city to city. That maybe, after a brief fling with Mush and his goddamn pretty hair, she'd realize I was actually the guy she'd always wanted, a guy who'd never bust her face. And later, she'd move in with me and Mom. I'd find work at the furniture factory, she'd take classes at Community.

"She's gone," said Mush. "Thank God." Then, after a beat or two, he frantically opened the glove compartment. "Jesus, she better not've ripped us off."

Which sent my heart skyrocketing. Our money, our passports, we'd spaced all of that. Everything we had, we'd left it sitting in plain view. How could we have been so stupid?

"Fuck, Juan. Where's our shit?" said Mush, digging through the contents like a dog on the beach. Gas station maps, gum wrappers, old registration cards, they all spilled out.

"Right there," I said, pointing. "Relax."

Between his feet lay our passports. He snatched them and thumbed the pages until he located our cash. "Jesus, sorry. Kind of lost it for a sec."

"I think you're still buzzed," I said, turning the ignition. "Let's go find that campground."

"Yeah, let's do it. I'm starving for some Beanie Weenies."

The campground sat on the Canadian side of the Niagara River, a mile upstream from the falls. We scored one of the last sites, tucked away in the far corner of the property. It was farthest from the bathhouse but a trail conveniently meandered from our spot through some steep woods down to the riverbank.

"You should go ahead and start putting up the tent," said Mush.

"Okay, but what're you gonna do?" I'd recently noticed that Mush had a "path of least resistance" mentality. That is, if the path involved work, he generally resisted it.

"I'm going back to the office to buy a firewood bundle. Get a fire going so we can cook the Weenies."

"There's a forest right here," I said, motioning toward the trail. "Why pay for wood?"

"Dude, it's dark. I'm not going in there at night."

I rolled my eyes. "Okay, whatever."

"Can I bum two bucks?"

Once he left, I opened the back doors. The tent was a three-man pup which I tossed onto the grass. My sleeping bag was still spread out from where Melody had stolen my strap for her tourniquet. I attempted to huddle the bag to my chest, as if gathering laundry from the dryer, when something hard and heavy prevented my progress. So I jerked on a corner, fighting the mysterious weight until it finally surrendered. In that precise moment, my entire life changed. Hidden beneath was Melody's body, the strap still taut around her arm, yellowish bile crusting her face. My lower jaw inadvertently grated side-to-side as I stared in wonder. In horror.

"So the dude gave me two bundles for the price of one," said Mush, dropping the loads into the fire ring. "We can build a rager."

How long had I been standing there, gazing at dead Melody? Five minutes? Ten?

"Dude," I said, though Mush interpreted it as a question rather than a flat, deflating statement.

"Yeah, the dude at the office. Pretty cool for an old geezer. Said he'd give us a twofer on inner tube rentals tomorrow if we wanted to float the river."

"Dude," I said again, "get over here."

Mush finally caught my tone. "What's your deal, man?"

"We got a problem."

He sidled up, warily, then saw her. "Jesus...fucking...Christ."

"She must've shot up again," I said.

"Holy shit, Juan."

"Or maybe spazzed out. A seizure or something. Got twisted up in the blankets."

"This is not..." Mush grabbed his springy locks and yanked hard as if trying to rip out a clump, "...this is not good."

"No, this is bad, Mush. Like really fucking bad." Families chattered at distant campsites. Little kids laughed and chased one another around picnic tables. A dog barked. "Like, we-could-go-to-prison bad."

"Jesus."

"There's a dead girl in my van," I said, probably way too loudly, "and we might've killed her."

Mush squeezed my elbow. "Keep it down," he said, glancing at the various fires dotting the campground. "Are you crazy? We didn't kill her."

"We didn't help her, did we? Saw her flipping out, just left her here. We're accessories or whatever."

"We were tripping balls. We didn't know this was gonna happen."

I moved away from the van, kicked one of the firewood bundles. "You wanna tell the cops that? 'Yeah, Officer, we were tripping balls, so, not really our problem.' Mush, we're screwed. All because you wanted to get laid." My jaw started grinding again.

"Listen, calm down. I've got an idea. No one knows she was with us, right? Not a soul. So we're fine."

"We're not fucking fine. There's a body in my van. A dead body. Holy Christ, is Canada prison worse than American prison? We gotta call the cops."

Mush grabbed my shoulders and shook them. "Calm. The fuck. Down. No cops. No way. I said I've got a plan."

Mush returned twenty minutes later with a fully inflated inner tube.

"That's your plan?" I said. The whole time he'd been gone, I'd paced the fire pit, contemplating using the pay phone by the bathhouse. *Call the cops, don't call the cops.* A year back, Mush had done six months for possession, and something had happened while he'd been locked up. Something he'd never discussed with me. So I guess I understood his hesitation. "And what took so long?"

"The guy was closing the office. Had to wait until he left. Then I jumped the fence and snagged the biggest one I could find. He's got a shit-ton back there."

"But I don't get it."

"I'll explain as we go. For now, grab our passports and money."

"What're we doing? Escaping by river? Like goddamn Huck Finn?"

"Just grab our stuff. If we have to run or split up, at least we'll have the necessities. Have a way back into the States."

I followed his instructions blindly. One thing about Mush, he was always planning ahead. I gave him his passport and stuffed mine into my pocket along with the van keys, then divvied up the cash. After that, we got to work.

We set Melody on her back across the inner tube, then Mush cut a rope from the tent's rainfly, tied it around the tube, and held the opposite looped end like a rein.

"I'll pull and lead, you push and keep her steady. We'll glide her right down to the river."

"Fine. Let's just hurry and get it over with."

"No, we can't hurry," said Mush. "One rock, one sharp stick, and we're screwed. We can't puncture the thing."

"Can we just go already?"

The progress was slow as we push/pulled the tube along the wooded trail. The descent was far steeper than we'd anticipated, and our feet slipped as we fought to keep Melody upright. For the first ten minutes it went pretty well, Mush and I feeling each other out as we worked the tube—not too fast, not too slow—down the incline. Then the inevitable happened. The tube collided with a hidden stump and capsized, ejecting Melody.

"Mush, we're losing her," I yelled.

Mush clawed at her ankles, I reached for a handful of dress, but she slipped away, logrolling down the hill the same as kids getting dizzy. Leaves kicked up in her wake as she gained momentum. "You were supposed to hold her, goddamnit," said Mush.

"Don't blame me," I said. "This was your stupid-assed idea, not mine."

Seconds later, though it seemed like forever, her torso snagged at the base of a pine sapling, the trunk no bigger round than a fencepost. Mush bolted, the vacant inner tube bouncing behind him.

Fifty yards downhill, I caught up.

"You know," he said as we both looked into the darkness, out of breath, trying to discern the remainder of the steep descent, "it might actually be easier if we just let her keep rolling."

"What? Have you lost your mind?"

"Why not? Let momentum do the work. Like rolling big-ass logs of firewood down a hill."

"She's a human being, not firewood."

"She's dead," said Mush. "What's the difference? Shit, we're about to send her over goddamn Niagara Falls for Christ sakes."

"I don't care."

"Johnny-boy, we're dumping a body so we don't go to prison. Got me? The respectful ceremony bullshit train left a long time ago."

I considered arguing, but what could I say? He was right. So we dislodged her from the pine and used the vague tree silhouettes to map out a course. Then, on three, we aimed her as if sending an old rubber tire down a steep embankment. She veered a few times, got hung up once, but eventually rested near the bottom.

The entire distance, from campsite to river's edge, had been less than three hundred yards, but it took half an hour. A million little frogs chirped along the riverbanks, as did other loud, mysterious tree insects. A half-moon lit up our surroundings enough to partially see, though we would've preferred total darkness. Melody's corpse lay at my feet, once again atop the rubber tube. Only hours earlier I'd been fantasizing we might get married someday. Kids even. Now I was preparing to send her off to Valhalla like a goddamn Viking.

"We gotta weigh her down," said Mush.

"Yeah," I said, my voice lifeless, just wanting it to all be over.

We placed rounded river stones beneath her clothing, setting them on her stomach, then her legs and chest. Mush tied the bottom of her long skirt into a knot so none would leak out. He said, "Once she goes over the falls, she'll separate from the raft, but the rocks will sink her straight to the bottom."

His plan seemed foolproof, but I hated what we were doing, hated what had happened. When I showed some hesitation, he put things in perspective. He was good at that. "It sucks that she died, but we didn't ask her to do heroin. Why should our lives be ruined because some crazy hippie chick chose your van to shoot up?"

"Oh, so *now* it's my van?"

"What? What the hell're you talking about?"

I shook my head. "Never mind."

"Anyway, I think we're good," he said, stuffing the last rocks into her armpits, trying to wedge them in neatly like puzzle pieces. "Let's launch this thing and split."

"This better work," I said, still holding a stone. We'd been fully occupied in our work, as absorbed as little kids building sand castles. I was creeped out, disgusted that my fingers had grazed her cold skin. I'd done everything to avoid her bare breasts. I'd refused to put any rocks in her panties. The whole enterprise seemed so disrespectful.

"Are you boys okay?"

Mush and I sprang up in tandem and spun around. Tiny pricks of heat stabbed my cheeks and forehead like armies of tattoo needles. We brushed shoulders in an attempt to shield Melody from view.

A man stood before us, his features hard to distinguish except for white hair glowing in the moonlight.

Somehow, Mush managed to respond. "Yes, sir. We're fine."

Slightly hunched, the man cocked his head, trying to peek around us. "What exactly you up to?" he said, his voice gravelly, the way my grandfather's had been.

"Nothing," said Mush. "We're just...nothing." Mush advanced a step, and I followed.

The man mimicked us, took a subtle step backward, his boot heels clicking against the river rocks. "Well, all right then. I'll be...I'll be moseying on." I couldn't see his face, couldn't read his eyes, but his tone revealed everything.

Something rippled beneath my skin, went straight to my brain. A strange sensation, not entirely unpleasant. I reared back, the stone still clamped tight in my fist, and smashed his head, catching him on the ear and temple. He crumpled on impact, imploding like one of those high-rise buildings you see on TV—the whole demolition over in seconds.

Except I continued. I wailed the old man twice more with the rock, caving his skull into a November jack-o-lantern. The frogs went silent.

I stood over his prone body, almost daring him to move or say something. He did neither. My fist was warm and goopy, my breathing controlled, my jaw no longer tweaking.

"Holy shit, dude," said Mush.

I glimpsed Mush's shadowed face, his wild, frightened eyes. "We're gonna need more rocks," I said.

We didn't talk, just acted. We set the old man perpendicular to Melody, forming a cross, then filled his trousers and flannel with rocks. A couple of times I said, "I'm sorry, Mush. I swear to God, I don't even know what happened."

I wanted him to reassure me. To tell me it was okay, to say he wasn't mad. But he'd gone silent. Shell-shocked, I think. It wasn't until we finished that he finally spoke. "So I'll take the rope," he said, "and wade out. You bend and push."

He wrapped the cord around his fist and slowly entered the water as if readying for baptism. I knelt, the stones, pebbles, and grit grinding into my knees. I drove my shoulder into the old man's torso and grunted, "Heave."

Mush was in thigh-deep, tug-o-warring with the cord while my sneakers dug into the rocks for purchase. On the fourth or fifth *heave*, the laden tube abruptly loosed itself from the bank's grip. I lurched forward, my face splashing the shallow water. Mush lost his balance, submerging completely before popping back up, but the current was far stronger than we'd anticipated. The tube, with its heavy cargo, started pulling away downriver, taking Mush with it. He flailed, white splashes visible in the darkness. Frantic splashes. "The rope," he squealed. "The fucking rope."

"Mush, what're you doing?"

"Johnny," he screamed, "undo the rope!"

But jumping into the river wasn't an option; I was a doggie-paddler at best. So instead, I scrambled along the bank, loose stones attempting to snap my ankles as I monitored that bobbing raft. Mush was nowhere to be seen.

Until another white splash erupted, like a fish breaking the surface. He came up for air, yelled something inaudible, submerged again. I sprinted, following the inner tube as it gained speed, coasting toward the world's most infamous waterfall. "Mush. Come on, man. Do something."

I kept running, but the black inner tube, the black outlines of the piled bodies, they vanished, leaving only the black of the silent water. The black of night. I imagined the paralyzing roar of the falls a mile downstream, of how the volume would steadily intensify as Mush drifted closer and closer.

I awoke sprawled on the van floor, partially wrapped in the Melody sleeping bag. Sunlight cut through the bubbled windows. Birds chirped innocently, as if they'd never known a bad day.

I hoped Mush was in the passenger seat, curled and sleeping. That he'd somehow returned. Which is why I didn't leave the campground last night—I couldn't abandon him. If he'd managed to get untangled, somehow swam to shore, staggered back to the campsite, well, I needed to be there.

Then true dread hit. I'd killed a man. Beat him. I couldn't comprehend it. I'd never even gotten into a fistfight before.

I had to leave. Immediately. Cross the border, back to the U.S. Figure things out later. Mush had no real family. Drunk mom, estranged, didn't give a shit about him. Some older sister he mentioned once. They wouldn't miss him. And Melody? Nobody could tie me to her. But the old man? His dried blood still on my hands? Splatter on my jeans? I had to go.

An odd, sickening pain formed in my foot arches as I

neared the exit. A Canadian trooper stood against his patrol car, conversing with a woman leaning on a cane, a cardigan hanging loosely over her shoulders. He raised his palm as I drove forward, not in a wave but a halt.

A few times in school, when I'd known my presentation was next, I'd felt a similar panic. I rolled down my window as he approached.

"Morning," he said. "You heading out?"

"Yes, sir."

He glanced at a clipboard, flipped a few sheets of paper. "You haven't seen Mr. Barrett, have you? Last night or this morning?"

"What?" I said. "Who? I'm sorry, I don't understand."

The cop glanced up from his papers, his eyes cold beneath the wide hat brim. "The owner. Mr. Barrett. Mrs. Barrett," he said, nodding across the hood, "hasn't seen him since last night. Have you?"

"Have I what?"

"Seen him, son. Or heard anything out of the ordinary?"

"Oh. No, sir. I just woke up."

He looked down, reexamined his clipboard, not seeming overly interested. I got the feeling he thought Mrs. Barrett was overreacting. Like maybe she was a confused grandma who'd simply misplaced her keys. She was super skinny, vulnerable as a dry twig. Wore a scarf over her head, tied tightly beneath her chin and clinging to her scalp. It was possible she had no hair. She wasn't crying, but her lips did a weird pulsing thing like she'd just sucked lemons. I felt bad for her, knowing she was screwed and I was the one who'd screwed her. But what good would 'fessing up do? Wouldn't bring her husband back. Sure as hell wouldn't save my ass. Or Mush's.

"What's your name?" said the officer.

"I'm John," I said, awkwardly sticking my hand out for a handshake.

He ignored my offer, instead ran his finger down the paper

before stopping halfway. "John Wheatley? That you?"

"Yes, sir."

"Where's your partner?" He stared past me, to the passenger seat.

"My partner?"

"Says here you and Danny Mush...what is it?... Mushkowski?...says you two checked in at eight-forty-five last evening." He peered past me again, this time trying to look into the rear of the van. "Where's Mushkowski?"

"I don't...I don't know what you're...who that is. What do you mean?"

The cop suddenly seemed a tad more interested. It was subtle, the way his head cocked. How his eyes narrowed. "Register says there were two of you."

"I guess that's a mistake." What had we been thinking, signing our real names? How stupid were we? Until I remembered we'd had no reason to lie. We hadn't yet known Melody was in the van.

Fucking Melody. Goddamnit. Discovering her seemed like days ago. Weeks ago. A lifetime. Was it possible this much insanity had happened in only twelve measly hours? "He must've signed in after me, put his name in the wrong spot."

The officer took a minor half-step forward. "Okay, could be. You got identification?"

"Yeah, sure." It seemed like he believed me. I reminded myself that if anybody appeared innocent, it was me; I was eighteen but looked much younger. "Got my driver's license," I said, forcing a smile. But when I reached for my back pocket, I remembered I'd left my wallet in my other jeans. "Actually, I've got my passport. Is that good?"

"Just give me some ID, son, so we can get this over with. I don't care what."

I pinched the edge of the passport tucked in my front pocket, slipped it out. "Here you go, Officer."

The cop flipped open my booklet, glanced, then hesitated.

He looked at me again, this time dead on. "When's your birthday?"

I told him.

"Spell your last name."

I did so.

"I need you to step out of the vehicle. Slowly."

"I'm sorry?" I knew my damn birthday. Knew my name. "What do you mean?"

The cop stepped forward, extended the passport, holding it open for me to see. My picture, like a mugshot, didn't resemble me. Because it wasn't me. It was Mush, smiling his stupid smile as he stared straight at the camera, those bouncy locks framing his face. To the right of the photo, his full name. Daniel Phillip Mushkowski. Then his date of birth. His other vitals.

"Get out of the damn vehicle," said the officer. He'd dropped the clipboard, now had a hand on his weapon.

The door swung open and I was sucked out of the driver's seat, my right cheek grinding into the gravel, intense pressure on the small of my back, my left arm chicken-winged, then my right. Steel clamped my wrists.

Little did I know, but at the same exact time I was being squashed into the ground, Mush's body was discovered swirling in an eddy below the falls, near the Rainbow Bridge. A Maid of the Mist passenger noticed something odd, pointed it out to the captain, who radioed in that he'd just found a floater. Attached to the floater's arm was a long cord connected to an inner tube—an inner tube with *Barrett's Campground* stenciled onto its side in white spray paint. Of course, my passport would be found in Mush's pocket.

When two more bodies were discovered shortly thereafter, within two hundred feet of each other, nestled along the shoreline, partially hidden in the reeds, with no evidence of even one rock remaining tucked in their ragged clothing, well, my future was sealed.

But I didn't know any of that yet.

So as the cop's knee pushed deeply into my spine, all I could think about was how beautiful that sky had looked from the top of the Ferris wheel. How I'd imagined I had the entire world at my fingertips, that I might actually make it in this life. For the first time ever, I'd really thought I might turn out okay. That I would get married or at least date Melody or Melanie or something with an M. That it was going to be a great summer. That life was good and magical and full of possibilities for a boy—no, for a young man—like me, as long as I was willing to take a few chances, was willing to live a little.

Here To Stay
Tanis Mallow

Five months, three weeks and two days ago Val crossed the Blue Water Bridge and entered Canada driving a borrowed car, and flashing a stolen passport, eight grand in cash hidden under the center console liner. No goodbye parties or tearful farewells. Val was not sentimental.

There were a myriad of reasons for Val to stay on in Toronto and never return to her homeland south of the border. She liked the pub where she tended bar, made decent tips to supplement her small nest egg. The city, itself, was interesting in a diverse eclectic kind of way, the people nice enough. She thoroughly enjoyed Jake's prowess in bed and tendency to rarely speak. Ditto for Lenny. And the fact that neither Jake nor Lenny knew about each other (or if they did, they didn't care) was an added bonus.

Others—had they known—might suggest that the warrant for Val's arrest stemming from that unfortunate incident in Chicago was the real motivation for her new love affair with Toronto, and they'd have a point. But in truth the most powerful reason for staying in The 6ix was Victor.

Victor lived in Chicago. Victor expressed a seriously misplaced sense of patriotic pride in the fact that he didn't own a passport. Victor was a nasty boil on humanity's butt. And Victor harbored a well-earned grudge against Val.

For all those reasons, Val embraced her new home enthusiastically. She could see living in Toronto for a very long time.

There was only one problem: in a few days, her one and only piece of identification would show she had outstayed her welcome. She needed a new passport. Preferably Canadian.

It was a dilemma.

The pub sat mostly empty mid-afternoon and Val contemplated her problem while rearranging the liquor bottles along the shelves at the back of the bar. A small group of regulars had recently switched brand preferences. It was—in her humble opinion—a ploy to force her to reach for inconveniently placed bottles off the top shelf. Val was not what you'd call a tall woman and her skimpy outfits did not lend themselves well to such maneuvers.

As she moved an obscure yet suddenly popular brand of tequila, Val caught a reflection in the mirror. A younger, dirtier, scrawny version of herself drifted between bottles of bourbon, and for a moment she thought she might be suffering some hallucinatory flashback. The disembodied doppelgänger came to rest next to the Maker's Mark. Val turned around.

The girl rubbed her hands together, red from the cold, and plunked a stained Grocery City tote bag onto the bar. Val made a mental note to disinfect the counter later.

"Beer," the kid said. "Whatever's cheapest."

The girl looked in need of someplace to warm up and something to take the edge off, and for a brief moment, Val considered serving her without asking for ID. If Lenny, her boss-with-benefits, hadn't been watching from a back table she might have done it. Though he was sympathetic enough to let Val work off the books for ten bucks and hour plus tips, he'd made it clear from the get-go that he had zero tolerance when it came to serving minors.

He raised an eyebrow and Val looked back to the girl sitting across the bar. Something rang familiar about the kid aside from her strange resemblance to Val. The kid pawed through her bag for a grimy Tim Hortons cup and started counting coins, and Val realized that over the last couple of weeks she'd passed the girl a few times, panhandling down the block. She'd even dropped a loonie into her cup once or twice without giving much notice. In her defense, the kid seemed incapable of direct eye contact.

"I'll need to see some I.D.," Val said.

The girl blew a hank of damp hair from her eyes. "I'm twenty," she said.

"Excellent. Prove it."

"Do I look like someone who carries a Gucci wallet full of platinum cards?"

Val empathized. She'd been there, done that, but her hands were tied.

"My boss is watching. I can't serve you liquor."

The kid looked over her shoulder at Lenny. "He's kinda cute." She turned back to Val. "For an old guy."

"Yeah? You think?" Like she'd never considered it before. "Look, feel free to stay a while, warm up." She poured the kid a cup of coffee and whispered, "Come back later with I.D. and I'll comp your first beer."

The girl came back that evening.

"This is your ID?" Val flipped through the decrepit passport—the decrepit Canadian passport—a couple of U.S. entry stamps and a lonely Mexican one. The kid's name was Jillian Edwards and she'd told the truth about her age, twenty, seven years younger than Val.

"Mexico?"

"Our last family vacation before my mom died and my stepdad kicked me out of the house. Wouldn't mind going back. Wouldn't mind traveling to a bunch of places."

Val held open the passport. "This expires in a month," she said.

"What?" The girl snatched it back and studied it herself. "That's just effing awesome."

"How much does it cost to renew?" Val asked.

"Dunno." Jillian chewed a nail and Val fought the urge to tell her to wash her hands first. "Whatever it is, it's more than I have." Like an afterthought, she reached into her coat pocket and pulled out a handful of coins. Made a tower of them on the counter.

"First one's a comp, remember?" Val poured her a beer. "Do you have any other I.D.?"

Jillian chugged half the beer. "Nope."

"Driver's license?"

"Yeah 'cause, ya know, my Porsche is parked right outside." The kid scowled. "Used to have a G1. Never got my G2."

"Health card?"

"No picture. I think I was supposed to get one of those photo ones a while ago."

Val Googled passport renewals on her phone. They weren't cheap. She showed the screen to Jillian who cursed again and Val topped up her beer in a show of sympathy.

"Doesn't matter. Even if I had the cash—which I don't—and even if I wanted to spend it on this—which I wouldn't—I don't have a proper address, do I?"

Like Val should know. "Well, you aren't moving in with me."

"Didn't ask to, did I?"

"Do you always answer a question with another question?"

"It's called: *rhetorical.*"

"Whoa, big word," Val said. The kid looked hurt. A lumpy man sat down on the stool beside Jillian and grinned widely at Val.

"What can I get you," Val asked.

"The usual."

Shit. She had no idea. "Sorry, uh…"

He looked vaguely disappointed but not surprised. "Jared."

"Jared, of course. Sorry, been one of those days."

"Yeah, happens." He paused, maybe hoping she'd suddenly remember then sighed and said, "Southern Comfort and seven."

"Of course. Won't forget again."

"Uh, huh."

Val mixed the drink and Jared glanced over to Jillian, who was busy polishing off her beer. He looked at Val, then back to the girl again.

Jillian slammed her glass onto the counter, gathered up her coins and said, "Laters."

They watched her go.

"Sister?" Jared asked.

"Something like that," Val said.

The kid came around pretty much every night after that, stayed long enough to warm up, always paid in change. Never tipped.

Tuesday night she stayed longer than usual. Three hours. Kept looking at Val like maybe she wanted to ask something but never did. Left before Val could ask what was up.

The pub was quiet and Lenny let her leave an hour early. She'd kind of hoped he'd ask to drop by later but his wife had been suspicious of late and Lenny was on his best behavior. Maybe she'd call Jake instead.

She stepped out into a night cold and crisp, everything clearly defined like the crazy mental clarity that came from a line of good coke, but without the euphoria or paranoia. She pulled her coat tighter. Her place was only four blocks away but the thought of flagging down a taxi was tempting.

A small bundle huddled against the brick wall across the road. Val might have dismissed it as trash bags if not for the foggy drift of condensation. Breath. Jillian's breath.

Val crossed the street and nudged the girl with her toe. "Why aren't you at the shelter, it's freezing out." Jillian sat on her haunches on a small pile of newspaper, arms wrapped around her legs, head tilted and resting on her knees. She wore a toque Val had never seen on her before and a sketchy-looking blanket over her shoulders. "Well," Val asked.

"Avoiding someone," she said. Val didn't press her.

"You can't stay outside tonight."

"I was in there," she said, pointing to a coffee shop down the street, "but the fat dick running the place said if I wanted to stay all night, I'd have to do him a 'special favor.'"

"Really?" Val knew exactly who the kid was talking about. "Maybe I'll have a friend of mine pay him a visit."

"Whatevs."

Jillian's breath left a patch of white frost on her coat sleeve. She shivered and Val said, "Let me see your arms."

"What?"

"Your arms, let me see them."

"No." Val glared at her, Jillian glared back. After a moment she flung off the blanket, stood and stuck out her arms. Val took the left one and shoved the sleeve of the girl's coat past the elbow. No track marks. There was, however, a cobweb of thin white scars. She checked the right one. Same thing. The kid was a cutter. Jillian tugged down her sleeves until they covered her hands and crossed her arms. "Happy?" she asked.

"You can crash on my couch tonight," Val said. "One night only." Then to save the kid from the embarrassment of a thank you she turned and walked toward home. Jillian didn't move for almost a whole minute and there was a flurry of activity as she gathered her meager possessions and chased after Val.

Val sublet a small one-bedroom apartment on the first floor of an older building on a busy street. She'd paid six months up front in exchange for keeping her name off the lease. The guy had just painted and the appliances—including a much sought-after washer and dryer—were relatively new. The first-floor location, normally not an asset, wasn't necessarily a bad thing tonight. It meant the blinds were already drawn before they entered the place.

She flicked on a light and Jillian looked around with an expression of neither approval nor disapproval, more curiosity. She made no move to take off her coat or put down her possessions.

"Shower," Val said, pointing to the bathroom.

"What?"

"If you're going to sleep on my couch, you're going to have a shower first. It'll warm you up."

Val lent her a towel, an oversized Raptors T-shirt that belonged to Jake and a pair of lime green fuzzy socks. She persuaded a tentative Jillian to hand over her clothes to be laundered.

Mistrust prevailed. Jillian took all of her bags with her into the bathroom and locked the door. Val spent a few minutes moving whatever she had of any value (there wasn't much) to the bedroom where she could guard over it. She moved her money stash from the closet and stuffed it between the mattresses. She loaded the washing machine, and opened a tin of cream of tomato soup and a package of strawberry scones. They didn't really go together but she hadn't been to the store in a while.

Jillian looked younger without the heavy eye makeup. Almost innocent. Val fed the kid, moved her clothes to the dryer and tossed a spare blanket onto the couch. "Long night. I'm going to bed," she announced and handed Jillian a pillow. Jillian hugged it to her chest then held it away and made a face.

"What?" Val asked.

"It smells." The kid sniffed at it again and wrinkled her nose. "Like a guy."

Val laughed. Jake always did overestimate the seductive power of his cloying aftershave. "Beats the smell of garbage." She pointed to the couch. "Go to sleep. And, Jillian?"

"Yeah."

"Don't make me regret this."

Val closed the door and, based on her own past behavior, wondered what would be missing in the morning. She listened to the girl in the next room toss and turn and punch the pillow until finally the kid fell asleep. All was quiet save for the faint tic toc of the black Kit-Cat clock in the kitchen, its tail sweeping back and forth, the sound mesmerizing like a meditation mantra, focusing Val's thoughts as she worked her plan.

The next morning, Val was surprised to find Jillian sprawled on the couch, one bare leg hanging off. She had expected the kid to bolt, to take with her anything that wasn't nailed down. She looked around at the crappy thrift store furniture and kitschy knick-knacks. There wasn't much to take. That realization put her in a cranky mood. She pulled Jillian's clothes from the dryer and dumped them on the coffee table. The kid could fold her own damn laundry.

"I have an idea," Val said as the girl scarfed down five pieces of toast with peanut butter in as many minutes. "If you let your passport expire, you're kind of screwed. I could help you with the paperwork."

Jillian looked at her suspiciously. The kid was smarter than she acted. She chewed the crust off her toast and said, "I don't have any money," like that closed the argument.

"I know that. I was thinking I'd sort of lend it to you. You could work it off."

Jillian stopped chewing and squinted her eyes. "Doing what?"

"I don't know, running errands, maybe helping me clean up at the bar after closing." Jillian stared at her, holding the remainder of her toast in the air, halfway to her mouth. "Nothing illegal I promise." The kid didn't say anything. "And you can use my address on the forms if you want." She pointed at Jillian. "But that doesn't mean you get to live here."

"Why?"

"Because this is my place and I don't want a roommate and sometimes I have guys over and—"

"No. I mean why would you help me?"

"I don't know," Val said. "Actually I do. You sort of remind me of me when I was younger." Jillian abandoned the toast and chewed a nail instead. "Look, whatever. Think about it. I don't have to be at work until four. If you want to do this, come back here around one o'clock and we'll go get your passport photos and fill out the forms. You decide."

The kid was back at quarter after one, fifteen minutes late but fifteen minutes earlier than Val would have guessed.

Because this was a passport renewal and not a new application, the process was easier. Still Jillian had trouble coming up with references, addresses and employment information for the last two years. Val helped her through it, guessing that the likelihood of anyone calling was next to zero.

"Ever been arrested?"

"Is that on the form?"

"No. Just curious."

"Nope."

Good, thought Val. No fingerprints on file and less chance she'll be flagged.

"How about you?" the kid asked.

"Oh you know, there's two or three warrants out for my arrest but I've never been caught." The kid didn't laugh. "That's a joke," Val said, even though she had spoken the truth. "Hey, what's the deal with that guy you're trying to avoid?"

"It's a girl."

"Okay, what's the deal with the girl you're trying to avoid?"

"She thinks I'm trying to steal her BF. Which I'm not." Jillian smiled. "Not my fault he wants to hook up."

"What are you going to do about it?"

"Dunno. Stay at a different shelter for a while I guess."

Val nodded. "Okay, as long as you stay warm. Sign these and let's go get your photos."

By the end of the day, Val had Jillian's information, her signatures and—most importantly—her soon-to-expire passport. Tomorrow she'd get a money order and her own set of passport pictures, and the package would be ready to send off.

There was only one remaining action item on her list: get rid of the Doppelgänger.

Val had a low tolerance for trance music, so she was relieved when it took no more than ten minutes to find a dealer. He was as unsubtle as they come, and Val wondered how he hadn't yet been busted. He might as well have been wearing a sandwich board—Party Drugs R Us—in flashing neon, blinking in time to the club lights.

Back home she pulled the small plastic baggie from the Grocery City tote—same kind as Jillian's—she'd taken to the club. She rolled it between her fingers, the row of six dark green pills rippling under her touch like strange vertebrae. Greenies, fake Oxycontin made with Fentanyl. She tucked them into a canister in the kitchen.

Lenny was coming over in a bit and Val figured there was just enough time for a quick shower. She glanced in the mirror and was shocked to see Jillian reflected back. Before she'd left for the club, Val had gelled her hair back and gone heavy handed with the black eyeliner. The effect was startling. For a brief moment, she felt sorry for the kid.

The feeling passed.

Val lay on her back, arms tucked behind her head, and thought about her future. Once the new passport arrived she would be golden and never have to give Chicago or Victor another thought. With it she could claim a stolen wallet. Apply for a birth certificate, a health card, a driver's license. Apply for a whole new life.

Beside her, Lenny mumbled in his sleep and cuddled up to her. She'd have to boot him out soon, she had stuff to do in the morning. Plus his wife kept calling and the buzzing of his phone was driving her crazy.

She poked him in the shoulder several times and he stretched and kissed her belly and gave her *that* smile and she thought, Screw his wife, maybe she didn't have to kick him out right away.

An hour later she stood in her fake silk kimono in the tiny front hall as Lenny put on his jacket. His phone buzzed and he frowned at the message, unsuccessfully suppressing a guilty look. Val narrowed her eyes and Lenny grabbed her wrists and held them spread against the wall and kissed her in a way that made her want to take him back to bed. In the next few minutes he managed to both relieve her of her robe and knock all the jackets off the hooks on the wall.

He touched his forehead to hers. "Gotta go," he said, panting.

Val retied her kimono and Lenny replaced the jackets on the hooks, stopping to examine a ragged hoodie that had probably been red at some point in time. Lenny plucked at the sleeve and gave Val a quizzical look.

"It's that street kid's. Tabby, I think her name is. She left it in the pub the other day. Thought I'd bring it home and wash it for her."

He gave her a strange look like maybe he didn't think she was capable of such acts of kindness. Pissed her off, even though it was mostly true.

"That's nice," he said. "How's she doing?"

"I'm not sure," Val said, forcing a dramatic sigh. "Truth is I'm kinda worried about her. Last time she came in, she was pretty out of it. I think maybe she's started using."

"Look at you getting all maternal."

"As if."

Val forced the air out of the plastic baggie, sealed it and dropped it into a second one. Repeated the process. She lay it on the counter and rolled a cheap bottle of rosé back and forth, crushing the greenies—no slow-release for Jillian. The pills were green all the way through, not white as they would have been had they been actual Oxy, and Val wondered what sleazy Chinese back-alley lab had manufactured the damn things.

Val put on her Jillian-esque makeup, an old toque she'd found at the thrift shop and the kid's faded hoodie. She bought a sub from some sandwich shop-slash-dry cleaners that she'd never been to before and stuffed it into the Grocery City bag.

Behind a dumpster, she switched the hoodie for her own jacket and donned a pair of dark sunglasses, even though the day was overcast and there wasn't much need. She took the back way into the pub and made it to the washroom before anyone could see her. She fixed her hair and make-up. Val is back, she thought, looking in the mirror. And she's here to stay.

She locked the bathroom door, closed the lid on the toilet and used it as a counter to unwrap the sub. It was kind of gross but E Coli was the least of the kid's problems.

She snapped on a pair of nitrile gloves and held her breath. Opened the baggies slowly, careful not to touch its contents. No evidence, no accidents. Fentanyl wasn't something to screw around with. She spread the powder between the layers of ham and Swiss cheese then flushed the baggies and the gloves, and re-wrapped the sandwich.

Jillian was at her usual post, jiggling her paper cup at passersby.

"You forgot your hoodie the other day," Val said, squatting beside the kid, which was harder than it sounded in her current outfit. "I washed it. Here, I'll stick it in your bag." Val crammed it in, and while some guy flung some quarters at Jillian that landed nowhere near her cup, Val tucked her stolen passport, the one she'd crossed the Blue Water Bridge with six months ago deep into the kid's other bag.

The passport belonged to Tabitha Brennan, AKA Tabby Cat, an American runaway last seen in Chicago. Hopefully, that's how they'd identify Jillian. It wasn't like they'd ever find Tabby, herself. Val had made sure of that months ago.

"I thought you might be hungry," Val said. "I bought you a sandwich."

"Uh, thanks," said the girl.

"See you around."

The pub was packed but even so the night moved in slow motion for Val. Every time she heard a siren—and there were lots of them—she imagined someone had found the kid's body.

Val walked home from the pub half expecting to pass yellow caution tape and the drama of a crime scene investigation but it was relatively quiet. Just as well. Jillian had probably been taken to the hospital and there was no way they'd be able to revive her. Just another street kid overdose.

She turned the corner to her building and there, lit by the shimmering street lights, Jillian sat on the stairs, still and quiet, slumped against the railing. Eyes closed.

Holy hell, holy hell, holy hell.

Val checked out the immediate area to see if anyone was watching before whispering, "Jillian?"

The girl popped up to her feet, bright-eyed and smiling. "Hey."

"Jesus, you just about gave me a heart attack," Val said, clutching her chest. "What are you doing out here?"

"I forgot to tell you about something that happened."

"Go ahead."

"I really have to pee." Jillian jiggled up and down. "Think I could use your washroom? I won't stay."

The sub stuck straight up out of grocery tote like it was giving Val the middle finger. She unlocked her door and the kid pushed past her without waiting for an invitation.

Val nodded to the bag. "You didn't eat your sandwich."

"I didn't want to be rude after you were nice enough to get it and all but it's ham. I'm vegetarian."

Damn it. Now she'd have to figure something else out, like fast, before the kid found Tabitha's passport.

Val unwrapped her scarf and hung up her coat. The kid left hers on and handed the sub to Val. "I brought it back for you in case you're hungry after working all night."

"It's probably past its prime."

"Oh, I dunno, it's pretty cold out there. Kinda like keeping it in the fridge."

"Thanks," said Val, "I'll have it later." She put it on the kitchen counter. "So, what did you want to tell me?"

"Can I pee first?" She jogged to the bathroom and locked the door before Val could say anything.

When Jillian came out, her head was down and she was typing away. On Val's phone. The phone she'd left on the hall table beside her purse. What else had the kid taken?

"The hell you doing with my phone?"

"Candy Crush. Sorry, it's been so long since I played." Jillian placed it back on the table with a sheepish grin. "Hey, is that my stuff?" She picked the application envelope off of the kitchen counter. "I figured you'd have already mailed it."

"I'm going to courier it tomorrow."

The girl nodded and tossed it to the counter. The contents spilled out, the application, Jillian's passport, the money order Val had paid for. It was the photos she most worried about but they fell upside down and the kid didn't notice.

"Can I have a beer?" Jillian asked. Val tilted her head and made what she hoped was a disapproving face. "Or a glass of water."

"Is this a long story?"

"Not really. But I'm thirsty."

"I'm out of beer," Val said and poured a glass of water.

Jillian drank greedily and wiped her mouth using the back of her sleeve. "So the other day," she said, "I was just hanging around, you know, collecting money." Like it was a legitimate job rather than begging. "And this big guy starts talking to me. At first I think like he's going to ask me to blow him or something but it's not like that. He's kinda nice. Not bad looking either." She grinned and rolled her eyes.

"And?"

"And, well, he starting asking about your pub and the bartender—he said *hottie* bartender—and I figured he was talking about you." She stopped to drink some more.

"And?"

"He kept going on and on about how good looking you were, which, like, I kinda took as a compliment 'cause, ya know, we kinda look the same in case you never noticed."

"I noticed." The kid was shredding Val's patience.

"Anyways, I told him about some of the nice things you've done for me and it turns out..." She flung her hands up in a mind-blown gesture. "Boom! You guys have a mutual friend."

"Okay," Val said, unsure of where this was going.

"Anyway, this mutual friend, Victor, is in Chicago. I just texted him," said Jillian. "He says, 'Hello.'"

"Oh my gawd. Do you have any idea what you've done?"

"Yeah. I have a pretty good idea. I guess I figured I should do something to pay you back for all the stuff you've done for me. Like that sandwich. What's in it anyway? Arsenic?" She flipped over the passport pictures—pictures not of the kid as they should have been but of Val—then Jillian reached into her back pocket and held up Tabitha's passport, the one Val had planted. "Nice try."

"Goddammit," Val said. *Okay don't panic, there's still time.* She'd grab her stash of money, leave everything else and take off. Jake would let her crash at his place for a couple of days, while she figured things out.

Someone banged on the front door.

"Guess that's Victor now," the kid said, snatching up the passport application envelope. "Thanks again for all your help."

As Ye Sow
Craig Faustus Buck

NOW

Ulya felt like her eardrums were imploding. Her stomach churned from the pungent smell of gun smoke. She'd never fired a pistol before, so she was shocked that she'd actually hit him. His body collapsed in what seemed like slow motion. Then she blacked out.

THEN

Owen Fester was sitting in his cubicle, rewriting a love letter from a Namibian seamstress to a Nebraskan dry cleaner, when he heard a commotion. He looked up to see the most beautiful woman he'd ever seen. She couldn't have been more than twenty-five, with wide-set emerald eyes and ink-black short-cropped hair. She was screaming in Russian and kicking at the shins of a tall, thick, fortyish man who was trying to subdue her. He held her in a bear hug, her back against his chest and her butt jammed against the beer belly that spilled over his belt.

Larch Holland rushed out of his office to handle the situation.

"You call this bitch on wheels a loving bride?" the man shouted.

"Now let's just all calm down," said Larch.

"Let go!" said the woman, lapsing into English. "You are big ox."

"I'll let you go, all right," said the man, and dropped her on the floor. Then, to Larch, "I want my money back!"

The woman pulled herself up, quiet but angry, brushing dirt from the floor off her flowered sundress. Owen thought she filled that dress like one of those perfect figures that graced the vintage dress patterns his mother used to collect. An artist's rendering of the ideal female form.

"All right," said Larch. "Why don't we all step into my office and talk about it."

"There's nothing to talk about," said the man. "She don't want me. I don't want her. You're going to give me my money back or I'll have my lawyers burn this mail-order outrage to the ground. Just make the check out to Oskar Sandvik. Oskar with a 'k.'"

"Okay, Mr. Sandvik, just relax. You'll get your money." Then, to the woman, "And you'll work here until you've paid him back."

She snorted like a bull.

Ulya deciphered the foreign letters on the matchbook like a four-year-old sounding out her first written words. "Wild Oats Tavern," she read.

Owen laughed. "Oaks, not Oats," he said. "Never could figure out why they call it that. Ain't nothing but pine and dry rot in this dungheap. You couldn't hang a cat from them rafters without bringing the roof down."

"My English not so good," said Ulya.

A frown bloomed on Owen's face as he fingered the small gold cross around his neck. "Don't be so hard on yourself," he said. "You're more than smart enough. Don't need much reading or writing anymore, considering that voice recognition we got now."

"That softvare is crap. Does not vork for me," she said. "Alvays spellink wrong."

Ulya stuck her finger into a recycled tuna can filled with bar mix and fished around until she found a mini-pretzel. She waved it under her nose to make sure there was no fishy smell.

"Could be your Ruskie accent," said Owen. "Anyways, the worse your spelling, the more you get the saps believing you're really in Russia or Africa or Thailand or wherever their dick is pointed. If I can teach you one damn lesson, it's that love is blind, deaf and dumb. You get that hook in good and deep, you can spell sucker with a double Q, won't make no never mind to the fish."

"How you put hook deep?" asked Ulya. "You get salesman of month three times in row. You must to teach me how to be good hooker."

Owen laughed again. She wondered what the joke was. She hoped she hadn't said something that made her look stupid. She sensed a shrewd mind beneath his aw-shucks country-boy facade and she found that attractive. She also liked his look. Tall and lean, amber eyes to complement wavy blond hair down to his shoulders, cute little freckle by his nose.

If Owen had been the man she'd found at the end of her journey from Eastern Ukraine, she'd have thought she'd hit the jackpot. He made her feel like a person, not a piece of meat, like most men she'd come across. Of course, life with any American would be better than the daily violence and corruption of her homeland. Except, maybe, Oskar Sandvik.

"Love is strange, girl," said Owen. "And you've got to be strange to make it work for you. I just happen to have a certain knack for romance. Kinda like Brad Paisley."

"Who?" She stuck her fingernail between her gapped front teeth to dislodge a big grain of pretzel salt.

"Never mind," said Owen. He picked up the bar mix can

and shot half of it into his mouth.

"Come on, love boy. What ees your secret?" She realized she was flirting. This seemed odd, considering that, even with his top sales bonuses, Owen wasn't going to make much money working at LoveGlobal.com. The only real money was the profit, which belonged to owner Larch Holland.

"She-it," said Owen, shaking his head. "Ain't no big secret. Just timing is all."

Owen glanced at the neon-ringed Budweiser clock.

"We best get going," he said, shooting his last Jack Daniels and stacking the glass to complete his six-shooter pyramid. "Five minutes until lunch ends. Larch has no toleration for latecomers."

The Colorado sun beat down on Owen and Ulya as if God were trying to fry them with a magnifying glass. The industrial space that contained LoveGlobal.com was just six doors down, but by the time they walked through the entrance, Ulya's underarms felt like shucked clams.

The long, narrow building had a line of twenty-nine windows down each wall, all of them blocked by cheap air conditioners purchased from the Pikes Peak Motel when it was closed due to an uncontainable outbreak of brain-eating black mold. The fifty-eight ACs made an uncontainable racket, but they were needed to keep the computers from overheating. The comfort of the workers was an unintended consequence, as was the perpetual gloom from the loss of natural light.

Ulya and Owen walked down the length of the building between two seemingly endless rows of cubicles. They caught slivers of conversation in a variety of accents, mostly Eastern European and African, coming from scores of multiracial women, all staring at screens and wearing telephone headsets.

"…wish I could smell your hair, feel your…refused to issue

my exit visa without...dream of you every night...had to cash in plane ticket for Mama's operation...smother you in rose petals...you would do that for me?...never thought love could feel so..."

The men answered emails and interacted with the lovelorn or lovestruck in chat rooms.

Photos of children and pets festooned the cubicle walls, along with plastic statuettes of Jesus on the cross, seeing as how Colorado Springs was the center of the Evangelical universe, home to the national headquarters of more than one hundred and forty churches. Completing the décor were two Stars of David and one copy of the Holy Koran.

"How long is usual for to string along...how you say... marks?" asked Ulya.

"I'll spend two, three months, to reel most of them in. I think my longest took around fourteen. Romance is a tricky scam. You pull the trigger too quick, they get spooked off. Love goes poof. No honey, no money."

"Da. But how you know when to pull trigger?"

"Me, I get this feeling in my testicular area. It's almost a sex thing. Like when you put your hand on a gal's leg in a bar and she don't push it off. She don't need to say anything and you know you're good to go. That's when you take your shot."

"Hey!" They turned to see Larch barreling toward them, hands flailing, red mullet bouncing high, bulging muscles molding the thin cotton of his Manitou Brewing tank-top. "Time is an infinite entity, Owen. Lunch is not!" His voice thundered like an unmufflered Harley.

A shiver ran up Ulya's spine. There was something unreadable about Larch that made her anxious, as if she were torn between fascination and fear. It wasn't only because the day he'd interviewed her for the job, his eyes may as well have been tethered to her breasts. She hadn't minded that so much because she knew the allure gave her power over him. It may take sleeping with him for her to harness it, but that might be fun. There was a certain appeal to his finely chiseled body, from rock climbing, she'd heard. They were, after all, at the foot of the Southern Rockies.

"You asked me to school her in the business," said Owen. "We were working over lunch."

"Don't bullshit a man who takes steroids, Fester. It can get ugly. And you," he turned to Ulya, "I want to see you in private." He pointed toward his office, the only one in the building.

Ulya saw Owen's jaw clamp, like he was locking a cage to contain a rabid pit bull. Then he slipped into his cubicle and started pounding at his keyboard so hard she thought it might crack.

As she followed Larch, she heard Owen dictate to the voice recognition software. "Darling Robert, that photo you sent me made me tingle in places I'm too embarrassed to name."

Since that first day, her opinion of Larch had remained in limbo. As befit the creator of a multi-million dollar match-making site, Larch had an ego. He could be harsh and he could be temperamental. She'd seen him dump a wheatgrass smoothie on his assistant's head because she'd neglected to add bee pollen.

Yet he'd been there for Ulya when she'd needed him. She'd been working the phone with a horny Iowa dairy farmer, telling him how she'd love to see his barn someday, watch him milk the cows, maybe pour a pail of the fresh milk over his naked body and slowly lick it off. By the time she'd finished describing what her tongue's sultry journey would do to him, the farmer was musing on the cost of a ticket from Kiev to Ames. She told him she loved him, but a flight to America was too exorbitant; he was not a rich man. As he started to argue that their being together was all that mattered, her smarmy Bangladeshi supervisor Mishkat leaned in to murmur in her ear.

"I like the sound of your tongue action," said Mishkat. "Come see me after work and you can practice what you preach. That's how day girls stay off the night shift."

He'd made her feel helpless, like her high school English teacher back in Ukraine who'd dusted her palm with chalk dust and threatened to flunk her if she didn't rub him the right way. At least that nightmare had allowed her to pass out of his class. Mishkat's humiliations had continued to mount every day, like Chinese water torture, with no relief in sight. Then, one day, a Nigerian coworker found her crying in the ladies room. The girl told Larch, who was of the opinion that unhappy workers were less seductive, costing him paying customers. It was Mishkat who wound up on the night shift.

Larch closed the office door behind Ulya and motioned her to a chair in front of his desk. The minute he'd first laid eyes on her, he'd been smitten. Fleshy breasts, long slender legs with a thigh gap you could slip the stock of a shotgun through.

"What's your name again? Anastasia?" he said, knowing full well both her name and her nickname. It was his usual opening power play to remind people who the boss was.

"Ulyana," she said. "By most people I am Ulya."

She had one of those dusky Eastern European voices that made him sweat.

"Ulya. I like that. Short and sexy. So how do you like working here so far, Ulya?"

"I like."

"Owen been giving you some good tips?"

"There is much to learn. He is good teacher."

"Just don't forget who's the rooster in this barnyard. Your future won't look so bright if you go poking your beak in the dirt, sharing seeds with co-workers. They've got the seeds of destruction. I've got the seeds of growth."

She took this for a sexual innuendo and shifted uncomfortably in her seat. He laughed and she took that to mean he was just kidding, though she wasn't sure he was.

"I'm the man who signs the checks around here. That makes me the alpha wolf."

"You said you was rooster."

He grinned. "I'm just teasing you. You play your cards right, you could go places. You got the looks and the brains to advance your career around here."

"Business all on Internet and telephone," she said. "What for I need looks?"

His grin twisted southward. "I meant that as a compliment."

"I am just hard vorker who vant no trouble."

"Trouble can be fun sometimes." His smile tried for sexy but settled for smarmy.

She held his gaze with a blank expression.

He laughed. "Go back to work, Ulya. We can revisit this discussion over a brew sometime."

As she left, he bent down to watch the light through her thigh gap.

Ulya returned to her cubicle next to Owen's.

"What'd he want?" asked Owen.

"I think, maybe, to sex with me," she said.

"He said that?"

"My English not so good."

"Son of a bitch."

Owen looked at her and she had a vision of steam coming off his eyes. It hadn't occurred to her that he might feel jealous. She didn't think they were that close. She was both thrilled and uneasy, as if she were victorious in a game she wasn't sure she wanted to play.

She realized he'd asked her a question she hadn't heard through her musings. "What?" she said.

"Bowling," he said. "They got that in Russia?"

The Peak Bowl lanes were half full by the time Owen and Ulya walked in after work. She'd been unimpressed by the cinderblock exterior, but was awed by the colorful strings of lights that lined the lanes, and the bright mural that filled the entire wall beside the first lane, depicting Fountain Creek running through the fall-colored aspens toward Pikes Peak.

This was the first time they'd been on anything approaching a date, and Ulya was nervous. Owen seemed in his element, as he strutted to the counter and retrieved shoes for her. He's brought his own shoes, purple saddle-shoe-style, along with his own purple ball adorned with some sort of smoky white swirls.

Owen picked out a red ball for her and then stood behind her, with one hand on her waist and the other under her ball, to show her, in slow motion, how to move. She could feel his body heat where his chest met her back, and she thought she could feel his heartbeat, but she wasn't sure. As he murmured instructions, his breath warmed her ear. It felt like a slow dance.

She was disappointed in her score on their first game, though she did manage to avoid the gutters most of the time. Owen crowed that she was a natural and she thought he was sweet to try to lift her spirits.

Before their second game, Owen flagged down a waitress and ordered a cheeseburger. Ulya ordered an open-faced burger called "The Slopper," with green chili and cheese, holding the onions, thinking, In case this date goes anywhere. Owen considered her for a moment, then told the waitress to hold his onions as well. Ulya felt a little thrill.

As she studied the beer choices, she heard someone shout

her name over the cacophony of the alley. She looked up to see Larch, striding toward them, ball in hand. She noted that he had no trouble remembering her name when he was horning in on a competitor.

Owen reacted to Larch as if he'd just seen the blazing lights of a police car in his rearview mirror.

From the march in his step, it was clear that Larch had been drinking. "You don't mind if I join you, do you, Owen? I'm sure Ulya won't mind."

Ulya watched Owen's fuse light up as he searched for words. "Well I don't know…"

"Of course you do," said Larch as if that settled the matter.

Ulya sensed a pissing contest coming on and knew that, no matter who won, Owen could wind up losing his job. She didn't want that on her conscience.

She leaped into the silence. "We'd love you to join us, wouldn't we, Owen?"

He kept his mouth shut, but his anger flashed like a neon sign.

"You two keep the lane," Owen said, tossing his ball into his bag. "I'm not feeling too good. You can get home okay, right?"

She nodded, living only a few blocks away in a rented house with three other LoveGlobal girls.

"No worries," said Larch. "I'll see her home."

Owen glared at Larch. For an awkward moment, Ulya feared Owen would dive over the ball return to strangle Larch. But, instead, Owen took a deep breath and trudged out in his purple bowling shoes, leaving her alone with the drunken boss.

Larch dismissed the waitress with, "I'll eat whatever he ordered."

* * *

Ulya looked around in awe. Everything was flawless. No stains on the antique rugs. No bald spots on the upholstery. No scratches on the polished wood. All original art on the walls, mostly abstract, in handcrafted frames. Larch's living room could easily accommodate her entire house. An enormous glass wall afforded a view of a turquoise pool in a tastefully lit and manicured yard that seemed endless. She'd never even dreamed that such a beautiful home was possible. Every detail was perfect.

Larch poured them each some sort of whiskey, with a name she'd never seen and couldn't pronounce. Then he led her outside to look at the stars. Even washed by the full moon, Colorado Springs boasted a skyful. Pike's Peak loomed before them, its snowcap reflecting the moon like a frosted lightbulb. Ulya shivered from the chill, even in her parka. Larch put his arm around her, pulling her close. She was surprised by a jolt of arousal.

"I'm sorry for today," he said.

"For what?"

"For being an ass after lunch. People think because I built a big business, because I'm the big boss, because I live in a big house, that I'm somehow a big man. I'm just a guy. And when I meet a woman like you, I get flustered. I say stupid things. I fall back on habits I should have outgrown in high school."

She slid her arm beneath his jacket, around his waist, and pulled him tight. His body felt both hard and soft. She imagined what it would feel like against hers.

"There is nothing for to be sorry," she said. "All men are teenage boys underneath. Some just hide it more better."

He chuckled at this.

"I've been attracted to you since I first saw you, you know," he said.

"Yes, I know." She also knew he was fishing for a reciprocal compliment, but she thought this would make her look weak. And he seemed like the type who liked controlling women.

"It's just gotten worse the more I've gotten to know you," he said. "I'm not sure what to do about it. It's awkward enough being your boss, but it's downright weird trying to work out a relationship when you're in the relationship business."

"Mail-order bride is far from relationship business."

She expected him to push back, to get offended, at least to become defensive. But he surprised her.

"I'm not proud of what we do. Roping men in by their loneliness, to get their money. But it's not all bad. These men lead loveless lives. We give them hope. We sell them a fantasy and every once in a while it sticks. Maybe only for a few months, but that's better than nothing, right?"

"I do not know."

She looked up and recognized Orion's belt.

"Do you think I'm a bad person?" he asked.

She turned to him.

"You have been good to me." She shrugged. "Except maybe this afternoon, you naughty boy." She gave him a faux frown and waggled her finger.

"I'll be a good boy, I promise." He looked at her longingly and she saw the lonely man in him. She felt a stab of pity and pulled him into a kiss. She wondered if she would have done this without the whiskey. She decided she didn't care. She just wished he was a better kisser.

He led her up to his bedroom. It had a glass wall, too. She felt like they were making love under the stars. As it turned out, he wasn't much of a lover. And his body felt too rock-hard when it pounded against her. On the other hand, she'd never felt such soft sheets. She could easily overlook a few minor irritations to move into his world.

* * *

Larch dropped her off a little after eleven that night. He waited for her to open her door before driving off. She stepped inside feeling slightly giddy. As soon as she closed the door, someone knocked on it. She looked through the spyhole to see Owen.

They sat at her kitchen table drinking tea, speaking in low voices so as not to wake her roommates.

"I was worried sick about you," he said. "It got so late, I thought something might have happened to you on your way home."

"Larch showed me his house," she said. "We had drink."

"Drink?" The word was laced with suspicion.

"What I do is not your business."

"I'm sorry," he said. "I was worried is all."

She put her hand gently on his face. "I am sorry, also," she said. "I know you just try to do good to me."

He took her hand and kissed it.

"That's all I want to do," he said, then after a moment's consideration, he added, "maybe forever."

Then he leaned over and kissed her. She parted her lips to admit his tongue and realized, after a long evening, how refreshing it was to be with a man who knew how to kiss.

BETWEEN THEN AND NOW

A year or so later, Larch asked Ulya to marry him. She left her job and moved into his house the next day. By that time, Owen had worked his way up through the LoveGlobal ranks to become Larch's right hand. There was no one better suited to be best man, so Owen was forced to watch Ulya marry Larch from only three feet away. He forced a smile and had to struggle to contain the contents of his stomach.

The wedding had been over the top, even for the historic Broadmoor Hotel, but Larch wanted nothing but the finest for his "czarina." She eased into a life of leisure as if she'd been born to it. She drove a new Mercedes, made weekly shopping trips to Denver boutiques with girlfriends from the country club, was asked to join the board of the Colorado Springs Philharmonic, and persuaded Larch to rent her a studio in Manitou so she could take up painting. It was there that she'd rendezvous with Owen.

It didn't take long for the honeymoon to end. Following the wedding, Larch gave Owen more and more management responsibilities, so that Larch could spend more time at home. Ulya resented his increasing demands on her time and attention. Her thrice-weekly Manitou meetings with Owen quickly dwindled to thrice-monthly. On paper—at least paper money—Ulya had everything she'd ever dreamed of, but she was feeling increasingly lonely, miserable.

The longer she lived with Larch, the more she resented him, and that quickly morphed into loathing. She couldn't complain to any of her country club friends because they wouldn't empathize. They all complained about their husbands, but none of them really meant it. Her only true confidante was Owen. He understood because he loved her, and hated Larch as much as she did, for keeping them apart.

Then, one afternoon, she was spooning naked in Owen's arms, relaxed in the cooling embers of their afternoon's sexual play, when he said, "You'll never guess who ordered up a bride today."

When she didn't reply, he said, "Your ex. Oskar Sandvik."

Her initial surprise took a moment to wear off, but then the larval stage of a plan began to weave its cocoon in Ulya's mind.

Sandvik hated Colorado Springs. It was too metropolitan for him, which is like saying tofu burgers are too meaty. But by comparison, the population of his town in Minnesota could be expressed in three digits. No house was less than a half-mile from the next. Downtown had a general store with an attached gas station that doubled as a restaurant on Sundays, after church, when they fired up the barbecue for hot dogs, assuming it was dry enough and warmer than thirty-eight.

Nonetheless, it had been several years since Sandvik's last wife experiment, and he'd slowly come around to believing that his failure with Ulya might possibly have been due to long-distance communications over the Internet. So he was ready to give it another try, but only face to face. So he'd decided to return to the scene of his last fiasco, LoveGlobal's headquarters.

He landed at the airport girded for battle, determined to procure the perfect bride at a decent cost, prepared to reject any loss leaders they tried to toss his way. What he wasn't prepared for was Ulya.

She was waiting for him by the curb outside the terminal, looking gorgeous beside a new, lunar blue Mercedes, wearing a matching blue outfit that revealed her toned midriff. She could have been a model in a Mercedes ad.

"What are you doing here?" he said.

"I want to make apology." Her emerald eyes caught the light like gemstones.

She opened the rear door and motioned him in like a limo driver, saying, "Please. You let me give you lift." And he felt one emotionally.

He threw his carry-on bag on the seat and climbed in after it. As she drove, his eyes were riveted to her profile. He didn't remember her being so exquisite. Clearly, she'd taken care of herself. Not to mention the improvement in her English.

"Where are you going?" she asked.

"Motel 6," he said.

"You are in hurry?" she asked. "It would please me to spend a little time alone with you. Maybe to make up for a small piece of the pain I have caused? Would you like some tea? My place is on the way."

He tried to assemble the words to respond, but his mind was flooded by the memory of the first time he'd seen her nude. It took all of his faculties to rein in the image in order to muster even an, "Okay."

Larch lounged by the pool, staring at his plaid board shorts. He flipped up the hem to read the tag. "Made in Bangladesh." He was musing about whether they were sewn by child slaves when he heard Ulya's car drive up.

Good, he thought. She can make me a ham and cheese.

Ulya parked the car and got out, wondering whether Sandvik would expect her to open his door. But he let himself out, staring in astonishment at the mansion before him.

"You live here?" he said.

"With my husband," she said. "But he's out of town."

She said it suggestively and saw Sandvik's radar go up. Had she overplayed her hand? He may live in the sticks, but he wasn't such a rube that he'd believe a woman who looked like Ulya, especially with their history, would be coming on to him.

She smiled. "I didn't mean that the way it sounded. It was just a statement of fact. But I have thought a lot about you over the years. When we met, I was upset about the mail-order situation; I never really gave you a chance. I'm sorry for that. You're a kind man and I treated you badly. Can I offer you a drink?"

She led him into the house, surprised to be feeling a little remorseful.

Sandvik couldn't figure her out. But she looked so good he was happy to give her the benefit of the doubt. What a pathetic hormonal male you are, he thought, remembering the pheromones he'd used with his farm animals to promote breeding. But those thoughts did nothing to subdue his fantasies about the contours that sculpted her blue dress.

"A little schnapps would be nice," he said.

She gave him a smile that could have powered a small city. If she thought she could play him for a fool, he'd disappoint her. But before he refused to bite at her bait, he saw no harm in letting her dangle it. He was titillated, just watching her move.

Sandvik followed Ulya through her home as if touring a fairyland. Then she led him out to the pool and the pixies died at the sight of Larch, sunning on the deck. The two men locked eyes like two deer caught in each other's headlights.

"What the hell?" said Larch.

Owen stepped out of the bushes and raised the Colt semi-automatic his father brought home from Nam. He felt the disappointment of his father's spirit as he aimed at Larch.

"What the hell?" said Sandvik.

Ulya pulled her own gun from her handbag and pointed it at the farmer from Minnesota.

"Over there, Oskar," she said, motioning toward Larch.

Owen lined his sights up on his sort-of-friend and mentor, thinking of the day he'd handed Larch the wedding band to put on Ulya's finger, not to mention the times he'd stared at that band on the nightstand as they'd betrayed Ulya's wedding vows. He imagined his father looking down from heaven, watching his only son planning to kill a man for his wealth and his scheming wife. How had he ever let Ulya talk him into sinking this low?

"What's this about?" said Larch.

"It's over," said Ulya.

"I love her," said Owen, more to himself than to Larch.

"And I love Owen," she said.

Owen watched Larch look from him to her, trying to make sense of it all. He watched Larch's face melt into an expression of profound sadness, and Owen's heart ached.

"You think the police won't figure this out?" said Larch.

"They'll believe me like men always do," said Ulya. "Sandvik came back for me and the two of you fought. It got out of control and you pulled a gun. He pulled one, too. It all happened so fast, I'm not sure who fired first. But before my eyes, you each shot the other."

Larch looked at Owen. "I trusted you," he said. "I treated you like a brother."

Owen's eyes watered as he lowered his gun, saying to Ulya, "I can't do this. I warned you I didn't think I could."

"Everything can be ours," she said, referring to Larch's fortune. "Just you and me. But we must do this now."

"Wake up, Owen," said Larch. "She's just using you. She hooked you, just like you taught her."

Owen ignored him. "I love you, Ulya. That's all I want. Why can't we just walk away?"

"Love is being there for me when I need you."

"I'm sorry."

"Then what for I need you now?"

She raised her gun toward Owen. Reflexively he raised his as well. He felt her bullet enter his chest. For an instant he stood still as a statue, waiting for the pain.

She got me spelling sucker with a double Q, he thought, as a red-hot crowbar tore at his insides. He heard a gurgling sound from his throat and felt his finger convulse on the trigger. The gun kicked as his legs gave out as he saw that she didn't blink when the blood from her forehead dripped into her eye. But he never felt the ground.

Dirty Laundry
Marie Hannan-Mandel

How is it when every other mode of transportation, including horse and buggy, is getting better, air travel continues to get worse? I don't expect an answer, I'm just throwing it out there. You'd think I'd avoid air travel, but instead, I do it for a living. I fly from place to place all around the country to interview goofy people for my even goofier boss's weird website. Said boss, Simon Shawell (not Shawl, but Shaw-well, as he points out to people who say it wrong, that is, everyone he ever meets) insists I go to where the subjects actually live and take pictures that show I've been there. Then I do this cheesy presentation on his website, no better than a high schooler's. He calls it "The Program." The man's a nut. And he makes me travel economy. So economy that it would be more expensive to ship me freight.

This latest trip to Florida is to meet a man who likes to eat entire loads of laundry—coloreds and whites—without owning a set of teeth. No teeth, that's the part that perplexed me. There are plenty of soft, non-chewy foods available. Why eat laundry? The sponsor of the show for the website that month was a national cut-price dentist outfit who wanted something about teeth. I told Simon that demonstrating that you can eat something as chewy as clothes without teeth wouldn't make the dentist company's point, but the CEO wants to take the line that he'd enjoy his linens so much better with a new set of choppers. This wasn't what I thought I'd be doing at thirty-six, but a job's a job, and a position in journalism isn't easy to find.

My rental car doesn't deserve the name. Oh believe me, they're charging me for it. It's a rental, but a car worthy of the name? No. It was the only one left in the lot after the snow birds, pasty faced and starved for warmth, had swooped through. It was, however, cheap. I think you're getting my drift. The criterion for acceptable in Simon's world, is that a thing is cheap.

I wasn't surprised to find Mr. and Mrs. Lowell Juniper, aka, laundry-eating man and his wife, living in a trailer park right by the Everglades. I *was* surprised to be met at the door by a woman wearing an orange scarf around her head. She didn't look like the wife of a man who ate his shorts. She *looked* like a woman waiting to be discovered and signed to a modeling contract.

"Hello, Mrs. Juniper. I'm here to write a story about your husband eating laundry," I said.

"What? Now? I wrote to you three months ago. It's too late." She twisted the dish towel in her hand like she was trying to wring it dry.

"Too late?" Simon was the one who chose the stories to match the advertisers.

"It was just such a long time ago," she said, smiling without opening her mouth.

"The story was such an interesting one..." I always said this. Getting the subjects to like me is important—how else can I get them to tell me everything, not just what they want me to know?

"Lowell always did want to be famous. You'd better come in." She walked away, leaving the screen door open for me to follow her.

The trailer was old but cleaner than most places I'd visited, and that includes my own apartment in Buffalo. I walked in and sat at the kitchen table in the chair she indicated with a nod of her gorgeous head.

"I'm Mary, Mary Juniper," she said, smiling that closed mouth smile of hers. She didn't sit down.

"I'm Jake." I put out my hand, but she ignored it, so I returned it to my side feeling something that might have been disappointment.

I took out the recorder, and settled my camera in front of me. No point in wasting time.

"And your husband?" I asked, when she didn't say anything but turned away to wipe down a swirly green laminate counter top that didn't need wiping.

"The thing is, Lowell is ill," she whispered without turning to look at me. "I warned him eating clothes would kill him, but he won't listen."

"Ill?" I echoed to keep myself from saying that any man who ate his laundry was definitely ill.

"Not feeling well. He might be better tomorrow, but today won't be possible." Her voice had gone back to normal. She scrubbed at the counter.

"I'm sorry. What's wrong with him?" I asked. Simon wouldn't agree to more than one night in the cheapest motel in town.

"He's got a cough," she said now knocking sparks off a saucepan with a scrubbing brush under the running tap.

"Maybe I can get some background and then, he might be feeling better?" I said.

"Okay," she said softly, still not looking at me.

I turned on the recorder.

"So, when did Mr. Juniper first show an interest in laundry?" I asked.

Her hand stopped moving. "About six months ago, I guess," she spoke so softly I wasn't sure the recorder would get her voice. I somehow knew I was lucky to get her talking at all, so I didn't say anything.

"And does he eat clothes that have already been washed or..." I didn't want to think of the "or."

"Washed, of course, always washed. You think we're savages around here?" She swung around, the sponge tightly clasped in her fist.

I stood up and considered telling her that no one as beautiful and graceful as she was could ever be considered a "savage." Instead, I said, "Of course not."

"Look. I'm sorry Lowell's ill, but you'll have to go away and come back—"

"I ain't ill, Mary. I ain't never been ill." The voice could have scoured the pot clean without the aid of water. "Come in here, will ya?"

I studied Mary. Her shoulders slumped. She dropped the sponge onto the counter.

"He'll have to meet you, I guess," she said.

"You'll come with me, right?" I asked. She'd been the one to contact us, so it was her story, really.

"Who's this, Mary? I didn't know anyone was coming," the man, Lowell, I presumed, said from the bed. He was splayed out, the blankets scattered around him as if he'd been shot by hunters and left for dead. The low ceilings and heavily curtained window gave the place the feeling of a dungeon. He was older than Mary, much older. A beauty queen and a troglodyte. There was something way off here.

"It was a surprise visit," I said. "I just thought I'd drop in."

"Who the hell are you?" he growled, protecting what was his.

"I'm Jake Harrison. I've come from New York to—"

"New York? I bet you like this weather better. Why y'all live up there with the cold and the snow, I can't figure."

Mary stepped in front of me and faced Lowell. "That's right," she said.

He grabbed her by her porcelain wrist and pulled her to sit down next to him.

"I've come here to—" I began my patter.

A sharp snap of Mary's head in the negative stopped me.

"I bet you're wondering how an old stud like me got me such a pretty wife." Lowell said, grinning and showing his gums.

When I didn't say anything, just stood there smiling politely, my hands shoved hard into my jacket pockets, he continued, "Well, me and her daddy was great friends. He had three girls, and I got me the best one. The pick of the litter. I'd just die without her." He wheezed like an elderly pug. Mary handed him a tall glass of a bright yellow drink.

"Kool-Aid," Lowell said when he'd downed a big gulp. "Only thing I drink exceptin' for whiskey." He laughed at himself again.

"What's your favorite flavor?" I asked.

"What? Whiskey's whiskey."

"He means the Kool-Aid," Mary whispered, still tethered by her wrist.

"What's my favorite?" Lowell asked her.

"I mix the two flavors they carry at the store," she said.

"She's real clever, ain't she?" Lowell said.

"Yes," I said.

"And real pretty. She's real pretty, ain't she?" He stared at me with his flinty-hard eyes.

"I have to go now. Nice meeting you," I said. I wasn't going to make Mary's life any worse than it already was.

"You'll see him tomorrow, Lowell. You'll be here at nine, right?" Mary said.

I nodded.

"Wait a minute, are you the guy that's going to interview me about my collection?"

"Yes," I said, playing along in a pretense I wasn't sure I understood.

"Make sure you come back when you say," Lowell instructed.

Mary made to get up to see me out, but he tugged at her arm and she winced.

I left without giving him the punch he deserved.

I drove out of the trailer park wondering what to do for the rest of the evening. A store just up the road advertised cold drinks and I felt in need of one. The sign over the door was worn to a shadow and read "Susan's Marketplace."

"Are you Susan?" I asked the woman behind the chipped plastic counter. She was probably in her fifties, though she might have just had a hard life.

"Nah, Susan left for Las Vegas to become a Priscilla Presley impersonator. That was years ago." She seemed happy to talk, so I thought I'd get some background for my piece.

"Is there much call for that kind of thing? Are there Elvis impersonators in need of a wife?" I ask.

"Don't think so, but she does look like Priscilla, and there's probably not a lot of competition."

"I guess not." I'd have to mention this to Simon. I'd love a trip to Vegas.

"You visiting?" she asked.

"I'm here to interview Lowell Juniper about the laundry." As soon as I'd said it I regretted opening myself up to what would certainly be ridicule. What kind of a person is interested in that sort of thing? And worse, what kind of person does a show about it?

"Lowell Juniper? You must be hard up. As for laundry, that man's never done a lick of work in his life. I see Mary lugging their stuff up there to the Sparkle and Clean every week, even though he's got a truck and could take her." The woman leaned on the counter so comfortably, I decided to join her.

"Why doesn't she drive herself?" I asked. I thought about turning on the recorder in my pocket but didn't want her to catch on. Besides, I knew I'd remember what she said.

"She can't drive. Not allowed to."

"She's got a medical thing?" I ask.

"That man is a jackass. Jack with a capital Ass. I'm Carrie," she said putting out her hand for a shake.

"Jake." I shook her warm strong hand briefly before we returned our hands to the countertop where they belonged.

"Why you ain't up there with them?" she asked. "Are you interviewing me for background?" She grabbed my hand. "You gonna use my name or just call me 'a neighbor.' Would you mind mentioning the store? I could use the business." The words tumbled out of her like children let loose for recess.

I dealt with this kind of thing all the time. You never knew if people would be happy to be interviewed and want a bigger part in the story or refuse to be involved at all and threaten to sue.

"I'd be happy to." I took out my camera.

"Wait, wait, I gotta get cleaned up." She ran through a door that led into what looked like a kitchen. The amount of banging that went on made it sound like she was building a robot, rather than smartening herself up.

Carrie came out with an inch of makeup on her face and lipstick red enough to stop traffic, literally. It was the same color as a new red traffic light.

"I know, I know you're thinking, 'there she is all done up and it's like putting lipstick on a pig.'" But her face didn't say that. Her face begged me not to agree.

"You look stunning!" I said. She wasn't unattractive, a large girl, but not unshapely. She wasn't a Mary, but then how many women are?

"In fact, I'm going to need a few shots of you around this place for my piece. You're just what I need to make this piece sing with local color."

"Really? You're not making fun, are you?"

Her vulnerability touched me. I wasn't kidding her. I don't take Simon seriously, but I do take my interview subjects very seriously. For the most part, they are people who just want someone to notice them, someone to tell them they matter. And they do. To me, at least.

"Let's take a picture of you at the cooler." I pointed down the row of soft drinks. The place was small and cramped, but the groceries didn't look like they'd been hanging around.

I scanned the aisles and saw two different colored tubs of Kool-Aid powder side by side, orange and ice blue raspberry.

"There you go, right between the soda and the beer," I said, taking her picture as she shifted around, tugging up her jeans and down her plaid shirt.

"You want a drink?" she asked when I'd finished.

I pulled a bottle of Mountain Dew out of the snapper in the cooler. Then I saw Birch Beer and wanted that instead. I tried to put the first bottle back.

"Don't you just hate these things?" Carrie said taking it from me and shoving it hard against the bottle at the front ramming it back.

"I do."

"So what else do you sell here? I want everyone to see what you've got."

She took me to the next aisle. This was truly an old-fashioned mercantile with sewing kits, computer wires, and car supplies cheek by jowl on the jammed shelves.

"Pick up something for the picture," I instructed.

She hauled the smallest bottle off the shelf and blushed as she tried to wipe the dust off. "Don't move much of this stuff," she said gesturing at the car fluid with a grimace.

"Smile," I said.

We walked back to the counter, and when I took out my wallet, she waved it away.

"You're a visitor here, I can't take your money."

"Thanks." I screwed off the top of the soda bottle and enjoyed a sugary swig.

"I can't believe anyone would want to interview Lowell. It's not like he's ever done anything. He just sits in that trailer drinking and playin' with his guns."

"He's got guns?" I didn't like the sound of that.

"Used ta have a lot until the deputy came and took'em all. Now he just plays with these." She held up a pair of beefy arms in a boxing position.

"His wife is much younger than him. How long have they been together?" I asked.

"A long time. Since she was legal. Her daddy gave her to Lowell like she was a gold fish at the county fair." She shook her head.

"Huh." I wanted to ask her if that kind of thing happened often down here, but knew I'd sound like a snot-nosed New Yorker, so I didn't.

"Mary's nice. So nice, real nice." She said each "nice" as if it were a different adjective and not the same one over and over. Maybe she thought the change of emphasis made up for the repetition.

"She certainly seems so," I said, taking another long drink of my soda.

"Let me give you a big ol' hug." Carrie swooped. "And be careful around Lowell. He's not a good man." She stepped away and watched as I walked out the door to my car.

The next morning, I was cruising along in the bright, but not hot sunshine, when Carrie flagged me down in front of her store. It was already after nine, but I wasn't turning up on time just because Lowell Juniper told me to.

"Business that bad, you gotta kidnap people from the road?" I said when I'd stopped and rolled down the window of my rusty steed.

"Mary's in trouble," she said, breathless even though she'd been standing still waiting for me.

"What? What's happened?"

"Lowell's dead."

I unlocked the doors. "Get in," I said.

She clambered in like a goat up a mountain with a lot of enthusiasm and no grace.

"Listen. We don't have a lot of time. I can get you in there to talk to her. You've got to stop her from telling the truth." She clutched at my arm.

"And what is the truth?"

"She poisoned him," she whispered, looking around like someone might be hiding outside the car listening.

"With the Kool-Aid." I hated that I hadn't come earlier so Mary could have said eating the laundry had killed him. Who knows if anyone would have believed her, but it would have been one hell of a distraction. Besides, people tend to accept what they see on the screen, even the computer screen.

"How'd you know that?" She reared away from me.

"He wasn't eating, but he was drinking, and mixing orange and ice blue raspberry powder does not make yellow. His drink should have been brown."

"Why didn't you stop her?" she demanded, outrage pouring off her in waves.

"Why didn't you?" I countered. I wasn't sure she knew ahead of time, but I'd wanted to find out.

"Because he deserved it," she whispered.

"I didn't do anything because I knew it was too late," I said.

Her disappointed look made me add, "And he deserved it."

"Come on, we gotta get up there," she said.

She motioned for me to pull into a drive alongside a trailer a few down from Mary's.

"This is Henry's place. He won't mind," she said.

There were two cars in front of Mary's trailer. One was a squad car and the second a dark sedan. A uniformed police officer stood at the bottom of the front steps.

"Now. You walk around the back of those trailers and wait until you hear me say, 'I can't believe you, David Hicks' and then you can go in the back door." The woman had thought this through.

"Okay," I said.

"You can climb over onto the deck at the back, right?"

"Of course I can." Whether she'd hurt my pride or I was just nervous, I wasn't sure.

"Sorry," she said.

"Me, too."

We got out of the car.

Carrie set up a storm of protest about not being allowed into the trailer and I was in position when she gave the code phrase. I climbed over the railing, through the back door, and crept into the hallway, right in front of the bedroom where Lowell lay, dead as the stump he'd been in life.

"What are you doing here?" Mary started as she came out of the bathroom.

"Yes, and who are you?" a male voice said full-boom. The man, about my age, was dressed in a suit.

"I'm Jake Harrison." I never give more information than I'm asked for.

"And do you always sneak in the back way?" he demanded.

"I told you about him, Greg. He's a nice man." Mary's headscarf was in place, her mouth pulled into a tight line, the words barely making it out.

"Look, I'm just worried about Mary," I said. "Who are you?"

"I'm Greg Saltzman," He put out his hand and I took it. I guess he'd decided we were on the same team.

"What happened to Lowell?" I pointed in the direction of the body behind us.

"He was poisoned."

"You sure? The man ate laundry, after all."

"Laundry?"

"Didn't Mary tell you?" I looked at Mary. I'd already figured it wasn't true, but I was too taken with the story to let it drop.

"She told me you'd come to buy something from Lowell, a backhoe." Now he was looking at her. She was looking at the floor.

Greg was being surprisingly forthcoming. If I'd been him, I would have insisted he answer my questions without any hints from me. A backhoe? Why, in the name of all that croaks, would I want to come from New York to buy a backhoe?

"Hm," I said.

"Come out here." He gestured toward the living room. "Mary, you just go into the guest bedroom and wait, okay?"

She nodded and did as she was told. I couldn't imagine that guest bedroom getting much use. Who'd want to visit Lowell? And who would he allow to stay?

"What's going on?" I asked when we'd reached the living room.

"You tell me," he countered. His suit was rumpled and his tie was on backward. "It might help Mary."

His face softened when he mentioned her name.

"I'm here because Mary contacted my boss's website and said her husband liked to eat loads of laundry and that he had no teeth."

"Do you know how crazy that sounds?" he asked. We sat on the wrap-around couch, covered in the kind of material designed by a drug-fueled color fiend.

"Please. Of course I do. Everything about this gig is crazy, but I do get to meet interesting people." I smiled. I tried never to explain what I did, but this was the time to lay it all out there.

"She made the laundry eating up," Greg said.

"I'm glad. The thought of that man chewing on her delicates makes me sick." I grinned, testing the waters.

"Yeah," he said.

"So, you think Mary did it." It wasn't a question.

"I'm afraid so. Antifreeze in his Kool-Aid. They ain't got but two flavors at the store, but they also got antifreeze."

"Of course, she could have gone to a different store, you know, to shake things up?" I suggested.

"Nah, she only ever went to Susan's Marketplace. Lowell wouldn't let her drive, and he wouldn't take her anywhere. Afraid she'd run off." The anger in his voice grew until I thought he might punch something.

"What's Mary hiding under that scarf, and why doesn't she smile?"

"He tore clumps of hair out a few days back and her two front teeth are broken." Greg grabbed at his tie like he might strangle himself.

"But if she was planning to kill him, then why bring me here? Why call attention to herself with such a crazy story?"

"Hey, that is strange. Why'd she do that?" he asked, screwing up his face in thought.

"From all I hear, Lowell was sick in the head. Didn't you guys have to take away his guns?"

"How d'you know that?"

"I'm a reporter, well sort of. I find things out. It's my job."

"Hah," Greg said. "Anyway, he was threatening the neighbors, so we took them away. He was working on getting them back, though."

"Only work he did, I'll bet," I said with a snort.

"You got that right." He joined me in the snort.

"Any chance he'd get them back?"

"Hell, no. He's, he was in too much trouble."

"The humiliation of you taking his guns for good might have been too much. It's probably suicide," I said.

"Suicide?" He sounded hopeful.

"Yeah, I have him on tape saying he didn't want to live. And he was drinking that Kool-Aid like it was going out of style. What with the antifreeze bittering laws, it now tastes awful. He'd have to have known what he was drinking."

"Antifreeze bittering?" Greg repeated.

"Yup, to stop animals drinking it by mistake. Even humans." I was pretty sure the law didn't hold in Florida, but I wasn't going to mention that.

"Huh," he said. He wiped his forehead less roughly. He was going with my flow.

"He was a proud man, right?"

"He was."

"He wouldn't be the kind of man who would go to a therapist if he was depressed, right?"

He laughed, "Of course not. Normally he just beat up on whatever woman was nearest."

"Eating weird things is called pica. It's a mental illness. Like I said, Lowell was ill." I waited for the objection to the assertion that Lowell actually did eat laundry, but Greg said nothing. He was with me now. I could feel it. I love the feeling when my subject is just along for the ride I set in motion. It's like setting someone flying back and forth on a swing. "He couldn't control his temper and he was a wife beater, so stands to reason he could have killed himself when he saw that he was going to lose Mary."

"Lose Mary?" Greg tore at his tie again. He was going to strangle himself and where would Mary be then?

"Oh yes, he said so himself. He said that he'd die without her." I played the recording for him.

"He nodded as he listened. "I think we may have got ourselves got a case."

The Last Train Out
Su Kopil

Fi's hands rest on the small, overnight bag, the brown leather soft beneath her fingers. She knows she should wait until the house is dark and Doug asleep, but Sundays are the worst, the emptiness hollowing her insides.

From the bedroom, she can hear the game blaring; Doug will be half watching from the broken recliner, half dozing, half drunk. He won't move except for the occasional stumble to the bathroom.

Unable to wait any longer, Fi closes her eyes, and pulls the bag's zipper along its track, breathing in the first puff of escaped aroma, something fruity—strawberry, maybe, or watermelon.

Keeping her eyes shut, she slides her hands inside, feeling the textures first, coarse denim, soft cotton, smooth silk. A shiver races along her skin. She pulls each item out and lays it on the bed. Jeans, tops, toiletries, panties, a makeup bag, a smaller drawstring pouch, and a red chemise trimmed in black lace, polyester, not silk, but a far cry from her own baggy T-shirts. A woman then. What is she like? Where is she going? Who is she meeting?

Fi picks up the chemise and holds it against her body. She smiles at her reflected image, feeling daring, flirty, completely unlike herself, because in that moment she is not herself. She's an exotic woman traveling alone to meet her lover someplace far from here. Then she turns. The light catches the bruise along her jawline, and the dream is shattered. She drops the chemise onto the dresser and goes back to the bed, picking up the drawstring pouch.

"Fi, where the hell are you? I need another beer. Fi."

Panic makes her movements jerky as she races to gather the items and stuff them back into the bag.

There's a crash from the other room. "Dammit." Doug's boots hitting the floor. Footfalls coming closer.

She shoves the travel bag into the back of the closet just as the bedroom door swings open.

Doug's pouchy stomach stretches his stained tank top. He scratches at the stubble on his chin, and she wonders why he doesn't just shave. "What are you doing in here? Game's on. I'm hungry." He turns to go. Stops. "What's that?"

She pivots back to the closet afraid she left it open. "What?"

"This." He's all the way in the room now staring at the red chemise lying like a pool of blood on the dresser.

He picks it up with one finger, sniffs it, looks at her. A red flush blooms on each cheek, spreading into the stubble. "You cheating on me?"

"What? No." Even when she tells the truth, it feels like a lie.

"Then whose is this? 'Cause I sure as hell know it's not yours."

"I don't know. A friend." The red flush has moved through the stubble, creeping toward his chest. It makes her mouth dry to watch it. "Not, not a friend. A stranger. Just someone."

The chemise slips through his fingers to pool back on the dresser. His gaze is steady on her, while his fingers curl around the handle of her hairbrush.

"It's not mine," she says.

His thumb strokes the stiff bristles.

"It's not—I can prove it." She hurries to the closet,

searches for the bag. It's gone. Wait. There in the corner. A sweatshirt half hiding it. "Look." She's breathless when she emerges.

Doug laughs, deep, ugly. "You think you can just pack a bag and leave?"

She shakes her head, tosses the faux leather bag onto the bed. "It's not mine. I borrowed it from the train station." She has his attention now. "The nighty was in the bag."

He moves to the bed, dumps out the contents. "So you steal other people's luggage from work."

"Not steal, borrow, from the lost and found. If no one claims it after a week, I borrow it, just to, I don't know, look." She won't tell him about all the people she pretends to be, the people she's imagined by the stuff they pack. How pretending to be someone else, if only for a small while, is the only thing that keeps her in the game, keeps her keeping on.

He opens the drawstring pouch. Jewelry spills into his hands. Not a lot, a gold band, earrings, and a necklace. He laughs again, softer, like he used to when she still thought he was one of the good ones.

It's morning. She doesn't eat. Can't. Nerves pinch at her stomach like a naughty child. Doug paces in front of her. Greed making his eyes too bright. He's never up this early. But today he's awake, making sure she doesn't forget what he told her last night.

"I want a man's bag. Someone who looks rich, sophisticated, you know. I could use some new threads. You'd like that, wouldn't you, babe?" He sidles up to her, exhaling stale beer, his beefy arm spilling over her shoulder. "Me in some fancy dude's designer clothes. I can use a new razor, too." He scrapes his stubble across her cheek.

She pulls away, pretending to search her bag for the car keys she knows are in there. "I told you there was no other luggage in the lost and found. It might be awhile."

He yanks the bag from her hands, shoves it onto the counter and grips her upper arms. "You're not hearing me, babe. Plenty of people in that train station, lots of confusion, luggage left alone. All you got to do is wait, then swoop in at the right time. Someone spots you, say you were taking it to the lost and found, right?"

She nods.

"You want your man looking good, now don't you? As good as you looked in that red number last night?" He pushes her lower back into the counter and grinds himself against her.

The pain in her back doesn't dull the memory of last night when he forced her to wear the chemise. She wasn't some exotic woman off to meet her lover. She was herself, in a woman's stolen lingerie, wrapped in shame.

The station's already open when she gets there. She has to rush to make the coffee, fill the packaged pastry bin, pile a stack of today's newspapers on the counter. Wally's pushing the broom across the main floor, his gray head down, humming to himself. When he passes the store, he looks up, catches her eye, nods. This is the first time she hasn't returned a borrowed bag. She wonders if he noticed. They all have access to the lost and found, but Wally's the one who keeps tabs on things.

When she finishes setting up the shop and waiting on the morning's first customers, she stands in the doorway. The passenger waiting area is filling up. Latisha, working the ticket counter, spots her and waves, Fi nods once and melts back into the store. It's a cycle. Each time she ventures out, she's like a cardinal in snow—obvious, vulnerable. Women watch her, children stare, men pull their luggage closer. She feels dirty just thinking about what Doug wants her to do.

Borrowing from the lost and found was different, she wasn't hurting anyone. But stealing will make her no better than him. When the six o'clock train rolls in, she leaves empty handed.

Doug is waiting at the door. The avarice in his eyes quickly turns to disgust. He makes her wear the lingerie again that night, and she does so because she wants to be needed for something.

Afterward, when he's snoring, she sits on the floor with the pouch from the borrowed bag. She pulls the drawstring and spills the jewelry into her palm. Something is stuck inside, a card with neat print. "If found please return to" and a Tennessee address. The jewelry is inexpensive, hardly worth the trouble. Taking the gold band into the bathroom where the light is brighter she sees an inscription on the inside, "Annie now and forever." Her fingers tighten around the ring. Silent tears fall.

The next day she helps Wally clean up a soda spill in front of the store. She asks him if it bothers him when people stare.

"They's not staring at me or you, Miss Fi. They's just staring." He leans on the mop. "Just trying to figure out how to get through the next problem in their lap. You could dance on your head and no one would pay any mind." He drops the mop in the bucket and rolls it away.

In between customers, she spends the day watching. Women scatter their attention from child to child or, if single, from man to man. Men focus on pretty women, newspapers, or their cell phones, oblivious to distractions. Children look at everything, but their interest is short-lived.

Humming loudly, she walks past a group of men. They ignore her. A mother sitting on a bench stares but her eyes are weary, unfocused, until she's roused by her child climbing on a garbage can. It dawns on Fi that she's not the cardinal in snow, but an owl in a tree, hiding in plain sight.

Armed with this new knowledge, her confidence grows. Mid-afternoon, Latisha walks into the store, stops, hands on hips. "Girl, what are you so happy about? You finally kick that man to the curb?"

The mention of Doug reminds her of what she still hasn't done, what she doesn't want to do. She rings up Latisha's candy bar, half-listening to the monologue about her wonderful husband, and knows Latisha would never understand what it's like to be a hare caught in a trap.

When the six o'clock rumbles in, Fi's back in the lost and found. There's no luggage among the sunglasses, key rings, and umbrellas, but there is a tattered copy of *Harry Potter*. She picks it up, thumbs the worn pages, wishing there were a platform nine and three-quarters she could disappear onto.

When she arrives home, Doug looks up from his chair, sees her hands are empty, and scowls. A string of rude names follows her into the bedroom. She opens the closet, pulls the Harry Potter book from her jacket, and slips it inside the overnight bag she has yet to return.

She backs out of the closet right into Doug.

He grabs her by the arm and jerks her around.

Every fiber of her body goes on high alert.

"I ask for one lousy thing and you steal a book?"

"No. No, it was in the lost and found."

"Can't you ever do anything right? Can't you ever think of anyone but yourself?" His grip on her arm tightens.

The pain to her flesh is nothing compared to the bruising inside.

"Tomorrow," she says. "I'll do it tomorrow."

It's raining—a cold, dreary, relentless rain. Doug is sullen when she leaves. His mood will last through the weekend or more. She doesn't think she can stand it any longer.

The trains run late all day. The station's cold, the passengers few. To keep busy, Fi helps Wally collect trash from the bins and load it onto a cart. Worry has settled between her shoulder blades. She shouldn't have waited so long. She should have stolen a bag when the station was full. She should have told Doug to come steal one himself. She should step out onto the platform and board the next train to anywhere...

She hears him before she sees him. A man yelling obscenities, wearing a black trench coat, waves his ticket in the air. He's standing at Latisha's window, threatening to have her fired, as though the train's failure to arrive on time is her fault. A small crowd forms, including Dugard, the station manager, who steps in front of Latisha.

But it's what's on the outskirts of the crowd, separated from its owner, which has Fi's attention. A black duffel bag.

She tells Wally she needs the restroom and walks toward the small throng. When she's two feet from the bag, the man starts yelling, pushing at the crowd, searching for the bag that is no longer at his side.

Fi stoops down, grabs the handles, and walks into the ladies room. She shoves the bag into the empty garbage can, tears off a half dozen paper towels from the machine and tosses them on top of the bag. Her mouth is dry and her hands shake. She grips the edge of the sink to still them. The restroom door opens. Looking into the mirror, her eyes connect with Latisha's. For a moment neither moves, then Fi lets go of the sink, and faces her co-worker.

"You okay?" she asks.

"Girl, I was about to ask you the same thing. You look ill."

Fi glances at her reflection. Her face is pale, her skin tight. She shrugs. "Not feeling so hot. How about that guy? Did he leave?"

"That crazy drama queen? First, he tries to blame me for the train schedule then he's screaming someone ran off with his luggage. Dugard offered to take his number, said we'd call if we found his luggage, but he stormed out onto the platform. The four-oh-five just pulled in. He's their problem now." She checked her makeup in the mirror, washed and dried her hands, and threw the towels into the garbage. "Girl, you really don't look good."

Fi waves her concern away. Resisting the urge to look in the garbage, she follows Latisha back onto the floor. She doesn't leave the shop again until her replacement on the night shift arrives. Waiting in the restroom until the day crew leaves, she digs through a layer of trash and lifts out the black bag. It's heavier than she remembers.

The rain has stopped. Clouds hang low, and the earth is damp and musky. She tosses the bag in her car and starts the engine. Somewhere else in the parking lot another car starts. A young couple walks behind her car. She waits until they reach the station entrance before pulling out. Her hands are clammy on the wheel. There's a sourness in her belly. Her eyes keep drifting from the road to the bag on the seat next to her.

The twenty-minute drive feels like an hour, but she finally turns into their driveway. Before she can cut the engine, Doug opens the front door, the houselights forming a fuzzy halo around him. He yells something to her, swaying against the iron railing.

She rolls down the window. "What?"

"Beer run," he slurs. "Need to make a beer run." He stumbles on the bottom step, straightens, and heads toward her.

"I'll go."

"I can drive."

"Have you eaten? I'll pick up the beer and some burgers."

He curls his lip, leans on the car door, but the argument leaves him when he spots the bag on the passenger seat.

She puts her hand on it.

"Baby, you did it." His breath is foul. "What's in it? Let me see."

"I haven't opened it."

He reaches across her.

"Not here." She pushes him back. "Take it inside." She glances at the neighbor's house, relieved to see their blinds are closed.

He opens the door, and she hands him the bag. "I'll get the beer and the food."

"Yes." He grins. "We're going to celebrate. This is just the beginning." He kisses her hard on the mouth. "I'll wait for you to open it."

She knows he won't, but she doesn't care. She doesn't want to know what's inside. She shuts the door and shifts to reverse, almost hitting a dark car parked at the curb. She doesn't remember it being there when she pulled in, but then she wasn't paying much attention.

The liquor store is empty. Wanda, the owner, recognizes her and asks how she's been. Fi considers telling her the truth, instead, she lays her last twenty on the counter.

"What's this?" Wanda picks up Annie's card.

Forgetting she stuffed it in her back pocket, Fi snatches it back. "Nothing, a note to myself." Her thumb strokes the card. She watches Wanda ring up her purchase and wonders if she believes in a world that is honest and good.

Fat raindrops hit the windshield as she pulls back into the driveway. The front door is open. Light spills out onto the stoop. She grabs her purchases and makes a run for it. The television is blasting. At first she thinks the room is empty, then she sees him, Doug lying on the floor near the kitchen. Blood seeps from a wound in his stomach and another across his bicep.

"Doug." She drops the beer and food at the door, moves cautiously toward him.

His eyes open, fill with loathing. "You did this." He draws

a painful breath. "This is all your fault."

"What?" She looks around the familiar room. "What happened?"

"The bag you took...full of stolen money...followed you home...cut me...took the money..." He tries to move, to come toward her, but falls heavily back.

She remembers the man at the train station, his frantic search for his bag, his refusal to leave his number, the dark car parked at their curb. Did she do this? She starts to apologize then stops herself. "You wanted me to steal a bag."

His lip curls. "You never could do anything right."

She backs away, his words like a physical punch. She's not sure when she made the decision. Maybe at the liquor store, maybe when she first put on the red chemise. Or maybe it was the card in her pocket, or seeing Doug's blood puddle on the floor.

In the bedroom, she collects a few things, essentials, stuffs them in the overnight bag. She takes the cash Doug keeps in his nightstand, considers it money due. She walks past the six-pack and greasy burger bag dropped at the door.

When he realizes she's leaving, a flood of curses follows her into the night. She doesn't know if he'll live or die, or if she cares. She arrives at the station with minutes to spare. The girl at the ticket counter is new to her, which is just as well. She buys a one-way ticket to Tennessee. In the distance, she can hear the eight o'clock coming down the track.

She hurries to the lost and found, pulls the copy of *Harry Potter* from the bag, and places it back on the shelf. She makes her way to the platform as the hissing wheels roll to a stop. With Annie's bag in hand, she boards the last train out.

The Haunted Hotel
Chris Grabenstein

Zack Jennings did not come to Canada looking for ghosts.

But they were definitely looking for him.

Zack, who was eleven, had traveled to Toronto with his stepmother, Judy Magruder Jennings. She was a world famous children's author whose Curiosity Cat books had been turned into a musical that was about to be given a pre-Broadway tryout at the Royal Alexandra Theatre in downtown Toronto.

Zack's dad—who had to work—and his dad's dog Zipper—who hated even thinking about cargo crates—stayed home in North Chester, Connecticut. Zack's school was on its spring break so he was totally psyched to make the trip north with his famous stepmom.

Canada became the first stamp in Zack's brand new passport because Judy requested it when they passed through customs at the airport.

"It'll be his first souvenir!" she told the obliging Canadian Borders Services Agent.

"Be sure to get some maple syrup, too, eh?" the agent said to Zack with a wink.

"Yes, sir," replied Zack.

"And maybe a loonie and a toonie."

"Oh-kay."

"Those are coins," explained Judy.

"Gotcha."

Once they'd cleared customs, Zack and Judy hailed a cab and headed to their hotel, which was practically right next door to the theatre.

"I can walk to rehearsals," said Judy. She still had to do some "minor rewrites and tweaks" on the script, even though the musical had already been staged at the Hanging Hill Summer Stock theater in Connecticut—a production that almost ended in disaster when the wackaloon director opened a doorway for demons down in the basement.

"I just hope no ghosts want to see the show this time," said Zack.

Judy nodded. "It's been rough, huh? Your 'gift?'"

Zack shrugged. He'd sort of gotten used to the fact that he could see ghosts and, more importantly, they could see him. That meant, if they had left behind any unfinished business on earth, they sometimes asked Zack to finish it for them.

"With great power comes great responsibility," Zack joked, quoting Uncle Ben Parker from his favorite *Spider-Man* movie.

Judy laughed. "Well, if any ghosts show up, tell them you're taking the week off from being responsible. You're here on vacation to have fun."

"And to eat maple stuff."

"Exactly."

The taxi dropped them off at the Twittleham Plaza, a very grand, old school hotel. A bellman helped them drag their rolling suitcases into the lobby.

"May I be off assistance?" asked a ramrod stiff man behind the check-in desk.

Judy and Zack stepped up to the counter.

"Yes. We're checking in. Judy Magruder Jennings?"

"Of course." The man behind the counter clacked a couple keys on his computer.

Then he frowned. His pencil-thin mustache drooped on his upper lip.

"Do you have a reservation?" he asked.

"Yes. We're with the Curiosity Cat company…"

"Curiosity Cat?" said the man, whose name, according to the brass tag pinned to his dark suit, was Jacques. "Are you here for a pet food convention?"

"No," said Judy with a nervous chuckle. "It's a show. We're at the Royal Alexandra Theatre. Just across the square."

"Indeed," sniffed the man behind the counter. He clacked a few more keys. Squinted at his screen.

"I have a confirmation number," said Judy, digging through a jumble of papers in her shoulder bag.

"I'm certain you do," said the man, sounding super snooty and semi-French. "However, it seems your reservation doesn't start until Tuesday. Today, as you must be aware, is Sunday."

"No," said Judy.

"Yes, it is. I have a calendar if you care to consult it."

"I meant to say, 'No. The reservation is for today.' This is when the production company told me to be here. Today. Sunday. They made the reservation."

"I'm very sorry if this causes you any inconvenience, madam. However, there is nothing further I can do. We are fully committed, until, of course, Tuesday. You have a very nice suite on Tuesday. One of our best."

"Can you give us a not-so-nice suite for today?" Judy asked sweetly.

"Please?" said Zack, eagerly. "This is my first trip to Canada."

"Is it?" said the man, sounding not in the least bit interested in any of Zack's trips—first, last or in-between. "Well, I'm sorry it's off to such an inauspicious start."

Judy found her cell phone. "Maybe you can talk to Ian Trembley. He's with the producers…"

"I'm sorry," said the man, looking down his nose at Zack and Judy. "Unless this Mr. Trembley also produces magic shows and can, somehow, magically make an empty room appear, there is nothing more he or I can do. Perhaps you'd like to discuss making alternate lodging arrangements with Mr. Trembley? Until Tuesday, of course."

The man name-tagged Jacques smiled. It looked like his lips were pinching his face.

"I'll do that," said Judy, sounding a lot less cheery than usual. "By the way, I didn't catch your name."

"Jacques," said the man behind the counter, tapping his nametag. He bowed slightly. "Sorry I could not be of further assistance." He signaled to whomever was waiting behind Zack and Judy. "Next?"

"Can I speak to your manager?" Now Judy sounded sort of mad.

"You already have."

Frère Jacques flicked a thin business card out of his vest pocket. Zack and Judy read what was printed there: "Jacques Boulanger, Manager."

"Next?" He signaled, once again, to the guest waiting behind Zack and Judy.

The man stepped forward. They moved out of the way.

"Don't worry, hon," Judy told Zack. "We'll find another hotel."

They trundled their suitcases over to a cluster of sofas and chairs so Judy could call the Curiosity Cat production company. Zack sat down in a fancy chair with all sorts of lumpy padding and flipped through an Official Toronto Tourism Guide he found on top of a glass table.

Judy said "uh-huh" and "I see" a lot into her phone.

Zack read about the Hockey Hall of Fame. And the CN tower. And the Royal Ontario Museum.

After about a dozen more "uh-huh's," Judy ended her call.

"There's some kind of convention in Toronto this week," she said with a sigh. "All of the downtown hotels are booked up. Except…"

"Except what?"

"Well, Mr. Trembly was able to find us a room at the Royal Duke. It's a few blocks west of here. It'd only be for two nights. Today, tomorrow…"

"Great!" said Zack. "Let's go."

"There's one slight problem."

"What?"

"Well, Mr. Trembly says there are rumors…stories…"

"About what?"

"The Royal Duke." Judy scrunched up her face the way she always did before she had to tell Zack bad news. "They say it might be haunted."

Of course they do, thought Zack. Because what would a Zack Jennings vacation be without a few ghosts, ghouls, or goblins?

"I could ask him to keep looking," said Judy. "But rehearsal starts in two hours…"

"With great power comes great responsibility," muttered Zack, grabbing the handle on his rolling suitcase. "Let's go see some Canadian ghosts. Maybe one will be a hockey player or a Mountie. Maybe they'll bring me maple candy…"

Zack and Judy rolled their suitcases down the sidewalk to the creepy old hotel. The bottom right corner of the "D" in the Royal Duke neon had burned out so the sign looked like it was for the Royal Puke.

There weren't any uniformed doormen out front under the dimly lit portico. Zack and Judy had to wrestle their bags through a narrow revolving door into the lobby, which was lined with dark wooden panels soaked with cigar smoke. Murky oil paintings of old-timey guys in white curly wigs hung on the walls. There was ratty red carpet stretching from wall to wall. Musty carpet. It smelled like a wet cat. One that smoked cigars.

"Welcome to the Royal Duke," said the ancient man behind the front desk. He looked like a cadaver wearing an ill-fitting striped suit he'd stolen from a funeral director. "We have you in room 1313." When he said that, thunder clapped and chandeliers flickered.

Seriously. Of course, thunderstorms had been in the forecast. But still...

"Is that one of the haunted rooms?" asked Zack, casually.

The ancient man bristled. "None of our rooms are haunted, young man."

"Sorry," said Judy, resting a gentle hand on Zack's shoulder. "We just heard some stories."

"Well, madam, rest assured, there are no ghosts in any of our rooms." Thunder cracked again. "They're in the hallways."

Zack and Judy rode a rattletrap cage of an elevator up to the thirteenth floor and unpacked their suitcases in 1313 as quickly as they could. They took turns freshening up in the bathroom. Fast. They didn't bother adjusting the thermostat or opening the window shades or checking out the minibar.

"Ready?" asked Judy.

"Ready!" said Zack.

They dashed off to rehearsal at the theatre.

They spent several hours watching the cast sing and dance their way through the slightly revised tale of the world's most curious cat. Then they went out to dinner with Tomasino Carrozza, the hysterically funny clown who played the title character, Curiosity Cat.

Finally, when they absolutely had to, they went back to the Royal Duke Hotel and creaked their way up to the thirteenth floor again in that old-fashioned elevator with the accordion cage door. They stayed up and watched Canadian TV until they both fell asleep—Judy on the bed, Zack, fully clothed, on the couch, with an empty Pringles tube rising up and down on his chest.

Zack's eyes popped open when the very loud, old-fashioned digital alarm clock in the room flicked over from three-twelve to three-thirteen a.m. He heard voices out in the hallway. These weren't guests checking into their rooms after a maple-syrup-soaked night on the town. These were ghosts.

Zack was sure of it.

Because they were moaning. And wailing.

"Mom?" Zack whispered.

Judy snored.

Zack went over to the bed to jostle her leg a little. "Mom?"

She snored louder.

She was completely conked out. Zack would have to investigate the wailing spooks in the hallway alone. Not that Judy would've been all that much help. She couldn't see ghosts. That was Zack's special "gift," one he sometimes wished had come with a receipt so he could take it back for something a little more useful like the ability to sink jump shots from the half-court line.

Zack put on a bathrobe, which, unfortunately, smelled as musty as the carpet.

He creaked open the heavy wooden door hanging on squeaky hinges.

And saw an apparition marching down the corridor.

A young woman. Maybe in her late twenties. She was dressed like people used to dress back in the olden days, the 1990s. She was wearing a brightly colored tracksuit. Her hair had been crimped into tight corkscrew curls. Zack could smell bitter chemicals wafting in her wake.

He could not, however, see her face. Only the back of her head.

"Business or pleasure?" she wailed as she walked. "Business or pleasure?"

"Are you okay?" Zack asked.

The woman slowly, very slowly, turned around.

Her mouth was a weeping red gash. Bubbly pink blood burbled out from between her lips and trickled down the front of her tracksuit jacket. In her hands, she held a blue passport book. It looked like Zack's. Only hers was drizzled with blood splatters.

"I am dead," she announced, coldly. "He killed me." She held up the slim blue book with the American eagle seal on front. "This was my passport...*to murder!*"

Now two children, a boy and a girl, entered the hallway on either side of the woman. They each had a plush stuffed animal dangling from their hands: a moose in a Mountie hat wearing a knit sweater with a bright red Canadian maple leaf embroidered on its chest.

"He killed us, too!" they howled in unison, swinging their stuffed toys like pendulums. "Ret-tub tuna-ep! Ananab!"

Zack wondered if the kids were chanting Canadian First Nations people words. It sure sounded like a foreign language to him.

"Avenge our murders!" cried the woman, who might've been the boy and girl's mother. They were both definitely clinging to the legs of her track pants like she was. "Avenge us, demon slayer! Avenge our deaths!"

Oh-kay, thought Zack. Demon slayer was what some of the ghosts back home in Connecticut called him. He figured word had spread up to the great white north.

"Ret-tub tuna-ep!" said the boy.

"Ananab! Ananab!" said the girl.

"What are you trying to say?" Zack asked the two blank-eyed kids. As he moved closer, he noticed their mouths were thin lines of burbling pink blood, too.

"Ret-tub tuna-ep!" said the boy.

"Ananab!" said the girl.

"Peanut butter and banana?" said Zack, flipping the nonsense words around. He had learned about backward talking kid ghosts by watching an old Stephen King movie called *The Shining* with his dad. He figured it was a rule. Kids haunting hotel hallways had to speak backwards.

The three ghosts pointed to the floor in front of Room 1313. All of a sudden, there was a room service tray sitting there that hadn't been sitting there when Zack stepped out into the hall, otherwise he would've tripped over it.

There was a silver domed plate on the tray.

Zack bent down. The dome rattled, shook, and then hovered over the plate to reveal a glass of ice water, a bowl of tomato soup, and a peanut butter and banana sandwich cut in half. Two large chomps had been bitten into the soft bread on each side. A spoon leaned against the edge of the soup bowl. A butter knife smeared with brown peanut butter lay alongside the plate, which had a frilly R and D inscribed in gold on its curved border.

"Poison!" wheezed the woman.

"Poison!" wailed her children.

"Poison!" they all shrieked together.

The Royal Duke room service tray vanished. So did the women and her two children.

Zack understood his new responsibility.

It was up to him to, somehow, find the poisoner and avenge their murders.

The next morning, Zack and Judy had breakfast at a nearby restaurant called Eggspectation because even the thought of ordering room service kind of creeped Zack out after seeing the disappearing tray act in the hallway.

"You sure you won't be bored at the theatre all day?" asked Judy.

"Probably," said Zack. (There were only so many times he could listen to the same *Curiosity Cat* lyrics about how "there will never be another cat like that" over and over and over again.)

"Do you want to hang at the hotel? Maybe rent an in-room movie or three?"

Zack smiled. "Sounds like a plan."

When they finished their breakfast burgers—eggs and meat

on a bun—Judy headed off to the theater. Zack went back to the hotel.

Not to rent in-room movies; to investigate a murder.

When he pushed his way through the revolving door, he saw that the cadaver was still on duty behind the desk.

"Uh, hi," Zack said, shooting out his hand, the way he'd seen his dad do at backyard barbecues when meeting a stranger. "I'm Zack Jennings. We're in room thirteen-thirteen."

The elderly man smiled. He had very few teeth. And the ones he did have were either pointy or gold. "Yes." He came around the counter to shake Zack's hand. "We met yesterday. When you checked in. I'm Liam Cavendish."

"Pleased to meet you."

They exchanged a few more pleasantries. Mostly about baseball and hockey and why, in Canada, a knitted winter hat was called a "tuque."

"Probably from the French," said Mr. Cavendish.

Zack nodded like he was super interested.

"Soooo," he said, since the ice was broken with the tuque talk, "I think I met your ghosts last night."

The old man nodded. "Woman with two children?"

"Yep. They told me they were poisoned."

"Did they?"

"Yep."

"Strange."

"Why?"

"Belinda Baker and her twins, Billy and Bonnie, don't usually talk to guests."

Wow, thought Zack. Guess I really am special. Whatta gift.

"So, uh, do you know anything about it?" Zack asked.

Mr. Cavendish's eyes narrowed. "June fourteen. Nineteen ninety-two. I was on desk duty that night. Police asked me all sorts of questions. I told them what I will now tell you: The cook did it!"

"Huh?"

"Travis McAllister! He was our chef, back in the day. Ran our restaurant."

The old man flapped his hand toward an empty room on the far side of the lobby. It was filled with dusty round tables and moth-eaten chairs. There was one waitress with a paper hat and doily apron standing guard but nobody eating anything.

"I saw Travis flirting with Mrs. Baker when she and the twins came down for breakfast early that morning. Cheeky little monkey. She rebuffed his entreaties. Rebuffed them most soundly!"

Mr. Cavendish sounded like a British major general with bushy sideburns and a pith helmet that Zack had seen in a movie on TV.

"Did the police arrest the cook?" he asked.

"Not for long. Oh, they hauled him away to the old Bailey in handcuffs, mind you. Locked him up in the hoosegow. Nary a week later, they let him go."

"Was he the one who made them their room service food? The tomato soup? The peanut butter and banana sandwich?"

"Indeed so. He was also, if you ask me, the one who laced the food with arsenic!"

"So why did the police let him go?"

"I'm not certain. Why don't you go ask him?"

"Who?"

"Travis McAllister. He's still a cook, right here in downtown Toronto. You can find him at the Bloor House, a greasy spoon not but two blocks away, for, as they say, the criminal always returns to the scene of the crime. This one never left!"

"What does he look like?" asked Zack, already checking a tourist map for the Bloor House.

"Easy," said Mr. Cavendish. "McAllister will be the

chuffed man with the bald dome working the manky grill and flirting with all the chicky birds seated at the counter!"

Since it was the middle of the morning and Toronto seemed more polite than dangerous, Zack decided to dig a little deeper. He'd go to the Bloor House and talk to the cheeky chef, Travis McAllister.

When Zack stepped into the cafe, the scent of hot corned beef walloped his nose. It was a good smell. Like a greasy mountain of sizzling hot dogs on a grill. A bald man in a soiled apron who had to be Travis McAllister was flirting with two ladies, office workers half his age, who were getting up off their stools.

"Come back this afternoon for high tea, lassies," said McAllister. "We'll be servin' jambusters. Because I am a Manitoba man!"

When the giggling women were gone, Zack sat at the counter. Travis McAllister came over with a green order pad and stubby pencil.

"What can I get you, squirt?"

"Um, what's a jambuster?"

"A jelly doughnut—if we were back home in Manitoba, which we ain't, eh?"

"Right."

"So, what'll it be, squirt?"

"How about some information?" Zack said, because he'd heard a movie detective say that in a shady diner scene just like the one Zack was suddenly in. (Yes. Zack and his dad watched a lot movies.)

"'Bout what?"

"The death of Belinda, Bonnie, and Billy Baker."

"What? That's ancient history."

"I know. I have to write a paper about their poisoning for school."

Mr. McAllister gave him a look. It wasn't a nice one, either.

Zack took a deep breath. "I talked to Mr. Cavendish at the Royal Duke Hotel…"

Mr. McAllister laughed and shook his head. "That old fart is still alive then, is he?"

"Yes, sir," said Zack. He didn't add "barely."

"He tell you I poisoned them people, eh?"

"Sort of."

Mr. McAllister shook his head. "Wait here, squirt."

He disappeared into the kitchen and came back with a yellowed newspaper clipping sealed inside plastic.

"Had this thing laminated. Mr. Cavendish has been spreading the same ridiculous rumors about me since nineteen ninety-two. It wasn't me, kid. The police never found no evidence suggesting it might be. Newspaper said it was the rats."

"Huh?"

"There was arsenic in the water on account of the rat poison they spread all over the hotel. My only crime? Putting a glass of tap water on that tray with the sandwich and soup."

He slid the laminated article across the sticky, stain-splattered counter.

Zack read about the rats found in the hotel's water tank. They'd eaten arsenic-tainted bait that an exterminator had tucked into all the hotel's many nooks and crannies. Rat poison "made the vermin extremely thirsty." To slake their thirst, the rats leapt into the water tower and drowned. As they decomposed, the arsenic in their bodies polluted the water in the hotel's cistern.

"So what do you want to eat, squirt?" asked Mr. McAllister.

Zack could taste a hint of vomit in the back of his mouth. Reading about poisoned rats drowning in a hotel water tank will do that to a guy.

"Um, nothing…right now…maybe in a second…"

Mr. McAllister snatched the laminated newspaper story from under Zack's nose.

"Pretty lady, that Belinda Baker," he said. "Hated to see her go before, you know, we could get to know each other a wee bit better." He gave Zack a skeevy wink. "Of course our bell hop felt even worse."

"How come?"

"Because the pretty lady was his ex-wife. Came up from Buffalo to win him back. But Jack moved up here to start a new life. One without a wife or two bawling brats."

Feeling like he had to order something, Zack had a bacon cheeseburger, which had normal bacon on it, even though they were in Canada. He'd been expecting Canadian bacon.

That afternoon, he hung out with Judy at the theatre.

That night, they went out to a nice dinner with the cast, came back to the spooky hotel, watched some TV, munched some more Pringles, and, once again fell asleep. Judy on the bed. Zack on the couch.

At exactly three-thirteen a.m. Zack, who was sort of half-snoozing with one eye on the digital alarm clock, heard wailing out in the hall. This time, he didn't even bother trying to wake Judy.

He stepped out into the hallway in his robe.

Belinda, Bonnie, and Billy Baker were there again. The kids were holding their souvenir moose dolls. The mom was holding her passport booklet. They waited expectantly for Zack to say something.

He could tell: they were counting on him, big time.

"It was the rats," he told them. "They ate poison, hopped into the hotel's water tank and poisoned the drinking water."

The instant he said it out loud, Zack heard how stupid it sounded.

If the dying rats poisoned the water tank why were the three Bakers the only victims? Why didn't everybody else in the hotel die?

The two children turned their backs on Zack.

"Sorry," he said. "My theory might be a little off…"

Mrs. Baker motioned for Zack to follow her.

He did. Mostly because he was feeling bad for jumping to such a stupid conclusion. Plus, in his experience, ghosts couldn't really harm people. They could just scare you into hurting yourself.

Mrs. Baker and her twins led Zack to an exit door.

He opened it. They were in a stairwell. There were steps going up and steps going down. Pipes and conduits carrying steam and water and electricity were bolted to the naked cinderblock walls.

Mrs. Baker pointed at a bend where one of the pipes curved to duck beneath the staircase riser.

Zack looked to where she was pointing.

If he squinted, he could make out something gray and lumpy tucked between the top of the pipe elbow and the staircase. He climbed up the stairs, knelt down, reached around, and, after a couple of grunts, tugged the cloth wad out from its hiding place.

It was a bundled-up, soiled napkin, gray with dust and lint. A frilly R and D were stitched near the hem. Zack unrolled the cloth. Inside were a butter knife and soup spoon.

The murder weapons?

Had someone stirred arsenic into the tomato soup and spread it across the peanut butter on the sandwich? Had they then wrapped up the evidence and hidden it here in the stairwell?

"Who did this?" Zack asked, turning around to face the three ghosts.

But they had vanished.

They couldn't give him any more clues. Crimes in the mortal realm could only be solved by mortals. It was another ghost rule.

Solving this particular murder was up to Zack.

The next morning, he walked with Judy to the theatre. He had the antique napkin wrapped around the spoon and knife safely secured in a plastic bag—the liner from the hotel room's ice bucket.

"You're awfully quiet," said Judy.

"Thinking," Zack mumbled.

"About what?"

So Zack told her everything about his two encounters with Belinda, Bonnie, and Billy Baker.

"Why didn't you wake me up?"

"Because you were snoring. Plus, you can't see ghosts. And they weren't very scary. I just wish I could figure out who poisoned them."

"Well, maybe it *was* that creepy cook," said Judy. "The one who fed you the rat story."

"Maybe. But, the more I think about it, the more I think it might've been the ex-husband. Jack. Jack Baker. He was a bellhop at the hotel. That means he would've carried the tray up to the room. He would've had a passkey. So he could've gone in and switched out the knife and spoon. I think his fingerprints will be all over the stuff I found in the stairwell."

"We should take them to the police," suggested Judy. "There's no statute of limitations on murder cases."

"Definitely," said Zack. "But, um, can we eat first? I'm sort of starving."

"Sure. How about a chocolate croissant?" Judy gestured toward a window pane with "Boulanger" painted in black and gold letters.

"They have pastries?"

"Sure," said Judy. "'Boulanger' is French for baker."

And that's when Jack figured everything out.

They went to the nearest Toronto Police Service station. Zack told them his theory. They took his evidence and examined it.

Judy and Zack went to the *Curiosity Cat* rehearsals and

dinner. They watched TV, ate Pringles, and slept through the night.

Zack had no ghostly visitors at three-thirteen a.m.

The next morning, Tuesday, they went back to the Twittleham Plaza Hotel to check in to their suite.

"Ah, Madam Magruder-Jennings," said the snooty man behind the front desk. "Bienvenue. Welcome."

"Thank you, Mr. Baker," said Zack.

"Pardon moi?"

"You can cut the French act, Jack. Everybody knows you're really Jack Baker, not 'Jacques Boulanger!' You poisoned your ex-wife and your own kids."

"Ha! That is the most preposterous..."

That's when the two police detectives, who had been pretending to read newspapers, the way they always do in the movies, folded up their papers and marched to the front desk.

"Jack Baker?" said the lead detective, flashing his badge. "You are under arrest for the murders of Belinda, Bonnie, and William Baker. Do you understand? You have the right to retain and instruct counsel without delay..."

Zack and Judy stepped aside while the police read Mr. Baker his Canadian rights.

Then they told him about the lab results they'd received that morning and the fingerprints they'd found all over the knife and spoon. They mentioned they might need a DNA sample, too.

"I had to kill them!" they heard Mr. Baker protest. "For my career. I came to Toronto to start a new life. But Belinda had to come up here, looking for me. Dragging along those two sniveling little brats from Buffalo..."

As he confessed, he didn't sound so French.

And Zack realized why the ghost of Belinda Baker had called her slim blue book her "passport to murder." It got her into Canada. It also got her dead.

After the police hauled Mr. Baker/Boulanger away, a very

helpful—and slightly embarrassed—concierge checked Zack and Judy into the Twittleham Plaza Hotel.

"Says here you were supposed to check in on Sunday," he said, consulting his computer screen.

"That's what I told Mr. Boulanger!" said Judy.

"Must've been a computer glitch," said Zack. "You know—a ghost in the machine?"

Judy smiled. "Riiight."

She understood what Zack meant.

Somehow—maybe by messing with their own electro-magnetic auras, or manipulating the ether or doing something similarly mysterious—the Baker ghosts had changed Judy and Zack's reservations inside the Twittleham Plaza's computer system.

Because they needed Zack Jennings, the American "demon slayer" to stay at the Royal Duke until he solved their murder mystery.

And maybe that's also why, when the nice concierge showed Zack and Judy their rooms, there was a "Thank You" gift waiting on each twin bed: A stuffed animal tucked up against the headboard.

A moose, of course.

Wearing a Mountie hat and a knit sweater with a bright red maple leaf embroidered on the chest.

Journey into the Dark
Marilyn Kay

Amira watched, her dark eyes wide and her body transfixed in terror, as two more youths—sputtering adenoidal expletives—hunched into wooden crates. Then it was her brother Adnan's turn.

She stared at her own wooden box and wondered how she could scrunch into it. At fourteen she was slight and only four feet ten inches, but the crate was so small.

The burly man gave her a push. "In! Now!"

The other man, Ralph, leaned over, patted her shoulder and casually brushed her chest. "Arlind, don't be so rough with the goods."

When they nailed down the top, it took all of Amira's courage not to scream out. Then they hoisted her up into the green and white lorry and wedged the container with the others jammed among the crated furniture.

The rear doors swung shut, the motor rumbled into gear, and they jounced toward the Eurotunnel.

Crouched in her carton and plunged totally into blackness, Amira wondered if her brother now regretted paying four thousand euros—nearly all the money they had left—to get them into the United Kingdom.

She had wanted to stay among the Syrian community in Oberhausen. But Adnan didn't like Germany. He insisted they could find work at Sayid's mother's restaurant in Cardiff.

Their journey started after their father died in the bombing at the University of Aleppo in January 2013. Overwhelmed with grief, her mother decided they should move to Beirut. They lived there for nearly two years until tightened immigration restrictions forced them to try Germany.

Then further disaster hit Amira. Her mother and little sister drowned when the dinghy capsized on their way to Greece. She and Adnan had survived, rescued by fishermen. After that, they managed to catch trains where they could and walk, wherever they couldn't, to Oberhausen before making it to the nightmarish jungle of Calais. Calais. Where men tried to do more than touch her breasts.

It was her brother's friend Sayid who had lured them into this predicament. His Welsh father had come as an architect and archaeologist, and had fallen in love with the country and Sayid's mother. His father had also perished in the bombing, but he and his mother got British passports and moved to Wales. Sayid had put them in touch with Arlind and Ralph, who did a furniture run between Amiens and England for Burrows Antiques of Gloucester.

The lorry slowed down and then began inching forward, before coming to a stop. This must be the Coquelles freight station. *Ya Allah.* Let them not search this truck.

The lorry started up again, edging into the train's loading wagon. The engine shut off.

Relieved, Amira whispered, "*Subhanallah!* We are on the shuttle."

The cab doors opened and shut, but no one came near the back. It seemed ages until the shuttle clattered through the chunnel toward Folkestone and freedom.

Cramped, thirsty and numb with cold, Amira could barely lift her head when they pried the top off her crate. They were in a layby somewhere in the middle of the countryside. As her eyes adjusted to the bright sun, she realized it must be close to noon. Then Adnan touched her shoulder and offered her a bottle of water.

"*Alhamdulillah*, Adnan, you are safe!" She cried, hugging him with all the strength her aching limbs would allow.

"Yes. We are in England now," he said, smiling broadly. He turned to Ralph and asked, "How long will it be to get to Cardiff?"

Ralph nudged Arlind and sniggered. "We're going to Gloucester, you pillock."

"Gloucester? But Sayid's restaurant is in Cardiff."

"There's no restaurant in Cardiff, you arsehole. Sayid works for the big house now. And that's where all of you are going," Ralph's lip curled as he glared serially at each of the six travelers.

The other four looked at one another and muttered as Arlind spoke rapidly in a nasal language.

"You must be wrong!" protested Adnan. "Sayid texted me this morning to say see you in Cardiff."

"Yeah. Well if you see Sayid you can tell that shite-faced little twat he's a liar. Tell him that for me, too."

Arlind began to laugh as Ralph continued, "Yeah. There's a special place waiting in hell for all Judases, right, Arlind?"

His eyes narrowing to slits, Arlind stopped abruptly and spat.

Fists clenched, brown eyes blazing, Adnan pulled himself up to his full five-foot-eight-inch, sixteen-year-old self and strode forward. "Leave us here, then. We'll find our own way," he demanded.

At that, Ralph raised his brows and glanced at Arlind. Arlind reached into his jacket and pulled out a gun. He walked up to Adnan and jabbed his chest. "You will do as you are told. Otherwise, it's back in your crate, you, *cope muti.*"

The youths chuckled nervously before quickly looking down to avoid Arlind's withering glare.

Amira grabbed Adnan's arm and said quietly, "We will do as you say."

He shook loose, but then put his arm protectively around Amira's shoulder.

"So. We understand each other now," said Ralph, all the while leering at Amira. "If you need to use the loo, it's over there at the service station. You've got five minutes and then I come and get you."

Amira stood her ground a moment before unsteadily walking to the service station. She shut and locked the door. Then grabbing the sink, she sobbed into the broken mirror. Realizing she had no time for tears, she washed her face and readjusted her hijab over her neck and chest. She got back just as Ralph started out to fetch her.

Arlind had already martialed the youths back into the truck bed, where they found places to perch amidst the crates. Adnan climbed in and held out his hand to Amira. Ralph, his hands crawling down her body, lifted her up to her brother.

"We've got a four-hour drive, so make yourselves comfortable." With that he slammed the rear doors shut.

The fresh air had awakened Amira's senses. Inside she smelled the scent of wood and polish and a heavy odor of sweaty fear.

She curled herself against her brother's shoulder. Silent tears cascaded down her cheeks, dampening his jacket. He lifted his arm to cradle her and spoke into the darkness. "I will get us out of this. I promise."

Muffled jabbering from the other four, combined with the purr of the engine on the motorway, lulled her into a fitful sleep.

She awoke to the swing of the rear doors.

"Anyone want to take a piss, better do it now. This is the last stop before Gloucester." Ralph began throwing bottles of water into the truck bed for them to catch.

"What about food?" Adnan asked.

"No food until we get there. I don't want puking in my lorry."

The others had already managed to scramble out. Adnan jumped down and caught Amira.

"You go one at a time. The loo's behind those bushes," cackled Ralph.

Arlind came around the other side of the truck brandishing his gun. "*Në një kohë. Shkojnë prapa shkurre.*"

"I'll take her," said Adnan.

"You fucking won't. I said one at a time."

Amira pulled all ninety pounds of herself up and with a fierce scowl at Ralph, said emphatically. "I'll go first."

She strode back, head high, her hijab still wrapped in folds covering her breasts.

As soon as she appeared, her brother headed out. As they passed each other he nodded. A faint smile touched her lips, but she didn't break her stride. She would show Ralph that she was not one to be trifled with. She stood, back against a rear door of the lorry, until Adnan returned.

By then, the others had gotten the message and, filing in front of her, took their turns behind the bushes.

Amira surveyed her surroundings. They were clearly on a minor road. Sheep grazed on grassy hillsides dotted with stands of trees and, on their side, a jagged bank of thorny bushes intertwined with the delicate pink and yellow of honeysuckle. The sweet smell wafted in the air, clearing her nostrils of the reek in the truck. The light was still brilliant. Maybe two hours to go before they reached their destination?

Arlind pointed to the rear of the lorry and waved his hands. "In! *Nxito!*"

Adnan grabbed Amira around the waist and hoisted her up into the lorry.

The doors slammed shut and they were off again.

Her brother retreated into his own thoughts, so she began fantasizing about Gloucester. Would it be a big city? Where would she go to school? All she'd seen so far was sheep and countryside.

The lorry crept more slowly now. Would this ride ever end?

"Shh, Amira," Adnan spoke softly, putting a finger to his lips. "We aren't the only cargo being smuggled into England. There is white powder leaking from one of the furniture crates. Sayid and these men are trafficking drugs. We are but small change compared to the real money. I will find a way out of this, *Insha'allah*. But we must be careful."

When the doors finally swung open, the light was waning. Amira looked around. This was Gloucester? It looked more like a farmyard.

"*Nxito! Nxito!*" barked Arlind, motioning with his gun.

They scrambled out, her brother gently lifting her to the ground. Over to one side they could see a grand stone house, a yellow stucco edifice trimmed with black wood, gatehouse castle towers, and other assorted buildings. They were parked by a low stone structure that looked like a stable, but there were no animals in sight.

Then she saw two older people approaching, one a tall, sandy-haired man of about fifty and a blonde-haired woman with aristocratic bearing.

"Leave those two Albanians here," the man pointed to two brawny youths, "and take the others into the barracks."

Adnan stepped forward. "I cannot leave my sister."

The woman glowered at him, then turned an appraising eye on Amira. "So this is what you brought me?" she said. "Come here. Let me have a closer look." She examined Amira with a piercing stare. "How old are you?"

"I turned fourteen in March."

"You speak English well."

"My father taught architecture at the University of Aleppo. He made sure we both learned to speak English."

"What's your name, girl?"

"Amira, if you please."

"Can you cook?"

"Yes. My mother was an excellent cook."

"Hmm." The blonde lady continued to assess Amira. "Then come with me. But you'll have to lose that veil. I can't abide anyone who covers herself up like that."

Amira gladly took off her scarf and shook out her long, ebony hair.

Her mother had worn a scarf only for prayers. It was Adnan who made her wear the hijab. He said uncovered hair was immodest and provocative. Now that she was in England, she could be free. But she did not want to be a cook. She wanted to go to school and become an architect like her father.

Adnan began to follow.

The sandy-haired man pointed and snapped, "Take him to the barracks with the others."

"With pleasure," sneered Ralph and shoved Adnan nearly to the ground.

"Those two can unload the furniture and store it in the Great Hall. I'll meet you back for tea, Caroline."

Amira turned to look after Adnan. *Ya Allah* keep Adnan safe.

Caroline's tight voice called her to attention. "Hurry up, Amira, before I change my mind. I expect your full attention and prompt obedience if you are to stay here."

Amira followed, willing herself not to look back.

Caroline brought her into the kitchen. Oak-paneled cupboards covered two walls, copper pots hung from an overhead beam over the central island, and a large fireplace with a spit dominated one wall. Amira gaped in awe and trepidation at its capaciousness and modern appliances—some she had never seen.

"This is where you'll cook. And your first duty today is to make tea for Reggie and me. I will quickly show you your other duties and where you will stay. Then you must come back to make our tea. Understood?"

Amira nodded, "Yes."

"Lady Caroline is the proper way to address me. And...Sir Reginald is my husband."

"Yes, Lady Caroline."

"Good. Now come with me and I'll show you the rest of the house and explain your duties."

As they quickly moved through the mansion, Lady Caroline detailed the cleaning and polishing that she expected. The first floor was a construction zone. "We are having extensive renovations. You must clean these rooms every evening and keep the stairs and ground floor free of dust. Here is your room."

Amira hesitantly stepped into the room. It was certainly the smallest of the bedrooms, but the bed looked comfy and the room had its own bathroom!

"There are some clothes in the wardrobe. They are probably too big, but you'll have to make do until I have them altered. I want no jeans and make sure you wear an apron when serving and cooking. Now get cleaned up, dressed and be back in the kitchen by ten to four."

Amira felt she had fallen into a fantasy. How could they treat her so well, when her brother was thrust into a barn with other men?

At precisely ten to four, she hurried into the kitchen, her hair tied back and wearing a black dress with a white collar and white apron.

"You listen better than your brother," noted Lady Caroline and proceeded to instruct Amira on what was expected for tea.

By the time Amira had cleared the tea, prepared dinner and washed dishes, mopped the stairs and areas where the workmen had been, all she wanted was to fall into bed. As she washed out her underwear, she realized she had no sleepwear. Then she saw her pack she thought was lost. "*Ashokrulillah,*" she murmured. Then thought of Adnan. "Please keep him safe."

The days spun into months. Amira grew more proficient at her duties, but there was always more to do. All the while, every time she passed by a window, she looked for Adnan. The men working in and on the house turned out to be all Albanians. He was nowhere to be found in any work team she saw.

It was now high summer, but she'd barely had time to enjoy the balmy weather. Sometimes Ralph and Arlind would appear with more crates to roll into the long building they called the Great Hall, with its grand, pointed windows blocked to the sun. Sometimes furniture appeared in the newly painted upstairs rooms. More often than not, though, she feared, the furniture was drugs.

One August morning as she clipped herbs from the garden for the night's meal, a figure jumped from behind, clasped his hand over her mouth and dragged her behind a bush. "*Oskoti.* Hush." he whispered. Adnan spun her around and put a finger to her lips. "Meet me in the black and yellow house tonight at ten o'clock. Bring a torch, but don't use it." Then he vanished.

Amira stood gasping. In a matter of seconds, her thoughts had raced from terror to joy. Adnan was here and she would see him tonight, *Insha'allah.*

Dressed all in black, Amira stole away to the black-timbered and yellow-painted building with its odd, attached dovecote turret. As soon as she arrived, the door opened and Adnan pulled her inside. "You have the torch?"

"Yes."

"Good. Keep it off. Hang onto me. We are going up the stairs." At the top, he led her along a wide corridor illuminated by moonlight filtering through the leaded glass windows toward a smaller staircase. He stopped to feel the paneling on the wall. Then motioned to where he was looking.

"Turn on your torch here."

Amira pointed her torch into a dusky black opening. It was a round chamber inside the dovecote.

"Point the torch down. There are chinks in the walls that let the light out," Adnan said as they stepped into the room. Then he shut the panel, moved farther in and sat down on the cold, wooden floor.

The room smelled dank and slightly like caged birds, but the faint cooing emanated from the floor above.

Amira knelt by her brother and clasped him. "I've prayed every day that you were safe," she sobbed.

He let her cry for a moment longer then said firmly, "Enough. We must talk."

"But where have you been? Why did you wait so long to find me?"

"They put me to work in their landscape team. The only reason I was able to reach you is that it was my turn to water the hash plants in the hall. I have watched and waited, until I knew you were alone.

"Amira, this is an evil place. Anyone angering the keepers gets hung by his wrists in a black pit in that gatehouse over there. Last week, they didn't pull Jovan back up. They unclasped the manacles and let him fall to the ground. Then they closed the trap and let him scream in darkness. When they came to get him the next morning, he was half mad and could only babble and drool for days."

"They have not done that to you, have they?" her quaking voice terrified he would say yes.

Adnan shook his head. "But things are getting worse. Men come and go. I think most are sent to work, but I'm not sure where. Some may become part of the trafficking team. I've seen a few girls your age, too," he spoke the last words almost in a hiss.

"Tomorrow night can you be ready to run?"

"But where will we go?"

"We will walk in the stream to fool the dogs. Then make our way into the hills, away from roads. We meet here at ten. Bring some food and water for us. You still have your pack?"

"Yes."

"*Assalamu Alaikum*. Go in peace until tomorrow night, Amira."

They embraced tightly. Then slipped back to their places.

Much to Amira's relief, Sir Reginald and Lady Caroline went off that morning to London for an extended weekend.

Despite their departure, the place bubbled with commotion. With house renovations nearing completion, she saw several of the workmen herded onto a pickup truck and carted away. An hour afterwards, a white van appeared at the Great Hall, loaded up and drove off, but only after a flurry of shouted activity around the hall and the barracks.

Ya Allah! Give me strength this night for our escape.

Dressed in her old clothes and carrying her pack, she slipped out under an overcast sky. Without the moon, she could barely discern shapes and had to watch her footing. She got to the dovecote building and groped up the stairs. Tracing her hand along the wall, she headed to the small staircase, bumped her head under the steps and felt along the panel until it clicked inward. Turning on her torch, she slipped inside. Her brother had not yet arrived. She shut the panel, sat down and waited.

Amira dozed. At midnight she jolted awake. Adnan had not come. Panicked, she found her way back to her room and cried herself to sleep.

A week later, Amira finally mustered enough courage to ask Lady Caroline if it might be possible to see Adnan sometime. Lady Caroline scrutinized Amira's beseeching outstretched hands and misted eyes.

"I'll speak to Reg–Sir Reginald."

"Thank you, Lady Caroline."

Three days later, while she was serving tea, Sir Reginald

said, "I'm afraid, Amira, it's not possible for you to see your brother. We had to...uh...send him...away."

Amira's hands shook so much she nearly dropped the tray she held. She put it down and said with as steady a voice as possible. "Away? Please, Sir Reginald, please tell me where."

"That's not...possible," he said as he continued to stir his tea. "It appears your brother's behavior was a tad irregular. So we couldn't keep him." Sir Reginald looked up at her, his eyes hardened and his tone deliberately harsh, "You know how Lady Caroline and I cannot tolerate irregularity, Amira."

Amira nodded, her eyes averted and said breathily, "I understand. Thank you, Sir Reginald." She curtseyed, picked up the tray and left.

She was shaking so hard, she barely made it to the kitchen without dropping anything before rushing to retch in the sink. *Ya Allah*! Do not let me lose my brother.

By the end of February the manor had taken on a new character. The workmen had left. The barracks had become a stable again. The big house looked like something out of the *Country and Garden* magazines that Lady Caroline often perused over tea. The plants and the boards covering the windows of the immense Great Hall had disappeared. And Amira was left to clean up the mess.

The skunky stench left her breathless and nauseous. Choking, she ran outside, taking great gulps of air until the feeling subsided. Even with the doors left open, she could only endure working inside for short intervals. Yet the hall inside was magnificent, with its tiled floor, beamed vaulted ceiling, carved wooden gallery at one end, and tall pointed windows pouring in light through leaded glass. It reminded her of Christian churches she had been in. It reminded her of Adnan, too. Each day she cleaned, she felt a knife stuck in her breast.

As her birthday approached, Amira noticed she had grown two inches and nearly filled out her maid's clothes.

Sir Reginald and Lady Caroline also seemed different. The

air about them tingled with excitement and expectation. Sir Reginald had taken to exploring the house and the other edifices, including the funny black and yellow one, and making lists. She wondered if he had discovered hers and Adnan's hideaway.

Her birthday passed without their notice and April bloomed. Large swathes of yellow and blue flowers decorated the hillsides and cheered up the garden. Pink and white blossoms blanketed the fruit trees in the orchard, their fragrance perfuming the air. Amira longed for home.

Then, one day, a small, rather battered looking car parked in the courtyard. A tall, bearded man emerged from the driver's side and a young woman with ethereal, honey-kissed red hair emerged from the other. They were back again the next day, touring the house, and Amira served them tea.

Amira thought the woman lovely in chic jeans, the neckline of her fine sweater artfully draped in a floral silk scarf. The woman had smiled at Amira, then looked quizzically at her for a long moment. Each time she served them, the man and woman thanked her. Amira had never thought Americans could be so polite.

The two came back several times and Amira learned their names were Laura and Jack. Sometimes she looked up from her work to see Laura, her brows raised enquiringly, watching Amira. At one point, Laura approached Amira and asked if this was some kind of training as part of her education. Embarrassed, Amira shook her head and moved quickly to another room.

Two days later, Sir Reginald announced they'd sold the manor to the American couple. Amira wanted to dance. Yes! Hello, Laura and Jack!

Sir Reginald looked solemnly at her. "We'd like to take you with us, of course, but we are leaving the country. We've arranged for you to go...elsewhere."

"But I could stay here and work for Laura and Jack," she pleaded.

"Pack your bag, the car will be here soon."

Amira went upstairs and packed. She felt discarded just like her brother had been. They had bought her and now they were selling her, but not to Jack and Laura.

The two men who appeared at the door looked as rough and crude as Ralph and Arlind. One grabbed her arm and practically dragged her into the car, then got in beside her. The locks clicked. As the car started up, he leaned closer, his cigarette and beer breath in her ear, while his other hand began unbuttoning her maid's dress. She struggled and kicked at the driver's seat.

"Oi! No shagging back there while I'm driving," yelled the other man.

"She's a real looker. They shoulda slipped her a peace pill before sending her out with us," grumbled stinky breath.

"You, bloody berk, the boss does his own breaking in."

The car headed toward Cheltenham Racecourse, but turned off on a country lane into a touring park. Here she was forced into a caravan on the park's outskirts. Another girl with dead eyes was already in there, shooting up drugs on one of the beds.

They kicked the girl out and left Amira locked in alone.

"*Ya Allah*! Give me strength to fight Satan."

She picked up the hypodermic needle dropped by the girl and put it into her dress pocket.

The lock clicked open. A dark-haired, beefy man burst into the caravan. He grabbed Amira by the hair and threw her on the narrow bed. She bit, scratched and kicked.

He kept punching her; then with his hand under her chin, he shoved her head down on the pillow, and tore off her panties. Her hands free, she began pounding on his back with one hand and groping in her pocket for the needle with the other.

As he began forcing his way inside her, she brought her hand up and with all her might stuck the needle in his eye. She kept jabbing as he howled. Fly open and eye suffused with blood, he stumbled out of the caravan.

Amira willed herself up, staggered out and sprinted toward the park office, screaming in high staccato gasps.

The office manager came running out. She pointed at the yowling man, now surrounded by several park dwellers. Then she was taken inside to wait for the police.

Trembling uncontrollably and frigidly cold, Amira vomited what food she'd had that morning. Then, shrouded in a blanket, Amira was taken to a hospital.

She spent two days recovering there, with periodic visits from officers of the Child Abuse Investigations Unit and members of Gloucestershire social services. At first she couldn't talk about anything. The experience replayed over and over. She wanted to shut it out. But gradually, she began to articulate elements of her life—Adnan, Ralph and Arlind, the big house and her betrayal to the rapist and his gang.

While officers continued to question her, she stayed under guard at the flat of Ms. Bartlett, one of the council's social workers. She was nice enough and stopped the interviews when Amira got too tired. But many questions remained. The caravan was stolen and the name and card registered with the touring park was fraudulent. They wanted her to look at photos of men to see if she could identify any of them. They couldn't locate Sir Reginald and Lady Caroline. It was already a week and the list of demands kept growing. Worst of all, nobody could help her find her brother. Adnan. Oh, Adnan. Where are you?

She was deep into her art therapy session at the kitchen table when Ms. Bartlett came in with two officers she'd never seen before. Ms. Bartlett moved behind her chair and asked her to put away her drawing. Detective Inspector Evans had some news for her.

Amira put her watercolor crayon down. A sense of fore-boding enveloped her in a clammy chill.

"Amira, we think we have found your brother."

Tears welled in her eyes, "Where? May I see him?"

"I'm sorry... He is dead."

"Nooo!" she wailed. "He was sent away!" She felt Ms. Bartlett's hands touch her shoulders.

"The American who bought the estate, Laura Westin, found his...remains in a pit in the gatehouse."

"*Ya Allah!* In the black pit?" Amira hugged herself and began rocking back and forth.

"It appears his death was caused by...starvation."

"While I waited, Adnan was left alone in a hole to die. They did not send him away. They sent him to horror and death."

D.I. Evans waited for a moment. Then held out her hand with an envelope and a small package. "Laura asked me to give you these."

Amira stared at them and then reached out and placed them in her lap. Wiping the tears from her eyes, she opened the envelope to find a card and a handwritten note.

Dear, dear Amira,

I am so very sorry about your brother and what happened to you. Please forgive me for failing to realize your danger. I failed you once. But, if you will let me, I will help you all I can to recover, go back to school and become the woman of grace and intelligence you are meant to be.

Please accept this as a small token of my promise to you.

Laura.

Amira considered the note. Then took her time opening the package. Inside was a large, azure silk scarf printed with small yellow flowers. For a moment, she let her fingers luxuriate in the soft folds. Then she put it down.

After her three days of mourning, Amira picked up the blue scarf again. Curious, she removed her drab, polyester hijab and began modeling the silk scarf in front of the mirror in various styles around her shoulders and neck.

For the first time since leaving Aleppo, Amira felt free and pretty and unashamed.

Then she remembered Adnan. She slipped the scarf atop her head and affixed it around her face.

Tomorrow. Maybe tomorrow I shall wear it another way.

But as she stared at her face encircled once more, Amira felt a spark ignite and flare within her.

Chin up and eyes burning with newfound determination, she addressed her reflection. "It is time. Time for me to become who *I* choose to be."

With a sudden jerk of her hand, Amira unfastened the scarf, letting it slip to her shoulders. Then, flipping one end of it over her shoulder, she turned and resolutely walked into tomorrow.

Burnt Orange
Shawn Reilly Simmons

Shelby counted the rows of trees from the back seat as her mom sped north on I-95, getting up to fifty-nine before losing track. She dug into the bag of cheese curls next to her on the seat, licking the orange dust off before crunching them between her teeth. Huffing on the glass, she fogged the window and drew a greasy heart in the center, then watched it fade, counting the seconds until it was gone.

"Have to pee?" Shelby's mom raised her penciled eyebrows in the rearview mirror.

Shelby shrugged. "I don't know."

"You don't know if you have to pee?"

Shelby watched her mom's skin pull tight across her jaw. "I guess so, if you do." White highway lines streaked across the lenses of her mom's sunglasses.

"I swear you'd curl up and die if you ever gave a straight answer, Shelby Marie. I tell you one thing, Nana isn't going to put up with your lip."

Her mom twisted the dial on the radio, maxing the volume to drown out any response. The Pointer Sisters sang about how excited they were, their voices vibrating the windows.

Shelby looked down at her fingertips, smooth and pink beneath the orange powder. She touched one to her bottom lip, remembering the burn she felt when she held it as long as she could over the flame. The memory stirred something in her and she ducked her head, her black feathered bangs falling across her reddening cheeks. Sometimes the smell of matches stayed with her all morning, especially if she didn't wash up before leaving the apartment.

The building's super had found one of her burning spots out by the trash bins. He huffed up the stairs and knocked on their door, then carted her mom out back to see. Shelby watched them down in the courtyard from the window, the old man's face shiny with sweat, her mom swaying on bare feet in her frayed jean shorts. He'd caught Shelby once before in the basement trying to burn a dryer sheet, but had let it go that time.

"Sign says there's a service station off the next exit," her mom shouted over the music. Shelby rolled her eyes then stared back out the window at the passing trees.

Carlene Hamilton, who had been Shelby's best friend before everything changed, had seen Shelby sniffing her fingers one day at school and told the whole ninth grade that Shelby was dirty. Everyone believed Carlene, no matter what the truth was, even the teachers. The girls at school giggled at Shelby behind sparkly nail polish when she walked by, cutting glances at her discount clothes and plastic shoes. Carlene had held a grudge against Shelby ever since those older boys had asked her to the beach after school. It had been Carlene's mission to make Shelby miserable ever since.

Shelby's mom lit a cigarette and rolled down the window, the blast of hot air sucking the weak air conditioning out in seconds. She pulled off the exit and rattled up to the farthest gas pump, clamping the cigarette between her frosted lips and grabbing her purse.

"Come on," her mom said as the door groaned open.

"You shouldn't be smoking around here," an old man pumping gas said as they got out of the car.

Shelby's mom gave him her work smile, the one she used when people wanted to send back their eggs. "Thank you, sir."

The old man shook his head and scowled as their flip flops slapped across the soft asphalt. "Asshole," her mom muttered under her breath as she jerked open the door of the service station. She dropped her cigarette on the ground and smeared it out before stepping inside.

A disheveled older woman punched keys on the cash register behind the counter, her hair teased on top of her head in a melting beehive. The men who stood in line at the counter turned to look at Shelby and her mom, the cowbell clanging on the glass behind them. Shelby watched as their eyes moved away from her quickly, then fell on her mom, sliding up and down her long tan legs, taking quick glances at her thin pink tank top, her black bra showing through from underneath.

"Go ahead to the Ladies. I've got to pay for the gas," Shelby's mom said, jerking her head toward the rear of the store.

Shelby shuffled slowly down the center aisle, her fingers brushing lightly over the slick candy bar wrappers. The smell of motor oil was strong from the adjoining garage, and Shelby wondered how fast it might catch on fire.

A woman near to her mom's age and two girls wearing matching sweatshirts stood outside the door marked WOMEN. Shelby eased up behind them and pretended to read the magazine covers on the nearby rack. An older woman emerged from the bathroom, an embarrassed grimace pinching her face when she saw the four of them waiting. She hurried away, wiping her hands on her flowery shorts.

Shelby picked up *Tiger Beat* and flipped randomly to an article.

"She goes to Coconut Creek," one of the girls mumbled. Shelby looked up from the magazine and was surprised to see the girl was staring at her.

"No, I don't," Shelby stammered.

"Go ahead of us, hon," the bony woman said, waving

Shelby ahead. A row of white teeth appeared from behind her tan lips. The younger girl crossed her legs and tapped the toe of her tennis shoe on the linoleum, staring at the floor.

Shelby placed the magazine back on the rack. "You guys were here first."

"Go on ahead. And be quick, will ya?" the woman urged.

Shelby pushed her way into the bathroom where a single toilet sagged in the corner. She held her breath while she peed, hovering over the dingy seat. She spun the faucets on the sink and listened to the rush of water as she swiped faded pools of blue eyeliner from the corners of her eyes. Looking up to wipe under her lashes, a small piece of cardboard tucked behind the mirror caught her eye. She exhaled sharply and snatched the pack of matches, her heart skipping in her chest. She pulled the pack open and counted. Seven left. Putting the matchbook to her nose, she breathed in the sulfur, then carefully pulled one off, dragged it across the striker, and watched the flame burn down the cardboard. She shook it out just before it got to her fingers, then tossed it in the toilet. As she started to pull another one off, a loud knock on the door made her jump. Shelby closed the matchbook and tucked it in the waistband of her shorts, flushed the toilet and turned off the water.

"It's all yours," she said to the woman and two girls. The three of them went into the bathroom together and latched the door behind them.

Shelby walked back down the aisle, hearing her mother's raspy laugh long before she could see her. She was using her superior voice, the one she saved for when she had friends over or when they ran into one of the other moms from school around town.

Shelby remembered once at Winn-Dixie when her mom's card didn't work and they had to put back all their groceries. It was the only time she'd seen Carlene out shopping with her dad. Shelby's mom had to use change from the bottom of her purse to buy a box of mac-and-cheese and a couple of bananas. The next day Carlene told everyone at school that Shelby needed to go on food stamps.

Picking up a bag of chips, a candy bar and some gummy worms, Shelby made her way to the soda fountain and filled a large plastic cup with blue syrupy ice. Pinching the cup in the crook of her arm, she sidled up behind her mom who was next in line to pay at the counter.

"And what do you think you're doing with all that?" her mom asked loudly.

"I'm hungry," Shelby murmured.

"You haven't had lunch yet, Shelby," her mom said. "There are sandwiches in the car."

The man ahead of her in line took his change and turned to go. "Safe travels to you," he said as he headed to the door. A ring of salt stained his baseball hat, the patch on the front a picture of a snarling bulldog curling at the edges.

"Thanks, and nice chatting with you," Shelby's mom said breezily. "Now you see what I mean," she added, tilting her head at Shelby.

The man chuckled and stepped outside.

"Go on, put it up there," Shelby's mom said with a sigh.

Shelby placed the items on the counter and sucked on her straw.

"And ten bucks on pump three," Shelby's mom said, pouring some change into her narrow palm from her wallet. The cashier watched her slide the coins around the counter.

"Go on and wait in the car. I'll be out in a minute," her mom said.

Back outside, Shelby opened the back doors of the car to let the warm breeze flow through. She breathed in the gas fumes and watched her slushy cup sweat onto her thighs.

The woman and the two girls emerged from the station a few minutes later and shuffled across the asphalt, the woman in the rear, talking to the back of the girls' heads. Their legs reminded Shelby of the newborn colts she'd seen at the fair, sleek and fragile, kneecaps just below the skin. Shelby looked down at her own round thighs and quickly back up, then touched the matchbook in her waistband.

One of the girls tripped and the other reached out to steady her. The woman bumped into them, almost knocking all of them over. They were too far away for Shelby to hear, but she saw the woman's face crease with anger. Shelby snorted a laugh as they continued on their way, slipping behind the building and out of sight. Something small and white on the ground where they'd collided caught Shelby's eye.

Shelby's mom said people were always throwing money around, and it was good to be nearby when they did. One time Shelby had found five dollars in the sand and she and her mom had celebrated by eating hamburgers at the bar on the beach. Shelby slid off of the seat and casually walked over, nudging the object on the ground with her toe. It was a piece of paper folded into a triangle so many times over it was solid, like a pebble. Shelby picked it up and strolled behind the store just in time to see a gray pickup truck rumble down the road back toward the highway. She bounced the paper on her palm, then pretended to throw it like a baseball at the truck before squeezing it in her fist and heading back to the car.

Shelby pulled off her shirt and adjusted her bikini top, then opened her new bag of potato chips. A minute later her mom came out and yanked the pump nozzle from its holder, propping her rubber sole on the side of the car as she watched the numbers ping by. Shelby unfolded the paper and pressed it against her leg. A series of lines and shapes were spread across the page in faded pencil. Shelby turned the paper around, looking at it from different angles, trying to make sense of the marks.

"Want a sandwich?" her mom asked as she pulled the door closed.

"No," Shelby said, crunching another chip. Her mom's ham sandwiches were soggy with yellow mustard smeared on the inside of the baggies.

"You keep eating that junk, you're not going to fit into your new uniform. You're pushing your luck with that bathing suit, too. Might have to start wearing a one piece, you can't keep from stuffing your face."

Shelby looked down at her tan stomach puffing out over her shorts until the tears blurred it, then swept the chips and paper onto the floor. She slipped on her sunglasses and leaned her head against the window, pretending to sleep as the car pulled away from the station.

"Wake up, Shelby," her mom hummed.

Shelby sat up and rubbed her neck. "Where are we?" The sun was setting, streaks of orange and purple shot through the sky over the orange trees.

"Motel, close to the state line. I can't drive anymore," Shelby's mom said, stretching her arms over her head. "Come on, let's check in."

While her mom talked with the woman behind the glass in the front office, Shelby pulled on her shirt and got their suitcases from the hatchback. There were only a few other cars in the parking lot and most of the motel windows were dark, just a couple with the privacy curtains pulled across. A neon sign buzzed orange and green, "Vacancy" and "Hot Tub" alternating against the night sky. Shelby could feel the beat of the highway just beyond the orange grove.

"Room fifteen, second floor," her mom said. Their bags bounced on their hips as they climbed the chipped cement stairway, Shelby's mom yawning as she fumbled with the room key. Shelby's eyes roamed over the faded bedspreads and the thin towels hanging outside the bathroom next to the sink.

"Get some ice, Shelby," her mom said, handing her a brown bucket from the bedside table.

Shelby walked to the end of the dark breezeway. A soda dispenser glowed in the corner of an alcove at the end, and an ice machine leaked into a drain in the center of the floor. A woman drummed her fingers on the side of the machine, then slapped it with her open palm.

"Don't let it eat your change too," the woman said, keeping her eyes on the machine.

Shelby mumbled, "Okay," then hid behind her bangs as she flipped open the door on the ice dispenser.

"Now I got to walk all the way to the damn office to get my money back." She gave the soda machine a sharp kick then stomped away.

Shelby ducked her head into the hallway and watched the woman she'd seen earlier that day outside the bathroom at the gas station trot down the stairs to the front office. She pulled her head back in when the woman glanced back over her shoulder. A truck horn blared in the distance and Shelby looked out over the grove, then down at a row of big rigs parked behind the building. They were lined up like dominoes, positioned to topple each other if pushed from either side.

Shelby's mom sat against the wall on one of the beds in her underwear, drinking red wine from a motel tumbler and staring at the TV. A man in a yellow blazer was reading the news but the air conditioner drowned him out. Shelby set the ice bucket on the table and perched on the edge of the other bed.

"Want to watch something?" her mom asked.

"Not really," Shelby said. She looked at her mom's bra, her flat stomach, the gold ring through her belly button.

Her mom took a sip of wine, then turned to Shelby. "You're going to have to learn how to get along with people, Shelby. In your new school, you can be whatever you want."

The loose bun of hair on top of her mom's head bobbed as she spoke.

Shelby felt the matchbook press against her stomach. "I don't know how to make friends," she mumbled.

"Sure you do," Shelby's mom said, topping off her glass from the bottle on the bedside table. "When the other girls ask, just say you had to move to Macon for your dad's job."

Shelby looked at her in disbelief. "It's a reform school, Mom. It's not like anyone goes there on purpose. And I don't have a dad."

The glass clinked against her mom's teeth. "Well, they don't know that. It's a story that will get them on your side."

Shelby rolled her eyes and glanced at the television.

"They won't know anything about you except what you tell them. Clean slate."

"When will I see you again?" Shelby asked, her voice wavering.

"I'll be back up to visit," Shelby's mom said. "I have to pick up some extra shifts, save up some money."

Shelby felt tears coming and pinched her thigh, her gaze drifting back to the television. "Wait, turn that up," she said.

Shelby's mom looked languidly at the bedspread.

"Mom!" Shelby said, jumping up and twisting the dial on the TV. A girl's face filled the screen.

"...family says has gone missing. Anyone with information on the whereabouts of Jessica Palmer is asked to call the authorities immediately," the man's voice droned. A phone number with a Florida area code flashed at the bottom of the screen.

"I saw that girl today!" Shelby said, staring at the phone number.

"Who?" Shelby's mom leaned forward and squinted. A woman in a pink sundress was standing in front of a weather map, pointing to areas of northern Florida.

"The missing girl they were just talking about. I saw her

today when we stopped for gas," Shelby said. "I think I saw the lady she was with just now."

"If you saw the girl, she's not missing," her mom said, easing back down. She poured herself some more wine and set the bottle down unsteadily on the table.

"Mom," Shelby said loudly. "What if she was kidnapped by that woman?"

Shelby's mom gazed at her. "What woman?"

"The one I just saw when I went to get ice."

Shelby's mom threw her head back and laughed. "So now they're staying here, too? Did this missing girl say anything to you?"

Shelby chewed her lip. "Yeah. Something about a school."

"Did she say 'please help me, I've been kidnapped' or anything like that?" Shelby's mom's teeth were tinted purple.

"No," Shelby admitted.

"You and your stories," her mom said. "If you're going to lie, make sure it's for a good reason, not just for attention."

"I'm not lying," Shelby whined. "Can I call the number from the TV...tell them what I saw?"

Shelby's mom stared at the weather map. "And spend five dollars for a phone call? Stop playing around, Shelby."

"But, Mom!" Shelby said. "I'm not making this up."

"Shelby, you're always making things up. That's why we're here in the first place. You're not getting us into trouble again, understood? I mean it, Shelby Marie."

Shelby thought about the stack of books and papers in Carlene's locker, the blue flames licking up the sides, toasting the pages brown, then brittle black, the stitched letters on her jacket melting. Shelby had been welded to the spot, staring into the locker, her blood pulsing, breaths coming quickly. She couldn't move, even after she heard the others running, yelling at her to get down, pulling the fire alarm. Her mom told the police Shelby could stay at the station forever, that she wasn't coming to get her, which Shelby believed until she showed up hours later to take her home.

"This is your second chance, Shelby," her mom said, attempting to sharpen her words. "You won't get another one."

"I know, Mom," Shelby said, watching her move the glass slowly to her lips. An orange vial stood open on the sink outside the bathroom, her mom's nighttime pills. Shelby sulked in silence for a few minutes until her mom's expression relaxed.

"Mom, can I get some change for a soda?"

"Sure," her mom sighed. "In my purse."

Shelby went through her mom's bag and listened to her light up a cigarette, then turned around and watched her tuck the lighter back under the pillows behind her back.

Shelby palmed her mom's car keys against her thigh and headed for the door. "Want anything?"

"Nope," her mom said, exhaling smoke. She picked up the TV remote and closed one eye to look at the buttons. "Don't be gone too long, now."

Shelby slipped out the door and down the steps, pausing for a moment at the three rooms on the first level with the closed curtains. She could hear the faint sound of a television through the middle window but no voices. Easing the car door open, she rifled through the debris in the back seat, a touch of panic quickening her search when she thought the paper she'd found at the service station had been lost. Finally seeing the corner sticking out from beneath the seat, Shelby snatched it from the floor. She gazed at it, letting her eyes drift over the marks, the folded the paper into a diamond shape. The marks came together to reveal *Jess Palmer. GA AAX 1979 HELP ME*

"Help you?" the woman behind the glass in the office said when Shelby stepped inside.

"Can I use the phone?"

"Sure, we can charge it to your room," the woman said, picking up the large black receiver.

"Um, this is an emergency," Shelby said. "Is there a charge for that?"

The woman tilted her head back and looked down at Shelby through her smeary glasses. "What kind of emergency?"

"Yeah, it's just…" Shelby stammered.

"Spit it out," the woman said impatiently.

"I saw a missing girl earlier today and I need to call the police," Shelby said. Sweat pricked her armpits and she shifted her weight to her other foot.

The woman considered her for a few long seconds. "There's a payphone out back, you really want to make a call."

"Okay. Do you know who's staying in room six?" Shelby asked, hooking her thumb at the breezeway.

"Young lady, that is none of your business," the woman said. Her glasses slipped down her shiny nose and she slid them back up with her finger.

"Sorry," Shelby muttered. "Where did you say the phone was?"

Shelby followed the smell of chlorine down a narrow hallway and out to a courtyard behind the motel. A hot tub sat in the middle of a grassy area, surrounded by faded lounge chairs and a rickety wooden fence. Shelby crept to the payphone in the rear and picked up the grimy receiver, running her finger over the metal cord. "I found a note," Shelby said to the woman who answered the phone at the police station. "I think it's a license plate number. Georgia maybe."

After she hung up, Shelby sank to her knees in the grass and pulled the matches from her waistband. A feeling of calm washed over her as she lit the first one, but was quickly replaced with anxiety when she realized she only had five left. Glancing around the overgrown courtyard, Shelby gathered a couple of twigs and some dry grass, and piled them on top of a slate stepping stone. Watching the flames lick the pile and begin to grow, Shelby breathed in the smoke and felt the familiar pulse of blood rush through her body. She closed her eyes and counted to fifty, waiting.

"What are you doing over there?"

Shelby sucked in her breath and stood up quickly, stamping on the fire with her flip flop, scattering the embers across the slate. "Nothing," she said. Her heart skipped in her chest when she saw the woman from the gas station staring at her, shadows falling across her thin frame.

"Doesn't look like nothing to me," the woman said. She moved toward Shelby, one of her hands tucked behind her back. The only way in or out of the courtyard was behind her and she was getting closer every second. "Playing with fire, huh?"

"Not playing," Shelby muttered. She stepped out of her shoes, feeling the cool blades of grass between her toes.

The woman let her hidden hand drop to her side, a slender blade flashing in the dark. Shelby's heart began to pound and her legs went rigid.

"You're nosy. Asking questions about me, I hear," the woman said. She'd almost closed the gap between them.

"I thought you were someone I knew from school. My mistake," Shelby said. When the woman reached the hot tub, Shelby bolted, heading straight for her. The woman took a step back, startled, then Shelby shoved her as hard as she could. She flew backward and landed hard on the grass, stunned, as the knife bounced away.

"Help!" Shelby yelled as she ran down the hallway, banging on doors as she went. She stopped to pound on number six.

The door opened and Shelby looked into Jessica's eyes. "Come on!" Shelby said, grabbing her wrist. "Where's the other girl?"

"They gave her to one of the truckers," Jessica whispered. "Then he said he'd kill my family if I left this room."

"That's a lie," Shelby said. "We have to go now."

Jessica nodded, and followed Shelby outside.

"Hey!" the woman shouted from behind them as she staggered down the breezeway, gasping for breath and waving her knife.

"Run!" Shelby yelled. Jessica followed her across the parking lot and into the orange grove, the woman limping behind them.

"Stay quiet," Shelby said as they darted between the trees. "I called the police, gave them the license plate number from your note. We just have to hide until they get here." They ran a bit farther, then crouched down between two trees. Shelby was surprised to see blood on her toes, the skin scraped away. She was numb, and her head was buzzing. A metal pot sat on the ground next to them, a thin chimney pointing at the sky. Shelby touched it and put her fingers to her nose.

"Quiet," Jessica said. "She's getting closer."

Shelby squinted in the dark, listening to the woman's footsteps and the rustling of the trees, her back stiffening at the sounds. Shelby exhaled when she heard the woman move away from where they were hiding.

"I'm going to find you," the woman taunted. She'd recovered from Shelby's tackle, her voice clear and strong. "You're not going to get away."

A gray pickup truck rumbled up to the motel, and Shelby peeked out from behind her tree.

"He's back," Jessica whispered, her eyes glassy in the dark.

"Who?" Shelby asked.

"The man who took me," Jessica said. "The one who's going to kill us."

Shelby peered through the branches and watched the man step out of the truck. He was still wearing the baseball hat she'd seen at the gas station, the snarling bulldog bobbing as he flirted with her mom. The woman emerged from the orange grove and waved her arms around. Shelby couldn't make out exactly what they were saying, but she could tell he was angry. He grabbed her roughly by the arm and jerked her toward the truck just as a police car pulled into the parking lot.

"The police are here." Shelby sighed with relief as she watched the officer approach the couple. He bent at the waist to read the license plate number on the truck.

"We're safe," Jessica said shakily, standing up.

"Wait," Shelby said, watching the conversation. The man's demeanor had changed from threatening to polite as he spoke to the officer. The policeman nodded, his hands on his belt. He swept a glance at the orange grove then folded his arms across his chest.

"Okay, let's go," Shelby said.

When the gunshot sounded, Shelby grabbed Jessica by the shoulders and pulled her backward, ducking behind another tree.

"Oh no, what's happened?" Jessica sobbed. Shelby ignored her and stared at the police officer lying on the ground, the man standing over him, gun in hand. The woman put her hand over her mouth and staggered against the bumper of the truck. The man tucked the gun in the small of his back and grabbed her by the arm, pulling her up. Shelby's stomach dropped when his eyes fell on her, and he pulled the woman into the orange grove, heading straight for them.

"Come on!" Shelby said, pulling Jessica back to the metal pot next to the tree. "There's kerosene in here," Shelby said as she pulled the cap off the chimney.

"It's a smudge pot," Jessica said. "To keep the frost away."

Shelby kicked the smudge pot over and watched the kerosene spill over the ground. "Do that one," she said to Jessica, who toppled the neighboring pot over. Shelby pulled the matches from her waistband, the cardboard damp with sweat.

"What are you doing?" Jessica whispered.

Shelby pulled the match across the striker. "Slowing them down. We're going to run as fast as we can to the highway," she said as she tried to light the damp match again. Jessica stood frozen to the spot, staring at her.

"Get back here!" the man shouted. Shelby jumped at the closeness of his voice. She pulled the match across again, sparking it, then dropped it on the ground. The blue flame spread quickly. "Go!" she whispered. Jessica turned and ran for the road. Shelby dropped the matchbook and watched it ignite before following Jessica's path, knocking over smudge pots as she went.

"I told you I wasn't making it up," Shelby said from the back seat.

Her mom raised her eyebrows in the mirror, the afternoon sun glowing on her cheeks. "I know, Shelby. You did good."

"Do I still have to go to St. Anne's?" Shelby asked quietly.

"Yeah," her mom said wistfully. "But you saved those girls. Everyone at school will know you're a hero."

"If they believe me," Shelby said quietly.

"They will," her mom said. "A big story like that will be in all the papers. The police captain said they suspected shady things were going on at that motel for a long time. Now they know for sure."

Shelby sat back and smiled, holding her breath and making a wish at the exact moment they crossed the state line.

Hidden
Karen Pullen

Memory is a funny thing these days. I forget appointments, misplace keys, wander about Kroger's parking lot looking for my car. But the past springs to life vividly, sparked by the smallest nothing. Combing my short gray hair I fall into a memory of Emma, her musical Dutch-accented voice muttering as she detangled and braided my hair. I hear the bark of a nervous dog and my heart races, remembering Rudi's sharp yip-yip of warning. When I walk with my grandchildren through the woods near their home, a sudden rustle from the underbrush bathes me in adrenaline, my breath quickens and I fight the urge to run. And smells! Sardines, starch, Pall Mall cigarettes—all carry me to long-ago and far away.

In May 1942, after our father died in a sea battle, Mama, Giles, and I left our home in Rouen and went to live with Grand-papa in a village outside Lille. His house was tiny, with only two rooms; mattresses on the floor in one room, a stove and table in the other.

It was an unhappy time. There were no servants, and Mama had too much work to do. She hated cooking and besides, food was scarce. She fixed brick-hard bread, applesauce, carrots, and eggs, always eggs. Grand-papa drank apple brandy all day and fussed at me for being loud and bouncy. But what was I to do? I missed my friend Anna, our games in the schoolyard, ballet lessons. I pouted and whined until Mama said, "Leni, your incessant crying is making me crazy. Go into the bedroom, shut the door, and count your blessings."

"What blessings?" I shouted between dramatic sobs. "The Nazis want to kill us!" I slammed the door and buried my wet face in sour-smelling blankets. "I hate it here! I hate my life!" My tears flowed until I was bored and went out to find Giles.

I would pester Giles, follow him into the woods, down to the trickle of a creek, watch him climb and dig holes and catch tiny fish. He was thirteen and I was seven, a mile-wide chasm. If Giles ever humbled himself to play with me, we constructed forts, stocked them with stick-guns and knives. I had to be the Nazi soldier. The soldier ran, hid, was caught and tied up with rope. Giles was cowardly in most situations, but brave enough to capture this little Nazi.

In the village, real Nazis stood on the sidewalk, looking us over, staring at the yellow stars on our coats with sour expressions on their cold faces. One of Giles's eyes wandered outward, especially when he was anxious or upset, and he was self-conscious, worried a soldier would notice him. He had a bad stutter, and the Nazis knew it. "B-b-b-bumble b-b-b-bee eyes," they jeered, as Giles lurked behind Mama and me. "Stand tall," Mama told him, but he skulked along, like he was trying to be invisible.

One day a man in a black suit drove up to Grand-papa's house.

"The doctor will take you to a place where you will be safe," Mama said.

Giles said, "I won't g-g-g-go. I'll run away. He'll take us to a c-c-c-camp to be k-k-k-killed!" His stutter was worse when he was upset.

We had heard stories of trains to death camps. It scared me

that he was so upset. Mama calmed us, saying, "You will be safe. The Nazis won't find you. I promise."

We put on almost all our clothes until we looked like stuffed bears. I clutched my doll, Giles carried a small suitcase. His face was white and stony. Mama stood at the iron gate, blew kisses, smiled, though her face was wet with tears.

The doctor unpinned the yellow stars from our coats. He told us, "At the checkpoints, I will say I am taking you to a hospital. You must pretend to be sick. Cover up with blankets until you are hot and feverish-looking. Close your eyes and be very quiet."

Wearing so many clothes, I was burning up and it was easy to look hot. The doctor drove for hours, it seemed, until reaching a small farm on the outskirts of a Belgian village.

Be very quiet. An order we were to live by.

"Call me Tante," the woman said, though she was not our aunt. She helped us remove most of our clothes, clucked and hissed, "Too thin!" After a meal of fried sausage and potatoes, she led us to her bedroom, opened a hatch in the ceiling and pulled down a ladder. She shooed us into an attic, a dirty space filled with boxes, bundles, and broken furniture. There was a window with a black curtain, and a pile of blankets for a bed.

"You will stay here, because people gossip and there are collaborators," Tante said. "Never come down unless I tell you."

In the corner of the attic stood a tall oak dresser and next to it, a stovepipe through the floor and up out the roof. She stooped and reached behind the stovepipe, tugged on a board until a cupboard door opened, revealing a dark space under the sloped roof.

"Here's your hidey-hole," she said. "You can latch it securely once you are inside. No one will know you are here if you are quiet. Go on, try it out."

The hidey-hole had a low ceiling but was big enough for Giles and me to lie down, elbow to elbow. We both sneezed from the dust. I began to cry. I missed my mother, I was afraid, and I didn't want to live in a dirty attic. Giles tried to shush me, sang silly songs, but I wailed until Tante climbed the ladder and poked her head into the hidey-hole. "The Nazis will hear you," she said, "and we will all be shot. Be very quiet."

Many times Tante fussed at me for crying. I learned to cry in silence.

Tante wore thick glasses, fixed her black hair in tidy braids wrapped round her head, and spoke with a strong Dutch accent. Her husband and three sons had been forced into factories in Germany. She worked the small farm with her father, Opa, and Emma, her sixteen-year-old daughter. The farm was perhaps five acres, with a chicken coop, rabbit hutches, and bee boxes. There was a small barn, a pasture for two cows, and a large garden for growing potatoes, beans, cabbage, carrots, and beets. Their nervous, cloudy-eyed dog, Rudi, walked slow from arthritis, and barn cats showed up every evening for pans of milk but scattered at the approach of people.

Opa was old, white-haired and bent over. He walked with a stick, but never rested until evenings. Then he sat by the stove and listened to Radio Belgique, turned low because it was forbidden, growling curses at the Boches until Tante shushed him.

Emma had thick chestnut hair in a complicated braid woven around her head. She was jolly with rosy cheeks and, like Tante and Opa, never stopped in the daytime—cooking, baking, cleaning, washing. Tante and Emma spent mornings outside in the garden, weeding, picking fruits and vegetables, then pickling and canning them. In the cellar they buried cabbage and turnips, laid out potatoes, onions, and carrots in boxes. Opa tended the rabbits and bees, repaired tools, hunted wild hogs in the oak forest beyond the pasture.

Tante promised to fatten us up. Giles joked we were like Hansel and Gretel, prisoners of a witch who will cook and eat us. His stutter was worse, or perhaps I just noticed more, being shut up with him all day and night.

We became Emma's project. She climbed the ladder with a food bucket and climbed back down with the shit bucket. Giles said it was shameful work for her, emptying that bucket. She was kind and cheerful, never severe like Tante. When the terrible smell of his feet made me gag, Emma filled a bowl with hot water and vinegar and he soaked his feet. It worked! Giles said we made a lot of extra work for her.

The attic's one grimy window was stuck closed but we folded back the cloth covering a bit to peek out: at Tante in the garden, Emma walking the cows to the barn at dusk, a person riding past on a bicycle. Sometimes we saw children and I was so sad, missing Anna, missing our play with our dolls under the lilac bushes behind her house. We couldn't even write letters to our mother, Emma said, since not even the postman could know about us. But on each of our birthdays—three of them—somehow Mama managed to get us a letter and some sweets.

After dark, Tante allowed us to come down the ladder and put us to work. My chore was churning butter, to burn up my energy; Giles helped Opa outside. Afterward we played tag and climbed the fruit trees. Giles wanted to explore the oak forest but Opa said, "No, the wild hogs will eat you."

Rudi was a good watch dog, with different barks for neighbors and strangers. The bark for neighbors was a deep woof woof. His tail wagged, and his ears perked up. He greeted strangers with a higher-pitched bark, a yip-yip, and he was stiff and alert. We knew to be quiet when someone approached; no one must know we hid in the attic.

As an extra signal, Tante banged a pot on the woodstove.

Two *clanks* meant *be very quiet.* Someone was coming, to talk, or to buy eggs or honey.

Clank-clank-clank meant *German soldiers, go into the hidey-hole.* Giles said, "They are d-d-d-devils and I wish I had a gun."

Five quick *clanks* meant *all clear.*

I was always frightened. I didn't sleep soundly; even dreaming, I was alert to small noises. The loud hoots of owls would wake me. One perched right outside our window and others answered it from the woods. During the night, Rudi barked, at stoats, deer, squirrels. In the dark attic, with only a crack in the curtain to allow moonlight, things in the room seemed to move. The floor moved like quicksand, a witch hid behind a chair, a bundle was full of slugs and snakes. Hands with long fingers worked the attic hatch. Nightmares took me down into dark places until I woke, terrified, grunting strangled screams. (Even asleep I remembered to keep quiet.)

Then I would sit by the window to watch the stars slowly rotate in the sky, clouds pass before the face of the moon. I wondered if Mama saw them too; maybe we watched together. Often, a pack of wild hogs came to dig for acorns beneath the giant oak in front of the house. Then, like Giles and me, Rudi was very quiet, holed up in his dog-house next to the chicken pen.

Late one morning Emma brought us a can of sardines, drizzled with vinegar. At the sight of the little black-eyed silver fish, I cried and refused to eat them but Giles said they tasted so good, mashed on a piece of toast, and after one little bite I decided yes, they were delicious. We were licking our fingers when came c*lank-clank-clank*. My heart beat with a terrible fright and I began to cry, I couldn't stop. Tante made Emma go in the hidey-hole with us, to calm me. Two soldiers stomped about below, talking harshly to Tante. Giles and I understood a little German—our grandfather had spoken German to our mother. The soldiers said Tante must give them butter, rabbit meat, and eggs every week. She will have to meet a quota.

The hidey-hole was hot as an oven. We lay quiet until the stomping and the voices ceased. *Clank* five times. I sat up, dripping with sweat. My heart would not slow down.

The soldiers took—no, *stole*—eggs, honey, jars of pickles and beans, and three loaves of bread that had been cooling.

Passing the time was so difficult. I made paper dolls, drew pictures. We played checkers. Emma brought us arithmetic and history books. Giles taught me a bit of English and read *Alice's Adventures in Wonderland* aloud to me. We studied a book of maps over and over, planning where we'd go. *After.* We listed ways to kill Nazis. Sharp things to stab them with: knives of course, ice picks, spears, arrows. Hard things like hammers to bash their brains out. Ropes, scarves, wire, string to strangle them with.

We talked constantly of *after*. After this, after the war, after the Nazis all died. It helped, to think about a future.

Every week, the German soldiers, always the same two, came on motorbikes for Tante's food. Spots was tall and pimply, Tiny Eyes had slicked-back black hair and, well, tiny eyes set back in his skull. After the first few times, as soon as Rudi began to yip and we heard the putt-putt of their bikes, Tante made Emma go into the hidey-hole with us.

Emma would lie squished between Giles and me, her eyes closed, her cheeks pale. She smelled like sweat and starch. I lay rigid, too frightened to sleep, breathing a sort-of prayer, angels surround us. *Anges nous entourent.* I imagined enchanted glowing creatures, their silver swords poised to protect. I buried my face against Emma's arm, silently wetting her sleeve with my tears.

Giles, too, turned his face toward Emma, watching her with one eye as the other wandered upward to the spider-webbed ceiling.

I thought she was there to shush us.

We were not the only hidden ones. Through cracks in the floorboards, we heard hushed talk about Allied airmen moving from farm to farm, eventually to Paris and escape routes into Spain. We were intensely curious but also afraid, because Tante, Opa and Emma would tell us nothing, and their silence only added to my worry.

Moving some boxes and bundles around in the attic, I found a wood rocking chair with arms and a carved back. One runner was missing, and Opa fixed it for me. I rocked all day, cradling my doll. Creak creak creak creak...Giles didn't protest.

Our third winter was frigid with lots of snow. Snow covered the farm, the road, and the barn with a pure white thick blanket. Another time, it would seem magical to us. But two feet of snow was no protection against Nazis, or a witch behind the chair, a floor of quicksand. The owl was just as loud, the dog just as nervous.

On the evening before his sixteenth birthday, Giles was shoveling paths through the yard, to the road, the barn, the rabbit and chicken coops, when Rudi began to bark. Giles ran into the house. A neighbor from a nearby farm had made his way through drifts and Opa let him in. We tried to overhear what they talked about, but they went outside, to the barn, without speaking.

I went back to my sketches. I was drawing a bouquet of flowers for Giles, for his birthday. Tante promised an apple tart, and Emma was making over some clothes of her father's for him.

That night, Tante made us stay in the attic instead of coming down for chores, play, and warm milk. She didn't explain, but said firmly: "Be very quiet."

It was late, after curfew, when Rudi started to bark again. *Strangers.* "Something's going on," Giles said, and we crowded together to peek out the window. A half-moon cast a dim light over the yard, crisscrossed with shoveled paths. Two men walked into the yard. Opa went outside, hushed the dog, and led the men into the barn.

"Nazis?" I asked. "Should we get into the hidey-hole?"

"No. Civilians," Giles said. "Wait and see." His voice was a man's, now.

One man came out of the barn and walked away. Opa returned to the house. We put our ears to the floor to listen, and heard Emma ask, "Who is he?"

Opa said, "An American airman. He has a concussion."

"Oooo," Tante said. I could almost see her pursed lips and frowning eyes.

Giles and I looked at each other with big eyes. An airman! An American!

"He will stay here at least a few days," Opa said. "Then he'll be taken to Paris."

"The Germans will be looking for him," Emma said.

"Of course," Opa said. "But Adrian burned his parachute and clothing, and we have hidden him well."

"He will want to eat," Tante said. We heard the crackle of

potatoes dropped into hot oil. Tante made the best fries.

"I want to see him," Giles whispered to me.

I nodded. An American airman!

The next day we were crazy to see the airman but Emma said, "It is too dangerous, for him and for you. What if he was captured? He might tell about you two." She had helped me bathe, and was trying to comb my hair, not an easy job. It was so long, almost to my waist, and tangled easily. But she was patient, working on it strand by strand.

"He wouldn't tell," Giles said. "He is a b-b-b-brave man."

She looked up at him, shook her head, then went back to combing.

"Don't tell him we're Jewish," I said. "Tell him we are your sister and brother."

"P-p-p-please?" Giles begged.

"No. It's not safe for you or him."

I was wildly disappointed, sick of being *safe.*

So, the next afternoon, when Tante and Opa had gone somewhere on the train, and Emma was in the garden, Giles and I crept out of the house and dashed into the barn. Cats scattered as we tiptoed around looking for the airman, going from stall to stall, climbing to the loft, peeking into cupboards. We couldn't find him! Emma caught us coming out of the barn.

"Idiots," she said. "What are you doing?" She carried a pan of rabbit meat.

Giles shrugged. "Nothing. Just looking in the b-b-b-barn."

Emma looked us up and down. Giles had grown a good six inches taller, and his pants barely covered his knees. "What did you find?" she asked.

"Cats," I said. "Many cats."

"Good. Now back inside. I'll bring you some stew later."

Just then, Rudi's sharp yip-yip and the rumble of a motorbike coming down the road jolted us into a panic, and we ran across the yard, inside and up into the attic. Giles pulled up the ladder, and we squatted by the window and opened the curtain a tiny sliver to see who it was. Tiny Eyes, by himself. He banged on the door and Emma let him in. We crept into our hidey-hole. My heart thumped the way it always did when a Nazi soldier was in the house.

"Is he looking for the airman?" I whispered.

"He asks her for the food," Giles told me. He frowned. I could hear arguing and Emma yelling, "No, stop."

"What shall we do?" I whispered. "What's he doing?"

We heard thuds, like chairs falling over, and Emma screeched, "No, no!" The soldier yelled, "Quiet, you bitch!" and more thuds then suddenly she was silent.

"Has he left?" I whispered.

Giles was so red I thought he would ignite. He opened the door to the hidey-hole. "Stay here," he said.

But I followed, scrambling down the ladder. Whatever was happening, I wanted to be part of it.

The soldier was on top of Emma, on the floor, struggling with her. He had one hand around her throat, and the other pulling on her clothes, and she squealed and squirmed, pushing against him. His pants were down and his bare bottom shoved against her. It was a horrible sight and as I started to cry, Giles lifted Tante's big black fry pan and swung it onto the side of the soldier's head, knocking his face into the floor. Giles whammed the fry pan into the soldier's head over and over as Emma wriggled away and her noises changed from squeals to sobs, just one or two, then she stopped. Emma was as tough as they come.

The soldier lay still. Blood poured from his head. "He's dead," Emma said, but when Giles nudged him with his foot, the soldier moaned. He wasn't dead. More blood. Oh, so much blood. The soldier's pants were clumped around his ankles, and I couldn't help seeing his stiff penis, like a mule's, in its hairy nest. Disgusting. Poor Emma.

She was all right. "You two saved me," she said. "He didn't get very far." She took our hands—Giles's all bloody and sticky and trembling—and we stood, joined in a circle, over the soldier's body, until she kicked him, then I gasped and kicked him too. Oh, how Emma and I kicked that Nazi soldier until our shoes were bloody. We tried to be quiet, choked on strangled laughter, excited, though I wanted to shriek to the heavens *Filthy Boche! Dead Nazi!* Giles backed away, watching us celebrate. When the Nazi stopped moaning, Emma and I turned to Giles to praise his bravery, but he stood rigid and the color was gone from his face.

"They will hang us from trees for this," he said. "Your mama and *grand-père* too. They will find the airman and shoot him."

"No. He will help us," Emma said, and she darted outside.

We listened to the soldier gurgle through his broken nose. "You were brave," I said to Giles. He ignored me and walked back and forth.

Emma came back with the airman. He was sandy-haired and stocky, and there was a big lump on his forehead. At the sight of the Nazi, he took out a cigarette and lit it.

"Nice job," he said. "Who are you?" His French was very good.

"I am Giles, and this is my sister Leni," Giles said.

"That's a Nazi soldier," I said. "He was hurting Emma and Giles hit him!"

"Good for Giles," the airman said. "Let's get rid of the bastard."

"Get rid of the bastard," I yelled. Emma grinned. She went into her bedroom, came out with a sheet. The airman and Giles rolled the Nazi onto the sheet, wrapped him up. He was still breathing. They dragged the bundled soldier outside, and

I watched through the open back door as they heaved him through the yard, past the chicken pen, the garden, the bee houses, the sheds and into the woods.

Emma fetched cloths and a bucket of water. "We have to clean this up," she said. "They'll be looking for him." I set to work, frantically sopping up bloody water, emptying the bucket, filling it again, over and over. We washed the floor, cupboards, our shoes, the woodstove, chair legs until every speck of blood was gone. She wrung out the cloths, put them into soapy water along with the small rag rug that lay before the sink.

We sat by the attic window, hip to hip, and waited. I lay down onto Emma's lap, but my muscles felt tight and shivery and I couldn't rest.

It was dark when Giles and the airman came back. They stopped in the yard and pumped water to wash, and I climbed down the ladder and ran out to them, crying, so glad the Nazis hadn't caught them and hung them from a tree.

"Where's your mom? The old guy?" The airman asked. He squatted to rub Rudi's ears.

"They will be back late tonight," Emma said. "Come in, have something to eat." She cut bread, spread butter and jam.

"What did you do with the Nazi?" I asked.

Giles and the airman shared a glance. Giles said, "We took him very far into the trees, burned his clothes, then waited."

"For what?"

"For the hogs to smell his blood."

The airman shook his head and said, "We got pigs back home, but I never saw them do a man like that."

A feeling of glee stabbed me. Glee on top of terror and exhaustion, and I couldn't help it, I let go of a warm gush of pee, pee I'd been unable to release all day.

"Poor girl," Emma said. "But that will explain the wet rags, and the clean floor. Now go up to bed."

* * *

The airman left with the motorbike.

"Where's he going?" I asked.

"To ditch it," Giles said. "So no one will know Tiny Eyes was here."

"Is he coming back?"

"I don't know."

I pulled a blanket around me and curled onto the rocking chair. I was wide awake, worried about the airman. When Rudi woofed softly, I peeked out the window; the moon was bright enough to see Tante and Opa, returning in the mule-driven wagon. Emma had said it was better that they didn't know what happened, and we should say nothing to them.

Then I must have slept because the next thing I knew, the hatch to the attic was opening and the airman was climbing through it. "Hey there, kids," he said. "There's German soldiers coming up the road and the old man told me to hide up here with you two."

"You had a good hiding place in the barn," Giles said. "We couldn't find you."

"I wasn't in the barn. I was off in the woods having a smoke because the old man told me not to smoke in the barn. Anyway, what's the plan up here?"

"Follow me," I said, and opened the cupboard to our hidey-hole. We crawled in, latched the door, and lay down with the airman in the middle, squashed together in a sandwich. My head was under his arm, and I could feel his heart thump, his ribs move as he breathed. He smelled of cigarettes, of hay, and leaves.

Rudi barked hysterically as motorbikes pulled into the yard. *Bam-bam* pounding on the door, then sharp voices questioning Tante about Tiny Eyes. She would be in her nightdress and robe, black braids hanging down.

"No, no soldiers were here today," she told them. "Should

I wake my old father and child?"

The soldiers stomped through the kitchen, into the small parlor, then outside. As Rudi barked and barked, I guessed they were searching the barn. We lay in silence until we heard the motorbikes putt-putt away.

"We'll live another day, guys," the airman said. "Say, how long you been hiding here?"

"Almost three years," I said.

"The war's almost over," he said. "We're bombing the shit out of Berlin."

My brave brother Giles smiled, and I felt my muscles uncoil, for the first time since I put on all my clothes for the car ride from Lille. I stretched a little to get more comfortable, and rested my head on the airman's chest. His heart had slowed, but I could still feel it thumping beneath the scratchy wool of his shirt. *Anges nous entourent,* I breathed, closing my eyes to conjure up flickering lights, tiny silver swords.

The airman asked what I had said.

"*Anges nous entourent,*" said Giles.

"Indeed they do," the airman said.

ABOUT THE CONTRIBUTORS

ERIC BECKSTROM writes crime fiction, horror, and some literary fiction. The publication of his story, "Pick-Up and Delivery," in the Bouchercon 2017 anthology *Passport to Murder* marks his first time in print. Beckstrom grew up in Minnesota, majoring in English and Film Studies, with a subsequent Master's Degree in same. His thesis, "The Rhetorical Function of Tragic Components in American Film Noir: Appropriating Aristotle's Poetics as a Tragedy Noir Critical Paradigm," was awarded Saint Cloud State University's inaugural Distinguished Master's Thesis Award. Beckstrom cofounded Indiana University's City Lights Film Series, which will soon celebrate its 20th anniversary.

MICHAEL BRACKEN, 2016 recipient of the Edward D. Hoch Memorial Golden Derringer Award for lifetime achievement in short mystery fiction, is the author of several books, including the private eye novel *All White Girls*, and more than 1,200 short stories published in *Alfred Hitchcock's Mystery Magazine, Crime Square, Ellery Queen's Mystery Magazine, Espionage Magazine, Fifty Shades of Grey Fedora, Flesh & Blood: Guilty as Sin, Mike Shayne Mystery Magazine, Weird Menace,* and in many other anthologies and periodicals. He lives and writes in Texas.

Author/screenwriter **CRAIG FAUSTUS BUCK** has been writing network series, pilots, movies, miniseries and cable specials for more years than he cares to admit. In addition to dozens of produced television credits, he was one of the writers on the seminal miniseries *V: The Final Battle* and he wrote the Oscar-nominated short film, *Overnight Sensation.* His debut neo-noir novel, *Go Down Hard*, has won numerous awards as have his short stories. He is an active member of

Mystery Writers of America, International Thriller Writers, Sisters in Crime, Writers Guild of America, and Southern California Aquatics, and Bouchercon Poker.

SUSAN CALDER is a Calgary writer, who grew up in Montreal. She is the author of two mystery novels, *Deadly Fall* (TouchWood Editions) and *Ten Days in Summer* (Books We Love Ltd.). Her short stories have won contests and appeared in magazines and anthologies, including *AB Negative, Long Lunch/Quick Reads* and *Writing Menopause.* Susan is a member of Crime Writers of Canada and serves on the board of Calgary's When Words Collide Festival for Readers and Writers. In her non-writing time, she loves hiking and travel. Her story, "Zona Romantica," was inspired by a recent holiday in Puerto Vallarta, Mexico.

HILARY DAVIDSON'S debut, *The Damage Done*, won the 2011 Anthony Award for Best First Novel and spawned a mystery series that continues with *The Next One to Fall* and *Evil in All Its Disguises.* Her latest book is the dark stand-alone thriller *Blood Always Tells.* Her widely acclaimed, award-winning short stories have been featured everywhere from *Ellery Queen* to *Thuglit,* and in a collection titled *The Black Widow Club.* A Toronto-born journalist and the author of eighteen nonfiction books, she has lived in New York City since October 2001. www.hilarydavidson.com

MICHAEL DYMMOCH is the author of ten novels, includeing the John Thinnes and Jack Caleb mysteries, and the West Wheeling series. Michael ventured into romantic suspense with *The Fall* and *M.I.A.* In preparation for a writing career, she took classes on law enforcement, "Gunshot and Stab Wounds", crime scene investigation, and screenwriting. She's attended autopsies and worked as a baby sitter, veterinary assistant, research tech, recycler, and professional driver. Michael lives and writes in Chicago.

JOHN M. FLOYD'S work has appeared in more than 250 different publications, including *The Strand Magazine, AHMM, EQMM, The Saturday Evening Post, Mississippi Noir,* and *The Best American Mystery Stories.* A former Air Force captain and IBM systems engineer, John is also a three-time Derringer Award winner, an Edgar finalist, and a three-time Pushcart Prize nominee. His sixth book, *Dreamland,* was published in 2016.

CHRIS GRABENSTEIN is a #1 *New York Times* bestselling author whose books include the Lemoncello Library series, the Wonderland series, and The Island of Dr. Libris. He is also the coauthor of fun and funny page-turners with James Patterson, including *I Funny, Treasure Hunters, House of Robots, Jacky Ha Ha* and *Word of Mouse.*

MARIE HANNAN-MANDEL was raised in Ireland and is Associate Professor and Chair of the Communications Department at Corning Community College in Corning, NY. Marie was shortlisted for the Debut Dagger in 2013. Her short story, "The Perfect Pitch" appeared in the 2016 Malice Domestic anthology, *Murder Most Conventional.* Her essay, "Bringing Hope" is included in *Soap Opera Confidential* (McFarland and Company 2017). Her story "Sisters, Sisters" will be in the soon-to- be-published *Adirondack Mysteries 3* (North Country Books). Marie has two grown children, one husband, one most unruly dog, and many aunts, uncles, cousins, and friends who all make her life worth living.

JANET HUTCHINGS has been the editor of *Ellery Queen's Mystery Magazine* since 1991. She is a co-winner of the Mystery Writers of America's Ellery Queen Award and the

Malice Domestic Convention's Poirot Award, and in 2003 she was honored by Bouchercon for contributions to the field. Her previous jobs included a stint at the Mystery Guild and mystery editor for Walker & Company. While at *EQMM*, she has edited many anthologies, including 2007's *Passport to Crime*, culled from *EQMM's* monthly department of translated stories. Her own short fiction has appeared pseudonymmously in anthologies from MWA, Sisters in Crime, and elsewhere.

After a long career not writing fiction, **MARILYN KAY** debuts two crime short stories this fall: one in the Bouchercon 2017 anthology, *Passport to Murder*, the other in the Mesdames of Mayhem anthology, *13 Claws*. Marilyn began as an academic contributor to the *Dictionary of the Middle Ages*, before moving into the commercial world as a business journalist, then communicator within and outside of government. More recently, she operated her own social media consultancy. She is a member of Sisters in Crime and an executive member of Sisters in Crime—Toronto. When she is not at work on her Toronto police procedural novel, you can find her blogging at marilynkay.me or on Facebook.

Obsessed with books, dogs, and creepy old houses, **SU KOPIL** writes short fiction about peculiar people. Her stories have appeared in various magazines and anthologies. She is the owner and founder of EarthlyCharms.com , a graphic design company that has been working with authors since 2000. Visit sukopil.com or follow @INKspillers.

ROSEMARY MCCRACKEN hails from Montreal, and has worked as a reporter, editor, editorial writer and reviewer at newspapers across Canada. Her first mystery novel, *Safe Harbor*, was a finalist for Britain's Debut Dagger award in 2010. It was published by Imajin Books in 2012, followed by

Black Water in 2013 and *Raven Lake* in 2016. Rosemary's short fiction has appeared in *Room of One's Own* magazine, *The Whole She-Bang I*, *Destination: Mystery*, *Black Coffee*, *World Enough and Crime*, *Thirteen*, *Thirteen O'Clock* and *Thirteen Claws*. Rosemary now lives in Toronto and teaches novel writing at George Brown College.

Editor **JOHN MCFETRIDGE** is the author of four novels in the Toronto series, and the Eddie Dougherty trilogy set in Montreal in the 1970s. He is also the co-editor, with Kevin J. Anderson, of the anthology, *2113; stories inspired by the music of Rush*, and co-editor with Jacques Filippi of the anthology *Montreal Noir*.

TANIS MALLOW wrangles her dark and twisted imagination into short fiction found in anthologies and selected online magazines. Full length novels are in the works. She co-hosts Toronto's Noir at the Bar. Facebook: tanismallow, Twitter: @TanisMallow.

LD MASTERSON lived on both coasts before becoming landlocked in Ohio. After twenty years managing computers for the American Red Cross, she now divides her time between writing and enjoying her grandchildren. Her short stories have been published in numerous anthologies and magazines, most recently *Still Me After All These Years*, *Fish Out of Water: A Guppy Anthology*, and *Busted! Arresting Stories from the Beat*. LD is a member of Mystery Writers of America, Sisters in Crime, the Short Mystery Fiction Society, and the Western Ohio Writers' Association. Catch her at: ldmasterson-author.blogspot.com or ldmasterson.com.

Born under a bad sign, **GARY PHILLIPS** must keep writing to forestall his appointment at the crossroads. He is editor of the anthology of sweaty paranoid pulpiness, the *Obama*

Inheritance: 15 Stories of Conspiracy Noir, and with Christa Faust co-wrote *Peepland,* a gritty crime graphic novel set in the last bad old days of 1980s Times Square New York. Bookgasm.com said of his *Treacherous: Grifters, Ruffians and Killers,* "So do whatever it takes to secure a copy, because contemporary crime short fiction doesn't get much better than *Treacherous.*"

KAREN PULLEN is the author of two mystery novels, *Cold Feet* and *Cold Heart,* both from Five Star Cengage, and the short story collection *Restless Dreams,* from Bedazzled Ink. She has an MFA from Stonecoast at the University of Southern Maine, serves on the board of Sisters in Crime, and lives in Pittsboro NC.

KM ROCKWOOD draws on a varied background for stories, such as working as a laborer in steel fabrication and fiberglass manufacture, and supervising an inmate work crew in a large state prison. These positions, as well as work as a special education teacher in alternative education and a GED instructor in correctional facilities, provide material for numerous short stories and novels, including *Abductions and Lies,* 6th in the Jesse Damon Crime Novel series by Wildside Press.

SCOTT LORING SANDERS is the author of two novels, as well as two new books out in 2017: a short story collection of dark mysteries, *Shooting Creek,* and a memoir, *Surviving Jersey: Danger & Insanity in the Garden State.* His work has appeared in *Best American Mystery Stories,* and he's a frequent contributor to *Ellery Queen Mystery Magazine.* His nonfiction has been noted in *Best American Essays* and widely published and anthologized in various literary journals. He was recently a Writing Fellow at the Edward F. Albee Foundation. He teaches creative writing and mystery writing at Emerson College in Boston.

SHAWN REILLY SIMMONS is the author of the Red Carpet Catering Mysteries (Henery Press), which feature Penelope Sutherland, an on-set movie caterer, as well as several short stories in various anthologies. Shawn is a member of Sisters in Crime, Mystery Writers of America, and the Crime Writers' Association in the UK. She serves on the Board of Malice Domestic and is an editor at Level Best Books, publishers of the annual Best New England Crime Stories anthology series.

JOHN STICKNEY is a poet/writer from Cleveland, Ohio and Wilmington, North Carolina. A retired Special Agent, U.S. Treasury Department—Criminal Investigation Division, his poetry has appeared in numerous publications including *The Line-Up*. A collection of his poetry was published as *These American Moments* (Burning Press). John's crime fiction has appeared in *Demolition, Beat to a Pulp, Hardluck Stories, Thuglit, Needle* and in *Borderlands Noir: Stories, Essays of Love and Death across the Rio Grande*. Visit him online at onedownoneup.blogspot.com.

VICKI WEISFELD'S short stories have appeared in *Ellery Queen Mystery Magazine* (three times), the literary magazine *Big Muddy*, Level Best Books' spring 2017 anthology *Busted: Arresting Stories from the Beat*, and elsewhere. Her cop tale "Breadcrumbs," which appeared in Issue 3 of *Betty Fedora*— "kickass women in crime fiction" Yes!—was shortlisted for a Derringer Award. She's debriding a pair of novels and maintains an active website that includes book, movie, and theater reviews, topics for writers, and grist for the creative mill: www.vweisfeld.com. She's a reviewer for the UK website crimefictionlover.com and thefrontrowcenter.com (theater).

OTHER TITLES FROM DOWN AND OUT BOOKS

See www.DownAndOutBooks.com for complete list

By J.L. Abramo
Chasing Charlie Chan
Circling the Runway
Brooklyn Justice
Coney Island Avenue

By Trey R. Barker
Exit Blood
Death is Not Forever
No Harder Prison

By Eric Beetner
Unloaded (editor)
Criminal Elements
Rumrunners
Leadfoot

By Eric Beetner
and Frank Zafiro
The Backlist
The Shortlist

By G.J. Brown
Falling

By Angel Luis Colón
No Happy Endings
Meat City on Fire (*)

By Shawn Corridan
and Gary Waid
Gitmo

By Frank De Blase
Pine Box for a Pin-Up
Busted Valentines
A Cougar's Kiss

By Les Edgerton
The Genuine, Imitation,
Plastic Kidnapping
Lagniappe
Just Like That (*)

By Danny Gardner
A Negro and an Ofay

By Jack Getze
Big Mojo
Big Shoes
The Black Kachina

By Richard Godwin
Wrong Crowd
Buffalo and Sour Mash
Crystal on Electric Acetate

By Jeffery Hess
Beachhead
Cold War Canoe Club

By Matt Hilton
Rules of Honor
The Lawless Kind
The Devil's Anvil
No Safe Place

By Lawrence Kelter
and Frank Zafiro
The Last Collar

By Lawrence Kelter
Back to Brooklyn
My Cousin Vinny (*)

(*)—Coming Soon

OTHER TITLES FROM DOWN AND OUT BOOKS

See www.DownAndOutBooks.com for complete list

By Jerry Kennealy
Screen Test
Polo's Long Shot (*)

By Dana King
Worst Enemies
Grind Joint
Resurrection Mall

By Ross Klavan, Tim O'Mara
and Charles Salzberg
Triple Shot

By S.W. Lauden
Crosswise
Crossed Bones

By Paul D. Marks and
Andrew McAleer (editor)
Coast to Coast vol. 1
Coast to Coast vol. 2

By Gerald O'Connor
The Origins of Benjamin Hackett

By Gary Phillips
The Perpetrators
Scoundrels (Editor)
Treacherous
3 the Hard Way

By Thomas Pluck
Bad Boy Boogie

By Tom Pitts
Hustle
American Static

By Robert J. Randisi
Upon My Soul
Souls of the Dead
Envy the Dead

By Charles Salzberg
Devil in the Hole
Swann's Last Song
Swann Dives In
Swann's Way Out

By Scott Loring Sanders
Shooting Creek and Other Stories

By Ryan Sayles
The Subtle Art of Brutality
Warpath
Let Me Put My Stories In You

By John Shepphird
The Shill
Kill the Shill
Beware the Shill

By James R. Tuck (editor)
Mama Tried vol. 1
Mama Tried vol. 2 (*)

By Lono Waiwaiole
Wiley's Lament
Wiley's Shuffle
Wiley's Refrain
Dark Paradise
Leon's Legacy

By Nathan Walpow
The Logan Triad

(*)—Coming Soon

77203556R00201

Made in the USA
Columbia, SC
24 September 2017